TO THE SHORES

Book One: The Empire's Corps
Book Two: No Worse Enemy
Book Three: When The Bough Breaks
Book Four: Semper Fi
Book Five: The Outcast
Book Six: To The Shores
Book Seven: Reality Check
Book Eight: Retreat Hell
Book Nine: The Thin Blue Line
Book Ten: Never Surrender
Book Eleven: First To Fight
Book Twelve: They Shall Not Pass
Book Thirteen: Culture Shock

TO THE SHORES

CHRISTOPHER G. NUTTALL

The characters and events portrayed in this book are fictitious. Any similarity to real persons, living or dead, is coincidental and not intended by the author.

Text copyright © 2016 Christopher G. Nuttall
All rights reserved.
No part of this book may be reproduced, or stored in a retrieval system, or transmitted in any form or by any means, electronic, mechanical, photocopying, recording, or otherwise, without express written permission of the publisher.

ISBN-13: 9781542362214
ISBN-10: 1542362210

http://www.chrishanger.net
http://chrishanger.wordpress.com/
http://www.facebook.com/ChristopherGNuttall

All Comments Welcome!

AUTHOR'S NOTE

Dear Reader,

To The Shores is the sixth book in *The Empire's Corps* and is a mainstream novel, following the adventures of the Marines stranded on Avalon when the Empire fell. I've done my best to keep it accessible to readers who haven't read previous works, but honesty compels me to admit that long-term readers will probably get more out of the book. In particular, the previous mainstream adventures are *The Empire's Corps, No Worse Enemy* and *Semper Fi*.

Chronologically speaking, *To The Shores* takes place roughly four years after *The Empire's Corps*.

The story of the final days of Old Earth are told in *When The Bough Breaks*, although the characters on Avalon are only starting to become aware of the end of Empire.

I hope this meets with your approval. Please feel free to post your opinions on my website discussion board or facebook page (links above.) And if you liked the story, please don't hesitate to write a review.

As always, if you spot any spelling errors and suchlike, drop me a note. I offer cameos!

Thank you for your attention.
Christopher G. Nuttall

DEDICATION

Ten years ago, I had my first formal introduction to the Marine Corps through Bing West, who chronicled the 1st Marine Division's advance on Baghdad in *The March Up* (2003). Since then, he has written several other books, most notably *No True Glory*, *The Strongest Tribe* and *The Wrong War*, all of which looked at modern war and those who fought it.

I write about fictional warriors, fictional defenders of civilisation. Bing West writes about *real* defenders of civilisation, the men and women who sacrifice their rights, their freedoms and (in some cases) their lives to preserve yours. Without the spirit of grunts, as he correctly points out, America cannot sustain itself.

This book is dedicated to him and the others who tell those stories to the world.

CHAPTER ONE

> The simplest definition of diplomacy might be the art of dealing with people in a sensitive and effective way. People use diplomacy every day, from negotiating with their partners to trying to convince their boss that they're worthy of a raise. However, in this article, we are primarily concerned with international diplomacy.
> -Professor Leo Caesius, *Diplomacy: The Lessons of the Past.*

Colonel Edward Stalker, Terran Marine Corps, rose to his feet as Lieutenant Jasmine Yamane entered his office and saluted smartly. Edward returned the salute and then motioned for her to take a seat, which she did, never taking her eyes off him. He studied her back, looking for signs that her ordeal on Corinthian hadn't crippled her permanently. No one became a Marine without an inhuman ability to handle pain and stress, but torture could break even the strongest minds.

She was tall and muscular, her hair grown out slightly in the months she'd been on the beach while the medics and headshrinkers put her back together again. Vanity was not a common Marine failing, but Edward couldn't help noticing that she'd had the scars on her face surgically removed, leaving her looking like a very dangerous predator. She might not be beautiful in the classical sense, certainly not like the holographic stars who had dominated the arena and public viewscreens before the Empire had collapsed, but she was definitely striking. And, he could tell, impatient to return to work.

"I received the final report from the medics yesterday," he said, without preamble. Marines rarely had time for small talk. "You are cleared to return to duty."

Jasmine nodded, slowly. Her face seemed unreadable, but Edward picked up the subtle signs of relief that showed just how concerned she'd been, even after passing a series of increasingly difficult tests intended to weed out the unsuitable or the unfit. Like Edward himself, she'd spent years turning herself into a Marine – and losing it might well have crippled her.

"Thank you, sir," she said, finally.

"However, there are other issues," Edward admitted. He winced inwardly as her shoulders twitched, slightly. "I cannot return you to 1st Platoon."

"I understand," Jasmine said, tonelessly.

Edward felt her pain. Command of a Marine formation was a honour – and Jasmine had commanded 1st Platoon during the covert operation against Admiral Singh. But she'd been taken off duty just after the operation had concluded, forcing him to place command of 1st Platoon into the hands of Blake Coleman, who still held the post. Before the Empire had withdrawn and then collapsed, a Marine officer who returned to duty could be assigned to a different company or spend a few months attached to a headquarters platoon. Neither one was an option on Avalon.

Traditionally, few Marine ranks were permanent – and an unsuitable officer could be reassigned without denting his pride or setting a bad example. But Blake Coleman seemed to have matured since his shaky start and there were no grounds to deprive him of his new post, even though he'd replaced his former commander and teammate. Besides, he did have another post in mind for Jasmine.

"Tell me," he said, falling into the informality that Marines adopted for private discussions, "where do you see your career going?"

Jasmine blinked in surprise – and Edward smiled, amused at her expression. It *did* sound like a silly question, particularly with so few Marines within the Commonwealth. Jasmine couldn't replace Edward himself – the company's CO – or take command of one of the five remaining full-strength platoons. Her career, on the face of it, had nowhere to go.

"I honestly don't know," she said, carefully. "I could return to the ranks…"

"You could," Edward agreed. Even among Marines, it would be impolite for her to suggest that she might take *his* place. If the Empire had still been in existence, she might well have been a Captain by now. But the Empire was gone. "I had something else in mind."

He met her eyes. "Have you been following the diplomatic updates?"

Jasmine nodded. "The Wolfbane Sector?"

"Yes," Edward said, simply. "Governor Brown may pose a significant threat to the Commonwealth."

The thought made him scowl. Four years ago, there had been the Empire…and no significant independent states worthy of the name. Everyone had known that even a nominally independent star system wouldn't stand a chance if the Imperial Navy came knocking one day. Now, there was the Commonwealth and a handful of other successor states taking shape among the stars. One of them had already posed a major threat to the Commonwealth. Another might be far harder to take down before it was too late.

Little was known of Governor Brown. According to the files, he'd been third or fourth in line to the sector governorship of the Wolfbane Sector, a man so unremarkable that the famously-complete files gathered by the Imperial Civil Service said very little about him. Edward could only imagine what might have happened to boost him into a position of power; civil war, a coup, perhaps even the mass desertion of his superiors. It wouldn't be the only time that high-ranking officials had fled the chaos looming along the Rim for the bright lights of Earth, if Earth was still intact. Some of the rumours that had reached them through the Trade Federation – another successor state – had been horrifying.

Edward tapped a control and a holographic star chart shimmered into existence. "We have no way of knowing just how powerful the Wolfbane Sector is," he admitted. "In theory, he should have five squadrons of battleships and several hundred smaller craft under his command, but we don't know how many of them are still there – and in working order. We *do* know that we want to establish diplomatic relationships and eventually determine a practical border."

Jasmine frowned, one finger stroking her chin as she studied the chart. "You don't intend to try to convince him to join us?"

"We don't know enough about him to even *guess* at how successful such a ploy would be," Edward said. It was galling to admit that his long-term objective, the restoration of humanity's unity without the cracks in the Empire that had eventually torn it apart, might be in jeopardy, but he couldn't avoid considering the possibility. "For the moment, we merely want to establish relations and trading links."

He pointed to one of the stars, situated roughly midway between Avalon and Wolfbane. "We've been talking to his representatives through the good offices of the Trade Federation," he continued. "Eventually, the Governor agreed to a conference between our representatives and his here, on Lakshmibai. We will be sending an Ambassador with authority to negotiate on the issues that concern us, as will he."

"That should be interesting," Jasmine said. "Why *there*?"

"Lakshmibai has nothing that anyone wants, us included," Edward said. "The planet is neutral by default. According to the files, there was little contact between it and the Empire, apart from a half-hearted attempt to intervene in the planet's civil war. Brown…seems to feel that it is a suitable place for two interstellar powers to hold talks."

He shrugged. "I would prefer to send a mission to Wolfbane, but that suggestion was rejected," he added. "To be fair, we rejected their suggestion of sending a mission to Avalon too."

"Because they might be trying to spy on us," Jasmine agreed. "And they have the same worries about us."

"They would be right," Edward said, wryly. He switched off the hologram and leaned back in his chair. "After a great deal of argument in the Council, it has been decided that we cannot afford to refuse his offer of talks. Accordingly, a mission will be setting out to Lakshmibai. That mission will be headed by me."

Jasmine scowled. "Sir," she said slowly, "with all due respect, it might be a trap."

"It might be," Edward agreed, unemotionally. It was equally galling to realise that he might be irreplaceable on Avalon, even though he was a mere Colonel. "But the mission needs ambassadors of considerable authority. Professor Caesius will make up the other half of the ambassadorial team."

He smiled at Jasmine's expression. No one would have expected the professor and her to have become friends, but they had. And Jasmine was also a close friend of both of the professor's daughters. Having relationships outside the Corps was good for his Marines, even if civilians did have the strangest ideas of what the Marines did for a living.

"There will be a substantial security element embarked on the transport," he continued, putting that thought aside for the moment. "I believe that this is a good opportunity to carry out a deployment of the 1st Commonwealth Expeditionary Force, now that we have *finally* put most of its order of battle together. You will be given the brevet rank of Brigadier and take command of the force."

Jasmine stared at him, no longer able to *try* to hide her surprise. It was a colossal jump in rank and responsibility – and it would have been unthinkable before the fall of the Empire, where an officer required years of seasoning or extensive political connections to rise so high. Even in the Marine Corps, it could be decades before an officer had a chance at divisional command. But Avalon had a shortage of experienced officers, particularly ones who had served on multiple worlds. Jasmine was among the handful of relatively experienced officers under his command.

There were other considerations, he knew. The Commonwealth's constitution limited the deployable forces available to the central government. In theory, the Marines should be able to provide reinforcements if they were needed at short notice – it had been one of their roles in the Empire – but there simply weren't enough Marines to handle the task. Instead, they had to put together a light force from Avalon, which had its own problems. Few Knights of Avalon had any experience operating at the end of a shoestring logistics chain.

And then there are the political faultlines between the former Civil Guardsmen and the Crackers, he thought. *And the reluctance of Avalon's Knights to serve off-world…*

He pushed the thought aside and smiled at her. "Hopefully, this will be nothing more than a full-scale exercise," he informed her. "An exercise conducted under extremely realistic conditions. However, just in case we do run into trouble…"

"It would be well to have a large force accompanying us," Jasmine finished. "What is the situation on the planet's surface?"

"Good question," Edward said. "Unfortunately, the last update in the files from Lakshmibai is over seven years old. At the time, there was a large Imperial Army garrison and supply dump on the planet's surface. Now…we don't know."

"It's unlikely that the garrison is still there," Jasmine said, thoughtfully. "And the weapons in the supply dump might have been taken by one of the factions on the planet's surface."

Edward nodded, concealing his annoyance. If the files were to be believed – and he knew through experience that the Imperial Army's manifests were sometimes nothing more than elaborate works of fiction – there was enough war material on Lakshmibai's surface to outfit several full-sized divisions of troops. He would have given his right arm for such a supply dump during the war against the Crackers on Avalon; now, however, it wouldn't be so useful for the Commonwealth. One of the major differences between the Marine Corps and the Imperial Army was that the former's weapons and vehicles were lightened to make them more deployable, while the latter could take months or years to build up the logistics base for operations. Hauling supplies from Lakshmibai to Avalon – or anywhere else in the Commonwealth – might be more trouble than it was worth.

"It is unlikely," he agreed. "And it's even more unlikely that there was anything in the supply dumps that would make a difference now. But I'd still like to know what happened to the planet, if only to add to the files."

He shrugged. "Assuming all goes to plan, you will have several months to run exercises on the planet's surface while I and the professor take part in the discussions," he informed her. "If not…we may have to improvise."

Jasmine didn't look daunted, he was pleased to see. But then, she'd never had to command such a large force on exercise, let alone in actual combat. She didn't really know what she was getting into, any more than Edward had truly realised it when he'd been offered command of the company.

Sink or swim, he reminded himself.

"You'll assume command of the assembling force tomorrow," he concluded. "Do you have any specific requests or requirements you wish to raise?"

Jasmine hesitated, then nodded. "I would like to request that Joe Buckley be assigned to my command," she said. "He...is running out of patience on the training grounds."

Edward smiled, rather dryly. The Marine Corps had a proud tradition of rotating training officers through combat units on a regular basis, a tradition that the Knights had copied...but there were still considerable shortages of experienced training officers. It required officers and sergeants who could come across as sadistic brutes, while carefully not *becoming* monsters who abused their trainees or pushed them too far. Joe Buckley had been doing an excellent job, ever since his marriage, but Edward could understand his wish to return to active duty.

"I dare say that he can be spared," he said, after a moment's thought. "I'll have a word with Howell and have him attached to your command. He'll have to deal with his wife on his own, though."

"I think Lila will understand," Jasmine said. "She did know what she was marrying."

Edward wasn't so sure. Military wives *might* be able to deploy with their husbands – or they might be left behind, to make do as best as they could while their partner did his duty in another star system. The military wasn't kind to married soldiers; it wasn't unknown for a soldier to return home, only to discover that his wife had left him for another man. Even the Marine Corps had problems handling married Marines. The stresses of never knowing when one's husband might be called away – or die in the line of duty – placed colossal stress on even the strongest marriages.

"Let us hope so," he said, neutrally. Had Lila and Joe Buckley been separated for more than a week since they'd married? It was unlikely; Buckley was currently based at Castle Rock, where there was more than enough room for married couples. As a training officer, he was entitled to quarters suitable for both himself and his wife. "You should tell him that the whole deployment will take at least four months."

Jasmine nodded. "I'll brief him personally," she said.

"There is one other issue," Edward said, diffidently. He didn't miss Jasmine's eyes narrowing as she registered his tone. "You will be…*shadowed* by a reporter."

"A reporter?" Jasmine repeated. "Why?"

"It is important to showcase how far we've come since the Cracker War," Edward said, truthfully. "And equally important to show Avalon the importance of the Commonwealth to their security. We cannot risk losing public support."

He couldn't blame Jasmine for being irritated by the mere suggestion. The Empire's corps of reporters had been staunchly anti-military – or at least their editors, who took orders from the Grand Senate's vested interests, had been anti-military. Every commanding officer had learned to dread the well-connected reporter sticking his nose into military affairs, asking stupid questions on one hand and breaching operational security on the other. Edward had heard rumours that half of the problems on Han wouldn't have occurred if a handful of reporters hadn't leaked military secrets to the rebels. It didn't strike him as particularly unlikely.

"This reporter does have some experience from the war," he added, as reassuringly as he could. "And besides, he won't be sending live dispatches from the battlefield."

"Good," Jasmine said. She still didn't sound pleased. "I look forward to meeting him."

"You'll have a chance to review some of his work tonight," Edward said, picking a datachip off his desk and passing it to her. "He hasn't broken any of the agreements he made when he started his relationship with the military, at least as far as we have been able to determine. And he's going to be under military discipline while on deployment. If he gets in the way, feel free to put him in cuffs somewhere out of the way."

Jasmine snorted. In the Empire, an officer who put a reporter in irons could kiss any future career advancement goodbye, even if his peers silently cheered him on. But Edward had written the new protocols for interacting with reporters personally. If they did give one of his officers real trouble, they could spend the rest of the trip as a prisoner; Edward would back the officer responsible to the hilt.

"We need to have the CEF ready for deployment as soon as possible," Edward concluded. "I don't know where the next threat will come from, but there *will* be a next threat. We *still* don't know what happened to Admiral Singh, among other things."

"Yes, sir," Jasmine said. She *sounded* confident, he noted, although Marines were taught to sound confident at all times. It helped reassure the civilians – and the Civil Guard, when Marines were deployed to stiffen their spines. "I won't let you down."

She saluted, then turned and marched out of the office. Edward watched her go, then looked down at the papers on his desk. There was just more and more paperwork for him and the other senior officers, no matter how hard he struggled to keep it under control. The rapidly-expanding military seemed to practically *breed* paperwork.

That's why I have to go on the mission, he told himself. *It will be a change from paperwork.*

Pushing that thought aside too, he picked up a datapad and returned to work.

CHAPTER TWO

International Diplomacy can be defined as the profession, activity, or skill of managing international relations, typically by a country's representatives abroad. This is, however, the simplest possible view.
-Professor Leo Caesius, *Diplomacy: The Lessons of the Past.*

"Damn it," Lieutenant Michael Volpe muttered as his wristcom started to bleep urgently, driving away the last vestiges of sleep from his mind. "All right, all right."

He picked up the wristcom from where he'd left it on the bedside table, checked to ensure that he wasn't being summoned back urgently, then clicked off the alarm. The temptation to stay in bed was almost overwhelming, but he knew better than to delay his return to the base any longer than strictly necessary. Instead, he looked over at where the girl was buried under the blankets and then around her apartment. He hadn't had a chance to take in the decor when he'd picked her up last night and allowed her to take him home.

"Hey," he said, poking the girl's shoulder. He realised suddenly that he didn't even know her name! "Where's the shower?"

"Next room," the girl muttered, sleepily. "What time is it?"

"Seven in the morning," Michael said, as he pulled himself out of bed and stood upright. "I'll leave you in bed, if you like."

He fought down a sense of embarrassment as he padded across to the door and opened it, wishing that he'd thought to ask more questions before going to bed with her. There was no way to know if she shared her apartment with other girls, her parents or if she was alone…no, that was unlikely. His memories of the previous night were a blur, but he was fairly sure that she was a student and few students could afford to live on their own. The bathroom held enough supplies, he decided as he stepped inside, for a small army of girls. He stepped under the shower, lowered the temperature as much as possible and closed his eyes as the cold water washed away the last remnants of exhaustion. Just how much sleep had he gotten last night?

Not much, he thought, with a sense of heavy satisfaction. Two weeks spent preparing the 1st Avalon Mechanized Infantry Battalion for deployment had been rewarded by four days leave, which he'd spent in Camelot. Like almost all of the battalion, he'd spent the time looking for sexual partners and trying to relax. The girl – and he still couldn't remember her name – had merely been the last of a string of partners.

He stepped out of the shower, dried himself with a towel that was almost ludicrously small for him and walked back into the hallway. There was a gasp from behind him and he turned to see another girl wearing a nightgown that left almost nothing to the imagination. Michael, who had lost any sense of body modesty he might have had in training – or when he'd been a pirate captive – merely nodded to her and stepped back into *his* girl's room. She was sitting upright in bed, her bare breasts marked from their lovemaking. Michael felt a surge of lust which he ruthlessly pushed aside. There wasn't time for any more fun and games.

"Look me up when you come back to the city," the girl ordered, as he pulled on his uniform and inspected himself in the mirror. All the nice girls on Avalon loved a uniform, he'd discovered; it was almost a guaranteed lay to wear one's uniform on leave. The Empire might have banned its soldiers from wearing uniforms when they weren't on duty, but there was no such rule on Avalon. "And thank you."

Michael shrugged, fought down the temptation to ask for her contact code and walked downstairs, leaving her behind. Outside, the streets were already starting to fill up with people, mainly soldiers and spacers in uniform. He wasn't the only person who was expected to report back to base early in the morning, or the only soldier who had tried to spend his last hours of freedom with a pretty girl. Quite a few of the men on the streets looked considerably worse for wear. He hoped that they would have the presence of mind to use sober-up tabs before reporting for duty. A soldier who turned up unfit would be lucky if he merely spent the next week in the guardhouse.

Churchill Garrison was located to the east of Camelot, close to a small port that provided a sea link to Castle Rock, where the Marines and most of the training facilities were based. It had expanded rapidly ever since it had been founded, during the height of the Cracker War, until it consisted of over a hundred barracks, hangers and supply depots. A chain link fence ran around the complex, guarded by armed soldiers with authority to shoot anyone who tried to enter without authorisation. The Crackers might have been largely defeated and assimilated into the new order, but everyone knew that there were some factions that remained as unrelentingly hostile to the Commonwealth as they had been to the Empire. No one expected them to remain silent forever.

At least the bandits are gone, he thought, as he signed in at the guardhouse and entered the garrison. Thousands of uniformed soldiers were thronging over the base, most of them heading for the barracks where their sergeants would sort them out, match them up with their vehicles and equipment and then take them out to the exercise grounds. In the distance, he could hear the sounds of shooting as the infantrymen practiced on the shooting ranges. The sharpshooting competitions between the different units were intense, deliberately encouraged by senior officers. Michael took some pride in knowing that his unit had taken the cup for sharpshooting several times before losing it to other units.

His wristcom bleeped, ordering him to report to the briefing complex. Shaking his head, he turned and walked down towards the large concrete building. They'd been promised that there would – finally – be answers about their planned off-world deployment. Despite his curiosity, Michael was almost disappointed. The rumours had been fun.

There was a refreshing air of informality, Jasmine was pleased to note, as she entered the briefing room. Unlike the Imperial Army, which had over three thousand years of precedent and protocol to draw on, the Knights of Avalon and the other Commonwealth military organisations were new. Given time, Jasmine was sure that they would evolve traditions of their own, but for the moment they were not burdened by the past. It should give them more flexibility, she told herself, than the Imperial Army had ever shown.

The officers came to attention as she took the stand, looking at her with obvious curiosity. A gathering of Imperial Army officers would have found her beneath their notice, even though she was a Marine; she was just too junior to garner their attention. And the Imperial Army officers would probably have been decades older than her, at the very least. Rejuvenation treatments had ensured that officers held their posts for *years* before finally moving on or retiring from the service. But the Knights were young…even their senior officers were younger than Jasmine herself. Only a handful had served in the military for longer than any of the junior Marines.

The Colonel was right, she realised, as silence fell over the assembly. *They don't have the experience they desperately need.*

"At ease," she ordered, projecting as much confidence and command personality into her voice as she could. "We have a great deal of ground to cover."

She paused, then pushed onwards. "We will be deploying to Lakshmibai," she continued, knowing that few of them would have *heard* of their destination. A handful of officers began to surreptitiously look it up on their datapads. "Once there, we will provide security for a diplomatic mission and exercise as a combined unit on hostile soil, away from our logistics bases on Avalon or any other Commonwealth world."

The officers didn't have the experience to hide their reactions, she noted. Several of them looked confident, others looked worried at the prospect of operating away from their homeworld. A handful definitely seemed to relish the challenge. None of them, even the ex-Civil Guard officers, seemed to show any resentment at her being placed in command. They knew their limits. Besides, Avalon knew how much it owed to the Marines.

She smiled to herself as she caught sight of Michael Volpe – Mandy's former lover – in the audience, then looked away from him. There would be time to catch up with him later.

"We are expected to embark on the transports in three days," Jasmine informed them. "That gives us two days to carry out what joint planning and exercising we can before we leave."

She'd deliberately picked a deadline she didn't expect to meet, knowing that it would encourage her new subordinates to look for ways to speed up the process. Embarking even a relatively small military unit on a transport could take hours, particularly when it included tanks, aircraft or other vehicles. The entire CEF might take *days* to embark on the four purpose-built transport starships. Still, the only way to practice the operation was to actually *do* it. Paper exercises *never* worked out well in real life.

"I have worked out a rough deployment plan for you to consider prior to departure," she said. There were officers who would have refused to consider asking their subordinates to comment on their plans, but Jasmine knew that the men who'd handled their units since they'd come into existence would know more about their operations than she did, even though she'd spent most of the evening skimming through their reports. "However, our first priority remains the security of the diplomatic team."

She scowled at the thought. There was relatively little information on Lakshmibai in the databanks, even though the Imperial Library was supposed to contain exhaustive information on every world within the Empire – and she knew that it was outdated by several years, at the very least. The situation on the ground had been nasty even before the fall of the Empire; there was almost nothing to suggest what it might be like now. It was possible, she supposed, that peace and prosperity might have broken out, but that struck her as unlikely. Civil war seemed a much more definite possibility.

Which leads one to wonder why Governor Brown picked the system in the first place, she thought, sourly. *What was he thinking?*

"I would suggest that you review the information on our destination once we're on our way," she concluded. "I want to run a full-scale exercise tomorrow, if possible, and that must take priority. We need to be as practiced as possible by the time we leave."

She looked around the room, her eyes moving from face to face. "I don't need to tell you just how important this operation is," she said, firmly. "Failure is not an option. Dismissed!"

The officers saluted, then stood up and headed for the doors. Jasmine watched them go, feeling the weight of responsibility settling down on her shoulders. The 1st Commonwealth Expeditionary Force was a new formation, composed largely of individual units that had barely even *practiced* working together. They really needed several months to practice and prepare for their first off-world deployment.

But we need to practice rapid deployment, she told herself, remembering why the Marines had been called the Emperor's Firemen. A Marine unit could expect to be summoned at a moment's notice and then thrown into battle, without time to muster a colossal logistics base to support its operations. The 1st Commonwealth Expeditionary Force had to function along the same lines, which wouldn't stop the whole experience from being painful for everyone involved. They'd learn lessons, all right, but they'd also be dispirited…

Her wristcom buzzed. "Brigadier," Joe Buckley said, "you have a visitor waiting for you in your office."

Jasmine nodded, even though she knew he couldn't see her. "Understood," she said. Joe Buckley had politely but firmly taken a place as her aide as soon as he had arrived on the base. "I'm on my way."

One of Colonel Stalker's decisions when he'd been creating the new army had been to ban comfortable offices. Jasmine had approved, although she hadn't really understood why it had been necessary until she'd assumed command of 1st Platoon. There had been a temptation – a very slight one - to withdraw into seclusion and leave the platoon to the sergeants. It had to be much stronger, she suspected, if the unit she commanded was large enough to prevent her having such strong emotional ties to its personnel. No wonder some of the Imperial Army officers had created luxurious offices for themselves and then hidden inside. The weight of the responsibility had beaten them.

Assuming they were aware of their responsibilities, she told herself, darkly. *Some of them didn't seem to know what planet they were on, let alone which units they commanded.*

Her office was a simple concrete room, furnished with a desk, a computer terminal, a handful of metal chairs, a coffee machine and little else. One wall was covered with operational diagrams, including the CEF's order of battle; the other three were bare, leaving her with the uncomfortable sensation that the walls were closing in on her. Jasmine was hardly claustrophobic – and if she had been, she would have been unlikely to graduate from the Slaughterhouse – but she couldn't escape the urge to leave the office and go out onto the field.

A man was seated on one of the chairs, watched by a scowling Joe Buckley. Jasmine studied him as he rose to his feet, quietly evaluating the reporter as best as she could. He was of medium height and very thin, with strikingly pale skin that contrasted oddly against very brown hair and eyes. The coverall he wore hid most of his body from her eyes, but what little she could see suggested that he was more muscular than she had expected. Not up to Marine standards, or even those upheld by the Knights, yet hardly a weakling.

"You must be Brigadier Yamane," the reporter said. His accent was pure Avalon, although his face suggested a level of genetic modification that was somewhat unusual for a world settled by the Empire. "I am Emmanuel Alves, *Avalon Central*."

"Pleased to meet you," Jasmine lied, as he held out his hand. She took it, taking the opportunity to further gauge his strength. Definitely not a weakling. "Welcome to the 1st CEF."

She hadn't had to deal with reporters personally before, certainly not as a senior officer. There had been thousands of reporters on Han, but most of them had largely ignored the junior Marines as being beneath their notice. Besides, only a couple of the hordes had gone out into the field with the soldiers, even in the safer regions of the planet. Most of them, from what she'd heard, had preferred to file largely fictitious dispatches from the secure zones and reap the plaudits from their fellows who hadn't even dared to go within light years of the planet.

"Thank you," Alves said. He sounded as though he actually meant it. "It is a honour to be here."

Jasmine nodded, impatiently. "I understand that you have reviewed the operational requirements," she said. "Is that correct?"

"I *have* embedded before," Alves assured her. "*And* I do understand the value of security. I was trying to outsmart the Council a long time before you arrived."

"So I heard," Jasmine said.

She *had* taken the time to review his file – and she had to admit that it was impressive. The Council that had ruled Avalon – and fought a losing war with the Crackers – had clamped down on the media, turning the few reporters that lived and worked on Avalon into their propaganda department. Alves had been one of the handful who had tried to set up an independent newspaper, something that had been technically illegal in the Empire without the proper permits. Under the circumstances, he'd been lucky to merely be thrown in jail by the Council. The Crackers had broken him out a few months before the Marines had arrived and he'd helped to run an underground newspaper that had gone mainstream after the Battle of Camelot and the truce that had ended the war.

"I don't think that you will be able to file dispatches until we return home," she said, shortly. One of the other requirements for the diplomatic summit was that both parties would keep their ships outside the Lakshmibai Star System, at least until there was some level of mutual trust. "However, I must caution you that revealing any sensitive data will have the most unpleasant consequences."

"I do understand," Alves reassured her. "And besides, I doubt that anyone on that world has access to a computer datanet."

Jasmine shrugged. The reports on the planet's exact level of technological development were contradictory, as well as outdated. Some of them had suggested that the world was effectively an agricultural planet, with no modern technology; others had implied that outside traders had shipped in everything from fusion power plants to modern weapons and equipment. There was simply no way to know what they were getting into until they arrived.

"We will see," she said, softly. She sat down on one of the uncomfortable chairs and crossed her legs. "I will do my best to make time for you, but when I don't have time to talk I suggest that you stay out of the way. You are welcome to interview soldiers who *volunteer* to be interviewed; you are *not* welcome to push them into an interview or film them without their permission. Do you understand me?"

"Yes," Alves said. "I understand perfectly."

"Good," Jasmine said. She stood upright and grinned at him. If he wanted to follow her around all day, she'd see just how long he could keep it up. "Now that we have that clear in our minds, let's go inspect the troops."

CHAPTER THREE

> A rather old view of diplomacy defines it as the art of getting what one wants without a fight (and all the attendant risks.) A rather more cynical view defines it as the art of patriotically lying for one's country. As we shall see, both views have a great deal of validity.
> -Professor Leo Caesius, *Diplomacy: The Lessons of the Past.*

"There isn't enough baggage allowance," Fiona Caesius grumbled. "Can't you convince the Colonel to give us some more?"

"I doubt it," Leo said, as his wife picked up one of her suitcases and shoved it down the hallway towards the door. "We already have three suitcases and that's more than enough."

"Perhaps for you," his wife snapped at him. "But I have to look my best at the Ambassador's Ball."

Leo sighed, inwardly. Life on Avalon had been good for Fiona, although she would have preferred to have her teeth pulled out one by one rather than admit it. The woman who had lost enough weight to make him worry about her health when he'd been kicked out of Imperial University was gone, replaced by a healthy woman in her early forties. It was strange to realise, sometimes, that both of their daughters were effectively grown adults…but then, they'd both taken to Avalon far quicker than their mother. They'd had to grow up quickly when they'd left Earth.

Fiona, on the other hand, had taken it badly. She'd married a respectable professor, which had given her status in the endless social whirl surrounding the staff and students of Imperial University. But then Leo had started asking the wrong questions and – in his naivety – started talking about his answers in the wrong places. It was astonishing just how quickly a life could be ruined on Earth if one made powerful enemies. If the Marines hadn't taken them under their protection, for reasons that still escaped Leo, he doubted they would have lasted much longer.

And if half of the rumours are true, he thought grimly, *we might have been lucky to leave Earth before it fell.*

But it had still taken Fiona years to adapt to Avalon. She'd tried to build up status with the former Council, only to lose it when the Council was arrested and permanently disbanded. It had shocked her badly and she'd been depressed, only crawling back out of her shell when it became clear that her husband was becoming an important man on Avalon. But Avalon had little room for someone whose sole achievement was marrying well. The whole experience had left his wife terrifyingly brittle.

"I think you always look beautiful," he said, truthfully. Fiona *did* look healthy, even if she had been denied the rejuvenation treatments that would have ensured that she looked younger than her daughters for several decades to come. "And we still don't know if there is *going* to be a ball."

He'd had mixed feelings about allowing his wife to accompany the delegation, but the invitation had been made and he'd accepted, even though he knew that Colonel Stalker would be unaccompanied. His affair with President Cracker was an open secret, but there was no way that she could leave Avalon. Leo privately wondered why they didn't marry. It wasn't as if anyone thought they were founding a dynasty.

"Liar," Fiona said, crossly. She picked up the second suitcase, opened it and tried to stick a few more dresses inside. "I haven't looked good for years."

Leo was spared having to answer by the sound of a horn outside. "I have to go now," he said, shortly. There was going to be one final meeting before they left Avalon and headed to the meeting with Governor Brown's representatives. "Can you have the final bag packed before the van arrives?"

"I'll do my best," Fiona said. "You really should have hired a maid."

Leo shrugged. They'd had a maid on Earth – a sign of status – but he'd never really liked having a stranger in the family home. Besides, Avalon's economic boom meant that he would have to pay high wages just to attract a maid – or any other servant, for that matter.

"It wouldn't look good," he said, tiredly. It was an old argument, one that he was tired of fighting over and over again. "This isn't Earth. The people here do not look up to those who hire servants to do the chores."

With that, he walked out of the house, leaving his wife behind.

———

Edward felt vaguely guilty as Professor Caesius walked into Gaby's office, even though he hadn't caught him exchanging passionate kisses with his lover. Gaby and he had an agreement, of sorts, that they wouldn't be anything other than colleagues outside their bedrooms, where they were largely unobserved. Even so, the thought of leaving her for longer than a week was distracting as hell. He couldn't help feeling sorry for Joe Buckley, whose wife would also be left behind. There had been no room on the transports for her.

"Please, be seated," Gaby said, as Professor Caesius closed the door. "I trust that you have reviewed the briefing notes?"

"Such as they were," the Professor said. He'd spent hours in the Imperial Library, trying to pull files on their destination out of the archives. Edward had heard that there had been problems caused by a simple misspelling of the planet's name. "The Governor hasn't said much about what he wants from us."

"He may be trying to feel out our strength," Edward said. "We don't know just how strong his bargaining position is."

The absence of intelligence made him scowl. Just how powerful *was* Governor Brown? Did he have the ships and manpower to overwhelm the Commonwealth – or was he desperately worried that the Commonwealth would overwhelm *him*? Edward knew that traders from Avalon – and the Trade Federation – were probing the Wolfbane Sector, but there were no real answers to their questions. The Governor, according to what little intelligence there was, appeared to be hiding his strength. There was no way to know if that represented weakness or confidence.

Gaby cleared her throat. "At least we can talk to him," she said. "He doesn't seem to be another Admiral Singh."

Edward's scowl deepened. A year ago, Admiral Singh had vanished into deep space with a formidable force…and hadn't been seen since. It bothered him more than he cared to admit; in theory, the Admiral's fleet should have worn itself out without access to repair yards and stockpiles of spare parts, but she hadn't even *tried* to steal what she needed. Where *was* she?

But Admiral Singh had been focused on her own power to the exclusion of all else. Governor Brown seemed to be very different.

"For the moment," he said, grimly. "But what will he do if he believes that he has clear military superiority?"

The Commonwealth was building up its Navy as fast as it could, but Edward knew that it would be several years – perhaps a decade – before he felt safe from attack. It was simply impossible to cover every inhabited planet within the Commonwealth, which meant that worlds along the frontiers were dangerously exposed. Even a comparable force could cause a great deal of damage if it was turned against the Commonwealth. One of his recurring nightmares was Admiral Singh's fleet appearing above Avalon and bombarding the world into a lifeless ruin. The battle would be costly – and the Admiral's fleet might not survive – but rendering the world lifeless would be relatively easy.

And there was no way to know what had happened to the hundreds of thousands of ships that had made up the Imperial Navy. A relative handful had been accounted for, but the fog of war had descended over the Inner Sectors and the Core Worlds. The ships might be gone, destroyed in civil war, or they might be in the hands of a warlord who intended to reclaim control of the Rim. Who knew just how many ships were in Governor Brown's hands?

Gaby made a face. "We won't discuss our own forces with him," she said, softly. "Instead, we will focus on establishing a border line and trade agreements."

Edward had his doubts. The idea of establishing a border in space was absurd. A starship in Phase Space would remain undetected until it entered a specific star system – assuming, of course, that the star system had the sensor arrays it would need to detect a starship's arrival just outside the Phase Limit. Given sufficient time, *any* star system could be entered covertly, without detection. Governor Brown had to know that a border line could be little more than an empty formality at best.

Trading might get them further. But what did they have that the Governor might want?

Technology, he thought, sourly. The Commonwealth had made a number of improvements to Imperial-standard technology...and the researchers had promised that, given a few years, they might be able to completely revolutionise the Commonwealth's technological base. Edward would believe it when he saw it – he'd heard too many exaggerated claims from designers and technicians over the years – but he had to admit that some of their work showed definite promise. But he didn't want to share anything with Governor Brown, not when his ultimate aims remained unknown. It might end up being pointed back at the Commonwealth.

"And try to agree on a formal exchange of ambassadors," Professor Caesius said. "Now that we have diplomats on Madagascar, we can certainly urge the Governor to send diplomats here and accept ours there."

Edward nodded. The Empire had never been very diplomatic, certainly not since the Unification Wars had come to a victorious conclusion. If the Empire wanted something, it generally took it first and came up with the excuse later. Now, however, the whole field of diplomacy had to be re-established. If they could open friendly relationships with Wolfbane, they might learn a great deal more about conditions in towards the Core Worlds.

If nothing else, it would be a relief not to have to worry about another war, he told himself, thoughtfully. *We don't want to fight if we can avoid it.*

"That does lead to another problem," Gaby said, out loud. "What if he intends to demand our surrender?"

Edward had considered the possibility, before deciding that he simply didn't know enough to come to any real conclusions. Governor Brown did seem to be going to a great deal of trouble if he intended to merely deliver an ultimatum; besides, it would have been far more impressive if the ultimatum had been delivered by a battlefleet entering the Avalon

System. Instead, he seemed intent on keeping the Commonwealth at arm's length...

The analysts had argued backwards and forwards over what it might mean, but they'd finally agreed that the most likely possibility was that the Governor was satisfied with what he had and didn't want to expand – or allow the Commonwealth to corrupt his people. It was quite possible, Edward knew, that the Commonwealth's economic boom would set an example for the rest of the former Empire...and if Governor Brown was in firm control, he might not appreciate his population seeing that there was a better way. But, once again, there was no way to know for sure.

"We tell him to make some more impressive threats," Edward said, finally. "And to give us proof that he can actually back them up."

Professor Caesius frowned. "The files say that he has a formidable force under his command."

"The files say a great many things that are outdated," Edward countered. "What do they say about Avalon now?"

The Professor nodded, ruefully. Outside the sector, the files in the Imperial Library would say that Avalon was a minor colony with its own cloudscoop. There would be nothing about the defeat of the Crackers or the birth of the Commonwealth. Edward knew that the Professor wanted to restart the Imperial Library – or establish something new along the same lines – but that would be a very long term project. There was just too much else that needed doing.

"Hopefully that won't make the situation worse," Gaby said. She looked over at Edward. "Is there no intelligence from the Trade Federation that we can use?"

"They're having problems penetrating the sector," Edward reminded her. "Besides, everything we have from them is second-hand at best."

Gaby nodded. "The Council has authorised you to serve as negotiators," she said, producing a datachip. "There's a formal confirmation of just how far you can go on the chip, but if you're expected to offer much more..."

She shrugged. "Delay as much as you can," she added. "And don't make any representations about joining the Commonwealth unless you think there's a definite chance that he will accept."

Edward shrugged. The Commonwealth hadn't assimilated any multi-star political entities; even Admiral Singh's empire had come apart after her defeat. Her former captive worlds had entered the Commonwealth as separate entities. But as they expanded towards the Core Worlds, they would encounter multi-system political entities that had considered themselves one entity before the Empire had come into existence. And assimilating them would create a whole series of new problems for the Commonwealth.

"We shall see," he said, softly.

Gaby gave him an understanding look. She seemed to have aged in the time he'd known her, ever since she'd been elected President of the Commonwealth. The stresses and strains of holding the Commonwealth together were taking their toll, despite the best rejuvenation treatments available on Avalon. Edward was privately relieved that she wasn't legally allowed to serve more than one term in office, although he did worry about what would happen when the time came to transfer power. *That* would be the first true test of the Commonwealth's stability.

"I trust you both – and so does the Council," she said. "Good luck."

The Professor nodded, threw them both an unreadable look and then left the room. Edward felt a moment of sympathy, knowing that Professor Caesius was going back to a wife who didn't really deserve him. It was beyond his understanding *why* the Professor stayed with the woman, unless there was genuine love there. But who would fall in love with a woman who could be haughtily aristocratic one moment and a nervous wreck the second?

She's been broken, Edward thought, grimly. Not everyone could meet shifts in fortune with the internal fortitude the Slaughterhouse sought to install in its graduates. At some point, further defiance and struggle just seemed useless and people gave up. Fiona Caesius had gone from being a social queen to a desperate woman in poverty so quickly that she'd had no time to adapt. And then she'd been taken away from Earth…

"You're boarding tomorrow," Gaby said, softly. "Is your escort ready to depart?"

"I think so," Edward said. He'd skimmed over the reports from Lieutenant Yamane, but he'd purposely not kept a close eye on her.

"Loading up the shuttles will commence tomorrow, with the aim of having the entire formation embarked by the end of the day. We'll learn a great deal from doing it."

Gaby nodded. "I'll miss you," she admitted, changing the subject. "Four months without you to warm my bed."

"I'll miss you too," Edward told her. It would be the longest trip he'd taken from Avalon – and it would put a strain on their relationship, even though they weren't married. He tried to tell himself that it didn't matter if she found someone else while he was gone, but his heart refused to believe it. "I'd take you along if I could."

Gaby laughed. "And what sort of example would *that* set for your troops?"

Edward laughed too. He'd always hated the officers who took luxuries – and wives, lovers or concubines – with them when they went into war zones, knowing that they were taking up valuable space that could have been used for more supplies. Besides, knowing that their officers had access to women while they didn't wasn't good for moral among the enlisted men. There might be no shortage of prostitutes outside army bases, but there was no way they could be taken onboard ship.

"A poor one," he said. He reached for her and pulled her into a hug. Her lips met his and they kissed deeply. "I'll be back before you know it."

"Tell your men to take very good care of you," Gaby said. She fixed him with a stern expression that dared him to disagree. "That's a direct order, by the way."

Edward sighed. Command Sergeant Gwendolyn Patterson – his senior sergeant – wouldn't be accompanying him to Lakshmibai, but that hadn't stopped her issuing strict orders to Blake Coleman. 1st Platoon was to accompany him at all times and keep him out of trouble, even if they had to sit on him. Technically, Coleman outranked the sergeant, but few lieutenants would defy an order from the chief NCO.

"I will," he promised.

He kissed her again, feeling her body pressing against his. It would have been easy to take it further, no matter what they'd privately agreed about not showing affection outside the bedroom. He had to force down the temptation and step backwards before it was too late.

"You know," he said slowly, "once I get back, we could get married."

Gaby laughed, although there was an undertone of sadness in it. "You're already married," she said, reaching up to tap the Rifleman's Tab on his collar. "The Marine Corps is a jealous mistress. I don't think she would approve."

"I know," Edward said, quietly. Even now, with most of his duties keeping him firmly on Avalon, they could never be truly together. And she too had her own duties. The President of the Commonwealth couldn't marry her senior military officer without one of them surrendering their position. "And I'm sorry."

He kissed her one final time and walked out of her office.

CHAPTER FOUR

It may seem absurd to think of nations as people (although humans do believe in national characters), but there is a great deal of truth in it. While most nations try to govern themselves according to geopolitical imperatives, hurt feelings and other emotions can and do affect international affairs.
-Professor Leo Caesius, *Diplomacy: The Lessons of the Past.*

"He isn't doing too badly," Joe Buckley muttered.

Jasmine shrugged. Every soldier in the CEF – they'd avoided the Imperial Army's concept of rear-echelon motherfuckers as much as possible – was required to undertake a two-mile run every day and she'd insisted that Emmanuel Alves join them. She'd half-expected him to decline, or to insist on being ferried around the battlefield in a luxury vehicle, but instead he'd put his head down and run with the best of them. His timings weren't very good – certainly not up to Marine standards – yet he wasn't as out of shape as most civilians.

"I suppose he isn't," she said, reluctantly. He'd actually stayed in the background as she hammered the CEF into shape, only asking her questions when it was clear that she had time to spare. "Maybe this won't be so bad after all."

"Wait until he's on the transport," Buckley advised. "You'll see what he's *really* like when he's cooped up with thousands of sweaty soldiers."

"True," Jasmine agreed. The best efforts of air scrubbers couldn't purge the air of the stench of thousands of men sharing the same compartment. She'd known otherwise promising soldiers who'd been unable to cope with the thought of spending so much time in close proximity to hundreds of others. "But he did survive living rough while the war was being waged over Avalon."

Buckley snorted. "But he was still out in the open air," he pointed out. "This time, he'll be in an interstellar transporter."

He gave Jasmine a rather sardonic look. "I think he's interested in you," he added. "Didn't someone tell him that you could take him with both hands tied behind your back?"

Jasmine glowered at him. "I don't think that's likely," she said, crossly. "I think he's more interested in his story than me personally."

"You could ensure he writes a good story about you, if you're careful," Buckley teased. "Or perhaps if you broke up with him…"

"Stop channelling Blake," Jasmine ordered. She shook her head in rueful disbelief. "It doesn't suit you."

"Blake's got his hands full right now," Buckley reminded her. "*Someone* has to take his place as regimental joker and asshole."

Jasmine rolled her eyes. "How come *I* never reached that high rank?"

"Too responsible," Buckley told her. He stuck out his tongue in a thoroughly childish manner. "By the time you could be considered for the post, you were already too serious and boringly mature for the position."

Jasmine smiled. She'd been new to the company on Han, when the entire planet had exploded into chaos and she'd probably worked too hard to fit in. But it had been worth it, she knew, even if she *had* had to put up with Blake's sense of humour. Playing pranks on FNGs was an old military tradition. So was playing pranks on other units, but that was rare in the Marine Corps. Jasmine still wondered who'd suggested it to the Knights.

"Me and my bright ideas," she said. She gave Buckley a long considering look. "How's Lila taking the forthcoming separation?"

"Not too well," Buckley admitted. "She knew that I would have to leave eventually, but I think she hoped that it wouldn't be until much later. Right now, she's talking about returning to her family and putting our stuff into storage until I return. Pity we can't take her with us…"

He gave Jasmine a beseeching look that made her roll her eyes. "I can't make those decisions," she said, shaking her head. She had absolute authority over the CEF – certainly more than any Imperial Army officer would have enjoyed – but she had no authority to allow anyone outside the military to accompany them. Besides, Lila Buckley couldn't really make herself useful. "Ask the Colonel."

"He doesn't want to be bothered by me," Buckley said. He looked down at the concrete ground for a long moment, then back up at Jasmine. "You do realise that you technically outrank him now?"

"I told you to stop channelling Blake," Jasmine said, tartly. It was true that a Brigadier outranked a Colonel, at least formally, but Colonel Stalker was also the senior officer in the Army of Avalon. Like most of the detached Stalker's Stalkers, he held several separate posts at once. "I don't think I can give him orders."

"At least not now," Buckley said. He elbowed her significantly. "What about when you're on the ground?"

"We'll deal with that when it happens," Jasmine said. It was true that there were situations where a senior officer had to defer to a junior, something most junior officers dreaded. Legal rights or no, they might still incur the wrath of a superior officer and their careers would suffer. "Anyway, it isn't as if the Colonel is going to be with the CEF."

"One would hope so," Buckley agreed. He elbowed her again as the men reached the end of the two-mile track. "Look; he's finished…and he isn't even winded. Much."

Jasmine smiled, remembering her first day at Boot Camp. They'd been ordered to run a mile and a half…and a third of the new recruits had been gasping, wheezing and coughing by the end of the run. She'd thought herself in great shape until she'd discovered just how far she had to go before she could even graduate from Boot Camp, let alone the Slaughterhouse. But, for a civilian, she had to admit that the reporter had done very well.

"We'll give him more time on the range," she said, as the first flight of shuttles came into view, heading down towards the landing pad at the far side of the base. "I don't want him behind me with a weapon until I'm *sure* he knows what he's doing with it."

Buckley smirked. "And what sort of weapon do you have in mind?"

"I'll tell Lila you said that," Jasmine said. "I'm sure she'll be very impressed."

"No," Buckley said, quickly. "Anything, but that!"

Jasmine concealed her amusement and started to walk towards the main building, pulling her datapad off her belt as she walked. The first Warriors from the CEF were already being prepped for transfer to the shuttles – and then to the transports, waiting in high orbit.

And then they could finally start moving.

"All right," Sergeant Grieves barked, as the hatch slammed open. "Everyone out!"

Michael gripped his rifle tightly as he led the way out of the Warrior AFV. It was a thoroughly ugly vehicle, without even the brutal elegance of the Landshark Main Battle Tanks, but he knew from experience that it was extremely tough. The vehicles were designed to take incoming fire from machine guns, RPGs and even heavy IEDs without being disabled, let alone wounding or killing the soldiers inside. During exercises, the only injuries the company had suffered had been aching ears; the sound-proofing was far from perfect.

He knelt down as the rest of the platoon formed up in a protective circle, ready to repel attack. For a long moment, they held the pose and then the Sergeant blew a whistle and they relaxed – slightly. It was quite possible that the endless exercises and simulations they'd carried out over the last two days had not yet come to an end. He looked back at the vehicle, then over at the massive shuttle waiting on the landing pad. It seemed an odd place to carry out an ambush.

But even a main battle tank is hopelessly vulnerable in a shuttle, he thought, remembering some of the campaigns he'd been forced to study when he'd gone back to the Knights. The Marines had been called upon to storm entire planets in the past…and the defenders, knowing just how deadly the Marines were on the ground, had fought hard to thin out the shuttles as much as possible. A single hit could take out an entire platoon of Marines and their support vehicles.

"At ease," he ordered, when he saw the signal from the Sergeant. The exercise was definitely over. Ahead of them, the shuttle was already opening its hatches. "Corporal Peotone, take the Warrior forward, into the shuttle."

He smiled as the Warrior hummed forward, weapons and sensors already retreating inside the heavily-armoured hull. It still surprised him just how *quiet* the vehicles actually were, particularly when compared to the primitive designs Avalon had been forced to use before the Marines had arrived. He hadn't believed that someone could actually sneak up to an enemy position in a tank – or an AFV – until he'd actually seen it done. The vehicles were almost impossible to hear unless one was at very close range.

But they would probably have a sensor net out too, he told himself. The Warrior shuddered slightly as it entered the shuttle, then carefully positioned itself in place to be secured to the deck. Michael stowed his rifle over his shoulder and followed it into the shuttle, where two crewmen were already checking its moorings. The driver shut the vehicle down completely and scrambled out, dogging down the hatch behind him. Michael watched as the Warrior was secured to the deck, then checked it for himself. He'd been warned, time and time again, to take nothing for granted.

"Good," he grunted finally, and straightened up. The remainder of the platoon was waiting outside. "Come on in; the water's fine."

Michael smiled at their expressions. It was odd, but he was one of a handful of officers and enlisted men who had any experience in operations outside the planet's atmosphere. His men were brave, naturally, yet space held plenty of terrors for those who had never experienced it before. He recalled how nervous he'd been the first time he'd flown into space and carefully refrained from taking official notice of the more nervous soldiers. They'd grow used to it.

Unless they're natural-born groundhogs, he thought, remembering what the RockRats had sneered about those they called dirty-feet. They'd believed that humanity had no place on a planet's surface and the only place to realise humanity's destiny was out in space. There were times when he was tempted to agree with them, but then he went out to hike through the countryside and knew better. The RockRat habitats lacked the natural beauty of a planetary biosphere.

The Sergeant checked the men as they sat down and buckled in, then sat down next to Michael and passed him a datapad. Michael took it and skimmed quickly through the final series of readiness reports, confirmed that they were accurate and then pressed his thumbprint against the sensor, sending a copy to the brigade's CO. He in turn would report to Brigadier Yamane that the 1st Avalon Mechanized Infantry Battalion was at full combat readiness.

Or it will be once we're on the ground, he thought. A dull rumble ran through the shuttle as its drives powered up, then it shook violently as it lifted off and clawed frantically into the sky. There were no portholes, unlike the civilian shuttles he'd used during his brief stint with the RockRats; he had to admit that the experience was a little unnerving, even before the gravity field began to shift slightly, compensating for the loss of Avalon's gravity field. As always, the artificial gravity field made him feel lightheaded as it shimmered into existence, although the technicians swore blind that it was his imagination. He made a mental note to check how many others were equally light-headed as the shuttle left the atmosphere and then closed his eyes. There was just enough time for a brief catnap before the shuttle docked with the *Koenraad Jurgen* and they had to disembark.

And then they would finally be on their way.

———

"She isn't very pretty, is she?"

Jasmine smiled at the surprise in the reporter's voice. *Civilian* starships were designed with a sense of aesthetics; military designers could hardly allow themselves such a luxury. *Koenraad Jurgen* – named for a Marine who'd died in combat against pirates – was a blocky mass, studded with sensor and weapons blisters. She would definitely not win any awards, Jasmine knew, but she would do the job. There was no need to ask for anything else.

"She's designed to allow us to disembark and deploy as quickly as possible," Jasmine said. The starship's underside was a teeming mass of assault and transport shuttles, attached to the hull rather than being taken inside the starship. In an emergency deployment, every second counted.

Disengaging a shuttle from an airlock was much quicker than launching it out of a shuttlebay. "And she's tough."

But not battleship tough, she added, in the privacy of her own mind. A battleship could ride out a nuke detonating against her hullmetal, but *Koenraad Jurgen* would be devastated by a single direct hit. The shuttles and other attached elements would be wiped out of existence, even though the main body of the ship would survive. *We dare not take on an enemy warship in space.*

The Terran Marine Corps had operated its own force of purpose-built transports, but none of them had been left at Avalon for the Commonwealth to put to work. Instead, a new class of transports had been designed, drawing on the centuries of experience in the Marine datafiles – and, more practically, the experience of the Marines serving under Colonel Stalker. Jasmine had never had to carry out a forced landing on a heavily-defended world – sneaking onto Admiral Singh's capital didn't count – but she knew that they could be hellish. The designers had done their best to ensure that their transports were capable of getting the Marines where they were needed and then escaping before they could be destroyed.

She smiled at the reporter's expression as the transport loomed up, suddenly becoming a wall of metal hanging against the endless field of stars. For a long moment, it looked as though they were going to ram the transport – the reporter blanched and clutched at his seat – before they came to a halt. A faint quiver ran through the shuttle as it docked with the transport, followed by a dull click as the hatch unlocked, allowing them to enter the ship.

"Optical illusion," Jasmine said, softly. "We weren't in any real danger."

"Thank you," the reporter said, quietly. "It's my first time off-world."

Jasmine nodded as she unstrapped herself from the seat and stood upright, pulling her duffel back from under the seat and slinging it over her back. It always struck her as strange just how few people in the Empire had been into space, even though the Empire had controlled over a third of the galaxy. But then, not everyone had the thirst for adventure – and the desire to prove herself – that had led Jasmine to leave her homeworld and join the Marines.

She led the way through the hatch and saluted the flag painted on the bulkhead, then led the way down to where the soldiers were flowing onto the giant transport. The reporter followed her like a stray puppy, with Joe Buckley bringing up the rear. Her HQ staff would finish unloading the shuttle and then take their place in their compartment, ready for the trip.

The reporter muttered a curse as they stepped through an airlock and into one of the holds. A dozen Warrior AFVs were secured to the deck, having been transported up from the planet's surface and unloaded into the transport. Behind them, a pair of Landshark tanks dominated the hold, their main guns looking thoroughly intimidating even without ammunition. Jasmine looked at their treads – which had left marks on the hullmetal that would have to be cleaned, once they were under way – and smiled to herself. The Landshark tanks were primitive, but no one could deny that they did their duties very well.

"I always wondered," the reporter said, "why you don't produce hovering tanks."

Jasmine smiled. She'd wondered the same thing herself, back when she'd gone to Boot Camp. It was a far from uncommon question.

"The more complex a piece of equipment is," she said simply, "the more likely it is to fail on the battlefield. A Landshark tank's treads are easier to repair than an antigravity generator. And besides, an antigravity generator can be detected from quite some distance. It's much simpler to rely on something so primitive that it can be hard to detect."

She would have continued, but they were interrupted by an all-hands announcement that echoed through the entire ship. "NOW HEAR THIS," a voice barked. "DEPARTURE IN SEVEN HOURS, FORTY MINUTES. I SAY AGAIN, DEPARTURE IN SEVEN HOURS, FORTY MINUTES."

"That's us told," Joe Buckley muttered, from behind her.

"See that everything is stowed away before the loadmasters come to inspect it," Jasmine said, turning to face him. They shared a moment of pure understanding. It was unlikely in the extreme that the loading would proceed without problems. They weren't commanding experienced Marines this time, but soldiers who'd never travelled on an interstellar transport before. "And then pass the word down the chain. Everyone is to have time to rest before we return to the training simulations."

The reporter looked surprised. "You intend to keep training while *en route*?"

"Of course," Jasmine said, dryly. "What do you think this is? A luxury cruise?"

"Hard training, easy mission," Joe Buckley said. "Easy training, god-awfully hard mission."

"You need to keep up with your exercise too," Jasmine added, before the reporter could say a word. "You never know what might happen once we reach the ground."

The reporter frowned. "You really expect trouble?"

"Always," Jasmine said. She doubted that there had ever been a Marine deployment that *hadn't* attracted trouble, even if it had just been nothing more than surreptitious punch-ups with the Imperial Army. "It's best to be prepared."

CHAPTER FIVE

> This should not be surprising. One nation may control access to another nation's supplies of raw materials; another may be a potential threat or ally when/if war threatens on the horizon. Diplomacy may ensure that the supplies keep coming, the borders remain calm and – perhaps – there will be armed support if war breaks out.
> -Professor Leo Caesius, *Diplomacy: The Lessons of the Past.*

Edward watched through the observation blister as Avalon fell away behind the transport, feeling a strange mixture of relief that they were finally on their way and despondency at leaving Avalon behind. It was odd, but Avalon had become his *home*; despite all the warnings about becoming too attached to any one duty posting, he had wound up falling in love with his new homeworld. Leaving Avalon – and Gaby – hurt worse than he had expected.

You knew that was a possibility, he told himself, sternly. He'd never resigned himself to spending the rest of his life on a single world, but somehow an…*acceptance* had crept up on him when he hadn't been watching his own thoughts. Unlike his subordinates, he hadn't been able to leave the planet frequently, even to visit the other Commonwealth worlds. Now…he was paying the price.

Marines weren't *supposed* to be become attached to any specific world, not even Earth. It was vanishingly rare for a Marine unit to remain on a single world longer than a year or two – or, rather, it *had* been vanishingly rare. Edward had wondered, during the sleepless nights he'd had when they'd been told that they were on their own, just what had happened to the rest of the Marine Corps. It was a question that had never been fully answered. Surely, the Commandant had set up other bastions of civilisation – Avalon couldn't have been the only one – but Edward hadn't been told anything about them. Operational security had to be maintained. He touched the golden cross the Commandant had given him and scowled, remembering the last time he'd seen him. Who knew where the Commandant was now?

He caught sight of a light cruiser effortlessly holding pace with the transport and smiled to himself. Civilians believed that a Marine transport starship could operate on its own, but only a fool would risk so many soldiers when it wasn't absolutely necessary. A small escort squadron would be enough to deter pirates, without seeming an overwhelming threat to Governor Brown and his subordinates. And they could hold the line long enough for the transport to escape, if they ran into serious trouble.

The hatch hissed open behind him. He turned to see Professor Caesius. The Professor looked tired and wan, but surprisingly enthusiastic about being on the way at last. Edward had a sudden flash of *Deja Vu*, remembering their departure from Earth. They'd spoken in the observation blister then too.

"Leo," he said, welcomingly. "How are you?"

"Just finished writing a letter to Mandy and Mindy," the Professor said, as he joined Edward in front of the transparent blister and stared out into space. "Just in case…you know. I wanted them to know that I was proud of them."

Edward nodded. Both of the Professor's daughters had been brats when they'd been shipped to Avalon – and bitterly resented having to leave Earth, even though they'd had little real hope of a life even before their father had wound up in hot water. Now, Mandy was a Captain in the Commonwealth Navy and Mindy was working her way up through the Knights of Avalon. They would never have achieved *that* on Earth.

"So you should be," he said, shortly. "And Fiona?"

"She doesn't like the cabin," the Professor admitted. "I told her that there weren't any bigger ones available."

"There aren't," Edward said. "This isn't a battleship – or a flagship. My cabin isn't any larger than yours."

"But there's only one of you," the Professor pointed out. "I have two people in *my* cabin."

"It could be worse," Edward pointed out. He grinned, relishing the opportunity to tease the older man. "You could be sharing a compartment with a hundred soldiers. Some of them will snore, some will take a really stinky dump in the middle of the night and some will be jerking off under the blankets. Compared to that, sharing a room with one's wife might be heaven."

He smiled at the Professor's expression. The Professor had admired the whole ethos of the Marine Corps from a distance, but he hadn't actually *met* a Marine until he'd been exiled from Earth. Or, for that matter, anyone else from the military, even the Civil Guard. But then, that hadn't been uncommon on Earth or the rest of the Core Worlds. The gulf between the military and the civilians they defended had been light-years wide even before the Empire had entered its final downward spiral. The reality…had been a mild shock for the Professor.

"I know," the Professor admitted. He scowled. "But the cabin is still very small and I…needed to get out."

"I am not the best person to ask for relationship counselling," Edward warned. "And I wouldn't really trust anyone who thought they *could* help you."

He gave the older man a sympathetic look. "Perhaps you need to help her find something to do," he said. "Something that allows her to develop herself. Something that would win her respect for being *herself*."

"I know that," the Professor muttered. "But what is there that she can do?"

Edward understood his dilemma. A civilian from Earth, no matter how many degrees he or she might have earned, would have real problems finding a post on the Rim. Most of Earth's emigrants found themselves working as grunt labour – or winding up in real trouble when they tried to act as if they were entitled to accommodation and food without actually working for a living. And Fiona Caesius was too old to try out for the military, or start working on a farm, or even take care of children. If, of course, she was *trusted* to take care of children on Avalon. She'd been born on Earth, after all.

"Medicine, perhaps," Edward said, finally. "There are quite a few training courses she could take that might help her to build her own career. And a word in someone's ear would at least give her the chance to try."

"That might work," Caesius said. "But what if she doesn't succeed?"

"She won't succeed if she doesn't try," Edward pointed out. A thought struck him and he frowned. "Can she *read*? And write?"

"Yes," the Professor said. He didn't seem surprised or insulted by the question. "I thought she might actually be able to work in the Imperial Library, but she's from *Earth*..."

Edward nodded. Earth's illiteracy rates had been the worst in the Empire, with an estimated sixty percent of the population – the officially-acknowledged population – being unable to read or write. It was blamed on Earth's pathetic schooling, he knew; it *was* possible to get a reasonably decent education, but someone had to really *work* on it. The kids on Earth generally found it far easier to sink into a morass of ignorance, amply fuelled by public entertainments on the datanet. And they tended to be thoroughly awful human beings.

"They won't hold that against her if she works hard and becomes a medic," Edward assured him. He gave the Professor a long considering look. "Do you love her?"

The Professor hesitated. "I think so," he admitted, finally. "But there are times when I feel as if we're doomed to lose what remains of our relationship."

"I think you need to concentrate on finding something for her to do that will give her life meaning," Edward said. "She *is* going to be the hostess while we're planet-side, isn't she?"

"That's true," the Professor said. "But will she do a good job?"

Edward shrugged. "No one has hosted a diplomatic meeting between equals for centuries," he pointed out. The meetings with the Trade

Federation had been as informal as meetings with the RockRats. "I think no one will notice any minor errors."

He looked back out towards the stars. "And it will definitely boost her confidence," he added. "Having something to do will *definitely* help her."

———

"Is now a bad moment?"

Jasmine rubbed her eyes as she looked up from the desk. Emmanuel Alves was standing in the hatchway, looking quizzically at her. Jasmine hesitated, remembering the endless paperwork she had to do, then put the datapad aside. *Anything*, even talking to a reporter, was better than reading the same documents time and time again.

"It shouldn't be," she said, waving for him to enter the compartment and close the hatch. If anything, her office on the transport was smaller than her office on Avalon, with barely enough room to swing a cat. The meetings she had to host for her senior officers had to take place in a briefing compartment. "What can I do for you?"

"Call me Emmanuel," the reporter said. "And I was hoping for some background information."

Jasmine scowled. "All the background information I can give you on the CEF is already on the open-access datanet," she pointed out. At least the reporter – Emmanuel, if he insisted – hadn't tried to hack into the secure databanks. *That* had happened on Han, if rumour was to be believed. "And I don't have time to go through it with you."

She grimaced down at the latest fitness reports. Her subordinates were taking advantage of the passage from Avalon to carry out a battery of health and general fitness tests. Thankfully, no serious problems had cropped up, apart from one soldier who seemed to have developed a taste for Crazy Juice. Jasmine had chewed him out *thoroughly* and assigned him to punishment duties for the next two weeks – and she devoutly hoped that was the end of the matter. Crazy Juice wasn't *illegal*, but it was banned from military units. Bringing several doses of the stuff onboard ship was a court-martial offence.

"I was hoping for some background information on *you*," the reporter said, diffidently. "My readers wanted to know what made someone a Marine."

Jasmine frowned, remembering Joe Buckley's comment that the reporter was interested in her. It had struck her as nothing more than the regular teasing exchanged between Marines – platoon mates were brothers and sisters – but was he actually *serious*? Or was she reading more into the situation than was actually there? It was difficult to know for sure.

"I don't think my life is *that* interesting," she said, after a long moment. "And…"

"Come on," the reporter interrupted. "I did some research. There's only four female Marines in Stalker's Stalkers, nine if you count Auxiliaries. Of *course* you're fascinating."

"Matter of opinion," Jasmine said, feeling oddly uncomfortable. She hadn't felt so…*exposed* since the first time she'd taken part in a live-fire drill, with very real bullets hitting the ground all around her. Stripping down with the rest of the platoon had been nothing in comparison. "There isn't much about my life I chose to remember."

The reporter quirked an eyebrow. "You ran away from home?"

Jasmine shook her head, running one hand through her hair. She'd meant to have it cut, but there just hadn't been time. "My family thought I was a little odd," she admitted, reluctantly. "I was always out and about, roaming over the countryside…it wasn't something they considered strictly appropriate for a young girl. But I just couldn't have stayed there for the rest of my life. I signed up with the Marines when I was eighteen and never looked back."

The thought made her wince. She'd had brothers and sisters, nephews and nieces, and she hadn't the faintest idea what had happened to *any* of them. The last she'd heard had been while the company had been on Earth. They'd still thought of her as odd, she knew from their recorded messages, but they'd been proud of her. And there were times when she missed them terribly.

"My world was boring," she added. "And I wanted to see the rest of the universe."

The reporter smiled. "And have you?"

Jasmine smiled back. "I've seen the Slaughterhouse, Earth, Han and a dozen other worlds along the Rim," she said. "I think I've seen something of the universe."

But it was a tiny fraction of the whole of the Empire, she knew. There were people who just travelled from world to world, working long enough on each world to build up the funds to buy another starship ticket and head onwards. They'd seen much more of the universe than herself, yet even they hadn't seen *everything*. There was always something else to see.

She chatted back and forth with Emmanuel until her wristcom bleeped, reminding her that she had an appointment with Colonel Stalker. When she looked at it, she was surprised to realise that she'd been talking for nearly an hour. She hastily ended the conversation, shoed him out of the room and bellowed for Joe Buckley. He was grinning from ear to ear when he entered her office and closed the hatch.

"You could have rescued me," she said, without heat. "Bastard."

Buckley's grin grew wider, somehow. "But you were having a good time," he said. "And you needed to relax."

Jasmine snorted as she stood up and pulled on her jacket. "This isn't a bar on the surface," she said, sharply. "I have work to do…"

"You're spending too long on it," Buckley said. "Ask Sergeant Harris if you don't believe me."

Jasmine snorted, again. "And how would you know that I was spending too much time on it?"

"I did a few months on flypaper duty," Buckley reminded her, using the slang term for being attached to an HQ staff. "You have to learn what is important and what isn't."

"Splendid," Jasmine said, evilly. "You can read through this shit" – she pushed one of the datapads into his hand – "and tell me what I actually need to know."

She was still smiling as she walked out of the hatch and headed up towards the briefing room.

———

"This is all fantastically complex," Fiona said.

Leo nodded. It had taken him a week to download everything the onboard library had on diplomatic meetings between equals, almost all of which dated back to the Unification Wars. Logic told him that there should have been a great deal more from the time before the Empire, but someone had scrubbed it out of the datafiles – if it had been there in the first place. The Empire had worked hard to try to create the impression that it had always been in existence, even to the point of censoring history textbooks and barring research into the deep past.

"These are the only precedents we have," he said, softly. "Everything else we have is for meetings between superiors and inferiors."

Fiona smiled as she worked her way through the protocols. "We have a place in the city, they have a place in the city…and we hold the talks somewhere else, *also* in the city?"

"Yes," Leo said. He could see the logic in it; there'd be a distance between the two delegations, allowing them to withdraw if discussions became too heated. And it would allow the locals to serve as mediators, as well as providing local security. "And you'll have to be our hostess."

He looked down at the datapad, which was displaying the files that Governor Brown's representatives had sent to the Commonwealth. There would be two senior representatives from the Wolfbane Sector, along with a relative handful of troops; Leo couldn't decide if that was a gesture of confidence or an admission that the talks were meant to be kept in confidence. Beyond that…there was a note that accommodation would be arranged by the planetary government and that no troops would be permitted in their capital city, apart from a handful of armed guards. The Colonel had told him that those guards would be a full company of Knights and a platoon of Marines.

"I won't let the Colonel down," Fiona assured him, quickly.

Leo had to smile, seeing the girl he'd married emerge briefly from under the bitter older woman she'd become. Fiona had enjoyed the social whirl of being married to a Professor far more than he'd enjoyed *being* a Professor; given time, perhaps she could work as a diplomat. It seemed absurd, but managing a large dinner party involved a *lot* of diplomacy…

He pushed the thought aside and gave his wife a hug. "And there's something else," he said, softly. "Would you like to train for a medical career?"

Fiona tensed against him. Doctors from Earth had a ghastly reputation, although Leo knew from his research that much of it came from the conditions the bureaucrats forced on them or the poor quality of medical supplies on Earth. Those who could afford off-world doctors did; everyone else took their chances or chose to go without treatment. And Fiona already keenly felt the discrimination against Earth-born settlers along the Rim.

The Colonel's from Earth, Leo thought, with a flicker of resentment. *Why doesn't he face it too?*

But he already knew the answer to *that*. Colonel Stalker had proved himself, while Fiona had tried to cosy up to the old Council. It didn't encourage the settlers on Avalon to take her very seriously, or to treat her with respect.

"You'd be studying here," he said, keeping his voice calm. "They'd know that you weren't trained on Earth."

"I'll do this first," Fiona said, finally. She looked down at the datapad. "This is going to be enough hassle for the moment."

Leo nodded. At least she wasn't dismissing the idea out of hand.

"We have three weeks before we arrive," he said, giving her another hug. "You'll have plenty of time to revise."

CHAPTER SIX

> There is a general perception that all treaties are negotiated between equals. This is simply not true. As a general rule, some countries are considerably more powerful than others. The more powerful countries have a stronger negotiating position than the weaker countries.
>
> -Professor Leo Caesius, *Diplomacy: The Lessons of the Past.*

"Normal space in twenty seconds," the helmsman said. "All systems report full readiness."

"Weapons and point defence grid online, ready to engage," the tactical officer added. "Sensors powering up, ready to go to full power."

"Good," Captain Hardy said. He keyed his console. "All hands, prepare for return to normal space; I say again, all hands prepare for return to normal space."

Edward settled back in his chair, resisting the impulse to take command and give orders. It would have been a severe breach of protocol; he might be the force's nominal commander, but Captain Hardy was the ultimate authority onboard his ship. Instead, he counted down the seconds until *Koenraad Jurgen* returned to normal space and the display filled up with new icons.

"Holding station at waypoint," the helmsman reported. "FTL drives spooling up; jump readiness in six minutes, fifty seconds."

"Nine contacts in detection range," the sensor officer added, as the yellow icons of unknown starships turned green. "All Confederation; I say again, all Confederation."

Edward let out a breath he hadn't realised that he'd been holding. The worst nightmare of any spacer was coming out of Phase Space right into a carefully-prepared ambush, with the enemy ships armed and firing before their victim's sensors had even registered their presence. It was almost certainly impossible – even if potential aggressors had known the exact coordinates they'd intended to arrive, there would be no guarantee that they'd arrive in precisely the right location – but that didn't stop officers and crew worrying about the possibility. The entire squadron could be wiped out before it knew that it was under attack.

"Hold the drive at thirty seconds," Captain Hardy ordered. It would place considerable wear and tear on the equipment, but the military-grade systems could take it. "Can you detect anything within the inner system?"

"Negative," the sensor officer said. "Wait…picking up a handful of radio beacons, unknown origin."

Smugglers, perhaps, Edward thought. Lakshmibai had no space industry at all, unsurprisingly. The system had no gas giant or asteroid belt to attract investment, or even a hidden RockRat colony. According to the datafiles, the original settlers had wanted a planet where they would be undisturbed by the rest of the universe. They'd been largely disappointed.

"Colonel," the Captain said, catching Edward's attention. "I believe that we should proceed into the inner system."

"Agreed," Edward said. There was nothing to be gained by lurking along the edge of the system, not when they had an appointment in orbit around Lakshmibai itself. "Take us into the system."

He settled back and forced himself to relax as the small squadron headed into the inner system, its sensors picking up four rocky worlds and a bare handful of comets. The system was surprisingly empty; Lakshmibai's only companion was a single moon, which appeared to be largely uninteresting. Most of the radio beacons seemed to be mounted on the comets, apart from one orbiting the outermost rocky world. A standard challenge received no answer.

"There are a handful of signals coming from Lakshmibai itself," the communications officer reported, "but they're all very primitive. I don't think they've even detected our presence."

Edward shared a long look with the Captain. It wasn't uncommon for a world along the Rim to have no deep-space tracking arrays, but Lakshmibai was light-years in towards the Core Worlds. But then, it's founders *had* wanted to turn their back on the universe. No doubt they'd thought that the universe would oblige by ignoring them in turn.

"Contact," the sensor officer snapped. "Captain, I'm picking up seven medium cruisers, holding station near the planet. They just brought their drives online!"

"Send them the prepared greeting," Captain Hardy ordered. They'd known that they would meet Governor Brown's representatives near Lakshmibai. "And launch a flight of probes in their direction."

It was nearly forty minutes before they picked up a response from the newcomers. "They're welcoming us to Lakshmibai," the communications officer said, "and informing us that we may take possession of the orbital station at our leisure."

"Thank them," Edward said, shortly. "Can you ID the ships?"

"Not at this range," the sensor officer said. "Their drive fields suggest *Proctor*-class medium cruisers, but two of them seem to have unusually enhanced drive emissions. They may have been extensively refitted."

"Or they might be new-build," Captain Hardy said. "Wolfbane has a shipyard, doesn't it?"

"Yes, sir," the sensor officer said.

Edward put the matter to one side as the planet grew closer. It was quite possible that Wolfbane was producing its own starships, just like the Commonwealth – and Admiral Singh. Unfortunately, there was no way to know just what had come off the slips since Avalon had lost contact with the Empire. Even the most astute intelligence officer had had to admit that all he could do was *guess*.

"The orbital station is still powered up," the sensor officer reported. "They're pinging us, inviting us to dock."

"We don't need to," Captain Hardy said. "Colonel?"

"Send 1st Platoon to sweep the station," Edward ordered. Finding it intact, let alone powered up, was a surprise. The Empire had installed it decades ago, but he'd assumed that it would have been abandoned along with Lakshmibai itself. It wasn't as if the planet had shuttles it could use to keep the station functional. "And then take us into high orbit."

Jasmine felt a flicker of envy as she listened into the conversations between 1st Platoon as they boarded and swept the station for potential surprises. The station should have been unarmed, but it would have been relatively simple to bolt a handful of missile launchers or plasma cannons to the hull – and understandable, in a system where there would be no help if pirates arrived to ransack the station. But nothing showed up, apart from a handful of ex-Imperial Navy technicians who wanted to go somewhere else. Anywhere else.

"That can't be right," the reporter said, as Blake Coleman reported to the Colonel. "They just *abandoned* the techs?"

"Why not?" Jasmine asked, dryly. "They abandoned *us*."

"It seems that they do have *some* links to the former garrison," Colonel Stalker said, through the intercom. "From what they're saying, the base is still manned."

Jasmine considered it, briefly. It seemed hard to imagine a caretaker crew keeping the locals out, but stranger things had happened. Besides, if half of the files were accurate, the locals feared and hated off-worlders. The garrison's crew might have decided that it was better to keep themselves isolated rather than surrender to the planet's inhabitants.

"Then we have to check it out," she said, calmly. "I suggest that the 3rd Avalon Infantry Battalion be dropped on the garrison to provide security."

She could practically hear the Colonel thinking it over. The Knights needed to practice disembarking onto potentially-hostile landing zones, even though 1st Platoon would probably be able to carry out the mission quicker. But then, it would take time to bring the Marines back from the orbital station…

"Make it so," the Colonel ordered. "We'll try to raise the garrison first, then drop the infantry if they refuse to answer."

Jasmine nodded. "Understood," she said. "I'll prepare them for deployment."

"Quite a few local women on the station," Blake Coleman reported, flatly. "They were sent up as comfort women, without any men."

Edward scowled. *That* didn't sound good.

"It seems that the garrison used the station to threaten the locals with planetary bombardment, if they tried to get across the causeway," Coleman continued. "They're being a little cagey about their strength, sir; I'm not sure they *can* bombard the planet."

"It's unlikely, unless they shipped the weapons in from outside the system," Captain Hardy put in. "This system has a shortage of asteroids that can be mined for cheap weapons."

"Picking up a response from the planet's surface," the communications officer said. "Sir?"

"Put it through," Captain Hardy ordered.

"This is General Joseph Raphael, Imperial Army Commandant of Manikarnika Garrison," a thickly-accented voice said. "Please tell me you're coming to take us away."

"This is Edward Stalker, Terran Marine Corps," Edward said. They could explain about the Commonwealth later. "I require a full SITREP and permission to land my men."

"Granted," the voice said. "I'll have the landing beacons powered up for you. But what are you and the others doing here?"

Edward frowned. "It would be easier to explain on the surface," he said, tightly. Had the garrison not communicated with Governor Brown's ships? Or had the ships simply maintained radio silence and waited for Edward's arrival? "What's the local security situation?"

"Tense," Raphael said. "Your forces are cleared to land at the garrison spaceport. Be advised that some rebel forces have access to HVMs and other antiaircraft weapons; I strongly advise you to come in over the ocean and not overfly the land. The garrison is relatively safe, but that may change at any moment."

"Understood," Edward said. "How long has it been since you heard anything from the Empire?"

"Five years," Raphael said, after a pause. "We haven't even been able to pick up any news from trader ships."

Edward blinked in surprise. Five *years*? The planet would have been abandoned before Avalon!

"Something about this doesn't quite add up," Captain Hardy mused, too quietly to be picked up by the microphone. "Sir…"

"I have to go down," Edward said, equally quietly.

He raised his voice. "Bring back 1st Platoon," he ordered. "They can follow the Knights down to the planet's surface."

"Prepare the remainder of the CEF for rapid deployment," Jasmine ordered, grimly. The Colonel should send her or another senior officer, not go down to the planet's surface – and into a possible trap – himself. "And get the first deployments down there as quickly as possible."

The planet was too primitive for communications intercepts to provide anything useful, but orbital observation *was* filling in some of the gaps. Manikarnika Garrison was on an island – not unlike Castle Rock – linked to the mainland through a long causeway that was only usable for an hour or two every day. There was a colossal city on the other end of the causeway, surrounded by rolling hillsides and countryside that would be ideal for an insurgency…they'd already picked up a string of what *had* to be military bases scattered across the countryside. Hundreds of thousands of armed men were scattered across the countryside, watching farmers who seemed to be struggling to grow crops. It didn't look very reassuring.

"The first shuttles are on their way," Joe Buckley assured her. "And we're loading up the others now."

"Good," Jasmine said. She looked over towards the near-orbit display. Governor Brown's ships were keeping their distance, but she knew that could change at any moment. If they decided to turn hostile, they might well catch her forces while they were deploying. "But hold them until we get confirmation that the LZ is secure."

Manikarnika Garrison looked fairly typical for an Imperial Army garrison, although it *was* larger than the files had suggested. Edward studied it thoughtfully as the shuttle descended towards the landing pad, noting the handful of automated weapons systems that had been deployed around the island. Clearly, whatever forces had been abandoned on the planet were insufficient to hold the base against a determined assault. A handful of remote drones seemed to be on constant patrol, watching for infiltrators who tried to land from the ocean.

He tensed as the weapons tracked them as the shuttle came in to land, then relaxed slightly as they touched down without incident. The hatch cracked open a moment later, allowing Blake Coleman and the rest of 1st Platoon to disembark and fan out around the shuttle, looking for possible threats. Edward gritted his teeth – training and experience told him that staying near the landing craft wasn't always a good idea – and waited as patiently as he could for the all-clear. When it came, he was out of the shuttle like a shot.

The warm air struck him as soon as he stepped out of the hatch, blowing in from the ocean and smelling vaguely of salt water and fish. Edward took a deep breath – after spending four weeks cooped up on a transport, it was refreshing to smell fresh air – and then looked down towards the nearest building. The base seemed eerily deserted at first, then he saw a trio of men appearing from the doorway and heading towards the Marines. They all wore Imperial Army dress uniforms.

"Welcome to Manikarnika Garrison," the leader said, as he stopped in front of the Marines. He wore the uniform of a General. "I had almost given up hope."

Edward grimaced. "I know the feeling," he said. "Can I ask for a briefing?"

The General grinned, toothily. "If you tell us what's going on," he said. "We've been frantic since the first ships arrived."

He paused, then pushed onwards. "There was a peacekeeping operation on this planet," he added, ruefully. "They pulled most of the troops out five years ago and promised that we'd be relieved within a couple of months. We've been here since then."

Edward shook his head in disbelief. "Absurd," he said, softly. "How have you managed to hold the base?"

"With difficulty," Raphael explained. "There's only seventy of us, so we set up guns along the causeway and engaged anything that tried to advance towards the base. They tried sending boats and we blew them out of the water, then…well, local political developments convinced them that leaving us to our own devices was a good idea. I think they thought that we could be starved out."

"But you're sitting on top of a mountain of supplies," Edward said. The Imperial Army would have brought along enough MREs to feed hundreds of thousands of men. Seventy soldiers would be bored stiff after five years of MREs, but they'd be alive. "And weapons and suchlike?"

"Enough to hold the line," Raphael explained. "We took in a handful of local women to help with the chores and…other purposes, but apart from that we've kept ourselves isolated. And now I've told you *our* story, you can tell me what's really going on."

Edward hesitated, then started to explain.

"The Empire is gone?" Raphael asked, when he had finished. "Gone *completely*?"

"We haven't seen any trace of organised Imperial power since they pulled back and abandoned us," Edward said. "Right now, a handful of successor states are organising themselves. If there's anything left of the Empire, it isn't likely to return any time soon."

He winced at Raphael's expression. The Marines on Avalon had had time to adapt to being on their own, even if most of them hadn't really accepted – *emotionally* – that the Empire was no more and they'd been abandoned. But they'd also had a great deal of work to do, while Raphael and his handful of men had been cooped up on an island base, surrounded by locals who would kill them as soon as look at them. They'd clung to the thought of the Empire returning to take them away, a thought that had been cruelly betrayed.

"We can take you with us when we leave," he commiserated, softly. "But right now we have other reasons to be here."

"I don't see why this…Governor Brown couldn't have communicated with us," Raphael muttered, darkly. "We didn't have the slightest idea what those ships were doing."

"We'll have to ask him," Edward said. "For the moment, I have to land my force. Would that be acceptable?"

"I don't think we have any objections," Raphael answered, dryly. "We only have two barracks currently in service; you'll have to help us reopen several more, unless you want to sleep out in the open air. I wouldn't advise sending anyone on leave either, no matter how much firepower you have. Off-worlders are not popular on this world."

"Hard to blame them," one of the other officers commented. "The locals had their planet turned upside down by the Empire. They never stood a chance."

"But they deserved it," the third officer said. Edward had the feeling that it was an old argument "There's little worth preserving in their society."

Raphael held up a hand and his two subordinates fell silent. "Land your men," he said, to Edward. "They can have full use of our supplies, as long as you take us with you when you go. None of us want to stay here."

"I quite understand," Edward said. The sooner they carried out the talks, the better. Perhaps they could arrange the next set of talks to take place in deep space or somewhere safer than a potentially hostile world. "I'd also like a set of briefings on local conditions, just in case we have to fight."

"It shall be done," Raphael assured him.

Edward nodded and keyed his wristcom. "Start bringing down the remainder of the troops," he ordered. "And then prepare the ships for departure."

Raphael made a face. "Is that necessary?"

"It's part of the agreement," Edward said, although he had his own doubts now. Perhaps he could convince Governor Brown's representatives to renegotiate the agreement. "We weren't given an alternative."

He watched as the second flight of shuttles came in to land on the landing pad, then started unloading their troops. It would be irritating if they were cooped up permanently on the island; perhaps they could deploy to the mainland and carry out exercises. But they'd have to come to some agreement with the locals first. The analysts suspected that the civil war on the planet's surface was still underway.

"And now," he requested, turning back to the General, "you can tell me more about this damned world."

CHAPTER SEVEN

> This puts them in a position where 'diplomacy' may boil down to an ultimatum that runs 'give us what we want or we'll beat the hell out of you and take it anyway.'
> -Professor Leo Caesius, *Diplomacy: The Lessons of the Past.*

"Welcome to the new base, same as the old base," someone muttered.

"As you were," Michael snapped, as they followed the Warrior out of the shuttle. The AFV rumbled across the tarmac and headed towards the vehicle park next to the empty barracks. "We don't know just what's going to happen here."

But the soldier had a point, he had to admit. The garrison didn't look *that* different from the bases on Avalon, apart from having a name he struggled to pronounce. Indeed, there was something strange about such a large base having a tiny population. The garrisons on Avalon that trained and based the Knights were thrumming with activity at all hours of the day, but this base had hardly anyone in view, apart from the newcomers. And there was a very different scent in the air.

The barracks smelt musty, he discovered, as they opened the doors and peered inside. Everything that might decay had been removed, leaving only the frameworks of hundreds of bunks, shower stalls and tiny compartments for the soldiers to stow their possessions. There were a handful of pieces of graffiti on the walls, but nothing else to suggest that the barracks had once played host to hundreds of soldiers. Someone had cleaned up the compartment *thoroughly*. It struck him as odd; the brief

SITREP they'd been given as the shuttle descended through the atmosphere had suggested that there were only a handful of personnel on the base. But then, if they'd been isolated for over five years, even a relatively small crew could have cleaned up everything.

He reached for his pistol as a door at the far end of the barracks banged open, then relaxed as he saw a dark-skinned woman carrying a colossal pile of pre-packaged bedding on her head. One of the soldiers wolf-whistled as she entered, even though the robes she was wearing hid her body's curves quite nicely. She was followed by several more, all carrying bedding of their own. Michael remembered that some of the locals had been recruited to help maintain the base and relaxed, slightly. It seemed odd to have servants doing *any* of the work – normally, they were expected to take care of themselves – but the base had clearly allowed standards to slip.

Sergeant Grieves evidently agreed. "Don't just stand there, you lugs," he barked. "Each of you take a piece of bedding, then set up by the numbers. Move!"

Michael allowed himself a smile as he took a package from the lead woman. She lowered her eyes, something that bothered him more than he cared to admit, if only because it reminded him of the women on the pirate-operated asteroid. They'd learned to keep their heads down too, knowing that the slightest hint of resistance would result in a savage beating – or worse – from their masters. He felt sick as he unwrapped the package, then spread the inflatable mattress out on a bunk close to the doors. It was alarmingly easy to forget some of the stories he'd been told about life in the Imperial Army – or the Civil Guard.

He looked down at his wristcom as it bleeped. "Briefing at 1700, local time," a voice said, shortly. The device had already adapted to the local time – Lakshmibai had a twenty-seven hour day, something he suspected would cause confusion when they started operating – and linked into the garrison's datanet. "All armoured vehicles are to be paraded on the grounds immediately afterwards."

"Understood," Michael said, dryly. They weren't going to get any time to relax, although he wasn't too surprised. If half of the muttered rumours in the shuttle were accurate, they were landing on a very rebellious and unwelcoming world. "We'll be ready."

He closed the connection, then looked over at the mechanics. The Warriors should be in perfect condition – after all, they hadn't been moved at all while they'd been in transit – but he knew better than to take that for granted. It would be much better to discover any problems *before* they went into operation.

"Pass out the MREs, then we can start working on the Warriors," he ordered the Sergeant. "I need to attend the briefing."

"Understood," the Sergeant said. He lowered his voice. "And you might want to ask about the local women too."

Michael blinked in surprise, then understood. Were the women servants, prostitutes or the wives of the garrison's maintenance crew? It would probably be good to know *before* there was an incident. His men had been starved of female company on the transport and the handful of local women he'd seen had been beautiful. Of course, if half the stories he'd been told were true, there hadn't been a garrison or army base at the height of the Empire that *hadn't* been surrounded by bars, brothels and other institutions intended to separate a soldier from his monthly pay.

"I'll ask," he said, softly. The Imperial Army had no regulations banning sexual contact with the locals, merely banning marriage until someone had several years of service under his belt. "And you can supervise until we *know*."

The briefing room was surprisingly ornate for a garrison on a world the sector government *couldn't* have considered very important, no matter how many people had seriously believed that the Empire could keep the peace right across the universe. Jasmine rolled her eyes as she saw the computer screens, holographic maps and even a near-space orbital display, each one more expensive than a Landshark tank. And there was no *need* for a communications system that could allow the CO to monitor the operations of an entire army…when she considered just how starved the combat arms had been for funds in the last days of the Empire, it made her more than a little mad.

"They don't seem to be working either," Joe Buckley pointed out, when she said her thoughts out loud. "There's no communications nodes out there for them to draw on."

Jasmine nodded. Apart from a handful of drones, the garrison had *no* presence at all on the mainland. There was a live feed from the orbital station, providing additional coverage of the sea around the island and the causeway – currently under the waves – but little else to justify such an expensive investment. She could have purchased enough equipment to raise a light infantry regiment for the price of everything in the garrison.

There was a paper map pinned to the wall, right at the front of the compartment, showing the countryside near the garrison. Someone had been marking on it with pencil, trying to keep track of the political situation. It looked oddly familiar, but it took her several seconds to place it; the maps she'd seen of Avalon, during the height of the Cracker War, had looked quite similar. The political situation shifted then, she realised, shifted so quickly that it was impossible to produce any permanent maps.

"At ease," Colonel Stalker ordered, as he entered the compartment. "Take some coffee or water if you want; this is probably going to be a long session."

Buckley motioned for her to stay where she was, then headed over to the coffee machine. It wasn't common for drinks to be served during Marine Corps briefings, although Jasmine could see some advantages when the briefer was too tedious to keep her attention. Some of the briefers she'd had to listen to on Han – the ones on loan from the Imperial Army in particular – hadn't known to focus on the important details. She'd even had to pretend to pay attention during a briefing on the ecology of the region they were going to use as a base.

She took the cup of coffee and sniffed it, feeling an odd sense of *Déjà Vu*. The Imperial Army had had, according to rumour, a whole series of worlds devoted to producing coffee that was foul-tasting, but very good at keeping soldiers awake. Jasmine hadn't tasted it in years, ever since supplies of pre-packaged foodstuffs on Avalon had run out. The stuff they produced on Avalon just wasn't the same.

"That's why we've come," Buckley muttered. "They want us to pick up the *coffee*."

Jasmine smiled, then suppressed it as one of the garrison's officers stepped forward. "I am Colonel Cindy Macintyre, Imperial Army Intelligence," she said, as the room quietened down. "As punishment for my sins, I was told to remain here with the garrison and monitor the local situation. This has been an immensely difficult undertaking and I cannot guarantee the accuracy of much of the following data. The situation simply changes too rapidly."

"Give her points for honesty," Buckley whispered.

"True," Jasmine whispered back. Intelligence officers, in her experience, tended to assume that they knew everything and that their conclusions were always correct, often ignoring facts that contradicted their theories. There had even been a handful of officers who had claimed that Han wasn't on the verge of exploding, even when Imperial Army garrisons and patrols had been coming under increasingly heavy attack. "But then, her career isn't going to go any further."

"To sum up a very long story, Lakshmibai was founded by a group of exiles from Hindustan, some seven hundred years ago," Colonel Macintyre said. If she'd heard Jasmine and Buckley whispering, she gave no sign of it. "These exiles believed that the key to paradise was to return to the caste system of their ancestors – or how they chose to interpret the caste system – and, after a brief civil war on their homeworld, they were transported here and dumped on the planet's surface, where they started to build their own perfect society.

"Everything went relatively well for them until some bureaucrat in the Imperial Civil Service, looking for a place to put refugees, decided that Lakshmibai would be an ideal destination," she continued, smoothly. "The refugees refused to fit into the caste system and civil war broke out, a situation made worse by an uprising among the lower-caste members, who were confronted by people who didn't care about birth. Their lives were so hopeless that they kept on fighting even after the Imperial Army landed a garrison to assist the local government in dealing with the mess. Right now, large parts of the countryside are effectively under rebel control.

Only the weapons and equipment supplied to the central government have allowed it to remain in power."

Jasmine winced. Avalon, even during the rule of the Council, would be preferable. At least Avalon hadn't had seven hundred years of population growth and development to fuel the fighting, or ensure that the hatreds were too deeply embedded to be removed by anything other than major bloodshed. In some ways, Lakshmibai even sounded like a rerun of Han…

But Han was a sector capital, she reminded herself. *This world isn't even remotely important to anyone else.*

"The caste system is outlined in your briefing notes," Colonel Macintyre said. "What you *need* to know is that there are five prime castes, ranging from rulers and warriors to those who do the shit work. There are actually gradations within the castes – some are more important than others, even though they share the same caste – and you'll be lucky to find someone who *isn't* intensely aware of his status. As a general rule of thumb, higher caste – or position within the caste – trumps everything else. The lower castes have few legal rights."

Buckley stuck up a heavily-muscled arm. "And they just *accept* it?"

"Their religion states that everyone starts out in the lowest caste and, assuming they have lived a good and blameless life, are reincarnated into a higher caste after they die," the Colonel explained. "They climb up the ladder until they pass through the very highest caste and then graduate into paradise. As you can imagine, that is actually quite an effective tool of social control."

Jasmine nodded. If the lower castes genuinely believed that they had to work hard to rise, they would; if the higher castes thought themselves entitled to their power – and that the lower castes existed for their use – they'd become monsters. And those who didn't believe, who questioned the very basis of their society, would be shunned by all of the castes, although for different reasons. Believers wouldn't want any truck with non-believers, for fear that it would rub off.

"Despite – or perhaps because of – their population density, conditions in their cities are actually quite wretched," the Colonel added, returning to her subject. "There is almost no social mobility at all, no way to make a living outside the castes; the vast majority of the population is really little more than property. Vast resources are lavished on temples and palaces for the elite, or military formations assembled from the warrior caste, but almost nothing is spent on the common people. They exist permanently on the verge of starvation, which helps keep them under control. It isn't uncommon for hundreds of lower caste servants to die during winter."

"Just like Earth," Buckley said.

"In many ways, yes," Colonel Macintyre agreed. "But while Earth has several safety valves – people could sign up with a colony development corporation or join the military – Lakshmibai has almost none. If you happen to be born to the untouchable caste, you'll spend half of your life shovelling shit and the other half scavenging for food. And you'll be a permanent victim. Should someone from a higher caste decide that he wants to rape or kill you, no one will stop him. Life will grind you down and you'll be lucky if you live past fifty.

"The rebels generally want to destroy the caste system and replace it with something else," she added. "However, they have several different visions of what they expect to put in its place; several of the rebel groups, I suspect, merely want to reverse the order of the caste system rather than destroying it altogether. Others would be happy if they could declare independence from the local government."

Colonel Stalker leaned forward. "Do you have any contact with the rebels?"

"We have tried to keep ourselves completely isolated from both sides," Colonel Macintyre said. "We didn't want to be drawn into the fighting – or to make it worse by handing over weapons and equipment from the garrison. However, we do know that Jhansi – the settlement on the other side of the causeway – is caught between rebels and the central government. I've been expecting them to start fighting for months now."

Jasmine looked up at the map, then frowned. "Are they worried about you intervening?"

"It's a possibility," Colonel Macintyre said. "But if they have an accurate idea of our strength, they'd know that we couldn't hope to intervene if fighting did break out again."

Major Lobo Villeneuve snorted. "How…*capable* are the local government's forces?"

"Generally, a very mixed bag," Colonel Macintyre said. "Those born to the warrior caste will generally be accepted into the military, regardless of their other qualifications. Some of them are very tough, capable fighters; some are little better than ceremonial units, prancing around in fancy uniforms and shiny vehicles. Right now, they don't have the force to eradicate the rebellion, while the rebels don't have the force to push them back and destroy the central government.

"However, they are capable of the most shocking atrocities," she added, grimly. "Even the Butchers of Bullhorn would blanch at some of their crimes."

Jasmine shuddered, a reaction shared by almost all of the experienced officers. The Butchers of Bullhorn had been an Imperial Army unit with a reputation for putting down uprisings and rebellions with shocking cruelty. Their CO, a man with enough friends in high places to shield him from any punishment, had actively encouraged his men to loot, rape and burn their way across a dozen worlds. By the time they'd finally been disbanded, they'd been responsible for thousands of needless deaths…and rumour claimed there had been millions more.

"Which leads to a different issue," Colonel Stalker said. "Why did Governor Brown choose *here* as a place for talks?"

"If I had to guess," Colonel Macintyre said, "he believed that this world's neutrality would allow it to serve as a meeting place. Besides, the locals wouldn't dare pick a fight with either side; they have absolutely no orbital defences at all. A single corvette could carry out punitive strikes that would bring the local government down in an afternoon."

Jasmine exchanged a long look with Buckley. It *sounded* plausible, but she knew that expecting religious fanatics to act rationally was asking for trouble. Besides, if the population on the planet's surface was so isolated from the external universe, they might not really comprehend what the outsiders could actually *do* to them.

"One other thing," Colonel Macintyre said, when she'd finished the rest of the briefing, "I'd advise dark-skinned personnel to lighten their skins and female personnel to pose as men. As a general rule of thumb, the darker the skin, the lesser the caste; they're not likely to take a dark-skinned officer seriously."

"Hell with that," Buckley muttered "I'd like to see Blake's reaction when they refuse to take him seriously."

"He can wear his battlesuit," Jasmine said, quietly. She looked down at her own skin, wondering if she should lighten it. Principle was all very well and good, but if she had to work with the locals…luckily, Marine BDUs could conceal her breasts, particularly if she wore proper body armour. "But I'm glad I don't live here permanently."

"Me too," Buckley agreed.

The meeting broke up, but Colonel Stalker called for Jasmine to remain behind. "You seem to be handling the CEF well," he said, once they were alone. "But we may have to rethink carrying out operations on the mainland."

"Perhaps it would help remind them of our power," Jasmine said, although she understood his concerns. "And maybe that would head off trouble at the pass."

Chapter Eight

However, this approach can be costly or backfire. In some cases – the Russian invasion of Finland in 1939, for example – the weaker party may still be capable of inflicting considerable harm on the aggressor. Or other weaker parties may collectively stand up to the stronger party, forcing the aggressor to fight on several fronts at once.

-Professor Leo Caesius, *Diplomacy: The Lessons of the Past.*

Sivaganga Zamindari barely noticed the servants prostrating themselves as he stepped into the Imperial Palace. They were beneath his notice, men and women whose sole role in life was to carry out orders, no matter what those orders happened to be. He allowed one of them to take his cloak, then walked up the stairs and down the long corridor towards the throne room, pausing every so often to study a piece of particularly ornate artwork. The palace had been crammed with golden trinkets by the Rajah's predecessors, men who had founded their society and then worked hard to maintain it. He reached the final set of doors and stepped into the antechamber.

A dozen women, wearing the red and yellow robes of Imperial courtesans, threw themselves to their knees and placed their heads to the floor at once. Their pale skins marked them out as *Brahmins*, women whose breeding made them suitable to carry the Rajah's children to term. It was a sign of prestige, he knew; no one else, even the Rajah's heir, was allowed courtesans from the highest caste. It was a grave insult for anyone else to even *suggest* the possibility.

The four guards at the far end of the room – also *Brahmins* – didn't prostrate themselves. Instead, two of them stepped forward and carried out a brief search, then ran a sensor the palace had purchased from an off-world trader over his body. The sword he carried as a mark of his rank was removed and placed on a table, just to ensure the Rajah's safety. Once the search was completed, the guards nodded for him to enter the throne room.

He sucked in his breath, as always, as he stepped inside. The throne room was covered in gold and silver leaf, casting an eerie light over the chamber. At the far end of the room, the Rajah lounged on his throne, watching his subordinates with a gimlet eye that belayed his indolent appearance. Rajah Gangadhar, the absolute ruler of Lakshmibai, had survived a power struggle with his brothers after his father had died, eventually claiming the throne for himself. It would be dangerous to underestimate him.

Sivaganga bowed, then lowered himself to his knees and pressed his head against the carpeted floor. It was a display of respect he found more than a little humiliating, but failing to prostrate himself could have resulted in his immediate beheading. The Rajah *might* decide that Sivaganga's family was too powerful to irritate by beheading their patriarch, or he might decide that he could endure their displeasure. It was never easy to tell which way he might jump, if pushed. And Sivaganga had no shortage of enemies who would drip poison in the Rajah's ear, given half a chance.

"Rise, my loyal servant," the Rajah ordered, in his high-pitched voice. "It is Our pleasure to speak with you."

"I thank you, Most Honoured Rajah," Sivaganga said, feeling his bones creak as he stood upright. One day, he suspected, he was going to be unable to rise when commanded, despite the rejuvenation treatments he'd purchased from an off-world smuggler. Rumour had it that off-worlders lived for thousands of years, but they'd never offered *those* treatments to his world. "It is my pleasure to attend upon your person."

The door opened again, revealing Mirza Khwaja – the Rajah's oldest son and heir – and Ramnad Zamindari, one of the interior ministers. The Rajah's son bowed shortly to his father, but didn't prostrate himself, even though his father could order him beheaded. But then, he was the *only* grown son the Rajah had. He was immune to his father's rage until his younger brothers reached adulthood. Sivaganga had a feeling that the boys would never see their twenty-first birthdays.

"The off-worlders have arrived," Sivaganga said, once the formalities had been completed. "They have announced their intention of heading to the capital in two days, where they will move into the old Imperial residence."

The Rajah scowled, his chubby fingers playing with the sword he wore at his belt. "It does not please Us to have interlopers in Our city," he said.

"Then we destroy them, father," his son said. "I have heard that the rumours have been confirmed. The Empire is gone."

"Then they are vulnerable," Ramnad said. "We could wipe them and their influence off our world, permanently."

Sivaganga kept his face expressionless. Like his fellow minister, he wouldn't shed a tear for any off-worlders who happened to die on his world, not after the Empire had turned their society upside down. The introduction of new ideas from the damned refugees – they should have just slaughtered or enslaved them all – had convinced the lower castes that they didn't *have* to be patient and work their way up the ladder to paradise. And then the Empire hadn't succeeded in exterminating the rebels. And sold the warriors weapons they barely knew how to use...

...He hated the Empire and all other off-worlders. But he also had a healthy respect for their power.

"They have brought heavy forces with them," he warned. "Destroying them may not be easy..."

The Prince rounded on him. "We have them heavily outnumbered," he hissed, lifting one hand as if he intended to slap Sivaganga across the face. "They can be destroyed!"

"And then their influence can be purged," Ramnad added. "We can rebuild our society along proper lines."

Sivaganga had his doubts. Even now, whispers of rebellion were making their way from city to city, suggesting to the lower castes that there might be another way to live. The priests and warriors were doing their best to keep it under control, but he suspected that it would take years to remove the poison from their society. If nothing else, they needed to exterminate the rebels to prove that open resistance was futile. But the warriors had been unable to carry out even *that* task.

"Most Honoured Lord and Master," he said, addressing the Rajah, "the off-worlders are powerful – and their worlds are beyond our reach. We should merely allow them to hold their summit and then depart in peace."

"But that would not be the victory we need," the Prince said, coldly. "We need to show our people that the off-worlders can be beaten."

Sivaganga understood. The Prince wanted – needed – something that would secure his position in the event of one of his younger brothers reaching adulthood. A victory over the off-worlders would make him untouchable. He might even be able to push his father into honourable retirement and take the reins of power for himself. And it would also solidify the position of the Imperial Family against challenges from the aristocracy.

But it might also cost them everything.

The Rajah's face became a blank mask. "We shall lure them into a position of overconfidence," he said, softly. "They *will* come to our city and they *will* hold their talks. And then we shall strike."

He looked over at his son. "It will be led by you, a rogue operation," he added. His voice lightened and became mocking. "If you wish to take it."

The Prince flushed angrily. "I *shall*, father," he said. "And I shall purge our world of outsider filth."

Sivaganga smiled, inwardly. If the whole operation went badly wrong, it would be blamed on the Prince – who would never survive to be handed over to the off-worlders. The Rajah wouldn't be overthrown or forced to pay colossal reparations. Once he was dead, the Prince would make a convenient scapegoat – and anyone who knew better would have a very strong motive to toe the party line. The off-worlders would never know the truth.

"They have also requested permission to deploy their forces away from the garrison," he said, smoothly. "Would *that* suit our plans?"

"It would indeed," the Prince said, touching his belt where his sword should have been. Even *he* wasn't allowed to carry a weapon into the throne room. "The garrison is not an easy place to attack. But on the mainland, away from the sea, they can be overwhelmed and destroyed."

"Yes, My Prince," Sivaganga agreed.

It was frustrating, but they had to face up to the facts. The garrison had been effectively impenetrable. All the attempts to get a force over the causeway or land from the sea had been ruthlessly smashed. He'd worried that the off-worlders would intervene in the rebellion, either by providing fire support or weapons to the rebels, but so far they'd done neither. Indeed, they hadn't even received any shuttles for nearly five years.

But if the off-worlders happened to be in the countryside, they could be targeted. They could be destroyed.

"Then We shall grant them Our permission," the Rajah said. "Let them come. Let them be treated as honoured guests. Let them suspect nothing until we strike. And then let them be exterminated like the vermin they are."

Sivaganga bowed his head. He still had concerns about the whole idea, but he knew better than to say them out loud, not now that the Rajah had made up his mind and his son was definitely rising to power. It would merely get him beheaded and accomplish nothing, nothing at all.

"I will have the Imperial Residence prepared for our guests," he said. If there was one thing all off-worlders seemed to have in common, it was that they wanted food, drink and women – and someone to take care of the laundry work. He'd provide them with all they wanted, knowing that his people would spy on the outsiders for him. "And, once they arrive, do you wish for them to be presented at the Palace?"

The Rajah grimaced. "We do not wish to set eyes on them," he said. No doubt he remembered how his honoured father and grandfather had been humiliated by envoys from the Empire. What sort of barbarians believed that a mere demand was sufficient to approach the Rajah in all his glory? "You will inform them that we will receive them after they have settled their own differences."

"Yes, Most Honoured Rajah," Sivaganga said.

"Go," the Rajah said. "Give them Our word. Ensure that they suspect nothing."

Sivaganga bowed again, then backed out of the throne room. He didn't turn around until after the doors had slammed closed, blocking his view of the Rajah. The guards returned his sword, then motioned for him to leave the antechamber. He couldn't help noticing that the women had vanished, probably afraid of spending too much time near the Prince. The guards had been fixed to prevent them from taking any interest in the women – assuming they dared, knowing that it would mean a painful death for both of them – but the Prince would inherit the harem after taking power.

But until then, they would be killed if they shared their favours with anyone else, Sivaganga thought, as he walked out of the Palace and down past the gardens that countless monarchs had built up over the centuries. He would have liked to spend a few hours merely contemplating the wonders of the gardens, which included a number of plants imported from off-world, but there was no time. The Rajah would not be understanding if he delayed purposefully.

He stepped through the gates and into the litter waiting for him. The four porters picked it up as soon as he sat down, carrying him back towards his own palace. Shaking his head, he pushed the curtains to one side and peered out into the city, marvelling – yet again – at the network of palaces and temples that made up the inner city. Outside the walls, he knew, there were countless hovels belonging to the untouchables, but they weren't really part of his home. No one cared about them. They existed to work and nothing else, to lead blameless lives that would see them start climbing towards paradise. It was something the off-worlders would never understand.

But it was the off-worlders who called it into question, he thought, as the litter lurched onwards. He allowed the curtain to fall back and leaned back into the cushions, forcing himself to relax. The die was about to be cast. *They didn't care about what they did to our world.*

Michael couldn't help feeling nervous as the Warrior nosed its way along the causeway, even though he knew that it was perfectly safe. Imperial

Engineers had designed the road along the line of rocks, ensuring that it could take the weight of tanks and heavy transports, let alone a relatively-light AFV. Even so, every time he looked towards the rolling waves he had the unpleasant sense that they might slip off the road and fall into the water, trapping them in the vehicle. The atmosphere filtering systems would keep them alive, if they battened down the hatches in time, but it still bothered him.

"Coming to the end of the causeway now," he said, pushing his fears aside. "Driver, take us onto the beach and hold us there."

The Warrior lurched slightly as it drove onto the sand. Michael wasn't sure what he had expected from the coastline – perhaps something like a fishing village on Avalon – but it was more than a little shocking to see the desolation. The beach was littered with debris, the remains of boats damaged or destroyed during the first attempt by the locals to force their way along the causeway, but the damage seemed far more extensive than he would have expected. A number of buildings at the far side of the beach had clearly been burned to rubble.

"The locals didn't want fishermen to live here," Sergeant Grieves suggested. "They destroyed their own fishing industry during the fighting."

Michael grimaced. The briefings they'd heard in the day since they'd landed had made it clear that the local government didn't really give a damn about its own people, but it was still shocking to realise the degree of malice they'd shown towards anyone who might just have been a rebel or a rebel supporter. He picked up his binoculars and looked around, hunting for signs that someone was alive nearby, yet he saw nothing apart from wild animals and birds. The sound of the second Warrior, approaching over the causeway, sent them fleeing for their lives.

His radio buzzed. "You are cleared to advance to the first waypoint," Brigadier Yamane said. "Keep a careful watch for any signs of trouble."

"Understood," Michael said. The Warrior lurched back into life and advanced towards the road leading inland. "We're on our way."

The landscape only became stranger as they advanced towards the city. He could see it in the distance now, a towering mass of strange buildings that were brightly illuminated by the sunlight, yet there was still no sign of people. There were more and more hovels by the side of the road, but half of them appeared to have been destroyed and the other half appeared to be deserted. He caught sight of a pig nosing through a bucket of scraps and felt a hint of pity for anyone who had to live in such conditions. No doubt they were hiding from the newcomers. The briefing had made it clear that most of the locals feared and hated off-worlders.

It wasn't until they reached the very edge of the city that they saw their first locals. Most of them looked beaten down and dispirited, staring at the Warriors as if they expected to be crushed under their treads – and not moving, as if they would placidly accept that fate if it were written in the stars. He couldn't help noticing that the locals seemed almost painfully thin, their bones clearly visible against their darkened skin. The stench of sick or dying humans hovered in the air as he took a long breath. He had to fight down the urge to don his mask.

"We should help them," he muttered, as he caught sight of a young girl who was missing an arm and one eye. Someone had removed it, leaving a sightless socket that chilled him to the bone. It was sickening, particularly when he knew that replacing a damaged eye was relatively simple. As it was, he had a nasty feeling that the girl wouldn't survive for much longer. The briefing had hinted that the ill or crippled – or the elderly – were often simply exposed to the elements and left to die. Their relatives just didn't have the food to keep them alive when there would be no return.

"If we handed out every MRE in the garrison," Sergeant Grieves said, equally quietly, "it wouldn't keep the population of this city alive for more than a few weeks."

"And to think I thought that the pirates were bad," Michael snarled. "Look at *this*!"

He keyed his radio. "Holding position at Point Beta," he said, forcing his voice to remain calm. "No visible threats; I say again, no visible threats. Should we enter the city itself?"

"Negative," Brigadier Yamane said. "Hold position and wait for reinforcements."

Michael nodded, then looked back at the people outside. Some of them were clearly begging, others were offering themselves…he swallowed hard as he saw a young girl undoing her tattered skirt and exposing herself to his men. It was impossible to be sure – she was all skin and bones – but he would have been surprised if she was of legal age. But how else could she survive?

"We can't feed them," the Sergeant said, softly. "They'd all come after us, demanding food."

"I know," Michael said, bitterly. It didn't make looking at such poverty any easier. "I know."

Chapter Nine

To some extent, this also took place after Hitler broke his word in 1939 and annexed the Czech Rump State (after poor Czech diplomacy had ensured that the Czechs were largely defenceless.) It underlined the fact that Hitler (and thus Germany) simply couldn't be trusted and provided the impetus for a unified front against the aggressor.

-Professor Leo Caesius, *Diplomacy: The Lessons of the Past.*

"Sickening," Leo muttered.

He stared down at the live feed from the advance forces, the drones and the orbiting platforms and shuddered. The Empire tried to ensure that each Earth-compatible world could feed itself before anything else – hell, a healthy surplus was something that could be used in trade with off-world colonies – but politics and war could interfere easily. Here, it was clear that most of the local population was starving.

It was worse than it seemed, he realised, as he parsed his way through the images. The higher castes were clearly eating well, while leaving the lower castes to struggle to survive. He knew that politics often had as much to do with food shortages as anything else; here, there wasn't any practical reason why Lakshmibai couldn't feed its own population. If nothing else, they could have set up an algae-plant and produced ration bars for the lower castes.

He gritted his teeth as the shuttles flew onwards towards Maharashtra. If it had been up to him, he would have removed the local government and replaced it with something more humane. But he knew that the

Commonwealth would never sanction such an operation, no matter how much the targeted government deserved to be removed. They'd had too much experience of the Empire's meddling in planetary affairs to allow themselves to go the same route.

"We could set up an algae plant," Colonel Stalker said, when Leo suggested it. "But how long do you think it would last?"

Leo frowned in puzzlement.

"The starving area just happens to be the most rebellious part of the planet," the Colonel explained. "I'll bet you anything you want to put forward that the government is trying to starve the locals so they are incapable of fighting when their soldiers finally march in and suppress the rebellion. Resistance will be difficult if the population has nothing in their bellies."

Leo glared at him. "How can you be so calm?" He demanded. "Don't you know what's happening down there?"

"I know *precisely* what's happening down there," Stalker said, softly. "The government has been starving people, destroying crops and infrastructure and trying hard to exhaust the rebels or force them into surrender. I know that countless innocents are dying because of this damned policy. I also know that there's no point in ranting and raging about it. If we had a mandate to intervene…"

"But we don't," Leo snapped. Even if the Commonwealth *did* agree to allow an intervention, they were on the border between the Commonwealth and the Wolfbane Sector. It was quite possible that Governor Brown would object to an intervention that would boost the Commonwealth's standing in the region. "And politics would get in our way."

Stalker nodded, grimly. "It always does," he said. "It always does."

Leo nodded and turned his attention back to the live feed from the shuttle's sensors as Maharashtra came into view. It would have been charming, he realised mutely, if the spectacular temples and palaces – and even beautifully-crafted apartment blocks – hadn't been surrounded by a sea of shacks and hovels. They were all on the wrong side of a colossal stone wall, preventing them from entering the inner city except under carefully-controlled conditions. He could almost *smell* the stench rising from the districts. It seemed impossible that *anyone* could live in such an environment.

He looked back at the files he'd downloaded from the garrison's datanet. The locals did have some genetic modifications – luckily for them, or disease would have wiped them out centuries ago – but they were still suffering the effects of their environment. Even for the higher castes, life expectancy was little more than eighty years – and the lower castes rarely lived more than forty. How could *anyone* live like that?

"Impressive," Stalker muttered, as a giant statue of a god – over fifty metres tall – came into view. It looked to be made of solid gold, shining out as sunlight streamed down on it from high overhead. "And to think that they made it without antigravity systems."

Leo shook his head in disbelief. The statue *was* impressive, even if it was tiny compared to Earth's towering cityblocks or the orbital installations surrounding Avalon and the other major worlds in the Commonwealth. But it must have cost thousands of credits – or the equivalent in local currency – to build, when so many people were starving. He couldn't help feeling that the government was thoroughly sick.

The impression didn't get any better as the shuttles descended over the capital city. There were five other statues positioned on the walls, glaring out over the countryside, while countless smaller ones studded the buildings. It looked as if the city's developers were competing to see how many statues they could produce; he shivered as he caught sight of one that looked like an angry angel, showing teeth and claws. Inside the walls, the city looked bright and clean, but there was still something about it that put his senses on edge. The locals didn't seem to care about the sea of human misery surrounding them.

He was still mulling it over when the shuttle touched down in the Imperial Residency, the complex the Empire had insisted that the locals produce for its representatives. It was surprisingly modest, compared to the rest of the city; it took him a moment to realise that it was intended as a studied insult to the off-worlders who had disrupted the peace and tranquillity of a very strange world. A handful of locals appeared on the edge of the landing pad as the hatches hissed open, then prostrated themselves in front of the first Marines.

"Curious," Stalker observed, as 1st Platoon surrounded the shuttle. "That's not the reaction we normally get."

Leo nodded, studying the locals through the shuttle's sensors. They were a mixture of male and females, all wearing fine clothes that seemed to signify wealth and power…but if they were aristocrats, why would they prostrate themselves? The files he'd taken from the garrison had seemed to suggest that the local aristocrats only bent the knee to their Rajah, never to anyone else.

"They're servants," Leo said. "And if you decide to reject them, they might be significantly punished."

Stalker scowled. "They offered us servants on Han too," he admitted. "Most of them turned on their masters when the shit hit the fan."

———

The air smelt of perfume, Edward was surprised to discover as he stepped out of the shuttle, rather than the stench of unwashed humanity from outside the walls. He looked down at the locals, who were still prostrating themselves, and coughed, feeling rather awkward. A life in the Marine Corps hadn't prepared him for dealing with servants of any kind, particularly ones who seemed to be completely submissive.

"You may rise," he said, wondering vaguely what the protocol was for addressing such servants. It hadn't been covered at the Slaughterhouse, an oversight that he doubted would ever be corrected. "Now, if you please."

He watched as the servants sat upright, a middle-aged man rising to his feet while the others – male and female – remained on their knees. Up close, it was clear that the women were wearing translucent garments that hid almost nothing, while the men were more modest with silken pants and shirts. They all refused to look him or any of the other Marines in the eye.

"Welcome to the Residence," the leader said, in oddly-accented Imperial Standard. "We have prepared your rooms for your stay and assigned guards to spare you intrusions and servants to care for your every want and need. Should you require anything, just ask."

Edward heard someone – probably Coleman – suck in his breath behind him. He fought down the temptation to reprimand him and, instead, nodded in agreement.

"We will have to inspect the quarters," Edward said, instead. "And our guards will be happy to work with your guards."

"All is prepared," the leader assured him. "We are at your service."

"Thank you," Edward said. He keyed his wristcom. "Disembark – but don't go beyond the walls."

The servants looked faintly surprised as the soldiers of 1st Company, 3rd Avalon Infantry Battalion flowed out of two of the shuttles and headed into the residency, while the Marines remained on guard near the shuttles. Edward listened to the brief snippets of conversation as the soldiers inspected their living quarters, then started to search the building thoroughly. If *he'd* been hosting a diplomatic meeting on Avalon, Edward knew, he would have been careful to have the residency bugged, looking for whatever advantages he could muster. He had no doubt that the locals would have done the same thing themselves.

"All blue-tango clear," Major Lobo Villeneuve reported, once the soldiers had finished their search. He'd been resistant to the idea of sending only a single company to provide protection for the capital, but Edward had overruled him. The locals would probably object if he'd tried to insist on landing the entire CEF in the city. "And a great deal of luxury."

Edward nodded. Blue-tango meant that they'd picked up bugs, but nothing actually *lethal*.

"Understood," he said. "Check the gates, then start unloading the shuttles."

The servants straightened up at their leader's command, then headed towards their own accommodation at one end of the compound. "I can give you a personal tour," their leader said, seriously. "It would be a honour."

"Please," Edward said, motioning for Coleman and two of the other Marines to escort him. They would hardly have let him go on his own, not after Gwendolyn had issued such dire threats about what would happen if they let a single hair on his head be hurt. "And I'm sure the Professor would like a tour too."

On the outside, the Residency was a long low building that was utterly overshadowed by the nearby palaces. Inside, it was spectacularly luxurious – and tasteful. The rooms that had been put aside for the soldiers were equipped with proper beds, baths and even curtains to ensure what privacy they could, while the rooms intended for himself and the Professor were staggeringly luxurious. There was a bed large enough for four or five people, a fridge full of delicacies and a colossal bath, all illuminated by a chandelier hanging down from high overhead. Just looking at it made Edward roll his eyes. Did they think that he could be seduced into relaxing so easily?

But it would be so easy to have a bath, he thought, ruefully. Marines took showers, if they had the time; Boot Camp had taught them how to wash themselves within two minutes and then leave before the water turned itself off automatically. Hell, they'd often preferred to use sonic showers rather than water, knowing that sonic showers didn't force one to undress before using them. But he'd always liked a hot bath. There had been a time when he'd booked a hotel, during his first official leave after graduating from the Slaughterhouse, and merely soaked in the water for hours.

He pushed the thought aside and inspected the remainder of the rooms. There was a conference room, a bare room of uncertain purpose and a large dining room that could have sat several hundred people at a dozen tables with ease. Below, there was a handful of rooms for the servants and a large kitchen. It was alarmingly clear that the servants weren't given anything like luxury apartments in the residence.

"Pass the word," he ordered, as he met Major Villeneuve in the conference room. "The servants, male or female, are not to be bothered."

The Major nodded. "That will upset some of the lads, sir," he said, "but I think they'll see the sense of it."

He sighed as he passed Edward a datapad. "This building is heavily wired," he added. "We found about four hundred bugs, mostly outdated crap. A handful were actually mil-grade from the last two decades or so. I'm not sure where those came from."

"They might well have slipped into civilian hands," Edward pointed out. It was clear that trader ships visited from time to time, even if the Empire hadn't transferred the bugs to the local government directly. The locals might not have wanted any cultural contamination, but they sure as hell wanted technology they could use to keep their population under control. "Is there anything completely new?"

"Nothing," the Major said, shaking his head. "I don't think that Governor Brown's representatives had a chance to bug our accommodations for themselves."

Edward studied the datapad. If anything, the Major had understated the situation. The locals had emplaced enough bugs to allow them to hear even subvocalised whispers, unless their guests were very careful. Hell, they'd be able to track everyone inside the building, an unacceptable security risk.

"Remove them all," he ordered, shortly. The locals would know that the bugs had been discovered, but he doubted that they would bother to complain. It was, he'd been told, an unspoken truth of diplomacy that everyone spied on everyone else. "Melt them down into scrap."

"Yes, sir," Villeneuve said. "I have teams ready to remove them."

"Good," Edward said. Villeneuve had clearly been thinking ahead. "And our security?"

"The walls are tougher than they look," the Major reported. "On the other hand, it wouldn't be too difficult for someone to get over them with the right equipment. The guardhouse is nice and solid; the local guards, however, look good but I don't think they could actually *fight*, if pressed. I've put a platoon on each of the three gates, with two more patrolling the ground and the remainder in reserve. You can keep your Marines as a close-protection force."

"Remember to rotate the scheduled patrols," Edward reminded him. "We don't want to fall into any patterns they can exploit."

He scowled. "And remind everyone that the servants, no matter how submissive they look, are probably primed to report everything we do to the local government," he added. "I want them kept out of our storage areas – hell, I want them escorted whenever they're outside their rooms."

"We could bug their rooms," the Major suggested. "Just to keep an eye on them."

"Possible," Edward agreed. He would have preferred not to have the servants at all, but he suspected that getting rid of them politely would be difficult. And besides, they would probably be punished if they were evicted from the Imperial Residency. "In fact, see if we can turn them into sources. We really don't know enough about what's going on here."

"I'll spread the word," Villeneuve assured him.

The Professor leaned forward. "What about our counterparts?"

"They're in the other set of buildings," Villeneuve said. "They have guards of their own on the west gate, so we merely exchanged salutes and kept our distance. I must say that their guards look professional, much more than the locals."

Edward smiled. He'd seen a handful of images of local soldiers in the city and they actually managed to make the Empire's Civil Guard look professional. Most of them wore fancy uniforms that made him wonder how they avoided getting them dirty while under fire…assuming, of course, that they ever *were* under fire. It was quite possible that the city, for all it was surrounded by a sea of poverty and misery, was relatively secure.

Or that they're sitting on top of a minefield, he thought, sourly. *Han looked relatively safe until it exploded into fire.*

His wristcom buzzed. "Colonel, this is Yamane," a voice said. "The *Koenraad Jurgen* is requesting permission to depart, along with the squadron and our new friends."

Edward had expected it, but it still left him feeling exposed. "Permission granted," he said. "Tell them to return to the system in four weeks – and make sure they run a full recon first."

He shook his head as he walked over to the window and looked out at the towering spires of the city. "And keep a sharp eye on your own security," he added, grimly. "You're far too close to rebel-held territory."

"Aye, sir," Yamane said. She sounded nervous, although it would be difficult for anyone to tell if they hadn't had the right experience. "Good luck with the talks."

The Professor caught his attention as he closed the channel. "When *do* we start the talks?"

"Tomorrow," Edward said. He grinned, suddenly. "You and your wife can have a long rest in your quarters" – he didn't begrudge the Professor some luxury – "and then you can join me tomorrow morning. It's time to finally discover just what Governor Brown actually *wants* from us."

"Well?"

The operator looked up as Sivaganga entered the chamber, then scrambled to his feet and fell on his knees as he realised just how important his visitor actually was. Sivaganga waved impatiently for him to get upright, then barked at him to report. The operator hesitated, then reported that the off-worlders had found and disabled most of the bugs. His voice made it clear that he expected to be beheaded for this failure.

"Not too surprising," Sivaganga mused, instead. "We knew that they kept some equipment for their own use."

He scowled down at the final reports. There were just over one hundred off-worlders from the Commonwealth and seventy from the Wolfbane Sector, all presumably heavily armed. He knew too much about the power of the Empire's weapons to be sanguine about the chances of eliminating them without heavy bloodshed. But they were in the Imperial Residency, caught like rats in a trap. And the trap was about to be sprung…

"I want full reports from the spies," he ordered, softly. "Let us find out all we can before it is too late."

CHAPTER TEN

It can get worse if the stronger party doesn't appear strong – or willing to back up its threats. If the weaker party believes that the stronger party doesn't have the will to carry out its threats, those threats will simply be disregarded.
-Professor Leo Caesius, *Diplomacy: The Lessons of the Past.*

Leo couldn't help feeling a twinge of excitement as he followed Colonel Stalker through the gates and into the third and final section of the Imperial Residency. The pre-meeting briefings had made it clear that they were going to be meeting their counterparts formally and opening talks – talks that might lead to permanent diplomatic relations and a treaty between the Wolfbane Sector and the Commonwealth. He smiled as he saw the third building – another low building, guarded by a handful of local soldiers – and the statues surrounding the walls. If nothing else, the location was remarkable.

The Colonel stepped through the door and into a large room, easily large enough to hold both delegations and their escorts without cramming people together. There was a large table in the centre of the room, illuminated by portable lanterns hanging from the ceiling, surrounded by a handful of high-backed chairs. On the other side of the room, two more people were stepping inside, both wearing modified Imperial Navy uniforms. It made him feel rather shabby in his academic suit and tie, although he suspected that he was more comfortable than the naval officers. He'd had to sit through hundreds of lectures before finally reaching a level where he could pick and choose where he went to be bored.

Nothing was said until Colonel Stalker and his counterpart had swept the room with security sensors. They found nothing, somewhat to Leo's surprise; he'd expected the third building to be as heavily bugged as their living quarters. He'd been disquieted to discover that there had even been surveillance devices in the bathroom, in prime position to watch as they went to the toilet or have a long bath. Colonel Stalker hadn't been surprised – he'd pointed out that most people who thought they were under surveillance used the sound of running water to conceal their words – but Leo hadn't taken it too calmly. He'd also been careful not to mention it to Fiona. After all, the bugs had been removed.

"Please, be seated," General Flora O'Donnell said. "There is little need for formality here."

Leo nodded. According to the notes provided by Governor Brown during the long pre-negotiation negotiations, she was his military representative – although there had been no trace of her in the files. *General* was an Imperial Army or Civil Guard rank, but she wore the uniform of an Imperial Naval officer with the rank stripes removed. It was impossible to tell if she was trying to confuse them or if she had absolutely no right to claim to be a military officer at all.

She looked formidable, he had to admit. The General wasn't as muscular as Jasmine or any of the other female Marines, but she was definitely no slouch. Her hair, cropped close to her skull, was brown; her eyes were sharp and moved restlessly from Leo to Colonel Stalker and back again. It was impossible to be sure of her age, yet it was clear that she was old enough to be quite self-confident in herself.

Alistair Lockhart – her companion - wore his uniform loosely, as if it wasn't something he was used to wearing. He was a paunchy man, although there was a glint in his eye that reminded Leo of the Dean of Imperial University, a shrewd man who had made himself the master of a small bureaucratic empire. Leo had to tell himself, firmly, not to confuse the two men; the Dean had been an ambitious little toad, incapable of looking beyond his own interests, but Lockhart might be very different. Governor Brown had trusted him to negotiate a treaty, after all. The man had to be trustworthy.

Unless Governor Brown doesn't have many people he can trust, he thought, remembering his studies of the empire Admiral Singh had built. She'd sat on top of an edifice built of human misery and fear, ensuring that anyone who dared step out of line was reported at once by their fellows, who were rewarded for their betrayal. But when cracks appeared in her foundations, her structure had shattered remarkably quickly. Governor Brown might be no better than her, merely more willing to consider co-existence as a viable possibility.

He wondered, vaguely, just what they knew about the Commonwealth's two representatives. The Empire's famously-complete files probably included references to Colonel Stalker – although they would probably identify him as a Marine Corps Captain rather than anything connected to Avalon – but he doubted there would be anything on him personally. All of his work had been wiped from the Imperial Datanet when he'd been unceremoniously sacked from Imperial University; it was quite possible that he was a non-person as far as the remnants of the Empire were concerned. It still irked him that all of the copies of his first papers, including his own personal copies, had been destroyed. No matter what he did, he was unlikely to be able to reconstruct his first pieces of work.

"That is good to hear," Colonel Stalker remarked, dryly. "Particularly as few people have any idea how to carry out a diplomatic meeting these days."

Flora gave him a smile that made her seem years younger. "Very true, Colonel," she agreed, lifting a hand to indicate the chairs. "Shall we be seated?"

She waited until they were all sitting down before continuing. "I meant to ask," she added, smoothly. "Was your promotion confirmed by the Promotions Board or was it merely handed out by the Commandant of the Marine Corps?"

Colonel Stalker smiled, although his eyes were very cold. "Honesty compels me to admit that I do not know," he replied. "I assume that the paperwork was handled in line with regulations. Even if it wasn't, the Commandant would have the authority to promote someone up to the rank of Major without requiring the Promotions Board to sign off on it."

"It is hard to tell these days," Flora said. There was a rueful note in her voice as she leaned forward, placing her hands on the desk. "Far too many people have been promoting themselves in the wake of the Empire's fall."

Lockhart cleared his throat.

"But my companion wishes me to proceed," Flora continued, without missing a beat. "I believe that we should start with an assessment of the current situation."

Leo studied Lockhart as covertly as possible. One of the other details the briefing papers had forgotten to mention – and he would have bet half his savings that it wasn't a simple mistake – was which of the two representatives was actually in charge. He'd assumed that the General was in command, but was it really Lockhart? And, if he was clearly no military officer, what *was* he? Secret Police? Or merely a trusted ally of the Governor?

"We have only heard rumours of the Fall of Earth," Colonel Stalker said, unable or unwilling to disguise his interest. "It would be interesting to hear what you know about it."

"The planet collapsed into chaos two years ago," Lockhart began. He spoke in an accent that dripped of Earth. "Details are scarce; apparently, there was a food shortage, followed rapidly by a breakdown into civil war. There was a major exchange of fire above the planet's atmosphere, ending when debris fell down and struck the planet's surface. It was the end of the world."

Leo shuddered. Earth had been building up its orbital installations for over five thousand years, a project that had started long before the Unification Wars. If a handful of the larger stations or habitats, particularly the ones built out of asteroids, had fallen out of orbit and impacted against the planet's surface, the results would have been disastrous. Earth's towering cityblocks would have fallen like ninepins as earthquakes swept over the planet. The death toll would have been utterly immeasurable.

There were eighty billion people on Earth, he thought. He'd known it was a possibility that Earth was gone – he'd worked out just how dependent Earth was on supplies from beyond the planet's atmosphere – but he'd shied away from considering the possible consequences. *Eighty billion – officially. God alone knows how many actually died.*

Colonel Stalker leaned forward. Only someone who knew him very well would have heard the hint of…fear in his voice. "And the Childe Roland? The Grand Senate? The Commandant?"

"We do not know," Flora admitted. She gave Stalker a long considering look. "We do know that the Grand Senators started fighting before the fall – and that civil war raged through many of the Core Worlds. However, we do not know any specifics."

Or are unwilling to share, Leo thought. The concept of keeping information private was not something that sat well with him, but he knew enough to know that it was done on a regular basis. After all, sharing one's information with someone else might allow them to steal a lead and move ahead – and claim all the credit. Besides, if the situation in the Core Worlds was really as bad as they claimed, it was quite possible that they didn't know anything for sure.

Flora smiled, although it didn't quite touch her eyes. "As the Governor sees it, the Empire is gone and it won't be coming back," she continued. "That leaves us effectively independent of any central authority – and you too, of course. Do you agree with our position?"

"We certainly have no intention of challenging your independence," Colonel Stalker assured them, calmly. He made a motion that suggested that he was laying something on the table. "We agree that the evidence suggests that the Empire is gone and that we're effectively on our own."

"Good," Flora said. "It is our intention to agree on precisely-delimited spheres of influence between Wolfbane and Avalon. We do not wish to have any other form of treaty at this time, merely an agreement on borders and…and on which worlds fall within which sphere. In particular, we wish to limit trading contacts between our worlds and your own."

"The Commonwealth Government does not limit the activities of independent traders," Colonel Stalker pointed out. "And, in any case, we do not control the Trade Federation."

"The Trade Federation is a different issue," Flora countered. "If you please, we need to discuss borders…"

Endurance was one of the prime requirements for passing the Crucible and donning the Rifleman's Tab that separated a recruit from a qualified Marine. Edward had marched and fought and marched again for days during the final examinations, somehow forcing himself to keep going when flesh and bone demanded rest. Few civilians really appreciated just how long a Marine could keep going, even without limited enhancement.

But if that were true, he asked himself dryly, *why can't I endure more than a couple of hours of talks?*

It was a relief when they finally separated for lunch, if only because the talks were going nowhere fast. The Commonwealth was going to be disappointed, Edward knew, if the representatives were telling the truth about wanting nothing more than delineating spheres of influence. He knew that the Council would accept that Wolfbane had political influence – just like the Commonwealth itself – but without diplomatic relationships it was hard to imagine it lasting. Besides, they knew almost nothing about the Wolfbane Sector's internal structure. There was no way to know if Governor Brown was barring them from worlds he controlled or worlds he intended to take under his wing.

There was another possibility, he acknowledged, as they walked back to their section of the Imperial Residency. Governor Brown might be trying to parse out the worlds controlled by the Commonwealth. After all, there were quite a few worlds that had chosen to remain independent – or join the Trade Federation instead. The Governor might be quietly assessing their potential strength before launching an invasion – or merely satisfying himself that they didn't pose a threat.

"I wonder how many times we can go over the same ground," the Professor mused, once they were back in the secure room. "They told us the same thing time and time again."

Edward heard the disappointment in his voice and felt a pang of sorrow. The Professor had been one of life's innocents, back when he'd been working at Imperial University. He'd learned hard lessons since, including the bitter truth that being right was no defence when someone wanted to shoot the messenger – or that power came out of the barrel of a gun. The Professor deserved much better…

…But if he'd been on Earth, if the representatives had been telling the truth, he would be dead by now, along with his family.

Edward's first deployment, after graduating from the Slaughterhouse, had been to a planet that had been struck by an asteroid. The civilisation had been nowhere near as compressed and integrated as Earth's and it had *still* been torn apart by the impact. Millions had died in the first moments; millions more had perished over the following weeks and months as the effects raged around the globe. And that had been *one* asteroid, tipped onto the planet by a revolutionary cell. If all of Earth's vast orbital network had been dumped onto the planet, everyone on the surface would die. They'd said that there were so many in orbit that they blocked out the sun, although Edward knew that was nothing more than hyperbole. Not that it would have mattered. Anyone who survived the first strikes would starve to death when the food supplies ran out.

"We can hold out for diplomatic relations as the price for considering establishing a border," he said, pushing his morbid thoughts aside. Who knew *what* had happened to the Slaughterhouse? The Marine Corps had had enough enemies to guarantee that at least one of them would try to destroy the training world, once the Empire collapsed into chaos. "But we really need to know more about what territory Wolfbane actually controls before we agree to a fixed border."

"And the traders won't stick to a border in any case," the Professor commented. "Mandy said that they'd go anywhere and do anything."

Edward smirked. They'd said that about the Marines too.

"They may well be trying to assert their own authority over the traders too," Edward theorised, pushing that thought aside too. "Or they may wish to separate us from the Trade Federation."

He shook his head, tiredly. The Commonwealth had a small tax on HE3 and interstellar trade, but the constitution had been carefully written to prevent the formation of shipping cartels like the ones that had done so much harm to the Rim's economy. Small traders were less efficient, but they weren't used as weapons against the colonies by interstellar corporations. Most of the corporations were gone now, or reduced to their local stations, but it was quite likely that others would form in the future.

But there was no attempt – there could be no attempt – to control the independent traders, let alone the Trade Federation. The Commonwealth could *advise* them not to enter space controlled by Governor Brown, but it couldn't *forbid* it. And, even if it could, Edward wasn't inclined to do it. The traders might be their only source of true intelligence.

He shook his head. "We've invited them to a formal dinner tomorrow evening," he reminded him, instead. "By then, we should have time to go over everything they said and make our counterproposals. If nothing else, they should be amenable to using this planet as a permanent point of contact…"

"If the locals don't object," the Professor noted. He'd taken the evidence of poverty and near-total neglect badly. "Or maybe we should set up a base in interstellar space we can use as a diplomatic station, now that we're actually *talking*."

Edward nodded as they reached the Residence and stepped through the doors. Lieutenant Coleman saluted, then ran a scanner over their bodies, looking for bugs or other unpleasant surprises. There was nothing, something that both pleased and worried Edward. It pleased him because it suggested that the representatives, for all their stubbornness, were being honest; it worried him because he hadn't been trained to be optimistic. He had to admit that it was quite possible that they were missing something.

"Get some rest," he suggested, once the scan was complete. "We'll discuss progress later."

The Professor nodded and started to walk towards the corridor leading to his quarters. "And tell your wife to plan out a dinner for them," Edward called after him. "She can source foodstuffs from the locals if she wants."

"I'll tell her," the Professor said. "Can she go out into the city?"

"If escorted," Edward stated, firmly. The planetary government would have to be insane to pick a fight with either diplomatic mission, but it wouldn't be the first time some rogue actor saw an opportunity and did something stupid. "Take a squad of Marines with you and have them escorting you at all times."

The Professor didn't bother to argue, although Edward suspected that his wife would complain once she realised that she wouldn't be free of the

Marines until after she returned to Avalon. Camelot had been a relatively safe environment; he rather doubted that Maharashtra was safe for anyone, even the higher castes.

He watched the Professor go, then looked over at Coleman. "Is there any update from the garrison?"

"They're deploying most of the CEF near the causeway," Coleman reported. "Apart from that, nothing specific."

"No news is good news," Edward said. Still, he had to admit that he felt nervous about being so distant from most of his command. "Anything else?"

"Private Doncaster was caught having his knob sucked by one of the servants," Coleman reported. "The Major took a dim view of it and ordered administrative punishment."

Edward rolled his eyes. Why was he not surprised?

CHAPTER ELEVEN

> This requires an accurate understanding of the balance of power. Imperial China, for example, never really grasped the disparity between the Chinese army and the invading Westerners. Instead of using diplomacy to buy time and refit their armies, they followed a course that brought them into inevitable conflict with a vastly superior foe.
> -Professor Leo Caesius, *Diplomacy: The Lessons of the Past.*

"This place," Jasmine muttered, "is far too like Han for comfort."

She looked around her as the small patrol made its way through Jhansi, wondering – again – just how anyone could live in such conditions. Vast piles of rubbish were scattered everywhere, flies buzzing angrily over food and human wastes. The stench was appalling; she'd had to admit defeat and order her escort to don their masks, just to allow them to keep walking through the city. The older buildings looked decayed, as if they were permanently on the verge of falling down; the only buildings that seemed reasonably clean were a handful of temples and a couple of large mansions for local government officials.

The sea of human misery was horrifying. Jasmine saw hundreds of young men wandering listlessly around the city, many of them carrying makeshift weapons and trying to look tough and nasty. There were few young women; the handful they'd seen had clearly been prostitutes or beggars. The majority, she guessed, were kept firmly indoors by their parents, something that had also been common on Han. There was no hope of bringing a rapist to justice in such an environment, assuming the girl survived the experience. It was much more likely that she'd be blamed for the heinous crime of being raped and killed by her own family. Jasmine found the concept sickening beyond belief.

From what the garrison's intelligence staff had said, Jhansi was technically under the control of the local government, but the rebels had a strong presence within the city's boundaries, priming the local population for an uprising. Jasmine suspected that they were right, although the more she looked around, the more convinced she became that resistance had been ground out of most of the population. Even if there had been some fire left in them, the near-starvation – she had yet to see a well-fed person outside the upper castes – would ensure that their uprising wouldn't last long.

But then, Han turned into a nightmare very quickly, she reminded herself. *This world might explode too.*

She looked across at Emmanuel Alves as they made their way down the road and out of the city, towards where they had set up their Forward Operating Base near the causeway. The reporter had been silent ever since they'd entered the city, barely taking the time to take photographs of their surroundings and what few people could be seen. Jasmine wondered, absently, if he'd been shocked into submission by the sight, or if he was trying to understand just what sort of people would do this to their fellow men. Even the Nihilists didn't try to grind an entire population's face in the dirt.

"This place definitely feels like Han," Buckley agreed, breaking his own silence. "As if it's on the verge of a final explosion."

Alves looked up at him. "Do you think that that's likely?"

"It's possible," Jasmine admitted, reluctantly. "But all we can do is stay on alert and pray that nothing goes wrong."

Once, she would have looked for a way to help the locals. But now she couldn't think of anything that *would* help, beyond removing their government and providing enough support to help them build up a new and better government. The task would be far beyond the Commonwealth, she knew, even if the remainder of the Knights were shipped to join them; the sheer level of hatred that burned through the population was terrifyingly powerful. When the lid blew off, the planet would dissolve into mass slaughter and starvation.

The FOB was little more than a handful of tents and prefabricated buildings, each one guarded by an armed soldier. Jasmine had issued explicit orders that no locals were to be allowed into the camp, even though she knew that *someone* would probably try to sneak in a local prostitute or two when they thought their superiors weren't looking. It wasn't uncommon on Avalon, where the prostitutes might try to drain the soldiers of their wages, but they wouldn't be actually dangerous. Here, it could be lethal. The medics had added to her orders by issuing dire warnings about the possibility of catching something nasty from the local environment.

"Brigadier," Captain Royce said, as they passed the tanks she'd positioned at the entrance to the base. The Landshark tanks were hellishly intimidating, perhaps enough so to discourage the locals from trying anything stupid. "We have a visitor. He wishes to speak with our commanding officer."

Jasmine gave him a sharp look. "And who, precisely, is he?"

"He claims to be Yin, the leader of the rebel forces," Royce informed her. "I've checked with the garrison and they've confirmed that there *is* a rebel leader by that name, but they don't have any ID data we can use to identify him for sure."

"Typical," Jasmine said, crossly. Trust intelligence officers to know nothing when it really counted. But perhaps it shouldn't have been a surprise. Even on Earth, millions of people – perhaps billions – had been excluded from the census. "Where is he now?"

"I put him in the guardhouse," Royce said. "He said he would wait until we were ready to speak to him."

"I'll speak to him," Jasmine decided. She looked over at Alves. "Do you want to come?"

The reporter nodded, once.

Yin was an old man, with bronzed skin, sharp dark eyes and a white beard that reminded her of her grandfather. His body was thin, although he was clearly in a better condition than most of the people in the nearby city. Jasmine wasn't too surprised; in an unstable location, like Han, everyone knew that the men with guns got to eat first. The Crackers hadn't stolen food from farmers on Avalon, but other insurgents had preyed on their fellow countrymen when they weren't fighting the government's forces. Why should Yin be any different?

"Two hundred years ago," Yin said, in poor Imperial Standard, "my grandparents were dumped on this world. Why were we then abandoned?"

Jasmine took a closer look at him. The locals – the original locals – shared the same genotype, with the only major difference being skin colour. Indeed, she'd seen thousands of mixed-caste children and adults within the city. But the refugees the Imperial Navy had dumped on Lakshmibai had introduced new genes to the planetary population. Up close, it was clear that Yin had inherited traits from both sides.

"The Empire lost interest in what it was doing," Jasmine said. She'd seen it before, a pattern that had become more and more common as the Empire approached the end of its lifespan. It would start on a project with the noblest of goals, then it would become a pork barrel for graft and corruption…and then it would finally be abandoned, leaving nothing but wreckage behind. "And I'm sorry about that…"

"We do not have long before they destroy us," Yin interrupted. "Please will you help us?"

Jasmine would have *loved* to help the rebels, but she knew that her hands were tied. The Commonwealth couldn't even ship in weapons and food-production facilities. She mentally cursed her helplessness, wishing that she'd declined the offer of command. All it meant was that she had to turn Yin away, without even giving him something for his trouble.

"I cannot," she said, softly. "There's nothing we can do."

"You have supplies on your island," Yin said. "If you gave them to us…"

Jasmine scowled. He was right; if they provided the rebels with weapons, the rebels would have a chance to take the local government out before it could adapt. But it was also possible that it would merely make the fighting worse, slaughtering thousands upon thousands more people before it finally came to an end.

"My wife died giving birth to my fifth child," Yin pleaded. "Three of them died before reaching their fifth year. We're being exterminated by the" – he spoke a word Jasmine didn't recognise, a word that sounded thoroughly unpleasant – "and we can't last much longer. I know what the Empire can do, young man; it can *help!*"

"The Empire is gone," Jasmine said. "There's just us now."

"Help us and we will help you," Yin offered. He leaned forward. "There has to be something we can do…"

"There isn't," Jasmine said, feeling her words tugging at her heartstrings. If there was something…but she knew there wasn't. They couldn't intervene and save the planet from itself. All they could do was provide security for the diplomats and then withdraw from the world. "I am sorry."

Yin stared at her for a long moment, as if he wanted to find the words that would force her to change her mind – or simply curse her for being so unfeeling – but nothing came out of his mouth. Instead, he turned and walked through the door, looking neither left or right as he passed the guards and headed out into the countryside. It struck Jasmine, suddenly, just how disgracefully healthy she and her subordinates must look to his eyes, a small army of men who were properly fed and trained, who could expect the best of health care if they were injured while on deployment. And three of *his* children had died in infancy.

She shuddered. Whatever else could be said about Avalon – or Earth - the infant mortality rate had been very low. But then, even Earth had been able to provide most of the population with food, although it had mainly been bland and boring ration bars. Lakshmibai didn't even try.

"That was sickening," Alves said. "When the people find out about it, they'll want to help."

Jasmine swallowed the first response that came to mind. "Maybe they will," she said, half-heartedly. "But will they be prepared to pay the costs of intervening here?"

Alves blinked. "The costs?"

"You'd need to deploy a small army to ensure security – and to take out the local government, if you didn't want to bombard the capital city from orbit," Jasmine informed him. "And then you would need to set up algae-production plants and then start handing out the food, while somehow preventing the locals from becoming dependent upon your produce. *And you would have to keep the downtrodden masses from brutally slaughtering all of their oppressors.*"

"Would that," Alves asked, "be such a bad thing?"

Jasmine nodded. "These people tell caste status by skin colour," she reminded him. "If the lower castes rise up, they'll kill everyone with lighter skin – men, women and children, all of them. And then they'll start killing those unlucky enough to be born to mixed-caste relationships. And then…"

She shook her head. "They'll smash the government, but they'll also wipe out those who know how to produce foodstuffs," she added. "It will take them time to learn the skills – and the food shortages will make them more dependent upon algae or simply cause most of them to starve. The newer government will start trying to take control of the food production systems and end up a tyranny just as bad as its predecessor."

Alves scowled at her. "How can you know that it will be that bad?"

"It's happened before," Jasmine said. "On countless worlds, all of which look very different…but share the same fundamental structural weaknesses. If the Crackers had won, would they have created a new government that encompassed all of society or would they turn on other enemies?"

"I don't know," Alves admitted. "But it would have been a better world."

"Probably," Jasmine agreed. "The question, however, is simple; better for whom?"

"There are some worrying signs," Colonel Macintyre admitted, two hours later. "We knew that the rebels were under intense pressure, but the local government has definitely been moving additional troops into the region. Mainly infantry, we believe, yet they're backed up by tanks and helicopters."

Jasmine winced. The memory of the sheer hopelessness in Yin's face refused to fade from her mind. If there was something they could do… it would be relatively easy to provide ration bars, she knew, yet even that would commit them to taking a side in the struggle.

"We can ask the local government to hold back until after the talks are completed," Colonel Stalker said. He had given them a brief outline of the talks and their progress – or lack of it – as soon as they'd established the connection. "But I don't know if they would listen to us."

"It wouldn't make any difference, sir," Jasmine pointed out. "The rebels are dying. So is most of the local population in this region."

The Colonel gave her a long considering look. "There's nothing we can do," he admitted, bitterly. "Even if we started distributing food now, even if we set up a full-scale production plant, what would happen after we left?"

Jasmine winced. The locals would crash back into starvation, made worse by the fact they'd had enough food to eat…if they *had* had enough food to eat. There were so many of them that providing food would be tricky until they could ramp up production.

"We could hand the production plant over to the rebels when we leave," she offered. It was unlikely that any of the former garrison's staff would want to stay on the cursed world a moment longer than they had to. "Or we could leave a small team of volunteers on the surface…"

"Which would make them a greater target," the Colonel pointed out, not unkindly. "The garrison might be tough, but it isn't invulnerable. We'd be involving ourselves directly in this world's affairs."

Colonel Macintyre cleared her throat. "With all due respect, sir," she argued, "we are already involved."

"We do not have the resources the Empire possessed at its height," Colonel Stalker said, firmly. "There is no way that we can make a long-term commitment to Lakshmibai, even if we didn't have to worry about our relations with Governor Brown and the Wolfbane Sector. I know; this world is heartbreaking. But there is nothing we can do that will do anything other than make the problem worse in the long run. Do you understand me?"

"Yes, sir," Jasmine said, feeling oddly like she'd disappointed her father. "But Emmanuel is intent on convincing the Commonwealth to intervene."

The Colonel smiled. "It's Emmanuel now, is it?"

Jasmine made a face to cover her blush.

"It would be nice to think that…*Emmanuel* could convince the Commonwealth to support a long-term intervention," the Colonel agreed. "But I think that it would be beyond our power, even if we had complete freedom of action. And we don't, because of Governor Brown."

"You could ask the representatives what they think," Jasmine suggested, slowly. "Perhaps we could agree not to install any orbital defences, or anything that would make this world a strategic target or a potential threat."

"I could," the Colonel agreed, "but right now the talks are…delicate. We don't want to upset them more than strictly necessary."

On that note, the discussion ended.

Prostrating himself in front of the Prince was humiliating – it wasn't as though he was his esteemed father – but Sivaganga Zamindari knew better than to omit the ritual, not when the Prince had formally taken command of the operation. He needed to maintain what influence he could over the younger man, even if it meant swallowing his pride and kowtowing before him.

"You may rise," the Prince ordered. "Is everything in place?"

"It is, My Prince," Sivaganga confirmed. The Prince had wanted to mount a headlong assault into the Imperial Residency, but Sivaganga had managed to discourage him, pointing out that it would make it far too clear who the aggressor had been. If the Rajah was wrong about the off-worlders leaving their homeworld alone, they needed *something* to make it seem as though the off-worlders on the surface had brought their fate on themselves. "We are ready."

The Prince smiled, darkly. "They suspect nothing?"

"Our spies have reported that they are cautious, but do not realise that there is a major threat," Sivaganga said. "One of them attempted to seduce an off-world soldier, but learned nothing of value."

"Of course not," the Prince sneered. "Who would tell a common soldier anything? Why are they not trying to seduce the diplomats?"

"One of them has brought his wife," Sivaganga explained. "Two others are clearly in a relationship; the fourth is seemingly uninterested in women or boys."

"Women," the Prince repeated. He'd laughed when he'd heard that one of the diplomats was a woman, pointing out that it proved that the off-worlders were truly effeminate. Even higher-caste women had no right to issue orders to higher-caste men. "Do they actually wish to come to any agreement?"

"There is a matter of some concern," Sivaganga told him, carefully. "One of the rebel leaders visited the camp which the off-worlders have established near their garrison…"

The Prince swore vilely. "What did he say to them?"

"We do not know," Sivaganga admitted. "It is possible that he sought their aid in waging war on us."

"He *would* have sought their aid," the Prince snapped. He glared down at Sivaganga, who hastily bowed his head. "They might already be shipping food and weapons to the rebels. We must stop them before it is too late. The operation is to begin tomorrow!"

"Yes, My Prince," Sivaganga conceded. The Prince was probably right; there was little else the rebels would want from the off-worlders. If there *was* an alliance between the two forces…it was hard to see how they could be prevented from overthrowing the Rajah and imposing a new government on the planet. "I will obey."

And with that, he knew, the die was cast.

Chapter Twelve

> Successful diplomacy requires, therefore, several different factors. First, there must be a clear understanding of just what is necessary and what would be nice to have. Second, there must be a proven track record of honouring treaties (even seemingly unfavourable treaties). Third, there must be a realistic understanding of the limits of the possible. Fourth, there must be a willingness to – in the immortal words of Theodore Roosevelt – speak softly and carry a big stick.
>
> -Professor Leo Caesius, *Diplomacy: The Lessons of the Past.*

"This is really quite a fascinating environment," Fiona commented, as she walked through the marketplace. "Don't you think?"

Leo shrugged. The marketplace was very different from anything on Avalon; there were countless stalls, selling everything from clothes to food supplies. It was hard to reconcile the supplies on display with the starvation outside the city's walls, or the gorgeous clothing with the rags and tatters the untouchable caste wore while slaving for their betters. But then, it seemed to be a common trait of the rich and powerful that they had to make a demonstration of their wealth.

He had to admit that the marketplace felt a little...*alien* to him. Avalon was a largely homogeneous society; Earth, or at least the parts he'd been familiar with, had claimed a legal equality for everyone, even though some citizens had always been more equal than others. But there was something weirdly disconcerting about Lakshmibai. The higher-caste men and women seemed to breeze through the marketplace, while the lower-caste either bowed their heads or prostrated themselves as their betters walked by. And some of the higher-caste men and women simply took whatever they wanted and didn't bother to pay.

The locals didn't seem to know what to make of the off-worlders. They stared at Leo, his wife and the four Marines, some of them making faces when they thought that the off-worlders weren't looking. None of them tried to bargain either, even though they were happy to bargain with their own people. Leo suspected, although he didn't know for sure, that there was a colossal mark-up price for the visitors. It was a fairly common problem when a planet played host to visitors from another star.

"Look at this," Fiona insisted, picking up a dress made of red silk. "It would go well with Mandy's hair."

Leo had his doubts – Mandy's red hair would clash badly with the dress – but he kept them to himself. It was worth it to see Fiona happy, even if they were going to spend a great deal of local currency. He was mildly surprised that the locals had even *provided* the currency, but he had a feeling that the government knew that the money wasn't going to leave the planet. It wasn't as if it was worth anything anywhere else.

"Or maybe this for Mindy," Fiona added, showing him a green dress. "If I can find one in the right size…"

There was a rustle running through the marketplace. Leo looked up to see a small group of men standing nearby, staring at the off-worlders menacingly. Cold ice ran down his spine – the last time he'd seen anything so menacing had been when he'd been forced to live on the very edge of Imperial City – and he reached for Fiona's arm, hoping to pull her back. The men produced clubs and moved forward, leering at Leo. He cringed back…

A strong hand caught him and pulled him backwards as two Marines moved forward to shield the civilians. The strangers didn't hesitate; they threw themselves forward, lashing out at the Marines with their makeshift weapons. Leo heard his wife cry out as it finally dawned on her that they were in danger, just as the Marines started to fight back. He stared in stunned disbelief as all seven of the newcomers were rapidly knocked down.

As if that had been a signal, the crowd surged forward, baying with anger. Leo froze, feeling warm liquid trickling down his leg; he'd heard stories about what happened to people who were caught up in a mob riot. And then the Marine grabbed him and pulled him along, away from the crowd. But the crowd was giving chase…

"This way," the Marine grunted. They moved into a narrow – and thankfully deserted – alleyway. Leo felt his legs buckle; if the Marine hadn't kept hold of him, he knew that he would have collapsed into a helpless puddle. Fiona seemed to be struggling with one of the other Marines; as Leo watched, the Marine threw her over his shoulder and carried her forward, ignoring her protests. "Sir, I…"

A shower of rocks rained down from high overhead. The Marine swore, unslung his rife and fired a handful of shots up towards the rooftops. Leo looked upwards and saw several young men scattering, one slipping and falling down towards the ground. He heard a growling sound from behind him and turned to see the crowd trying to press its way into the alley. The leader held a burning bottle in one hand, ready to throw. Leo heard the Marine swear again and fire a single shot towards the bottle. Liquid fire cascaded over the holder's body and he screamed.

Leo felt sick as the stench of burning flesh assailed his nostrils. The crowd flinched back from the heat, then started to come forward. Leo heard a crash and looked back, just in time to see one of the Marines kicking open a wooden door. There was no time to object before he was hauled inside and pulled up the stairs.

Somehow, he found his voice. "Where…where are we going?"

"Somewhere else," the Marine grunted. He pulled something off his belt and threw it back down the stairwell. A moment later, there was a flash of blue light and a faint electric shock running through the air that made Leo's hair stand on end. "*Anywhere* else."

Leo shivered. Outside, he could hear the sound of the crowd, baying for blood. His blood.

"They'll break in, won't they?" He asked, nervously. "What do we do then?"

"Go through the walls," the Marine said. "And then hope that the Colonel can put together a relief force."

———

"Report," Edward snapped, as he strode into the makeshift command and control centre. "What the hell is going on?"

"Mob riot, sir," Major Villeneuve reported. "The Professor, his wife and their escorts were apparently targeted."

"Shit," Edward hissed. A riot was always dangerous, particularly when the Marines caught up in the confusion had to protect civilians as well as themselves. And Blake Coleman and his squad weren't wearing full armour. "Get the QRF ready to go; tell them to use stunners first, but to be ready to switch to more lethal weapons if necessary."

He gritted his teeth, wishing that they had been able to bring vehicles into the city. But the landing pad by the Imperial Residency wasn't large enough to take the heavy transport shuttles. Maybe he should have had the shuttles landed outside the city…he cursed his own oversight, then pushed it aside. There would be time for self-recriminations later."

"Lieutenant Cradock has assumed command of the QRF," Villeneuve reported, a moment later. "They're ready to go."

Edward scowled down at the single map they had of the city. Intelligence was poor, but recon drones had suggested that the city was even more of a maze than they'd realised. The reports coming in over the communications network was odd; it puzzled him until he realised that the mob didn't seem to actually want to *catch* the fleeing off-worlders. But what had triggered the riot in the first place?

He gritted his teeth. Sending soldiers into a city was always risky, both for the soldiers and for any civilians who happened to be caught in the crossfire. Cities dampened down the advantages normally enjoyed by well-trained soldiers, levelling the playing field between them and ill-trained and expendable insurgents. He wanted to take command personally, to share the risks he was asking the Knights to bear, yet he knew that he had to remain in the Imperial Residency.

"Send them in," he ordered, tartly. "And then send a message to the garrison. Black Five; I say again, Black Five."

"Yes, sir," Villeneuve acknowledged. He paused. "May I make a suggestion?"

Edward nodded, impatiently.

"Inform the Wolfbane Ambassadors," Villeneuve advised. "They may be at risk too."

"I'll call them personally," Edward said. "Inform me if the situation changes, even slightly."

"Cover your ears," the Marine ordered. "Now!"

The wall facing them disintegrated with a thunderous crash. Leo looked up, alarmed, as plaster dust began to drift down from the ceiling. The Marine pushed him onwards, through the haze, and into another room. This one held a handful of young children who stared at the Marines with wide terrified eyes. Leo wanted to do something to help them, but there was no time. Instead, he was pushed through the corridor and up another flight of stairs.

"The QRF is on the way, but drones report that the marketplace is turning into a generalised riot," the Marine muttered as they reached the top floor. "They're already being hammered with sticks and stones from high overhead."

Leo nodded. "Can we get out of here?"

"We'll look after both of you," the Marine promised, understanding the unspoken question. "But you need to follow orders and keep your heads down."

He pulled open a hatch leading up to the roof and scrambled upwards, carrying a stunner in one hand. Leo heard the distinctive hum of the weapon as the Marine swept it around, then pulled his legs through the hatch and climbed out onto the roof. Another Marine followed him a moment later, then a third passed Fiona up through the hatch. Leo hesitated, unsure of what to do, but then the Marine simply picked him up – it was astonishing just how effortless it seemed – and passed him to one of the Marines on top. The other two scrambled up moments later.

"Shit," one of the Marines muttered. "They're trying to burn down the city."

Leo looked around and realised that the Marine was right. Piles of smoke were rising up from all over the city, including several that were alarmingly close to the marketplace. He could hear the sounds of fighting and looting everywhere, as if the rioters had decided to abandon the off-worlders and loot the market instead. It was easy to believe, he decided, even though it was impossible to be sure.

"This way," the Marine ordered. "Hurry!"

Somehow, Leo pulled himself to his feet and followed the lead Marine as he headed across the rooftop. Dozens of stunned locals lay everywhere, a handful moaning rather than simply sleeping it off, suggesting that they'd only taken a glancing blow from the stunner. He came to a halt as they reached the edge of the roof, even as the Marine jumped and made it across the narrow alleyway. Down below, he heard a roar as the crowd realised that their prey was escaping...

"Jump," the Marine snapped. The one carrying Fiona ran past him and jumped effortlessly across the chasm. "Jump now!"

Behind him, Leo heard the sound of rioters breaking out onto the rooftop. Somehow, he forced himself to jump across the gap. He landed safely on the other side and staggered, just as the remaining two Marines landed beside him. One of them turned and fired a handful of bursts from his stunner towards the crowd; Leo turned, just in time to see several rioters trip and fall over the edge, plunging downwards. The Marine caught his arm and pulled him onwards as they started to run, ignoring the hail of flying rocks thrown after them.

"What..." He coughed and started again. "What stops them jumping too?"

"Absolutely nothing," the Marine said. "Shut up and run!"

Leo obeyed, cursing the pain in his chest. Part of him just wanted to collapse; the rest of him knew that would be certain death. Instead, he somehow managed to run onwards, nearly tripping over other stunned bodies. Behind them, the mob kept coming...

"The QRF has reached the edge of the marketplace," Villeneuve reported. "They're driving back the rioters."

Edward nodded. Stunners made it easier to fire into a riot – reasonably healthy people would almost certainly survive being stunned – but there would still be deaths. Everyone who fell off the rooftops would be unlikely to survive, as would those who were crushed under their fellow rioters. Edward still had nightmares about the fighting on Han, when the howling mobs had attacked fully-armoured Marines with their bare hands. They hadn't stood a chance and yet they'd kept coming.

"Tell them to pull back as soon as they recover our lost sheep," he ordered. It was becoming alarmingly clear that the city was dissolving into chaos. He wondered, briefly, what the local warriors were doing, before realising that it was unlikely that they would be able to put down the riot without wrecking the capital city. They'd probably prefer to leave the off-worlders to their fate. "And then secure our walls."

He glanced down at the report from the sentries. So far, no one had attempted to besiege the Imperial Residency – on either side of the building – but it was only a matter of time. The local guards had been disarmed and taken into protective custody. Edward had no idea which side they were on and he didn't have time to worry about it. Besides, with a riot spreading through the city, he had a feeling that the guards would prefer to be under lock and key.

"We should take the servants into custody too," Villeneuve suggested. "They might be more than they seem."

"Do so," Edward ordered.

He sat back and tried to look confident, hating himself. There was nothing he could do now, but wait for his orders to be carried out. If he could have gone in person…he shook his head, understanding – once again – why the Commandant had been so reluctant to remain in his post. He'd known that, for all his rank and authority, he was helpless to do more than watch as his people risked their lives.

———

"They're waiting for us at the edge of the building," the Marine said, as they reached the end of the marketplace. "You're going to have to trust us here, understand?"

Leo swallowed, but nodded. "I understand. Why...?"

He gasped in pain as the Marine caught his hand and yanked, pulling them both off the edge of the building. There was a moment of absolute panic – and then he crashed into a vat of stinky liquid, breaking his fall. The stench was appalling; before he could say a word, strong arms pulled him out and over the side. Others caught on and held him upright.

"Stinky," someone joked. Leo's eyes were stinging so badly that he couldn't even *begin* to see who'd spoken. "What a mess."

"Shut up and run," the Marine growled. He was still holding onto Leo's hand, pulling him onwards. "You can make snide remarks later."

Leo blinked, forcing his vision to clear. Behind them, a line of people were falling off the rooftops and down to the ground. He looked down at his clothes and winced at the stench; he didn't want to even *think* about what they might have used to break their fall. And how had the Marine known it was there anyway?

"Drones say that there are bigger crowds heading our way," the Marine grunted as they ran, "but there isn't anyone in our path. We have a clear run back to the Residency."

Edward watched grimly as the Marines and QRF finally made it back to the gates. Their pursuers required some discouragement from the guards at the gates, but they broke and ran after the guards started firing live rounds over their heads. He checked that there had been nothing from the local government, then stood up and walked down to where the refugees were hastily undressing. Their clothes and uniforms had been completely ruined and their equipment would have to be checked carefully, but at least they were alive.

"Good work," he said.

"They didn't want to catch us, sir," Coleman reported. He might have a reputation – well-deserved – as a horny bastard, but no one had ever doubted his competence. "The whole riot was carefully controlled from start to finish. We were *allowed* to escape."

"I know," Edward agreed. It was the only conclusion that made sense. Mobs were about as smart as the stupidest person in them and they had a nasty habit of trampling on their fellows to get to their targets. The Marines would have given a good account of themselves if they had been backed into a corner, but they would have eventually been overwhelmed and destroyed. "But why?"

He looked over at the Professor and his wife. Fiona looked to have fainted; a female medic was cutting away her clothes for disposal. She could be carried into the makeshift infirmary and tended to there. Her husband looked stunned, perhaps on the verge of going into shock, but he was alive.

"You did well," Edward said, as reassuringly as he could. Civilians became hellishly unpredictable in warzones. "I'm going to have you sedated. Once you awake, we can decide what to do next."

Leo opened his mouth to object, but the medic pressed a sedation tab against his arm before he could say a word. Edward watched as he slumped over, then motioned for two of the Marines to carry him to his bed. It would be at least twelve hours before the effects of the tab wore off.

Edward's wristcom buzzed. "Sir, we're picking up a message from Sivaganga Zamindari," Villeneuve reported. "He is demanding an immediate meeting."

The penny is about to drop, Edward thought.

"Understood," he responded out loud. "I'm on my way."

CHAPTER THIRTEEN

> Looking at the first requirement, a country must analyse and then prioritise its requirements. For example, a neighbouring army division on the border represents a clear and present danger to the country's independence. Diplomatically, keeping that division away from the border is more important than whatever is happening on the other side of the globe. Concentrating on the latter instead of the former is asking for trouble.
> -Professor Leo Caesius, *Diplomacy: The Lessons of the Past.*

Sivaganga Zamindari shivered as he approached the Imperial Residency, wearing the full formal outfit of a Minister of State. The Prince – and his cronies – might believe that they could control the mob, but he had his doubts. Even the strict orders they'd issued to threaten and scare the off-worlders, rather than kill, might have been disobeyed in the heat of the moment. After all, the government had been telling everyone that their problems were caused by off-worlders and only their complete removal from the surface of the planet would allow peace and prosperity to return.

But it *had* worked, miraculously.

The guards who had been assigned to the Residency were gone, he noticed. In their place, there were off-worlders carrying modern weapons and looking at him as if they were about to unsling their weapons and use him for target practice. The lack of respect in their eyes saddened, but didn't surprise him. Off-worlders had never shown any real respect to the lords and masters of the higher castes. Humiliating them was a way to show their power.

One of the guards stepped forward and held up a hand, motioning for Sivaganga to stop and wait. He obeyed – and then cursed himself as two more guards came up to him and searched him quickly but thoroughly, removing both his communicator and the primitive datanet terminal that had been purchased from an off-world trader at considerable cost. Normally, even the Rajah's guards would never have searched *anyone* so thoroughly, but Sivaganga gritted his teeth and submitted without protest. As unpleasant as it was, going back to the Prince and reporting that he hadn't even been able to deliver the ultimatum would be worse.

"Come with us," the guard commanded, finally. There must have been some consultation with his superiors, although Sivaganga couldn't see how. "And behave yourself."

Inside, there was a line of men seated against one wall. It took Sivaganga a moment to realise that they were the former guards – and that they were helpless, their hands bound firmly behind their backs. He felt a flicker of outrage at how casually the guards had been treated, although he knew that the off-worlders had had little alternative. The Prince's plans had called for the guards to attack the off-worlders from behind, when the fighting finally started. It seemed that the off-worlders had anticipated that ploy.

"This is the Colonel," the guard growled, as a tall blonde-haired man appeared from the main building. He was wearing a uniform, including body-armour, with a pistol conspicuously buckled to his belt. Behind him, there was an older woman wearing a slightly different military uniform. "You can speak to him."

Sivaganga took a moment to study the two off-worlders. The woman seemed almost mannish, an odd thing in his experience; it was hard to truly grasp the fact that she *was* a woman. Indeed, if it hadn't been for the swell of her breasts, he would have automatically assumed that she was male. The man seemed younger, but there was a coldness in his eye that suggested that he had seen too much in his life to relax completely. Not for the first time, Sivaganga found himself wondering if the Prince – and, by extension, the whole planet – had bitten off more than they could chew.

He cleared his throat. "I come with a message from His Most Imperial Majesty," he said, making a deliberate decision to omit most of the Rajah's titles. "He wishes you to surrender the off-worlders responsible for starting the riot and killing upwards of a hundred citizens of this planet."

"I see," the man observed. "And the fact that they were just defending themselves doesn't matter?"

"We will establish the truth of such issues," Sivaganga said, blandly. Neither he nor the Prince expected the off-worlders to surrender their fellows – it would be in line with their arrogance – but it would make a suitable excuse for attacking the Residency. "I must insist that they be surrendered at once."

The two off-worlders exchanged glances. "Unacceptable," the woman stated, flatly. "We cannot simply surrender anyone to your idea of justice."

"And we cannot allow you to shelter fugitives from justice," Sivaganga retorted, forcing himself to take her seriously. Off-worlders believed that women could do anything a man could do. "If they are not handed over to us, we will be forced to take them from you."

Edward fought hard to keep his temper under control. It was now far too obvious what was actually happening. The locals had deliberately started the riot – carefully ensuring that no off-worlders were actually *killed* – in order to use it as an excuse to start a fight and invade the Residency. Even if he'd been inclined to surrender his people, something that would have been a gross betrayal of the men and women under his command, they would just have kept tacking on demands until they found something he physically couldn't give them.

"While Wolfbane would prefer to remain uninvolved in this affair," Flora maintained, "I feel that we cannot set the precedent of handing *anyone* over to you."

Edward could have kissed her. Defending the Residency would be hard enough at the best of times, but it would have been far harder if Flora's forces absented themselves from the fight. If nothing else, he would have needed to spread his own people thinner just to cover the walls…and if she'd decided to join the other side, the building might have become indefensible. But then, a few hours of shelling – if the locals had artillery – would have destroyed the building anyway.

"There will be a full investigation," he promised, "but we cannot allow you to simply *take* our people."

"That is unacceptable," Sivaganga snapped, so quickly that it was obviously pre-planned. "We will not allow you off-worlders to break our laws with impunity. It was hard enough to agree to allow you to hold your conference here. Now, we will take whatever steps are required to force you to surrender the criminals – and those who shelter them to us."

He took a step backwards, glaring at them both impartially. "You have two hours to reconsider," he added. "If you refuse to surrender them to us at the end of that period, you will be removed from our planet."

Edward looked over at the guard. "Take him back to the gate and kick him out," he ordered, sharply. A moment later, Sivaganga was hustled away. "We need to get ready for a fight."

Flora nodded. "I'll coordinate my forces with yours," she offered. "We're going to have to work together."

"Thank you," Edward said, surprised. But perhaps he shouldn't have been, he told himself firmly. The locals were unlikely to differentiate between two different groups of off-worlders. In his experience, those who played with mobs ended up losing control completely. "And I'll try to summon reinforcements from the coast."

He scowled as he led her into the building and down into the basement kitchen. The servants were seated there, their hands bound firmly behind their backs. Evicting them from the Residency was probably the smart course of action, but he had a feeling that the locals would punish them for daring to be thrown out of the complex. Or, if the mobs started attacking anyone who might have had any dealings with off-worlders, the servants would die before they had a chance to protest their innocence.

"It's two hundred kilometres from here to the garrison," he mused, thoughtfully. Shuttles could bring in reinforcements, but he knew that the locals had access to *some* antiaircraft weapons. God knew if they could shoot down a shuttle, but finding out the hard way would be costly. "We might have to hold out for several weeks."

Flora nodded. "We could try to break out of the city," she suggested. "Or would that be too risky?"

Edward scowled. If he'd had a company of Marines – and no one else – he would have taken the risk, relying on speed and armoured combat suits to prevent the enemy from pinning them down and exterminating them. But most of his soldiers were unarmoured and they would be accompanied by a handful of civilians. It was far too easy to imagine them being trapped by howling mobs and being torn apart, one by one. Maharashtra was simply too large for him to escape before the hammer came down.

"Far too risky," he muttered. "I think we'd better start preparing for a siege."

He looked over at Villeneuve. "Start moving all of our bedding into the basement," he ordered, grimly. "At least we'll have some protection under there."

But if they start shelling us, he thought, privately, *we won't have any protection at all.*

He pushed the thought aside and glared down at the makeshift map of the city. "Get a couple of drones in the air," he added, addressing Coleman. "I want to know when they start moving troops up to the walls."

"They'll probably put snipers in the nearest buildings," Flora offered, thoughtfully. "They could easily fire down into our complex from there."

Edward nodded, wondering just how long the locals had been considering their plans to attack the off-worlders. Had they had them in mind from the day they'd started designing the Imperial Residency? It was a large complex, but Flora was right. There was nothing to stop snipers firing down into the courtyard – and through the windows – from the nearby buildings. Hell, they wouldn't even have to be especially skilled!

"Put three of the Marines on the roof with sniper rifles," he ordered. "They can discourage anyone who wants to try to take shots at us."

He raised his voice, addressing everyone in the compartment. "From this moment on, you are cleared to engage anyone who tries to cross the walls or fire into the complex," he added. "Lethal force is authorised; I say again, lethal force is authorised."

"Understood, sir," Coleman said.

"The off-worlders rejected our demands," Sivaganga reported, as he returned to where the Prince had established his HQ. "They refused to hand the criminals over to us."

"Of course not," the Prince sneered. No one had seriously expected the off-worlders to simply hand over their men, not when they had good reason to suspect that the whole affair had been staged. "But I have several infantry units moving into the city right now. And the mobs, of course."

"I suggest evacuating the area surrounding the Residency first," Sivaganga said, mildly. "It would give us more time to get troops in position to storm the complex."

"They are already running for their lives," the Prince said, dismissively. He didn't sound too concerned, but most of the people who'd lived near the Residency had profited from dealings with off-worlders. They too would be purged once the off-worlders had been exterminated and all traces of their presence destroyed. "But the mobs will appear more spontaneous."

He looked down at his map. "The off-worlders in the garrison will move to assist their fellows," he added, sourly. "We have forces in place to block them. And others in position to destroy infrastructure if necessary."

Sivaganga nodded in relief. The Prince might be an ill-tempered zealot who saw the whole affair as a chance to render his position as Heir to the Throne unchallengeable, but he was not allowing his hatred of off-worlders to blind him completely. If the ground forces the off-worlders had landed were too powerful to be stopped directly, they could be forced to slow down by destroying bridges, canals and food supplies. Besides, even they had to run out of supplies sooner or later.

"The mobs can go in now," the Prince ordered. "Let the off-worlders feel our wrath."

"I'll send the CEF forward at once," Brigadier Yamane said. "How long can you hold out?"

"It depends on what they send against us," Edward reminded her. If there had been nothing between the Landshark tanks and Warrior AFVs, they could have reached Maharashtra in three to four hours. But drone and orbital surveillance were picking up signs of enemy troops moving into position to block their advance. "If they've decided to destroy us with artillery, it is unlikely that we can hold out long enough for you to reach us."

He closed his eyes for a long moment, remembering Gaby – and Avalon, and everything he'd hoped to accomplish. "If we are defeated, you are to pull back to the Garrison and wait for the starships to return," he said, cursing the diplomatic preconditions under his breath. A single destroyer would have been more than enough to prevent the locals from overrunning the Residency. "Do *not* throw away your people in a futile attempt to rescue us."

"I understand," Yamane conceded, with obvious reluctance.

Edward saw the mutiny in her eyes and understood perfectly. Marines did not abandon their own. If Marines were trapped, or captured, the entire force would do whatever it took to get them back alive – or avenge their deaths. But this was different. The CEF was simply too far away to make an impact in time. If they were facing obliteration, there was no point in wasting the CEF in a futile attempt to save them.

"I mean it," he warned. "There will be a chance to avenge us when the starships return."

He closed the channel and sighed, heavily. One way or another, this affair was going to leave scars on their souls. Assuming they survived, of course.

His wristcom buzzed. "Colonel, there are mobs advancing towards the gates," Villeneuve reported. "They're definitely under control."

Edward nodded and walked out of his office, into the makeshift situation room. Several consoles had been set up on the kitchen tables, each one showing the live feed from hand-launched drones orbiting over the complex. The mobs were advancing forward, controlled by a number of men in black robes. Even maddened as they were, the mobs seemed to defer to them. Edward wondered vaguely who they were, then dismissed the thought. All he needed to know was that they were in charge.

"The ultimatum hasn't run out yet," Flora pointed out. She didn't sound concerned, even though she would be more used to combat in space than on the ground. Spacers always considered their field to be *clean*. "Are they trying to intimidate us or are they jumping the gun?"

Edward shrugged. It was a mob – and mobs were unpredictable and unreliable. There was no way to know if the locals intended to attack before the ultimatum ran out, but it was quite possible that was going to happen anyway. He studied the dark-clad men thoughtfully, wishing he could hear what they were saying to the mob. Probably reminding them to rape, *then* loot and finally burn, he decided.

He looked down at some of the other views from the drones. Mob violence was breaking out in several other parts of the city, well away from the Residency. Men and women were being dragged out onto the streets and brutally lynched, while their homes and businesses were burned to the ground. It looked very much like the local government was losing its grip on its population already, Several smaller mobs were heading towards the slums surrounding the city, ready to attack the untouchable caste. In the chaos, he suspected, hundreds of thousands of private scores would be settled. It was very much like Han.

The mobs halted momentarily as the Residency came into view…then stumbled forwards, pushed by the men and women behind the first ranks. Edward winced as he saw several of the crowd falling over, knowing that they would almost certainly be trampled to death, then gritted his teeth as the mob pressed forward, advancing on the gates. The guards were already in position with stunners at the ready, but stunners had always been less than perfectly effective against mobs. They tended to use the first rows as human shields against stun pulses.

"Here we go," Villeneuve muttered.

Edward felt – again – a strange chilling helplessness as the mobs plunged forward, slamming into the walls. No amount of merely human strength could have budged walls made of hullmetal, but Lakshmibai was so backwards that it couldn't even *begin* to produce such composite materials. Thankfully, the mobs seemed more intent on attacking the gates rather than challenging the walls; if they'd fallen, the Residency would have rapidly become completely indefensible. Brilliant flickers of light shone out as the guards opened fire with stunners, sweeping them across the crowd. Hundreds fell to the ground, but thousands more kept coming.

Flora looked over at him. "We're going to have to switch to live weapons," she observed, bitterly. "All of the gates are under attack."

"Use gas first," Edward ordered. If nothing else, the gas might distract the crowds long enough for the stunners to take them all down. He knew that hundreds were already dead, crushed under the mob, but he didn't want to add to that number if possible. "And then prepare to open fire."

Another group of rioters appeared on the display, carrying ladders towards the walls. Edward gritted his teeth and issued orders, knowing that they couldn't risk people scrambling over the walls. The Residency was hard enough to defend as it was. Moments later, the Marine snipers picked off the ladder-carrying rioters, leaving their bodies lying in the streets. The ladders lay broken and shattered in their wake.

"There'll be more of them," Edward predicted, grimly. "Engage any other ladder-carrying…"

And then the crowds simply started to fall back from the walls.

CHAPTER FOURTEEN

> This is amply demonstrated by Anglo-Greek relationships in 1941. While the Greeks were facing a life-or-death struggle with Italy (and then Germany), the region was a third-order consideration for the British, who could survive a defeat in Greece, but not an invasion of the United Kingdom. Unsurprisingly, the Greeks did not care for this attitude and it blighted post-war relationships between the two powers.
> -Professor Leo Caesius, *Diplomacy: The Lessons of the Past.*

"Orbit Station can't drop anything on their heads," General Raphael admitted, through the intercom. "We can hit something the size of a city, but there are no precision weapons."

Jasmine scowled as she studied the map. The CEF was largely across the causeway already – thankfully – but they still had quite some distance to go before they reached the capital city, where they would probably have to fight their way through the streets. There was little data on the current state of the planet's infrastructure, which would make it harder to get there in time to save the Colonel and his men, yet it *was* clear that the planet's military was deploying to block their advance. Jasmine suspected that her force had the edge on manoeuvrability, but they would have to punch their way through. There was no time to be fancy.

She wished, not for the first time, for some heavy – and relatively cheap – transport aircraft, aircraft that could be risked in combat. The only craft she had that could ship reinforcements to the capital city were the shuttles…and if she started losing them in significant numbers, the war would be lost with them. If nothing else, re-embarking the CEF would be far harder without the entire complement of shuttles.

"Order the helicopters to provide air cover as the Warriors lead the way," she ordered, finally. It was relatively easy to track the enemy positions through their radio transmitters, but she had to remind herself that the enemy might *know* what she was doing. They might have an entire infantry unit dug in under strict radio silence, just waiting for her to poke her nose into a trap. "The tanks are to move up in support."

"Understood," Buckley said. He passed her orders on to her subordinates, then looked back at her. "Do you want to send the scouts forward first?"

Jasmine shook her head. Ideally, she *would* have preferred to send the scouts forward, but the advancing force was likely to overtake them very quickly. Instead, she would have to gamble and rely on the drones to spot any enemy forces lurking in ambush.

"Tell them to keep an eye on the city," she ordered, instead. "Is there any sign of a reaction from either side?"

"Not as yet," Buckley reported. "But they may not have had time to decide what to do yet."

He paused. "You should remain here," he added. "You're in command..."

"I'll be in the command tank," Jasmine declared, flatly. She would have preferred to command from a heavy battlesuit, but there wasn't one available for her. Besides, commanding anything larger than a company of Marines would have been very difficult from a suit. "I am not going to hide while others take risks on my behalf."

"Of course not," Buckley said. His voice hardened. "But you *will* stay back from the front lines."

"Yes, mother," Jasmine conceded, tiredly. "Which one of us is the Big Banana, anyway?"

"The Colonel," Buckley said. "And *he* said that you weren't to place yourself in too much danger."

Jasmine made a face. There really was no answer to that.

"This would be lovely countryside," Corporal Jason Briggs judged, "if it wasn't for the poverty."

Sergeant Andrew Wyrick shrugged as the helicopter raced eastwards, searching for enemy contacts. The countryside *was* lovely, he had to admit, although the war had definitely torn up most of the cropland and farming settlements that would have ordinarily fed the population. As it was, he honestly couldn't remember seeing anything worse in his career, even on Han. The handful of locals who looked up at the helicopter showed no curiosity; nothing but a listlessness that suggested that they were too far gone to care. Andrew had been on worlds where the helicopter might have been taken for something unworldly, but this was different.

"I suppose it would be," he grunted, keeping one eye on the threat receiver. No one was entirely sure how many ground-to-air missiles the locals might have purchased off interstellar traders, but he *was* sure that they would have been deployed to block the CEF from advancing towards the capital. The locals had little in the way of an air force – one of the reasons they hadn't been able to destroy the rebellion – and their forces could shoot at anything in the sky, confident that it belonged to the off-worlders. "But we have to keep our minds on the job."

He peered down at a tiny village as the helicopter skimmed over it, wincing inwardly at the complete absence of any modern technology. Even the worst parts of Avalon used combine harvesters and tractors to help the farmers reap a crop from the land. Here, the farmers had no choice, but to use their bare hands and whatever handheld tools they could obtain. He wouldn't be too surprised to see the locals using slave labour to break the ground, sow the seeds and then reap the harvest. And then most of their produce would be taken away by their superiors, leaving the farmers with barely enough to keep themselves and their slaves alive.

If that, he thought, remembering some of the other scenes from orbital observation. Vast tracts of farmland had been destroyed during the fighting, or abandoned so long that it had simply reverted to wilderness. It was quite possible that the local population was starving to death, even to the point where they could no longer provide even a minimum level of labour.

The threat receiver whistled in his ear and he cursed, automatically pulling back on the stick and yanking the helicopter into an evasive manoeuvre that should have allowed them to break the lock. Below them, he saw a flash of light as a missile was launched; not an HVM, he noted with some relief, but a more primitive MANPAD. Briggs automatically launched a air-to-surface missile back at the launcher, although Andrew suspected that it would be pointless, even if they did kill the man who'd fired the missile. The handheld launchers were designed to be used once and then thrown away.

"Deploying flares," he said, as the missile raced towards the helicopter. A moment later, it slipped to one side and struck a flare, destroying both of them in a thunderous explosion. The helicopter rocked as the shockwave struck home, but remained undamaged. "I think we found the enemy."

"Confirmed," Briggs reported. He was peering down at the sensors. "I'm picking up at least a dozen armoured vehicles and a few hundred infantry. They're dug in to block advance up the road."

"Pass the report back to the CO," Andrew ordered, as he took the helicopter upwards. Having realised that they'd been detected, the locals were opening fire with rifles and machine guns. It was unlikely that they would manage to bring the helicopter down, but it was quite possible that they would get lucky. "Tell them that we have located the enemy."

"Contact," Buckley reported, quietly. "It's a trap."

Jasmine felt a hint of relief. At least they knew where the enemy were, even if they *were* in the worst possible place. If she had to take her force cross-country, it would slow them down considerably. Instead, she would have to punch through and hope that the enemy hadn't had time to deploy mines, IEDs and other unpleasant surprises.

"Order the tanks to move forward," she ordered smoothly. If nothing else, there was very little on the surface of this blighted world that could slow down a Landshark. The orbital sensors hadn't revealed *any* plasma weapons. It was a curious oversight, but perhaps the traders who'd shipped in weapons had decided to honour the Empire's ban on exporting plasma weapons. And the locals might not have known to ask for them.

She looked over at the reporter, who looked back at her. He looked nervous, but not as terrified as she had expected. But then, he *did* have some combat experience of his own.

"They're trying to stop us from reaching the capital city," she said, calmly. Perhaps an explanation would help calm his nerves. "But they won't succeed."

"The off-worlders are coming," the sergeants shouted, as Mahabala and his comrades slipped into the trench they'd dug to provide some cover. "Get ready to repel them!"

He braced himself as the nearest sergeant glared at him. The price for being part of the warrior caste was absolute discipline; failure, any failure, meant a beating at the very least. It had been a hellish deployment even before they'd been told that they might have to fight off-worlders; the local peasants had kept their gazes lowered, but it was clear that they hated the warriors almost as much as they hated the rebels in the hills. At least he hadn't had to go hunting in the hills too; the stories he'd heard had made it clear that the rebels ruled the hillside. Every warrior who had fallen into their hands had died a very painful death.

His palms suddenly felt sweaty as he saw the off-world vehicle coming into view. It was *massive*, larger than most of the farmhouses they'd turned into makeshift barracks by evicting most of the farmers and taking their beds for themselves. Suddenly, the trench they'd spent hours digging felt as flimsy as a sheet of paper. Nothing he'd seen the better-connected warriors driving was larger than the off-world tank. Its colossal main gun alone was bigger than any of the artillery pieces that were being set up behind the lines.

"Hold your ground," the sergeant barked. Several of the warriors were showing signs of wanting to run, although the gods alone knew *where* they would have run. The rebels would have killed them if they'd been caught and the penalty for desertion was death. "Fire on my command."

There were two more tanks now, Mahabala realised; advancing towards the trench as if they didn't know that it was there – or didn't care. He tried to tell himself that it was the latter, just as one of the missile launchers panicked and fired his missile towards the lead tank. The sergeants swore out loud and barked a command, ordering the rest of the unit to open fire on the enemy vehicles. Mahabala pointed his weapon at the tank and opened fire, only to see the missiles slamming into its hull and detonating without causing any damage at all. It was hard to imagine that his rifle would do any better. Indeed, he couldn't even see sparks as the bullets bounced off the hull.

And then there was a terrifying noise as the tank opened fire with machine guns of its own. Mahabala dived into the trench, hugging the mud and praying desperately as thousands of bullets slammed into the ground, tearing apart his comrades if they didn't get out of the firing line in time. He saw one of the sergeants simply disintegrate as he was caught in the stream, almost wiped from existence by the off-world weapons. And then a dark shadow fell over the trench.

He had a moment to realise that the tank was driving right *over* the trench, it was driving right over *him*! There was a moment of absolute terror…and then the walls collapsed in on him. And then there was nothing, but darkness.

"The tanks have broken through the trench lines," Major Daniels reported, over the intercom. The CO of the 2nd Avalon Armoured Regiment seemed pleased with himself. "They're engaging the enemy tanks now."

Jasmine nodded, although she couldn't banish a vague sense of unease. It was understandable that the enemy would underestimate the sheer power of an off-world force, but surely they would have known better than to set up trenches and assume that they would be enough to stop her. Indeed, the trenches had done little more than slow the tanks down for a few seconds. If that was all the resistance they were likely to face, breaking through to the capital would be easy.

But it won't be, she thought, bleakly. *There are places where geography will make it easier for them to slow us down.*

She looked up at the live feed from the drones in contemplation. The local tanks were several generations behind the Landshark, unsurprisingly. No doubt the interstellar traders had taken advantage of the chance to unload junk on an unsuspecting planet. But she had to admit that the enemy tankers were showing no shortage of bravery. It was their tactical acumen that was in question. Their vehicles were so thin-skinned that her tankers didn't even need their main guns to deal with them, yet they were still charging forward, firing desperately. And other vehicles were following in their wake. Her tanks simply had too many targets to choose from…

Understanding clicked, too late.

"Those vehicles are bombs," she snapped. Her tankers had been so focused on the enemy tanks that they'd largely ignored the other vehicles. "Get the tanks back…"

It was too late.

———

"Jesus!"

Andrew stared as he saw a Landshark tank picked up and flung over by the sheer force of the blast. The tank was heavily armoured and it was quite possible that the crew had survived, but it was unlikely that it could be recovered in time. His threat receiver started screaming again as the enemy opened fire with artillery, shelling the off-worlders before they could back off out of the trap. Moments later, a second explosion sent another tank skidding to a halt.

"Two Landshark tanks appear to have been taken out," he reported, numbly. It was rare to lose a Landshark – and humiliating to lose two to such pitiful opposition. "Request permission to engage the enemy guns."

"Granted," a crisp voice returned. "You are cleared to engage."

———

Jasmine swallowed the rage that threatened to overwhelm her. She'd made a mistake and allowed her overconfidence to blind her to the threat, but there was no time for recriminations. Instead, she would have to extract her forces from this trap, a task made harder by the sudden appearance of enemy guns in the distance. They'd pound her to scrap if she let them. Maybe the Landshark tanks could survive a direct hit from a shell, but little else could.

"Order the remaining tanks to fall back," she ordered, shortly. "All enemy vehicles are to be engaged and destroyed at a distance."

"Understood," Major Daniels said. He didn't sound shaken, for which Jasmine was grateful. Quite a few officers in the Imperial Army had gone to pieces when they discovered that primitive didn't mean stupid. "We have survivors in the damaged tanks."

Destroyed, Jasmine thought. It was quite possible that the vehicles could be repaired, but recovering them would be far too dangerous. They'd just have to hope that the enemy didn't take the time to complete the task of rendering them irreparable before it was too late.

"Order the 1st Avalon Mechanized Infantry Battalion to move up and recover the survivors," she ordered, regretfully. "And then order the 1st Avalon Artillery Battalion to prepare to move out of the FOB."

The ground shuddered as more enemy shells crashed down on the off-worlders. She ran through it in her head, cursing her own mistakes. If she'd had the artillery moving with them…but it might not have made a difference. The enemy clearly had far more guns dug into the countryside, ready to duel with her own guns as well as hammer her advancing forces.

"Picking up a report from the garrison," Buckley said, chuckling with black humour. "The city's gone crazy and there are infantry units moving towards the FOB."

"Order the garrison to engage the advancing enemy forces with shell-fire," Jasmine ordered. It was galling, but she had to admit that the ambush had been carefully planned. The enemy had struck as soon as the CEF was away from the garrison's long-range guns. "There's nothing we can do for the city now."

The ground seemed to be glowing with fire from where the enemy guns were based, firing madly towards the trapped off-worlders. Andrew gritted his teeth as the threat receiver went off again and again, warning him of hidden enemy MANPADs, then ignored it as he activated the helicopter's ground-attack weapons.

"Weapons online," Briggs reported. "Sir?"

"Open fire," Andrew ordered.

The helicopter shuddered as it unleashed a spread of rockets and shells, firing down towards the enemy guns. Moments later, the level of enemy fire died away as explosions ran through their position, culminating in a final explosion that went up like a baby nuke. They must have hit an ammunition stockpile, Andrew told himself, as the shockwave buffeted the helicopter. Normally, ammunition would be kept away from the guns to prevent a lucky hit triggering a series of explosions, but the enemy had to keep the ammunition nearby if they wanted to maintain their level of fire.

"We used most of our ammunition," Briggs informed him.

"I'll take us back to the barn," Andrew said. They'd have to fly all the way back to the garrison, reload and then fly back. He hoped that the ground-pounders could remain alive until then – or pull back from the hell they'd stumbled into. "Tell command that we're moving."

They hadn't wiped out all the guns either, he realised, as they flew back towards the coastline. The enemy had other guns, all firing on the oncoming off-worlders. There were so many shells flying through the air that it was quite possible that one of them would strike the helicopter, if they weren't careful. And there were explosions billowing up from where they were landing, hammering the CEF…

It looked very much like hell.

CHAPTER FIFTEEN

Looking at the second requirement, failing to honour one treaty (no matter how minor) can convince outside powers that one will not honour other treaties. A reputation for bargaining in ill faith can blight a country's relationships with the rest of the world for decades afterwards, even if the government responsible is removed and replaced with a new government.
-Professor Leo Caesius, *Diplomacy: The Lessons of the Past.*

"Keep your damned heads down," Sergeant Grieves bellowed, somehow making himself heard over the sound of incoming shells and explosions. "Keep your heads down and you might live to see the dawn!"

Michael ran forward, keeping low as he led the way towards the wrecked Landshark. It was weird to see the tank flipped over, as if all it really needed was a push to right itself and start operating again. But the hull was clearly damaged, he realised as they approached, and the treads were broken. It would be able to move on its wheels, if he recalled correctly, but it wouldn't be able to make full speed.

A bullet pinged past his head and he swore out loud, then turned and fired back towards the advancing enemy soldiers. They were crawling towards the tank themselves, intending to claim the wreckage and capture the crews inside the vehicles. Michael found cover behind the tank as his comrades added their own fire to the maelstrom, driving the enemy soldiers back. He couldn't fault their determination, he told himself, or their willingness to close with the enemy.

Another series of thundering explosions ran through the ground as the enemy dropped more shells to the west, trying to take out more of the CEF's vehicles. Michael ignored it as best as he could, concentrating on activating his mouthpiece and trying to link into the tank's communications network. Convincing the tankers to come out of their vehicle was tricky; unsurprisingly, they felt that they were safer inside the tank, even if it was damaged. They might have been right, he knew, if the CEF was still advancing, but it was alarmingly clear that they would have to fall back and regroup. The tankers couldn't be left behind.

There was a dull click as the hatch opened, allowing the first tanker to slip out of the hull and drop into the mud. Michael couldn't help rolling his eyes at how clean the tanker's uniform was, or at the man's expression of disgust as he breathed in the stench of the battlefield. But then, he supposed that warfare would look cleaner if he had umpteen thousand tons of main battle tank wrapped around him too. He was followed by five more tankers, including two women. Michael silently promised himself that *they* wouldn't be allowed to fall into enemy hands. If the local warriors believed that they could do whatever they liked to local women, particularly those of lower castes, what would they do to captured off-worlders?

"Keep your damned heads down," he snarled at them, as the enemy fire intensified. He gave the leader a shove that sent him flying headfirst into the mud. "Stay down and crawl west."

The other tank crew didn't waste so much time climbing out, much to his relief. But then, their vehicle had been hit so hard that the hull had been cracked. They didn't have the time to delude themselves into believing that they were still safe. Michael detailed off half his force to escort the tankers back to friendly lines, then looked to the east. A line of enemy infantry were advancing towards them.

"Take aim," he ordered. If the enemy were obsessed with capturing the remains of the tanks, it might give the rest of the CEF time to withdraw in good order. Losing the wrecked tanks would be annoying, but losing the CEF would be worse. "Fire!"

Five of the enemy soldiers dropped as his men opened fire. The remainder hit the dirt and started to crawl forward, covered by their fellows. Michael motioned for the sergeant to unhook a grenade from his belt, then throw it towards the oncoming enemy; as soon as the grenade detonated, he led the way back towards better cover. If they were lucky, it would take the enemy several moments to realise that they'd changed position.

The sound of the guns grew louder for a long moment, then dimmed slightly; the dull thrumming running through the ground faded away. Michael hesitated, wondering what was going on, then pushed it out of his mind. It wasn't his job to worry about the overall battlefield, merely his small corner of it. The big picture was in the hands of his superior officers.

"I think they're running out of ammunition for their big guns," Buckley reported. "Their level of fire is dimming slightly."

"Let's hope so," Jasmine said. Civilians never quite understood just how rapidly a military unit could burn through ammunition – and nor could soldiers who had never fought a real battle in their lives. It was quite possible that the warrior caste hadn't appreciated just how much ammunition they'd use while trying to smash her forces. "Move the tanks to cover our escape, then pull back the point forces."

Buckley blinked in surprise. "We're retreating?"

Jasmine nodded, bitterly. There was no way to avoid the fact that the CEF had taken a bloody nose – and that it would only get harder as they pushed onwards towards the capital. They needed time to regroup and plan – and what? Make common cause with the rebels? Maybe they could do that now. Hell, there was no other option, apart from abandoning the Colonel, the Professor and their escorts to whatever fate the locals had in store for them. And she would sooner die than let that happen.

"Yes," she admitted, curtly.

She looked down at the reports from the city. They were hellishly confused; the garrison had some human intelligence sources on the ground, but not all of them were considered reliable, unsurprisingly. Intelligence sources could be subverted by the enemy, if they were detected. But if what they were saying was true, the local government and the rebels were battling it out for supremacy, with the population caught in the middle. She'd just have to wait and see who came out on top. Even if she hadn't been trying to extract her own forces from a trap, there was no way to know who was on what side.

"And tell the helicopters to rearm as quickly as possible," she added. Right now, they were the only mobile artillery they had. If they couldn't take out the enemy guns, or at least force them to waste time changing position, they would find it harder to withdraw in good order. "We need them back here."

"Understood," Buckley said.

———

"Incoming enemy tanks," the CO reported. "Five of them."

Corporal Sharon Jones nodded as she took control of *Hammer's* main gun. The giant Landshark tank normally gave her a comforting sense of invulnerability – and besides, it was the only combat arm open to females, at least outside the Marines. But now two tanks had been lost and a third had been badly damaged and ordered to make its own way back to the FOB. The sense of invulnerability was gone.

"Weapons locked on target," she reported. The enemy tanks were smaller, which didn't mean that they weren't dangerous. Standard high-explosive or armour-piercing shells wouldn't be enough to break Landshark-grade armour, but plasma warheads would melt their way inside and reduce the crew to ash. "Ready to fire."

The CO smiled. "Fire," he said.

Sharon keyed a switch and the first shell launched from the main gun, whistling out to strike the enemy tank. The other tanks opened fire at the same moment, one of them scoring a direct hit on the Landshark, rocking the tank without doing any major damage. Her firing sequence continued unabated, striking the remaining four enemy tanks and leaving them nothing, but burning wreckage. She found herself hoping that the enemy crews had had time to bail out, although she knew that it was unlikely. Even if they had, they'd have to make their way off a battlefield where both sides were firing at everything that moved.

"All targets destroyed," she reported.

"Pull us back," the CO ordered the driver. "We're being ordered to cover the infantry as they fall back."

"Aye, sir," the driver said. Something struck the tank hard enough to shake it, but didn't break through the armour. A moment later, the vehicle lurched into life and started heading back towards the coastline. "We're on our way."

The tankers were looking like drowned rats, Michael decided, as they finally reached the place where the Warriors were waiting for them. They looked so relieved that he decided not to point out that the Warriors weren't as heavily armoured as the Landshark tanks and that a single shell would be enough to reduce them to flaming debris. Instead, he watched as they were chivvied into the lead AFV and driven back towards the coastline.

His earpiece buzzed. "Remain with the tanks for the moment," a voice explained. "Then prepare to withdraw back to the FOB."

"That's most of our engaged forces out of the battlefield," Major Daniels reported. "The last of the tanks are pulling back now."

Jasmine sighed, relieved. The enemy guns were still trying to engage the retreating CEF, but their tanks seemed more inclined to stay back this time, rather than try to force the CEF to move faster. Maybe they thought they'd taken enough losses…or maybe they intended to launch a new attack as soon as they regrouped. Part of her hoped so; a mobile battle would play to her strengths, rather than her weaknesses.

"Good," she said. "And the helicopters?"

"Inbound, with full loads of ammunition," Buckley reported. "They're requesting permission to engage the enemy tanks."

"Denied," Jasmine said. "Tell them to concentrate on the guns. I need them suppressed."

Andrew wasn't too surprised as he led the four-ship squadron of helicopters towards the enemy guns. The tanks made tempting targets, but he could understand why higher authority would want to exterminate the enemy guns first. Their drones were reporting that the enemy rate of fire was actually increasing, as if they knew that their targets were slowly slipping out of their grasp. He flipped on the targeting computer and examined the possible targets. There were far too many of them.

"They've started to spread the guns out a little," Briggs commented. "And they're advancing others forward too."

Andrew nodded and activated his microphone. "Charlie-two, follow us in and engage the active guns," he ordered. "Charlie-three, Charlie-four; engage the moving guns."

Briggs keyed a series of switches. "Targets assigned, sir," he reported. "Ready to engage."

"Fire," Andrew ordered.

The two helicopters swooped down on the enemy guns, firing as they came. Andrew saw enemy troops scattering as the missiles and shells rained down, feeling the elemental force of destruction that was about to break over their weapons. The level of enemy shellfire dropped rapidly as the guns were destroyed or abandoned, even if there wasn't such a spectacular explosion this time.

They must have been running out of ammunition, he reasoned, as the helicopter clawed for sky after completing the sweep. *There wasn't enough left to cause a real explosion.*

The threat receiver screamed a warning and he dumped flares automatically, swearing out loud as he saw a pair of missiles lancing up towards the helicopters. One of them was misdirected by the flares and exploded harmlessly below them, the other refused to be diverted and slammed into Charlie-two, punching through the armour and detonating inside. The helicopter exploded into a colossal fireball before her crew had a hope of escaping.

"Charlie-two is gone," Andrew reported, bleakly. A further spread of missiles were launched from the ground and he accelerated to escape them. The remaining two helicopters completed their own sweeps and rose to join his craft. "No survivors; I say again, no survivors."

"Understood, Charlie-one," the CO said. "Ammunition status?"

"Down to 20%," Andrew informed him. Behind him, the second wave of missiles had lost their locks and headed down to the ground. Vengefully, he hoped they landed on enemy heads. Imperial Army equipment had safety features to prevent such accidents, but he doubted the locals would have bothered to enable them. "Do you wish us to reengage?"

"Hold position and wait," the CO ordered. "We're pulling out the remainder of the infantry now."

Andrew scowled. There was no escaping the simple fact that they'd lost. The enemy had given the CEF a bloody nose and forced it to retreat in disorder. And if they failed to break through to the capital, Colonel Stalker and his men were likely to be slaughtered out of hand.

He shook his head. That was not going to happen.

But, as God was his witness, he didn't know what they could do about it.

The IED was nothing more than a tiny packet of explosive, a motion sensor and a timer primed to activate the IED five minutes after it was placed under a stone. Michael carefully concealed it, pushed the activation switch and then moved away as rapidly as possible. He'd learned during the Cracker War just how unreliable IEDs could be, even the ones built with military-grade technology.

"That should delay them a little," he muttered. The rest of the squad was emplacing their own IEDs, knowing that even one explosion would deter the enemy from giving chase with enthusiasm. Unless, of course, the enemy soldiers were being followed by men with guns, who would shoot anyone who tried to slow down. "Sergeant?"

"All emplaced," the Sergeant reported, as they left the makeshift minefields behind. "The Warriors are waiting for us behind the next hill."

Michael allowed himself a sigh of relief as they rounded the hill and saw the AFVs. The noise of fighting was dying away, although he could still hear the thunderous *crash-crash-crash* of Landshark main guns as they engaged enemy vehicles at long range. He sagged as he clambered into the AFV and sat down on the bench, forcing himself to remain upright as the vehicle roared into life and took them away from the battlefield. It was funny how he managed to keep going while he was outside, but collapsed the moment he felt safe.

And those tankers felt safe too, he reminded himself, sternly. *He* didn't have a Landshark protecting him from the battlefield, even now. *You should know that you won't be safe until the war comes to an end.*

"That's the remainder of the infantry pulled out," Buckley reported. He sounded as tired as Jasmine felt. "The tanks are still providing covering fire."

Jasmine smiled. The enemy didn't seem to have realised just how far the Landshark could shoot, certainly not when the tanks were paired with invisible drones flying high over the battlefield. A handful of stunningly precise shots had deterred pursuit by anything larger than infantry – and the IEDs had kept them from pushing too closely – but she knew that the enemy knew that they had won. They'd taken on the CEF and forced it to retreat with its tail between its legs.

Colonel Stalker will not be happy, she thought, numbly. She felt exhausted, even though she hadn't been fighting personally. But being out in the field would have been preferable to watching her failure unfold on the display screens. Over a hundred soldiers – perhaps more – had been killed, because of her. And a handful more were unaccounted for. She'd failed them all.

Enough, she told herself. There was still no time for self-pity. *You have a job to do.*

"Keep pulling us back until we reach base," she ordered. Once they broke contact completely, they could relax and regroup – and prepare for future operations. "The long-range guns of the garrison can provide us with cover."

If nothing else, she added to herself, *it will give us time to think of what to do next.*

Private Mathew Polk felt himself moving in and out of consciousness, unsure of just what had happened to him. They'd been advancing against the enemy; he was sure of that, if nothing else. And then his vehicle had been hit, he'd fallen, and then…his memory failed him. He forced himself to sit upright and gasped in pain as he realised that his leg was broken. And the rest of his body hurt so badly that he was convinced that there were other broken bones.

Concussion, he thought. No *wonder* his thoughts were spinning through his head. *You can't think straight.*

He looked around, hoping to see someone coming to rescue him, but there was nothing in view apart from a burning AFV. The entire squad might be dead, he realised, or they might have thought that *he* was dead. They might have abandoned him…he opened his throat, intending to cry out, then stopped as hazy figures came into view. One look was all it needed to tell him that they weren't friendly. He started to reach for his pistol – his rifle was nowhere to be seen – but his hand refused to obey orders. And then they were on him, barking orders in a language he didn't understand.

They rolled him over, ignoring his cries of pain, and bound his hands and feet firmly together. A moment later, two of them hauled him up and carried him to the east, away from the rest of the CEF. Who knew what they would do to him? None of the rumours suggested that the locals would follow any of the POW treatment conventions the Knights had been trained to uphold. Everything they did to their fellow locals was horrifying enough.

He started to struggle, desperately, but it was already too late. One of them slapped him on the head with a club and he blacked out into darkness.

Chapter Sixteen

This doesn't just involve the two countries who signed the original treaty. A nation that shows bad faith to one nation will be suspected of being prepared to do the same to other nations.

-Professor Leo Caesius, *Diplomacy: The Lessons of the Past.*

Flora stared in disbelief. "They're leaving?"

Edward shook his head. The mob might be falling back, but it was clear from the drones that a large force of local soldiers was entering the city. It was hard to tell – their uniforms made it hard for him to take them seriously – yet it seemed as though the mob was scared of them. And yet mobs weren't known for being scared until they were lashed back into their component individuals…

"I don't think so," he said, grimly. "I think they're about to start round two."

He'd seen bodies piled high on Han, but this was almost worse. Hundreds of bodies lay in the street outside the walls, trampled flat by the mob after they'd fallen to the ground. Blood soaked the ground, flowing down towards the walls. The handful of remaining rioters stared at the walls as if they were coming out of a trance, then started to make their way away from the Residency. Edward watched them go, hoping that they'd learned a lesson from the slaughter. And to think that most of the dead had been killed by their very own mob.

"Almost certainly," Villeneuve agreed. He pointed to one of the consoles. "There's a small force of infantry approaching from the north. Somehow, I don't think they're here for our protection."

"Look for signs of heavy weapons," Edward ordered. *He* wouldn't have cared to unleash heavy weapons inside his own capital city, but it was clear that the local government didn't really care about their own people. They didn't even seem to be evacuating the nearest buildings, let alone setting up refugee camps or protection zones. The drones were picking up scenes of horror as fleeing refugees ran right into the mob. "Or are they just planning to run at the gates?"

He gritted his teeth as the enemy soldiers paused, taking cover beyond the Residency's walls. There was no sign of anything heavier than submachine guns, but it might not matter. It was quite possible that the enemy would just keep forcing their soldiers forwards until the defenders of the Residency ran out of ammunition, then overrun the walls and tear the defenders apart. Other troops appeared, heading towards the Wolfbane side of the Residency Complex. It looked as through the enemy intended to assault from both directions at once.

Clever, Edward acknowledged. It wasn't how *he* would have carried out the assault, but given the limitations of local forces they might not have a choice. *If they attack us at two or more points at once, it forces us to spread our defences thin and limits our reserves.*

"We have a mortar crew or two," Flora offered, after speaking to her subordinates. "We could drop a handful of shells on their heads."

Edward considered it briefly, then shook his head. "Wait until they start coming towards the walls," he said, flatly. "The longer we have to prepare our defences, the better."

He looked down at the live feeds from inside the Residency, feeling a flicker of pride at how well the Knights were coping with the unexpected fight. There was no panic; instead, the soldiers were setting up barricades, tripwires and other hidden surprises that would allow them to sell their lives dearly. Edward had no illusions about how long they'd last once the walls fell, but at least the locals would pay a high cost for their treachery. And they'd pay a higher one when the starships returned.

"Picking up movement in the surrounding buildings," Coleman reported, breaking into Edward's thoughts. "I think they're moving sniper crews into position."

Edward looked over at Flora. "Tell the mortar crews to target those buildings," he ordered, emotionlessly. They didn't dare let snipers start firing into the complex, or the defence would rapidly crumble. Edward doubted that the local snipers were up to Marine standards, but under the circumstances it hardly mattered. All they'd have to do was force his people to stay under cover, allowing the enemy infantry to storm the walls. "They're to fire at my command."

Flora nodded and started issuing orders.

"We may have to push out our defence line," Villeneuve suggested. "Right now, we're pinned down in the complex."

On the face of it, Edward knew, he was right. The walls were solid, but they had their limitations – and there were just too many places for the enemy troops to take up position and open fire into the complex. But he didn't have the manpower to seize and hold much in the way of additional territory, no matter what advantages he would derive from doing it. There was a good chance that it would shorten the fighting.

"We'll try and knock the buildings down first," he decided, finally. "General?"

Flora looked up. "The mortar crews are taking up position now," she informed him. "But they were unable to guarantee how much damage they could do to the buildings."

"Tell them to take their best shot," Edward said. There were other alternatives, but they'd mean exposing his Marines to the enemy forces. "And to fire on my command."

The Prince's crony commanders looked impressive, Sivaganga had to admit. They were dressed in the finest robes, carrying swords and rifles as if they were born to the military life – which, in a sense, they had been. Each of them came from the very highest levels of the warrior caste, direct descendents of intermingling between the ruling caste and the warrior caste. Some of them could even trace their descent all the way back to the Rajah's ancestors, although Sivaganga had his doubts. If the

Rajah had had so many bastard children, he would never have had time for ruling.

But would they suffice to lead the fight against the off-worlders?

He had his doubts about that too, although he wasn't fool enough to express them to the Prince. These were the men who had been completely incapable of destroying the rebellion, or overwhelming the Imperial Garrison, or even keeping the untouchables under control without resorting to mass slaughter. Maybe their forces weren't quite up to scratch, but it was a poor workman who blamed his tools. They spent more time posturing and carrying out military exercises than they did actually fighting.

"My Prince," the lead general said. "Our forces are in position to sweep the interlopers off the face of the planet."

The Prince smiled, cruelly. "Then destroy them," he ordered. "Let the offensive begin."

"Incoming sniper fire," Coleman reported. "They're aiming at the troops on the roof."

Edward scowled. "Order the mortars to open fire," he ordered. "And then tell the Marines to counter-snipe as best as possible."

Even underground, he heard the dull sound of the mortars as they opened fire. It was dangerously close range, but there was no choice. One shell slammed into the side of a building and detonated inside, wiping out the enemy position. Others were less fortunate; they plunged down around their targets or didn't inflict enough damage to take out the snipers. Even so, the level of incoming fire began to slack off rapidly. Having the buildings reduced to rubble around them *had* to be more than a little distracting.

"We only have a limited supply of mortar shells," Flora warned. "If we keep firing at this rate, we'll burn through them within minutes."

"Hold fire," Edward said, slowly. Most of the buildings were collapsing into rubble, clearly ill-prepared to stand up to modern weapons. A handful had been reduced to a framework; the walls were still standing, but the interior had been utterly destroyed. Flames licked through the rubble, forcing the enemy troops to fall back. "Let's see if that puts them off further advances."

"It hasn't," Villeneuve commented. On the display, enemy troops were advancing forward. "What are they doing?"

Edward had to smile at the note of disbelief in his subordinate's voice. The enemy troops seemed to be almost *dancing*, rather than inching forward while using every patch of cover they could find. It wasn't as if they were short of potential cover either; the destroyed or damaged buildings were solid enough to protect them from incoming fire. It took him a moment to realise what he was looking at and when he did, he laughed out loud. The enemy weren't throwing hardened soldiers against him, but pampered units more suited to display and pageantry rather than fighting.

But that makes sense, he told himself, as his men braced for the onslaught. *They will have to move their most experienced troops to the west to prevent the CEF from breaking through and rescuing us.*

"Household troops," he said derisively, remembering some of the private armies various Grand Senators had raised to protect their interests. They'd looked good…and their military value had been almost non-existent. The only such troops he remembered being of any value had been local defence forces created and operated by corporations and *they'd* largely been staffed by military vets. "They're sending household troops against us."

He sobered, quickly. It wasn't that funny. Every one of those men could soak up a bullet – and he only had a limited supply. Maybe some bright spark on the other side had decided to use the fancy troops to soften him up, then send in the more experienced soldiers once Edward and his men had been weakened. It suggested a level of callousness that even the Civil Guard's worst officers would have found hard to match, but he had to admit that it did make a certain kind of sense.

"Remind the troops to watch their bullet consumption," he ordered, looking over at his officers warningly. "We don't have bullets to spare."

Private Tomas Leloir stared in disbelief from his perch on the Residency roof as the enemy troops came into view. They looked like something out of a bygone age, bright splashes of colour against the rubble and bloodshed the first round of fighting had left in its wake. There was certainly no attempt to hide themselves against the background...but then, they *couldn't* have hidden themselves. They didn't even have anything reassembling urban combat BDUs.

Fighting the Crackers was harder than this, he thought, remembering the tales the old sweats had told him, back in basic training. His sole experience consisted of bandit-hunting missions, none of which had found a single bandit – or anything more exciting than wild animals and a handful of former Crackers living out in the countryside. But none of the simulated combat zones he'd fought in during training had been anything like this.

"Take aim," the Lieutenant barked, from his position. *His* voice was unflinching, as if he cared little for the bloodshed the rioters had left in their wake. "Prepare to engage."

There was a dull sound, echoing out over the city. It took Tomas a moment to realise that it was the sound of drums, beating out a four-beat pattern. On cue, the enemy soldiers lifted their rifles and started to run towards the gates, half of them providing covering fire while the other half were advancing. It would have been impressive, Tomas decided, if they had actually *had* some cover. As it were, they were merely making themselves targets. He wasn't even sure what they thought they were shooting at. Firing rifles at walls didn't actually wear them down, at least not outside bad combat simulations.

"Fire," the Lieutenant snapped.

Tomas squeezed the trigger and had the satisfaction of seeing his target – a gaudily-dressed enemy soldier who had been firing towards the buildings – drop to the ground, dead. He moved rapidly to the next target, then the next, picking them off one by one. The Knights were rapidly winnowing out the opposition, even though the enemy showed no lack of courage. They just kept coming.

"Squad two, load grenades," the Lieutenant ordered. "Aim for clumps of enemy soldiers."

Tomas sucked in his breath as he picked up the grenade launcher and clicked a switch, bringing the weapon to life. The enemy seemed to have forgotten their dance; they were just charging at the gates, howling strange words in a language Tomas didn't recognise. He took aim and fired, watching grimly as the grenade detonated inside a mass of soldiers, blowing them into bloody chunks. Other grenades wiped out other chunks of soldiers, breaking their discipline. They turned and fled back to the safety of their lines.

"Hold fire," the Lieutenant commanded. "Hold fire, I say."

The sergeants took up the cry as an uneasy calm descended on the Residency. Tomas fought down the urge to squeeze off another handful of shots at the enemy's retreating backs, but he knew that it wouldn't amuse his superiors. Instead, he took a breath…and was surprised to find out that he was sweating inside his BDUs. A glance at his wristcom told him that the entire engagement had lasted less than five minutes. It felt as if it had lasted for hours.

"Good work," the Lieutenant said. "Check weapons, then remain on alert. There will be another assault soon."

"Take the opportunity to have a drink," the sergeant added. "God knows when you will have time to drink again."

Tomas nodded. In the distance, he could hear the sound of drums growing louder.

"They're using them to coordinate their fighters," the sergeant explained, when he asked. "It isn't anything like as flexible as radios, but they probably know that using radios means identifying their superior officers to us. Besides, most of their troops probably think that radios are magic."

It seemed like hours before the next enemy force came into view. Tomas studied it through his sights, rapidly concluding that they'd learned nothing from the first engagement. Once again, they were *dancing* as they came forward…although he was sure that he picked up flickers of hesitation as they saw the bodies left behind by the first onslaught. Behind them, there were dark-clad men holding – of all things – whips, lashing out at any of the enemy troopers who didn't move forward fast enough. He stared in disbelief; basic training on Avalon had been hard, but he'd never heard of anyone being *whipped* into combat before. It wasn't as if Avalon *needed* conscripts when there were more volunteers for the Knights than they could take.

"That isn't uncommon in primitive societies," the sergeant growled, as mutters of disbelief ran up and down the line of soldiers. "The leaders don't trust their own people to press the offensive unless there's a gun held to their backs."

Tomas rolled his eyes. Unless he was missing something, none of the dark-clad men carried anything apart from whips. The soldiers they were forcing forward had loaded weapons; surely, they could just spin around and take the bastards out, then proceed to attack the dunderheaded superiors who had forced them into an unequal fight. But he remembered some of his training and shivered.

Some people are broken into unthinking servitude, he recalled one of the Drill Instructors saying, years ago. They'd been talking about the comparative merits of different military forces. *They're never allowed a chance to realise their own strength.*

"Squad one; take aim at the leaders," the Lieutenant said, calmly. "Everyone else, take aim at the incoming troops."

The drumbeat changed. A moment later, the enemy soldiers charged forward, chased by the men with whips. Tomas took aim at one of them and fired, then watched as the man spun around and collapsed to the ground. He switched aim to a second and then a third, sending them both into the next world. A fourth narrowly avoided death through a stroke of luck that sent him tripping over and falling on his face as a bullet cracked through where his head had been a moment previously.

And, again, the enemy troops seemed to take a number of losses and then fall back.

"Good work," the Lieutenant said, again.

Tomas looked down at his rifle and wondered just how long the bullets would last. But it wasn't a question he dared ask aloud.

"They're massing for another run," Villeneuve reported.

Edward scowled, shaking his head in disbelief. The enemy commander had to be incompetent – or completely unconcerned about his troops. If the definition of insanity was doing the same thing over and over again and expecting a different result every time, the enemy CO definitely qualified. But maybe there was method in his madness. Every attack they repelled drained their strength still further.

"The mortars could drop HE on their positions," Flora said. "It might dissuade them from massing so close to our lines."

"Make it so," Edward ordered. It would be harder to hit the enemy as they were protected by the surrounding buildings, but having mortar shells crashing down anywhere near them would be a nasty fright. He just hoped that it would be enough to force the locals to panic. "And then move out the reserves and replace the troops on the roof."

"Aye, sir," Villeneuve responded.

"We could take a team out under cover of darkness," Coleman suggested. "Give them a whole *series* of unpleasant surprises."

"We'll see what happens when night falls," Edward said, firmly. 1st Platoon was too important to be risked lightly, not when its Marines were the only real snipers his force had to deploy against the enemy. "But you're right. It might be a very good idea."

"Talk to the servants," Flora added. "They might know something useful."

"I'd better talk to the CEF first," Edward said. He had his doubts about the guards and servants; indeed, he suspected that the best course of action would simply be to expel them. "And then we might be able to decide what to do next."

CHAPTER SEVENTEEN

> Looking at the third requirement, there are strict limits on the possible, based on the strength (and internal politics) of the nations involved. A nation with limited military power (such as Kuwait, in 1991) cannot hope to stand up to a much stronger outside force. Nor, for that matter, could China or Russia realistically hope to prevent the American invasion of Iraq in 2003.
> -Professor Leo Caesius, *Diplomacy: The Lessons of the Past.*

Jasmine didn't spare herself. Mistakes were one thing, she'd been taught at the Slaughterhouse, but false reporting was a great deal worse. Her instructors had backed up their statements with a list of historical examples of disasters caused by someone trying to conceal their own failures or hide from the truth. Besides, Colonel Stalker needed to know precisely what was going on.

"I lost one hundred and thirteen soldiers," she finished, after a brutal examination of the disaster and the reasons for it. "And four more remain unaccounted for, sir."

"Understood," Colonel Stalker said. She was surprised that he didn't order her immediate relief on the spot. "And the FOB?"

"Secure," Jasmine replied. "The enemy underestimated the power of the garrison's guns, sir; they bombarded the enemy forces out of existence. Our one true success."

She winced at the thought. The CEF, for all of its power, had been saved by a tiny force the Empire had abandoned as it pulled out of the sector. It was more than a little humiliating, all the more so as the enemy commander had out-thought her. They were just lucky that they hadn't had to withdraw back along the causeway, or they would almost certainly have been obliterated by the enemy forces. As it was, they were holding a line on the very edge of the garrison's range.

"We're holding out here," the Colonel stated, "but we cannot hold out indefinitely. Sooner or later, they will wear us down."

Jasmine nodded, looking down at the display. Her drones were slowly parsing out the enemy's positions – and she had to admit that they were formidable. She simply didn't have the manpower to secure her supply lines as she advanced towards the capital city, even if she'd had the mobile firepower to outflank the enemy defence lines. Alone, the CEF could do nothing, but watch helplessly as its ultimate commander and his escort fought bravely, but futilely. They needed help.

She took a breath. "Colonel, I'd like to approach the rebels and ask for assistance."

The Colonel didn't object. He'd probably had the same thought, she realised, even though the rebels might not be able to provide mobile firepower. But they *could* help with suppressing resistance and guarding the supply lines…couldn't they? And it wasn't as if Jasmine couldn't reward them richly for their service. Perhaps they could overthrow the local government and help the rebels set up a replacement. Maybe even one that *wouldn't* slaughter all of the higher castes and replace them with a tyranny that would be almost as bad.

But it isn't our problem right now, she told herself. *Our problem is saving our people.*

"Make contact, if you can," Colonel Stalker consented. "Tell them that they can have the garrison's remaining supplies after we leave, along with the food-production vats and suchlike. Tell the garrison to start putting them together now, in fact. It won't take long to produce the first batch."

"Yes, sir," Jasmine acknowledged. She had a feeling that the rebels would be in touch, now that the CEF had openly engaged the local government's forces. If nothing else, they were in a stronger bargaining position. "But we also need to work out how to get supplies to you."

She'd contemplated the problem, but come up with nothing. Perhaps a shuttle could drop supplies from very high attitude, yet it would be chancy; they might accidentally wind up supplying the enemy instead. There was no way to be sure, not when they didn't dare fly too low. The MANPADs that had taken out one of her helicopters might well be able to damage or kill a shuttle.

"I don't believe that is possible without taking considerable risks," the Colonel said. He shook his head. "You are to concentrate on breaking through their lines and reaching us."

Jasmine felt her heart sink. She'd hoped that the Colonel, who had over a decade of experience in the Marines, would be able to think of a solution. But he didn't have one either.

"Yes, sir," she said, simply.

"And if we are overwhelmed, you are to pull back and hold the garrison until the ships arrive," the Colonel added, firmly. "I do not want you to throw away the CEF trying to change what cannot be changed. Do you understand me?"

"Yes, sir," Jasmine said, again. He'd said it before, as if he knew just *what* she was thinking. But she wouldn't abandon him as long as there was even the slightest chance that they could save his life and that of everyone else trapped in the Residency. "I understand."

"Good," the Colonel said.

Somehow, Jasmine wasn't surprised when Yin arrived, two hours later.

"I shall be blunt," Yin opened, in his oddly-accented voice. "You need our help and we need yours."

"That is correct," Jasmine agreed. Yin seemed to be more determined to bargain, now that he had something to bargain with. "What do you want in exchange for assisting us?"

"We want your assistance with overthrowing the government," Yin answered her. "We want weapons, supplies and training…and recognition as the legitimate government."

"Agreed," Jasmine said, curtly. She had no patience for bargaining; besides, she would have to hand over weapons and supplies in order to build up the rebels and turn them into a proper fighting force. No one outside the planet's atmosphere really cared who ruled Lakshmibai in any case. "In exchange, we need to move rapidly against the local government."

Yin gave her a long considering look. She realised, in a flash of irritation, that her sudden agreement might have worried him. He'd probably been expecting a long bargaining session, particularly if he hadn't realised just how strong a position he held. But what he'd asked for, she'd thought, was the bare minimum he needed. The rebels had to be on their last legs.

"You are willing to give us all that?" He asked, finally. "Just like that?"

"There are weapons and supplies – even food – in the garrison," Jasmine explained. "Handing them over to you would be a simple matter. I do have one condition, however. There are to be no reprisals against captured prisoners."

"I see," Yin said. His eyes bored into her face, as if he expected an underhand motive for her demand. "And why do you want that?"

Jasmine remembered the fall of Admiral Singh's government and shuddered. "Because if you start slaughtering prisoners, the remainder will refuse to surrender," she explained, patiently. She had a feeling that appealing to idealism would be a mistake. Idealism rarely lasted long in an insurgency war, certainly not as the hostile power bent all its efforts towards destroying the insurgency, root and branch. "In the long run, you can send the higher castes to their own island and leave them there to fend for themselves."

Yin surprised her by laughing. "They won't know how to *start* fending for themselves," he chortled. "They'll starve to death without workers to keep them fed, watered and clothed."

His eyes became calculating. "And no one can blame us for their deaths, eh?"

"No," Jasmine agreed. She had the distant feeling that the planet's future was going to be bloody. Even if Yin agreed to forbid reprisals, there would be millions of people who wanted to settle old scores or take land and property belonging to others. "But you might want to reintegrate them into your society."

Yin shook his head. "Let them have an island," he said. "Let them starve – or learn to live on their own. We don't want them."

His gaze turned calculating. "So, we have agreed," he continued. "What are you prepared to offer us?"

Jasmine pulled her notepad off her belt and looked down at it. "The garrison is unlimbering thousands of tons worth of supplies now," she said. "You can have weapons and ration bars first, followed by vehicles – if you can drive them."

She'd been astonished to take a look at the manifests the garrison's skeleton crew had kept religiously; they'd shipped in enough supplies from the sector capital to fight a major war. The shipping contractor must have been on the take, she'd decided finally. It was the only explanation that made sense. Someone had probably done very well out of shipping vast quantities of supplies to Lakshmibai, although *she* wasn't complaining. Those supplies might make the difference between success and failure.

"We don't have many drivers," Yin admitted. "There will be some within the city, if we can capture them…"

"Offer them and their families food if they work for us," Jasmine told him. In her experience, civilians worked better if they were paid for their labour, rather than forced to work at gunpoint. Besides, if they kept their families in a POW camp, they'd be able to use them as hostages. "We're going to need quite a few drivers, if only to move supplies."

"Then I shall start bringing some of my men to this camp," Yin remarked. "But what about the city of Jhansi?"

"I'll assign some of my people to assist you in securing it," Jasmine said. Jhansi was a road nexus. Securing it would be the first step towards pressing the local transport network into operation. "But I meant what I said about taking prisoners."

"We do not have the facilities to take prisoners," Yin objected. "Do you intend to take them to the garrison?"

"We have wire and other supplies," Jasmine pointed out, shaking her head. "We can rig up a POW camp if necessary."

Yin bowed as he stood up. "I look forward to working with you," he said, as he headed for the tent's flap. "And I hope that we will both get what we want."

Jasmine watched him go, then activated her internal communicator. "Have the supplies sent over the causeway as soon as the waters recede," she ordered, knowing that the FOB's communication nodes would pick up the signal and relay it to the garrison. "And I want to start work on a training and equipment camp for the rebels."

There was a pause, then Buckley answered. "Don't you trust them enough to bring them into the FOB?"

"No," Jasmine said, simply. Rebel forces, no matter how apparently committed to working with outsiders, always had their own agendas. And that wasn't the only problem. Even if Yin meant every word, it was quite likely that one of his people was actually a spy, working for the local government. In their place, Jasmine would have worked hard to infiltrate the rebellion, interdict their supply lines and locate their bases. "I want to keep our forces separate from them."

She looked down at her notepad, then moved to a new page. "And I want to work out a new operational plan as quickly as possible," she added. She'd have to speak to Yin again, find out just what his forces could do. Despite herself, she wasn't hopeful. "We have no time to lose."

―――――

"The defence of Jhansi seems to have collapsed," Andrew reported, as the helicopter flew high over the burning city. "Most of the resistance is now concentrated on the central complex."

He gritted his teeth as he saw the bodies lying in the streets. The local government had been shocked by the sheer scale of the uprising launched against them, but that hadn't stopped them using the most brutal methods to stamp it out. They'd killed hundreds of civilians, fired buildings and even called in artillery strikes until the CEF had managed to suppress them. Andrew didn't even want to *think* about how many people had died…

"Acknowledged," the garrison's fire control officer said. "Can you provide laser targeting?"

"That's a roger," Andrew said. He switched on the targeting system and angled the laser beam until it was pointed right at the central complex. The shelling from the enemy guns was largely inaccurate, but the heavy guns mounted on the garrison were an order of magnitude more sophisticated. "Laser locked on target."

"Firing now," the officer said.

Andrew tensed, despite himself. He knew that the odds were firmly against being hit by one of the shells the garrison had just fired, but accidents happened in wartime. Moments later, the shells fell past the helicopter and slammed into the central complex, sending colossal fireballs rising up towards the sky. The helicopter jerked as the gust of air struck it, then steadied as he fought with the controls. When he looked back down at the complex, it was clear that it had been devastated. Flames were rapidly devouring what parts of it hadn't been knocked down and destroyed by the direct hits.

"Direct hits," he reported, knowing that the live feed would show his superiors just what had happened to the central complex. "Resistance appears to have been badly hammered."

He watched as a swarm of locals raced for the complex, charging through the new gaps in the walls and throwing themselves into the remains of the building. One by one, the survivors were hauled out and brutally beaten to death; the rebels didn't seem any more inclined to spare the helpless than the local government. He watched helplessly as a family of young children was dragged out into the open and butchered by the rebels. Others fled into the chaos gripping the streets, looking for safety. Somehow, he knew that there was no safety to be found.

"Good work," the officer said, bluntly. "Fly to the next waypoint and scout for incoming enemy forces."

Andrew bit down the comment that came to mind, knowing that it would be futile. "Understood," he said, instead. "We're on our way."

Michael couldn't help feeling nervous as the Warrior nosed its way across the ring road and down into Jhansi. The city was a strange mixture of elegant and brutally functional, the buildings so close to the roads that it was terrifyingly easy to see how they might be ambushed and knocked out by one side or the other. Bodies lay everywhere, many gunned down or caught up in the chaos and killed by the mobs. Even the final terrifying moments of the Battle of Camelot hadn't been anything like as gruesome.

"The resistance has been largely eliminated," the dispatcher said, over the intercom. "You are to proceed to this location" – a light blinked up on the map – "and coordinate with the rebel forces."

Michael scowled as they saw their first locals, most of whom seemed to be engaged in looting. They stared back at the Warrior with open hostility, then turned their backs and ignored the AFV and its partners. It would be impossible to tell who was friendly and who wasn't, he realised. Just like the Crackers, the rebels didn't wear any uniforms.

And if the warrior caste soldiers have any sense, he told himself, *they'll dump their uniforms and try to slip out of the city.*

The location, he discovered, proved to be a park that had once been next to a temple. It had been devastated in the fighting, with dozens of statues simply destroyed out of hand, while the temple itself was a smouldering ruin. Michael had no idea how many people on the planet believed in their religion, but it was clear that quite a few of them had grudges to pay off. He'd done a little reading into the history of their religion and hadn't been surprised to discover that when a new religion, one preaching equality under God, had arrived, it had been very seductive to the lower castes.

He led his squad out of the Warrior as a line of pale-skinned men and women appeared at one edge of the park, being pushed forward by grim-faced rebels. Their clothes were ripped and torn – he suspected that jewels had been removed – but otherwise they seemed alive and unhurt. The children beside them were looking around in obvious confusion, some of them crying while others seemed unsure why their parents were being pushed around by lower caste members.

"Prisoners," a rebel explained, as the prisoners were forced to sit on the grass and wait. "You're to take them out of the city."

Michael looked at the prisoners, and then at the rebels looking at the prisoners, then nodded hastily. It was clear that some of the rebels wanted to butcher the prisoners, just to exterminate as many members of the despised upper castes as possible. If the CEF didn't take care of them, he suspected, the local rebels certainly wouldn't. He felt a moment of nostalgia for the Cracker War. As bloody as it had become, it hadn't been anything like as savage.

"I will, once a camp is set up," he said, firmly. "Until then, they can remain here under guard."

He keyed his radio as he walked back to the Warrior, motioning for the machine guns to be pointed just over their heads. The prisoners would have to be insane to try something, but he knew from his training that prisoners might try to escape, if they were given half a chance. And yet if they did escape, they would almost certainly be captured and butchered by the rebels.

"We have around two hundred civilian prisoners," he reported. In the distance, he heard the sound of gunfire. It seemed to be coming from the heart of the city. "Do we have a POW camp yet?"

"One is being set up now," his superior assured him. "Can you hold them until then?"

Michael looked over at the children and felt his heart break. "I think so," he said. The thought was unavoidable. "This is going to be a messy war."

"Copy that," his superior agreed. "I'm very much afraid that it is definitely going to be messy."

CHAPTER EIGHTEEN

> Diplomats who fail to keep the limits of the possible in mind tend to run into considerable problems, particularly when their bluffs are called. For example, if there is little enthusiasm for using military force to compel a country to do what the diplomats want, the diplomatic protests will be worse than useless.
> -Professor Leo Caesius, *Diplomacy: The Lessons of the Past.*

"How are you feeling?"

Leo rubbed the side of his head, wondering why it was so dark. "Like I picked a fight with…well, you," he said, recognising the Colonel's voice. "What happened?"

"He's fighting off the sedative," a female voice said. Leo didn't recognise the speaker. "I can give him a booster…"

"No," Leo said, before the Colonel could answer. His head felt like cotton wool. When he took a breath, he smelt…he didn't want to *know* what he was smelling, but he had the uncomfortable feeling that it was himself. "What happened?"

"You were attacked," the Colonel said. "Your escort got you back to the Residency before you could be overrun."

Leo managed to open his eyes. He was lying on a hard stone floor, in a darkened room illuminated only by a pair of portable lanterns. The Colonel was kneeling next to him, with a dark-skinned woman in military uniform studying a medical terminal with an air of disapproval. He was naked, Leo realised, in some puzzlement. It took him several minutes to remember that they'd been forced to use a septic tank to break their fall.

"Fiona," he said, turning his head from side to side in hopes of seeing her. "Where *is* she?"

"I saw fit to put her in a private room," the medic said. "She's still under sedation."

Leo tried to pull himself upright, but staggered as his head started to spin. "Lie still," the Colonel advised. "You haven't got all of the drug out of your system yet."

"Oh," Leo said. In the distance, he could hear the faint sounds of gunfire. "What's happening out there?"

"The Residency is under siege," the Colonel said, grimly. "They made four attempts to force their way in with troops, then they pulled back and concentrated on sniping at us from a distance. I think they're preparing for yet another try at our walls."

Leo stared at him. "But why?"

"Officially, they want to force us to surrender you and your escorts," the Colonel said. "I think that's just an excuse to start a fight. Their radio messages, such as they are, suggest that they're planning to kill the lot of us. You might want to try to remember those shooting lessons I gave you."

"…Oh," Leo said. The Colonel had taught him how to shoot, but he hadn't kept practicing, even when he'd been on Avalon. "Is it that bad?"

"Not yet," the Colonel said, standing up. "But it will be soon."

The medic pushed something against Leo's arm before he could object and the world faded away again back into darkness.

"I can see five of them," Private Tomas Leloir reported. Darkness had fallen over the city, but they didn't dare take time to relax. "Don't they know that we can see them?"

"They may not know anything about NVGs," the Lieutenant said, dryly. "Hold your fire; the CO wants to see what they're doing."

Tomas nodded, tracking the lead enemy soldier with his rifle. They seemed to have learned a few lessons about concealment after the first four attempts to break the defences, although they also seemed to have decided that darkness was sufficient cover for their misdeeds. Through the NVGs, they were easily visible, standing out clearly against the cold surroundings. They seemed to be carrying rifles in their hands and little else.

"They're reaching the wall," he whispered. They'd have some cover there, as long as they stayed low. A moment later, there was a chinking sound as a grabbling hook attached itself to the top of the wall. "Oh, you have to be kidding me."

"It looks as though they are trying to sneak into the complex," the Lieutenant said, over the intercom. "Request permission to engage as soon as they surmount the wall."

"Engage them with stunners only," the CO ordered. "I want them alive."

Tomas nodded and kept tracking the men with his rifle. If they had something clever up their sleeves…but they didn't; they were stunned as quickly and efficiently as the rioters had been, when they'd made their first charge at the walls. Moments later, they were frisked, secured with plastic ties and carried off to the main room.

"Keep your eye on the streets," the Lieutenant ordered. "They have friends out there."

Edward had to force himself to keep a straight face as he saw the newcomers in proper lighting. They were dressed like ninjas from a million bad entertainments, men and women who had mastered a mythical martial art that allowed them to be completely sneaky and go anywhere they wanted to go. But even Marine Pathfinders would have had trouble sneaking into the Residency without equipment that simply didn't exist on Lakshmibai.

"All right," he said, as they were secured to chairs. "Answer our questions and we'll let you go."

The ninjas babbled rapidly in the local language. None of them, it seemed, possessed a word of Imperial Standard, which made a certain kind of sense. The planet's governors were determined to keep outside influences from contaminating their people – and besides, Lakshmibai had been isolated for centuries before it had been unwillingly dragged back into the greater galaxy. It was quite possible that knowledge of Imperial Standard had been heavily restricted by the elite.

"The translation software can't follow them," Coleman advised. "Whatever language they're speaking isn't the official tongue for this planet."

Edward wasn't too surprised. Languages changed and evolved, even when there were datanets and entertainments using a shared tongue. A few centuries of isolation would probably have seen the planet's language evolve in all kinds of unanticipated directions. But, right now, it was a major hassle.

"Get one of the serving maids," he ordered, after a moment. The maids all spoke Imperial Standard, although their accents were abominable. "Tell her that translation services will be richly rewarded."

It was five minutes before Coleman returned with a very frightened looking maid. Once the first burst of fighting had died down, the Marines had transferred them to a large room and cut them loose from their bonds, but they wouldn't have found it very reassuring. If the Residency was stormed, they would be raped and then murdered by the mobs. Some of the radio transmissions they'd picked up had preached the destruction of all off-worlders and their spawn. Anyone who might have had *any* dealings with off-worlders was at risk.

I wonder, he asked himself, *if that includes the Rajah?*

"I want you to translate my questions for him," he said, as Coleman wrapped a lie detector band around her wrist. She eyed it in nervous incomprehension. "And then translate his answers for me."

She nodded, her dark eyes fearful. Edward couldn't help admiring her looks, although there was something oddly immature about her body, as if she were permanently trapped on the verge of adulthood. Some of the files had suggested that Lakshmibai's founders had used illegal genetic modification to help shape their insect colony of a society, but if some of the more extreme suggestions had been true, they would have wiped themselves out long ago. If the untouchables had been bred to be just a little less intelligent and capable than the rest of the castes, the poisoned genes would have spread to the others by now.

"Good," Edward said. He couldn't help noticing how she shied away from him and winced inwardly. "Ask him just what they thought they were doing."

The captive produced a series of words and finished by spitting at the maid. Coleman stuck out a hand and caught the spittle, then rubbed it into the captive's shirt.

"Ask him again," Edward said. If they'd thought to bring truth drugs… but somehow it had been overlooked when they'd been making preparations for the mission. No doubt someone had worried about what would happen if the negotiators were dosed. "Tell him that if he doesn't start answering, we'll start cutting his skin."

The captive babbled again; the maid started talking a moment later. "They were ordered to get inside and butcher you while you slept," she said, softly. "And then open the doors to allow the rest of their force to enter."

"Fucking idiots," Coleman muttered.

Edward shot him a sharp look, then turned back to the maid. "Ask him just what they think they're doing," he ordered. "What have they been told about us?"

There was a long moment of back-and-fourth, then the maid looked up at him. "He says that they have been told that you're going to kill them all – unless they kill you first," she said. "Your very presence is an offense against the gods."

"Bastards," Edward muttered. A world that largely hated off-worlders, mostly inhabited by people who were utterly unaware of the greater universe surrounding them. No wonder it had been so easy to whip up the mob; the real miracle had been keeping it under control long enough to allow Leo and his escorts to flee. "Who's in command of their force?"

"The Prince," the maid said, after some more talking. "He's been telling them that they will be richly rewarded once the Residency is destroyed."

Edward asked a few more questions, but the captive proved largely uninformative. He hadn't been told anything useful, certainly nothing about the Prince's future plans…although *that* wasn't too surprising. The only real question was if the Prince was maintaining operational security or if he had simply decided that the lower castes weren't to be told anything. Not, in the end, that it mattered. The final outcome was the same.

"We're going to release the rest of the guards," he said, leading the maid out into a side room. He didn't miss the look of terror that crossed her face. She'd probably realised that she and her fellows were included in the rewards for those who stormed the Residency. "Do you wish to leave too?"

The maid shook her head, frantically.

"Then I need you to help us," Edward said. It was a calculated risk; it was far too possible that the maids might be more than just spies, but he couldn't afford to feed them without putting them to use. The alternatives, either shooting them himself or sending them out onto the bloodstained streets, were unthinkable. "But you have to behave yourselves."

He left the maid to talk to her fellows, promising to return in an hour to see who wanted to leave, and walked up the stairs to the roof. A dozen soldiers lay on the rooftop, sweeping the surrounding area with NVGs, while two Marines in combat armour watched the remains of the nearby buildings for enemy snipers. Edward caught the telltale whiff of one of his soldiers sneaking a cigarette on duty and looked towards the smoker, then smiled to himself as he realised that he'd been smart enough to position himself out of sight of any watching snipers. If he had exposed himself to a watching sniper, the smoker might as well have drawn a targeting crosshair on his head.

"It's quiet, sir," Lieutenant Jaffna said.

"Too quiet," Edward finished, although it wasn't – not completely. In the distance, he could hear the sounds of rioters and shooting. There were parts of the slums where the local government had lost control completely, particularly after the first attacks had been so comprehensively defeated. "No further attempts at breaching our lines?"

"None," the Lieutenant said, as if Edward wouldn't have been immediately informed if another attack had been underway. "Did the prisoners say anything useful?"

"Just that we're all going to die if they overrun us," Edward said. He clapped the Lieutenant on the shoulder. "We're going to release the former guards in an hour, giving them a chance to make their way out of the city. And then we're going to hold our ground until help arrives."

"We will, sir," Jaffna said, with easy confidence. He didn't know how hard it would be for the CEF to punch through the enemy lines and make its way to the capital. "They don't stand a chance."

Edward smiled to conceal his grim thoughts, then looked out over the city. In the semi-darkness – Lakshmibai's moon was bright in the sky, casting an eerie light over the buildings – it looked fascinating, a strange mixture of styles from a dozen different eras. But several buildings were burning and he could smell smoke and human flesh on the winds. He heard someone screaming in pain, not too far away, and cursed his inability to do anything to help. The entire city – no, the entire planet – seemed to be tearing itself apart.

He spent several minutes briefly chatting with the soldiers, then walked back down into the lower reaches of the complex. The maids greeted him when he entered their chamber and explained that all but one of them had decided to remain in the complex. Edward eyed the lone dissenter suspiciously, before deciding not to object to her departure. It was unlikely that she could tell the Prince and his cronies anything more than they already knew. Edward would have been surprised if they didn't have a very good idea just what weapons and equipment had been unloaded from the shuttles before the starships had departed.

Coleman caught him as he walked back into the basement. "Do you really trust them?"

"They have as much reason to fight as we do," Edward pointed out, mildly. "Besides, we won't be giving them weapons or anything they can use against us."

"They'll be preparing food," Coleman objected. "Won't they?"

Edward shook his head. It had taken the enemy several hours to think of turning off the water and electricity supplies, long enough to allow them to fill every container they could find with water. Combined with the processors they'd taken from the shuttles, they shouldn't run out of water any time soon. Power was a more worrying concern; the batteries they'd brought with them wouldn't last indefinitely. If they *could* get some items flown in from the garrison, they'd have to include a portable generator in the list. And mortar shells.

And ammunition for everything else too, he reminded himself. *It's too easy to forget the little details.*

He caught himself yawning and covered his mouth with a sigh. "Get some sleep, sir," Coleman advised. "You'll need to be fresh when they launch their next attack."

Edward gave him a sharp look, then looked down at his wristcom. It was five hours until local dawn, when the enemy would probably resume their offensive. If *he'd* been in command, he would have been attacking at all hours of the clock, but the locals probably doubted their ability to command a battle at night. Judging from the ninja debacle, they were probably right.

"I'll get some rest," he said, finally. "Wake me the moment anything – and I mean anything – happens."

"Yes, sir," Coleman said. He paused. "And I'll finish putting together my operational plan."

"Please do," Edward said. All his objections to using the Marines in the city had faded away when the CEF had been so comprehensively repelled. Brigadier Yamane might be able to put together a combined force to make a second attempt, but Edward was too old a campaigner to take it for granted. Anything they could do to slow down the enemy's operations would be very welcome. "See how many likely targets you can find."

Coleman grunted. "There's the Rajah himself," he mused. "Wouldn't he make a good target?"

"Maybe," Edward said, reluctantly. "Or there's the Prince…"

He yawned again. "We'll discuss it in the morning," he said, heading to where he'd left his blanket. "And remember…"

"Wake you if anything changes," Coleman said. There was a hint of reproof in his voice. "I won't forget my orders."

"I do outrank the Command Sergeant," Edward reminded him, gently. "Good night."

"We took two prisoners," the warrior reported. The message had been sent via landline, rather than by radio transmissions. "One died during transport; the other is on his way to the capital."

"Good," Sivaganga said. He felt an odd burst of hope in his heart. Surely, if they *could* best the off-worlders in combat, they weren't so fearsome after all. "I shall inform the Prince personally."

He dismissed the warrior, then paused to consider what he'd been told. The first attacks on the Residency had failed spectacularly and the sneak offensive, which he'd been promised *would* succeed, didn't seem to have resulted in anything at all. It was possible that the Prince's elite had just sneaked off and deserted, but that seemed unlikely. The Prince was well-known for punishing any deserters heavily. Besides, with the streets as unsafe as they were, they'd be safer attacking the off-worlders.

But they *had* beaten back the off-worlders in open combat. That could not be denied.

I opposed this adventure because I felt that we couldn't win, he thought, *but we did beat them back. They're not invincible. They can be beaten.*

He looked out over the city, towards the darkened shape of the Imperial Residency. The battle had already been costly, both in lives and in their control over the population, but they had lives to spare. Indeed, eliminating many of the fancy troops that normally kept order in the city might improve the quality of the rest of the army in the long run. And besides, the enemy *had* to be running out of ammunition. Once their wondrous weapons were dry, their defeat would quickly follow.

The thought was seductive, but unavoidable. And, in truth, he didn't want to avoid it.

Perhaps they could win after all.

CHAPTER NINETEEN

> This leads neatly into the fourth requirement. Speaking softly and carrying a big stick (rephrased; speaking politely and respectfully, but firmly) works because it leaves feelings as undamaged as possible. Speaking loudly, without a big stick, merely irritates or amuses potential enemies – if nothing else, it convinces them not to take one seriously in future. The appearance of weakness can be dangerous because it can so easily become reality.
> -Professor Leo Caesius, *Diplomacy: The Lessons of the Past.*

He had never been in so much pain in his life.

Private Mathew Polk struggled to move as the vehicle bounced its way into the capital city. His hands and feet were so tightly tied that he'd lost all feeling; a quick glance had revealed that the skin had swollen up around the ropes. Even if he somehow managed to break free, he realised, it would be impossible to move. He was a helpless prisoner.

How long had it been? There was no way to tell. They'd beaten him, drugged him and then left him to recover on his own. He'd been warned that not everyone would take care of prisoners, even when it was clearly in their best interests to do so, if only to avoid reprisals against their own prisoners. The Conduct After Capture course he'd attended on Castle Rock had made it clear that he might be treated well – or he might be tortured for information. And, despite all the training, he'd also been warned that he might break.

The vehicle lurched to a halt. Moments later, the doors opened, revealing a trio of men in dark purple outfits and sneering expressions. One of them caught hold of Mathew's leg and dragged him out of the vehicle, dumping him on the hard muddy ground and searching him roughly. The other two produced a long shaft of wood and carefully inserted it between Mathew's hands and feet, then hoisted him up into the air. They were carrying him, he realised numbly, as if he was a dead animal being carried home by a hunter.

Voices assailed his ears as they carried him away from the vehicle and down the middle of a road. He glanced from side to side, despite the delirium, and saw crowds of men and women howling words at him in the local language. Their faces were twisted with hatred, as if they wanted to charge forward and tear him apart with their bare hands. His escort lashed around them with whips whenever the crowd came too close, but they chose to ignore a handful of rotten fruit and vegetables that were directed at Mathew's head. He could only grunt as something the size of a small apple cracked into his arm. For a long chilling moment, he thought the arm was broken.

They're showing you what you can expect when you escape, he thought, remembering some of his training. *A person from Avalon would stick out like a sore thumb on this world.*

There was a *clang* as a pair of gates opened in front of him, revealing a fairy tale palace made out of white marble. Mathew couldn't help wondering if he was seeing things; the palace seemed far too pretty to be real. His escorts carried him through the gate and up a long path towards the main doors, allowing him to see perfectly-designed gardens, fountains spouting water up into the air and even a handful of peacocks wandering through the grounds. It *had* to be a dream, he told himself. They'd drugged him while they were transporting him from the coast.

His escorts paused as a group of black-clad men appeared, carrying rifles in a manner that suggested that they'd had some proper military training. There was a brief discussion between the two groups – he found himself wishing that he knew just what they were saying – and then he was unceremoniously dumped on the ground. The shaft was removed and one of the newcomers cut away the bonds on his feet, then yanked him upwards into a standing position. Mathew's ankles screamed in pain and he collapsed the moment the newcomer let go of him.

The newcomer shouted at him, then helped him back to his feet and half-pushed, half-carried Mathew through the door and down a long flight of stairs. It was hard to believe that the interior of the palace was real; it seemed so fragile, like a glimpse of heaven. Tasteful artworks and paintings were scattered everywhere, while the air smelled sweet; he caught sight of a handful of girls in scanty costumes staring at him as he was taken down into the bowels of the building. They seemed too beautiful to be real too.

They stopped outside a heavy metal door – he vaguely recognised it as a blast door – which opened to reveal a darkened room. There was nothing inside, apart from a metal chair placed in the exact centre of the chamber. He was pushed inside, guided to the chair and forced to sit down. A moment later, metal cuffs were slipped around his wrists and ankles. His escorts cut off his clothes, leaving him naked, then walked away. He was alone.

"Welcome," a voice said, in oddly-accented Imperial Standard. It was toneless, as if it was generated by a computer. No matter how he strained his ears, he couldn't identify its source. "Do you know where you are?"

The advice he'd been given for use in the event of capture had been clear. Try to avoid talking to the enemy as long as possible. When forced to talk, say as little as possible; ideally, stick to name, rank and serial number. Try not to lie, but mislead the enemy as long as possible. And don't believe a word they say.

He said nothing, but the voice continued anyway.

"Your force has been battered into uselessness and most of your friends are dead," it continued. "You are one of a handful of prisoners; alone, hundreds of miles from any potential rescuers. There is no escape."

There was a long pause. "Cooperate with us, answer our questions and your life will be spared," it concluded. "Or refuse to talk and suffer as we *make* you talk."

Mathew felt a cold hint of despair at the words, even though he knew that the enemy was almost certainly lying. The CEF might have been battered – it had been clear that they had been forced to retreat – but he knew that it wouldn't have been rendered completely useless. They'd been trained to react, adapt and overcome; if they lost one fight, they would learn from the experience and come back loaded for bear the next day.

But it was hard to convince himself of that when he was so clearly alone.

Surreptitiously, he tested the metal cuffs binding him to the chair. They were solid, utterly unbreakable by anything short of an enhanced human. Indeed, the locals must have heard the standard exaggerated rumours about what enhanced humans could do, for they'd cuffed him far more than they needed to if they wanted to keep him in place. Or maybe they just wanted to underline his status.

Or maybe they're just sick bastards, he told himself.

"This is your one chance to talk," the voice reproved him. "If you refuse to talk, we will *make* you talk."

Mathew swallowed hard, wondering if he was in any state to be tortured. It was possible that the shock alone would kill him. But he'd seen enough of the enemy's treatment of their own population not to place any faith in their promises of safety. Even if he hadn't had his duty, he'd stay alive longer if he kept his mouth firmly closed.

"Very well," the voice said. He heard the sound of someone moving behind him, but he couldn't turn his head to see who it was. "How many soldiers are in your force?"

There was a faint whooshing sound…and then a whip cracked across his back. Mathew *howled* in pain, unable to believe that it could hurt so badly. The pain didn't fade either; his entire body seemed to be aching for long moments after the first stroke. A dark-clad figure moved into view, carrying a long whip that was sparkling with eerie blue light. Mathew felt a shiver run down his spine as he realised that it was no ordinary whip. It was a device designed to trigger the pain nerves, inflicting pain without causing any permanent damage. Pirates and slavers were fond of using them on their human cargo, just to keep them in line.

"I believe I asked you a question," the voice said, as the whip was raised for a second time. "How many soldiers are in your force?"

Mathew screamed as he was lashed again, and again. It was hard to think, hard to focus his mind and remember why it was so important to resist. The voice kept encouraging him, pointing out just how harmless it would be to tell his interrogators one little thing to make them happy and stop the pain. His entire world seemed to have become nothing, but pain.

"You're not in a good state," the voice whispered, seductively. "Tell us one answer and you can have the medical attention you so desperately need..."

"Not too tough," the Prince observed, as the first answer finally slipped out of the off-worlder's mouth. "Not as tough as we expected."

Sivaganga nodded, keeping his face expressionless. The Prince seemed to find a certain pleasure in torture, but Sivaganga preferred to take his pleasure elsewhere. But it wouldn't have been wise to suggest to the Prince that there was something wrong with enjoying his pleasures, no matter how perverse they might have been. The last thing he needed was the Prince's open enmity.

"Let us hope that the others are just as weak," he said, instead. It *would* please the Prince...and it gave him time to think. "But we need to take more captives."

He didn't trust torture, certainly not when it was difficult to verify what the interrogators were being told. Ideally, they would have several prisoners, all of whom could be interrogated separately and their answers confirmed, but only one off-world soldier had survived falling into their hands. A dozen warriors had died in retribution for lynching another potential captive, yet it had been too late. If the off-worlders knew what they could expect if they fell into local hands, they would do whatever it took to *prevent* themselves being captured.

And the off-world soldier had been strong. Most of the Prince's test subjects had been untouchables, or suspected rebels, both born to lives of backbreaking labour and endless sufferings. Untouchables might be little better than beasts of burden – there were members of the higher castes who cared more for their cows and horses than for their servants – but he had to admit that there was a solid endurance about them. They had literally nothing in their lives, something that gave them some resistance to torture. An aristocrat would have folded far quicker.

But the off-world soldier had held out for quite some time, despite serious wounds, before finally surrendering and offering an answer. Now, other questions were being thrown at him and answers were being dragged out, one by one, but he was still trying to resist. Some of his answers were obviously implausible – there was no way that the off-worlders had landed a million-man army – yet others couldn't be so easily dismissed.

He shook his head at the expression in the Prince's eye and tried not to shudder. Every single one of the former Residency guards had been put to the question, once they'd been caught trying to sneak away from the complex. They'd confirmed that the off-worlders were prepared to fight to the death, but they hadn't been able to say much more. The off-worlders, it seemed, were better at recognising how servants could spy than most of his own people. It was odd that they'd given sanctuary to the maids, but maybe it was for the best. He knew what had happened to the lone maid who'd chosen to leave.

"My Prince," he said, as the torturer approached the captive again. "I don't think we want to press it any further."

The Prince eyed him, an unholy gleam in his eye. "And you feel *mercy* for the off-world scum?"

Sivaganga kept his voice calm, somehow. The Prince was a hothead – and he'd chosen to surround himself with hothead advisors. If he drew his sword and gutted Sivaganga before he could react, the Rajah would probably refrain from punishing him. Sivaganga's family was important, but not as important as the lone Heir. But he had to advise the Prince as best as he could, no matter the risk. The entire planet was at stake.

"The prisoner might make a bargaining chip," he reminded the Prince. "Or he might have more to tell us, which he won't be able to if he expires in the chair. He was already badly injured before your man started to hurt him. No matter how tough he seems, his endurance won't hold out forever."

The Prince stared at him for a long cold moment, hopefully thinking it over. "I shall have him given time to recover," he said, finally. "But I will not waste a doctor on him."

Sivaganga wasn't surprised. The city's doctors were working hard to cope with all the higher-caste aristocrats who had been wounded in the fighting. If the Rajah hadn't ordered most of them to stay in the city, there would have been a flight to the countryside, even if there *were* outbreaks of violence among the farmers. The lower castes and the untouchables could take care of themselves. There was no shortage of replacements for everyone who died.

"We can also use the captive to show the off-worlders just how firm we are in our determination to destroy them," the Prince continued. "I shall have him prepared for his final role, once we have gained answers to all of our questions."

He slapped Sivaganga on the shoulder and walked off, heading back up the stairs towards the sleeping chambers he'd commandeered. Sivaganga took one last look at the off-world captive – in truth, the man looked to be on the verge of death – and then followed him, hoping to get some sleep. It wouldn't be long before dawn broke over the city…and the next round of attacks began.

And then, he assured himself, the off-worlders would be destroyed.

———

Mathew was barely aware of his surroundings until a sponge was pressed against his chest. His eyes snapped open, revealing a dark-skinned girl swabbing the blood away from his body and washing him clean. There seemed to be enough blood, he thought dimly through the haze, to leave him completely dry. But it had to be an illusion…

He opened his voice and tried to speak. "Who…?"

It came out badly. He cleared his throat and tried again. "Who are you?"

The girl shook her head sadly, then looked at him and opened her mouth. It took Mathew a moment to realise that she had no tongue. Someone had cut it out, along with most of her teeth. He felt his stomach churn as he remembered the stories he'd heard from the more experienced soldiers who'd stormed bandit camps after the Cracker War. If a girl had proved too determined to fight, they'd knocked out her teeth to stop her biting…

He would have been sick, if there had been something left in his stomach. Instead, he felt his head spinning. The girl didn't seem to be a doctor, or anything other than a worker. They weren't going to give him any medical attention at all. It was true that the whip wouldn't inflict any permanent harm, but the injuries he'd taken during the fight would fester if they were left untended. He might not last the night.

And he'd talked, he remembered, with a sudden burst of shame. The pain had grown unbearable and he'd snarled out an answer, only to open a chink in his armour. He'd been bombarded with question after question, each answer only leading to more questions…by the time they'd finally left him alone, he'd told them far too much. He wasn't even sure just how badly he'd managed to mislead them. It had been hard to keep remembering what lies he'd told as they'd kept altering the questions, or moving from topic to topic…

He grunted as the girl moved behind him washed his hands, even though they were still in the cuffs. It hurt when he tried to breathe, which suggested that he'd broken several ribs. Even if she freed him, it seemed unlikely that he could do more than crawl. She walked back in front of him and stared at him for a long sad moment.

It struck him, then, just how young she was. The clothes she wore were rags, revealing enough of her body to suggest that she was in her early teens…or that she was simply too malnourished to enter puberty. He felt sick as he stared at her, wondering why *anyone* would do that to an innocent young girl. But he'd heard enough to know just how unpleasant the universe could be to innocents who were mashed in the gears.

The girl turned and walked away, leaving him alone with his thoughts. Mathew shook his head, despite the pain; he was alone, trapped and a traitor. The thought kept running around his head. Even if they knew he'd been captured, they wouldn't bother to rescue him. He closed his eyes, feeling despair reaching up to overwhelm him. It was impossible to be optimistic. No matter how he tried to convince himself otherwise, it was unlikely that he'd live long enough to be rescued.

But who would want to rescue a traitor?

Chapter Twenty

The most dangerous possibility is amply summed up by Yosemite Sam, who once declared that 'well, I speak loud! And I carry a BIIIIIIIGGER stick!! And I use it too!'
-Professor Leo Caesius, *Diplomacy: The Lessons of the Past.*

Dawn broke over Maharashtra like a thunderbolt, heralded by chanting from the hundreds of temples in the city that blended together into an oddly melodious harmony. Corporal Paul Howard clutched his rifle tightly and tried to blink sleep from his eyes, fighting down an urge to yawn. The defenders – both Commonwealth and Wolfbane – had stood to as dawn approached, expecting a new round of attacks. But nothing had materialised. Even the probes under cover of darkness had stilled.

"All clear," he reported, as he peered down the street. No one had come to remove the bodies, even though he hoped that the higher-ups would agree to a limited truce to allow the besiegers to do just that. In the heat, they were already starting to stink. "There are no signs of enemy movement."

"Understood," the CO said. "Remain on guard."

Paul rolled his eyes, although he understood why the CO was nervous. The company that had been assigned to protecting the diplomats had been newly-raised, with most of its soldiers – including Paul – conscripted after the first wave of chaos had swept over the Wolfbane Sector. Paul didn't mind serving in the military – it certainly beat joining his brothers in the free labour pool – but he hadn't expected to be assigned to a thoroughly hostile world, let alone forced to work with another military to defend the diplomats. Indeed, the company had never been combat tested at all.

Until now, he thought.

The first attacks had been repelled with ease, but the sneaks trying to make their way up to the walls were a clear and present danger. It was all-too-easy to imagine one of them managing to knock down the walls, allowing the mobs to storm forward and pillage the Residency. Indeed, most of the supplies from both sides had been moved into the central building, where there was slightly more room to defend them if attacked. But if one of the walls fell, Paul doubted they could hold out for long.

He stopped as a motion caught his eye, snapping his rifle up to take aim. A moment later, he relaxed as the dog came into view, blood and flesh dripping from its snout. He felt sick as he realised what it had been eating and found himself wondering if he should shoot it out of hand, seeing that it had developed a taste for human flesh. But they'd been told in no uncertain terms to conserve ammunition as much as possible. The dog would be someone else's problem.

Maybe it will bite the enemy commander, he told himself, although he knew it was unlikely. There were just too many dead bodies on the ground for the dog to go hungry. He winced as a second dog came into view, followed rapidly by a third. They seemed to have gone feral very quickly.

The chanting faded away, leaving an unearthly silence echoing over the city. Paul shivered, wondering just what it portended. The old sweats had talked about facing religious fanatics, warning the new conscripts that they could convince their followers to do anything, even charge into massed machine gun fire. Some of them had even believed that their prayers could turn away bullets, although they'd learned *that* mistake very quickly. But people would seemingly believe anything if they were told it firmly enough.

There was a dull roar in the distance, snapping him back to full awareness. He muttered a brief update into the intercom, then peered down the road as the dogs scattered, heading back to their lairs amid the ruined buildings. Behind him, he heard more soldiers running out of the buildings or reinforcing the men on the rooftops. If trouble was coming, they'd be ready to deal with it.

The sound grew louder as a large vehicle came into view. Paul stared at it; at first glance, it seemed like an AFV...and then it became clear that armour had been bolted over a civilian vehicle. The driver gunned the engine and drove right at the guardhouse; Paul lifted his rifle and started to fire, realising that they intended to ram the gates. A moment later, a grenade was launched from the roof and detonated just underneath the vehicle. There was a colossal explosion, powerful enough to shake the entire complex; Paul felt himself picked up by the blast and flung across the grounds, right into the Residency wall. If it hadn't been for his armour, he realised numbly, he would have broken his back on impact.

A second fireball billowed up from the other side of the complex. The truck bombs had to have been targeted on all sides, he realised, just to prevent one group of defenders from reinforcing the other. As long as they broke through one set of defences, he told himself as he staggered to his feet, they would win the fight. There were no defences facing the Commonwealth's side of the Residency.

"Four more vehicles," he croaked, as the sound of fighting intensified. "They're coming in from the north."

"Understood," the CO said. "Are they truck bombs?"

Paul bit down the response that came to mind. How the hell was *he* meant to know? The only way to be sure was to hit them with a grenade or an antitank rocket and see just how big the explosion was. Two of the vehicles were hit in quick succession, both of them exploding violently enough to wipe out a handful of enemy soldiers who had been following in hopes of exploiting the expected gap in the walls. Paul felt a moment of hot satisfaction, then lifted his rifle and opened fire on the remaining soldiers. They fell back in some disorder.

"Stay alert," the CO instructed the squad. "The day is young."

"The day is young," Villeneuve said.

"Shut up," Edward ordered, not unkindly. The truck bombs had been a nasty surprise, even if they had been engaged far enough from the gates to leave the walls intact. No doubt the enemy could keep rigging them up until the defenders ran out of grenades. "What else do we have coming at us?"

"Enemy troops are massing here, here and here," Flora said. She looked as tired as Edward felt; neither of them had dared take a sleeping pill as the dawn approached. "They seem to have deduced our reluctance to use our mortars."

Edward couldn't disagree. The enemy troops were massing barely three kilometres from the Residency – well within mortar range – yet he knew he didn't dare waste their handful of shells to take them out. No doubt the enemy CO was hoping that he'd do just that; his men were cheaper and easier to replace than Edward's shells. Edward couldn't understand why anyone would throw away his own men so casually, but he had to admit that it was working out for the enemy. Edward's ammunition stockpiles were gradually being worn down.

He looked down at the live feed from the orbiting station and swallowed a curse. The vast majority of the enemy's professional forces were digging in along the route to Maharashtra, which would force the CEF to fight its way through a series of strongpoints before they could relieve the Residency. And they were doing whatever they could to slow down the CEF; taking out bridges, mining fields and emplacing other surprises along the route. But they were also bringing sizable numbers of troops to Maharashtra, as if they believed that they would need reinforcements to overwhelm the Residency and its defenders.

"We'll have to send out a raiding party," he said, looking over at Coleman. "Do you still want to volunteer for a daring commando raid?"

Coleman grinned. "Do bears shit in the woods, sir?"

"Take one volunteer and go," Edward said. "Sniping only. I can't afford to lose you."

Coleman saluted curtly and left the room.

———

Blake Coleman knew that he wasn't one of the Marine Corps' intellectuals. He'd joined up because he liked action and the Corps had seemed a good place to get it…and he had to admit that he'd been right. And he liked women and, on Avalon at least, a Marine uniform was a sure-fire ticket to a pleasant night of very little sleep. Sure, there had been one or two embarrassments along the way, but he enjoyed his life. The only downside was that the Colonel had promoted him in the wake of Lieutenant Yamane's period on medical leave. He would have happily surrendered 1st Platoon back to her, if he'd been given a choice. *She* could issue orders and he would carry them out.

He nodded at Rifleman Carl Watson and led the way out of the door and over to the wall. As far as they could tell, the enemy didn't have spotters in the rubble surrounding the Residency, although Blake knew that there were plenty of ways to keep an eye on the building without being obvious about it. Slipping over the wall was easy enough, once they'd informed the defenders that they were on their way. The real danger was accidentally being shot by the defenders when they tried to make their way back into the Residency.

"Disgusting," Watson subvocalised, using his implanted communicator. The intelligence techs had been fairly certain that the locals wouldn't be able to detect the transmissions, not if top-of-the-line Imperial equipment had problems. "They should at least clear away the bodies."

Blake nodded. He'd seen worse on Han, but there was something uniquely callous about the caste system and how the upper castes treated the lower castes. Even pirates didn't seem to have the sense that their victims were lower than animals. He pushed the thought to one side as they slipped through the rubble, watching carefully for dogs and refugees who might have hidden in the ruins. It was quite likely that some of the attackers who'd been forced back had chosen not to try to report to their superiors.

The damage grew less extensive as they reached an apartment block, one of the largest buildings within ten kilometres of the Residency. Blake had studied all the drone footage and concluded that no one had remained inside, but the two Marines swept it carefully as they made their way up to the roof. It was clear that none of the occupants had expected to find themselves in the midst of a shooting war; their apartments showed signs of having been abandoned in haste, even with food and drink left on the table. He found himself hoping that they'd made it away safely, although he knew that it was unlikely. The locals didn't seem to have made any provisions for refugees at all.

They braced themselves for trouble as they climbed out onto the roof – it was an ideal position for an enemy observer – but the rooftop proved deserted. Blake checked for hidden surprises, then lay on his belly and peered northwards through his scope. An enemy force was massing ahead of them, half-hidden by the buildings.

"Bingo," he said, as he unslung his rifle and peered through the scope. Beside him, Watson did the same. "They're well within range. See how many officers you can spot."

A Marine Corps sniper with proper equipment could pick off enemy personnel at over three kilometres, but even an average Marine made a pretty effective sniper. Blake studied the enemy formation, silently noting the officers and a handful of black-clad personnel who seemed to be supervising operations. Insanely, the locals seemed to have issued the brightest-coloured uniforms to their officers. *And* their men were saluting them. Didn't they *know* that salutes were unwise in a combat zone?

Blake smirked to himself. It was about the only time when an officer saluted enlisted men first.

"I make fifteen officers," Watson said, finally. "You?"

"Fourteen," Blake said, wondering who he'd missed. He switched his rifle to single-shot, then took aim. "Fire."

He squeezed the trigger. One of the enemy officers spun around and fell to the ground. He didn't waste time complementing himself; he switched the rifle to the next target and picked him off before they could react. The remaining officers were scattering rapidly; Blake tracked them with his scope and fired at them, one by one. Several escaped death, but a number were wounded or killed. Beside him, Watson did the same.

"Don't worry about the enlisted men," Blake ordered, as the enemy force scattered. It wouldn't take them long to regroup and try to flush the snipers out. "Let's go."

He crawled back to the hatchway, dropped down into the building and led the way down the stairs. In the distance, he could hear the sound of shooting, although he wasn't sure what they thought they were engaging. It was unlikely that they'd even be sure where they'd been hiding;

the rifles released no betraying spark of light, nothing that would draw the enemy right to them. Perhaps someone had panicked and ordered his men to open fire at random. It would certainly seem a logical explanation.

"First set of targets engaged," he reported, activating his communicator. "Enemy very upset."

He closed the channel without waiting for a response, then concentrated on leading the way back through the rubble. There were plenty of other places they could use as sniper perches and it would definitely discourage the enemy from advancing too rapidly. If nothing else, it should buy the Residency some additional time.

"They wiped out one enemy force's officers," Villeneuve reported. "Look at them scattering."

Edward grinned, savagely. There was little more terrifying than the sniper in modern warfare, particularly one who had the drop on you. Watching their officers mown down by unseen forces would have destroyed the enlisted men's morale – unless, of course, they hated their officers as much as they should. But even if they didn't, it would be hard for their officers to control their men if they had to remain under cover. He'd seen exercises on the Slaughterhouse where a pair of snipers had stalled an advancing armoured division for hours.

"Tell them to recon the west when they check in again," he ordered. "I don't like the sight of that enemy force massing there."

"Useless incompetent fool," the Prince roared. "What *were* you thinking?"

Sivaganga watched with some cold amusement as the officer – the sole survivor of a company of the Prince's personal troops – fell to his knees. He'd been marched back to the Prince's palace as soon as the news had come in; a dozen officers killed and more wounded…and an entire company coming apart at the seams. Rumour had rapidly turned it into a thousand officers killed…

"They should have stayed inside the Residency," the officer stammered, finally. "I..."

"Take him away," the Prince ordered. The officer was still protesting as he was dragged away. "Their new tactics are very worrying, but we shall prevail."

Sivaganga didn't doubt it. As irritating as it was to lose officers, the enemy force *had* to be running short of supplies. And besides, they were the *Prince's* officers. Losing them weakened his position.

"We need to reconsider our position," the Prince said. "The current tactics are not working."

It was hard for Sivaganga to keep the surprise off his face. The Prince was not known for rethinking his plans, not when admitting that he might have been wrong weakened his position. But perhaps losing so many of his officers – and executing one more, which would cause others to start considering *their* position – had taught him a salutary lesson. Besides, he was far from an idiot, even if he *was* a hothead.

"I want to bring up some of the heavy guns," the Prince said. "We will bombard the Residency into rubble."

Sivaganga hesitated, trying to choose the best argument to lose. "My Prince," he said, finally, "the gunners are not that accurate. We may do more damage to the city than to the Residency."

"I want this finished now," the Prince hissed. "We know from our captive that the enemy force will stop its advance if the Residency is overrun."

That was...*odd*, Sivaganga realised. Had the failure to actually win quickly convinced the Prince that he and his fellow hotheads might have bitten off more than they could chew? Or had he decided to abandon the aim of destroying the enemy force on the ground in favour of throwing everything at the Residency? If the enemy *did* reach the capital, the Residency's defenders would be in place to attack the Prince's forces from behind.

"Then you will have to explain the damage to your father," Sivaganga said, after a long moment. If the Prince felt strong enough to stand against the Rajah...at best, there would be a coup. At worst, there would be a civil war at the worst possible moment. The rebellion and the off-worlders would rapidly take advantage of any civil strife.

"My father will understand," the Prince hissed. He looked over at one of his officers. "Have the guns brought into the city!"

"Yes, My Prince," the officer said.

Sivaganga swallowed. There was no way, he realised, that this was going to end well. And yet he found himself swinging between two extremes. The off-worlders were going to be squashed like bugs…or the off-worlders would be able to hold out long enough to be rescued by their fellows. If the former, he knew that opposing the Prince would be pointless; if the latter…well, they *had* bitten off more than they could chew.

But he knew that he didn't dare oppose the Prince openly.

All he could do was wait and pray that the Prince was right.

CHAPTER TWENTY-ONE

> Sam's manic appearance is amusing on the cartoon set; in real life, it can be terrifying. A nation following the 'speak loud/big stick' policy will rapidly discover that its neighbours are arming to the teeth and preparing defensive alliances to prevent future expansion.
> -Professor Leo Caesius, *Diplomacy: The Lessons of the Past.*

Ekachraka sat in the middle of the park and tried, very hard, not to show his fear. His wife, two sons and three daughters sat near him, guarded by oddly-dressed off-world troopers and a handful of rebels. They were untouchables, the powerless and the despised, but they held weapons… and the glances they kept sending the women were far from friendly. It was hard to wrap his head around the fact that his world had turned upside down, that untouchables had thrown off their divinely appointed place and turned into rebels, but he couldn't avoid it, any more than he could avoid the consequences. He was no longer in control of his own fate.

He'd heard the rumours, even though the higher castes had ignored them. When untouchables rebelled, they became monsters; looting, raping and burning at will. The thought of his wife and daughters being violated was horrifying, as was the certainty that the untouchables would murder his son in front of his eyes, just to prevent him from growing up and avenging his family's disgrace. There was nothing he could do to save them, either. The one move by some of the young men to fight had ended with a quick burst of gunfire which had literally ripped their bodies apart. After that, they'd known that resistance was futile.

One of the off-world vehicles moved forward, a gray-clad man standing on top of the vehicle and pressing something against his lips. Ekachraka couldn't help noticing how disgustingly healthy he was, even though everyone *knew* that off-worlders lived in pigsties and ate their own excrement for food. He certainly didn't seem cowed by the prisoners, or by the rebels.

"Attention," the off-worlder said. "We require men to drive trucks. If you can drive a truck, we will take your families into protective custody as long as necessary. Should you die in our service, we will see that they are set up elsewhere and protected from those who would seek to do them harm. If you are interested, raise your hands."

Ekachraka hesitated. He *could* drive a truck, at least as long as it was of standard design. But did he dare leave his wife and children in their custody? He looked over at his wife and saw the fear in her eyes, the fear she was trying to hide from the children. She knew as well as he did that the untouchables would turn on them, eventually. They *hated* the upper castes…in a sudden burst of understanding, he realised that they'd felt as helpless to protect themselves and their families as he did now.

He held up a hand. Several dozen others, including some he knew, joined him.

"Good," the off-worlder said. He pointed to a set of buildings that had formerly belonged to the local government. "If you will stand up and take your families into the first building, we will process you as quickly as possible."

Ekachraka pulled himself to his feet and started to walk towards the building. If there were only limited spaces, he didn't want to miss out. Behind him, his wife followed him with the children. He could hear her praying silently under her breath. Quietly, he joined her as they reached the entrance. If the gods refused to provide…

Jasmine had never seen a group of more wretched men and women in her life, even during the arrest of the Old Council on Avalon. There, the councillors had been guilty of trying to build their own little kingdom, ensuring that civil unrest would continue to rage over Avalon. It was hard to feel sorry for them. But here, the men and women in the park had merely been born to the middle-level castes. Their only crime had been being born.

But it wouldn't save them, she thought, numbly. The reports of scores being settled kept flowing in from the soldiers patrolling the edge of the city. Yin's fighters seemed to be honouring their bargain, but other untouchables had clearly decided to loot, rape and kill…and, in some places, evict their former masters from their homes. Even those who had merely been made homeless were unlikely to know how to survive, certainly not with the world turned upside down. She had no doubt that the government would take full advantage of the reports of atrocities and use them to stiffen resistance further towards the capital city.

The reporter looked over at her. "Do you think that they can *really* drive?"

"I hope so," Jasmine said. One thing about the Empire that had always amused her was a bloody-minded insistence on standardisation. Components could be cannibalised and slotted into a very different machine; vehicles, no matter how different, had the same basic driving system. If the locals could drive their own vehicles, they could probably drive trucks removed from the garrison's stores. "And if they can't, we'll know about it very quickly."

Alves frowned, watching a little girl who was staring at the soldiers with wide frightened eyes. "And if they can't?"

"We'll see," Jasmine said. It went against the grain to threaten their families or to put them outside the camp. "There are other things they can do for us – or for the city. Help clean up the mess, for a start."

The rebels, at least, understood the urgency of removing the dead bodies. Mass graves had been dug outside the city, with work crews moving to pick up the corpses and transport them to the graves. It was cold and impersonal, but there was little choice. Besides, there was almost no hope of reuniting the bodies with their living relatives. Some of them had been smashed so badly that they were almost unrecognisable, while others had been mutilated to the point that they'd made hardened Marines sick.

Alves turned to follow her as she led the way back towards the Warrior. Coming to the city had been a risk – it was quite possible that there were still enemy holdouts in the buildings - but she'd wanted to see it for herself. And it gave her a chance to catch up with her subordinates and reassure herself that they were ready to go back on the offensive. Once they'd set up the POW camp and armed the rebels, they could start moving back towards the city. This time, she promised herself, it would be different.

"Jasmine," he said, very quietly, "do you think we can win?"

Jasmine tensed, despite herself. It was the same question that had been bothering her, ever since the CEF had been slapped back by the local defenders. Even now, with the rebels adding to their manpower, she had her doubts. The locals had more experience with their weapons than the rebels. Some of the more complex weapons required weeks or months of training before they could be deployed successfully.

"I think that we can," she said, finally. It was important to show confidence. "What about yourself?"

"I wish I knew," Alves admitted. "The rebels aren't quite what we want, are they?"

Jasmine snorted. "Are they ever?"

"We've secured two islands several miles off the coastline," General Joseph Raphael informed her, two hours later. "One of them will take the women and children; the other will take local upper-class aristocrats who refuse to work with us. The former will receive proper food and medical care; the latter will receive nothing but ration bars."

Jasmine nodded. The rebels had wanted to enslave the prisoners, but she'd pointed out that they didn't really have the manpower to guard them, certainly not when they began their offensive. Instead, those who refused to join the rebellion would be safe, if not entirely comfortable, on a prison island. Ration bars would keep them alive long enough for the war to be won and a more permanent solution to be devised.

"The waters around the islands are not safe," the General added. He sounded rather amused at the thought, although it had helped safeguard his garrison until relief had finally arrived. "If they manage to swim all ten miles to the coastline, surviving waves and dangerous critters...well, bully for them."

"Good," Jasmine said, shortly. She turned her gaze to the intelligence officer. "What do we know about the enemy positions?"

"Most of their armoured forces have held position here," Colonel Cindy Macintyre explained, tapping the map. "You'll notice that position is just outside bombardment range from the garrison. They have been trying to slip infantry through the defences and engage us and the rebels, but so far we've managed to keep them from doing any serious damage. Drone overflights report that they have been concentrating on establishing defensive lines blocking roads, knocking down bridges and other tricks intended to slow us down."

Jasmine had expected that, but it was still annoying. The Landshark tanks – and even the Warriors – could move underwater, if necessary. Blowing up bridges wouldn't do more than slow them down. But the other vehicles – and her infantry – would need bridges to get across the rivers, at least in large numbers. They'd need to bring bridging equipment along with them.

"In addition, they have been preparing numerous small towns and cities to serve as defensive strongpoints," Cindy continued, smoothly. "This one in particular" – she tapped a city situated between two mountain peaks – "is going to be a meatgrinder. There's no way to avoid it without making a wide circuit through the countryside that will add several more weeks to our operation. The enemy seems to know it too; they've been distributing weapons, sealing up the gates and rounding up untouchables who might otherwise serve as a fifth column."

Her lips thinned. "And they've also been telling their population horror stories about what they can expect if we capture their homes," she added. "We can expect most of the population to fight to the end."

"Wonderful," Buckley commented, sardonically. "A whole planet convinced that we're going to rampage through their homes."

Jasmine tapped the table for silence, then looked over at Major Bruno Adamson, CO of the 4th Avalon Infantry Battalion. "How are the rebels coping with the weapons we gave them?"

"Reasonably well, at least with the simple weapons," Adamson said. "Most of them are functionally illiterate; I doubt they can really master anything more complex than an antitank rocket launcher, but it isn't as if we were going to supply more advanced weapons anyway."

Alves leaned forward. "Why not?"

"It can take weeks – if not months – to learn how to operate a tank," Adamson pointed out, dryly. He'd been one of the officers who hadn't approved of having a reporter underfoot at all times. "And besides, we might end up having those weapons pointed back at us."

"A possibility," Jasmine agreed, when Alves looked shocked. "We don't know how the revolution is going to develop in the future. They may become as deeply xenophobic as the current government, or they might decide they want to massacre the upper-castes completely and turn on us when we object."

She tapped the map, drawing their attention back to the display. "I want our big guns moved over here," she ordered, tapping the ground near the rapidly-expanding FOB. "That should give us some additional range to hammer their positions, once the fighting begins. In the meantime, move our transport helicopters to the FOB; I want to use them to insert stormtroopers behind enemy lines."

Carefully, she drew out a line on the map. "We're going to advance up the main road," she added, "drawing their armoured forces into a trap and destroying them. That will not be easy."

"Of course not," Buckley warned. "That route is predictable."

"But also without an alternative," Jasmine agreed. The tanks could move off-road, but the trucks they needed for supplies couldn't. Clearing and holding the roads would be the first step towards advancing on the enemy capital. "Hold back a third of the Warriors; I want them in place to provide escorts for our trucks. We'll try and set the rebels up to patrol the roads, but we cannot count on it. Drones are to remain alert for IED emplacement teams at all times."

And good luck to us, she added, silently. It was often hard to tell if a person on the road was taking a dump or laying an IED for an unlucky vehicle. Sniper crews could deter them, but Jasmine had a feeling that a great many innocents were about to be caught up in the fighting and killed.

"All POWs are to be moved back to the camp, interrogated and then sent over the water," Jasmine continued. She'd issued such orders already, but they needed to be restated. As the fighting wore on, even experienced units could lose sight of their orders – or, for that matter, why it was important to treat prisoners well. They still had several soldiers unaccounted for, leaving her to assume the worst. "I don't want us to be responsible for a massacre."

"The rebels don't seem to care about the niceties," Adamson pointed out, grimly. "We've already seen them tossing people out of their homes or ransacking their houses. What happens when they decide to break the agreement and start killing their enemies directly?"

Jasmine made a face. If they tried to intervene, the rebels might turn on them – and ensure that the Residency would be lost. But if they didn't, they would be forever tainted by their complicity in a massacre. She'd heard stories of Marine units that *had* been tainted, merely through clearing the way for the Imperial Army's occupation battalions or newly-raised Civil Guard units, yet she'd never seen it directly.

"We try to stop them," she said, finally.

She stared down at the map for a long moment, then looked up, moving her gaze from person to person. "You know what's at stake," she said, quietly. "If we fail to break through to the Residency, we will lose our CO and his escorts – and our chance to establish diplomatic relationships with the Wolfbane Sector. And, even if *that* wasn't a consideration, we will suffer a defeat that might damage the Commonwealth's prestige. We must not lose. We *will* not lose.

"I intend to launch the offensive in three days from now," she added. Even that, she knew, was pushing it. The enemy would have ample time to prepare for them – and keep pushing at the Residency. "By then, we have to be ready."

She cleared her throat. "Dismissed!"

One by one, her officers left the room, leaving her alone with Alves. The reporter said nothing as she studied the map, trying to visualise the terrain. She knew from bitter experience that even the most comprehensive maps sometimes left out vital details, details that looked inconsequential to the officers at the rear, but terrifyingly important to the men and women on the front lines.

"It doesn't seem a very comprehensive plan," Alves observed, breaking the silence. "There were more complex and detailed plans on the base back home."

"No battle plan ever survives contact with the enemy," Jasmine explained. She scowled in bitter memory. "Our last battle plan certainly didn't."

She shook her head. "We'll have to improvise, depending on what they throw at us," she added. "If we tie ourselves too tightly to a specific plan, we'll run into trouble when we cannot adapt to something we didn't expect."

"Like the rebels doing something stupid," Alves said.

"Exactly," Jasmine agreed. "The problem with rebel forces is that they tend to start fighting over who should take power after the last government is defeated, often before the government has actually been destroyed. And if they turn on us, it could get very nasty."

She ran her hand through her hair, silently grateful that she'd found the time to have it pruned back to a Slaughterhouse haircut. It had been a shock, she recalled, to have her long hair sliced off in bare seconds, but long hair would have just got in the way. Besides, it took far too long to wash.

"You'll handle it," Alves said, calmly. "I have every faith in you."

Jasmine laughed. "I'm glad *someone* does," she said. The Colonel might have confided any doubts he had in his Command Sergeant, but who did *she* have to talk to? Buckley wouldn't have understood and she didn't know the other officers that well. "Right now, we're trying to manage a balancing act. If we fall off…"

Alves surprised her by giving her a hug. Jasmine hesitated, feeling oddly unsure of what to do, then slowly returned the hug. His body was relatively fit and muscular, but not up to Marine standards. But then, so few were outside the Special Forces. She found her thoughts whirling around and around in shock. Loneliness seemed to be part of life for a female Marine; the men she met were either fellow Marines – and thus off-limits – or intimidated by her. After all, she *was* stronger than the average man…

Did he want her? Did she want *him*?

"Thank you," she said, finally. She couldn't afford the distraction. Not now. There would be time to explore a possible relationship when they were back on the starships, heading home. And then the Colonel would be there…she could always talk to him, if nothing else. "I won't let you down."

Alves nodded – he seemed to understand, even though she hadn't said anything out loud – and then he withdrew, leaving her alone.

Shaking her head, she pushed her odd feelings aside and then reached for her terminal. She needed to update the Colonel and then return to the mainland. They had a war to plan.

CHAPTER TWENTY-TWO

> Hence, to some extent, an even more cynical definition of diplomacy – the art of saying 'nice doggy' while one prepares a big stick.
> -Professor Leo Caesius, *Diplomacy: The Lessons of the Past.*

"I think we have a problem," Villeneuve reported.

"Show me," Edward ordered. The truck bombs had been an unpleasant innovation – and, if they kept coming, the Residency would rapidly become indefensible. "What now?"

"One of the drones is reporting that they're bringing guns into the city," Villeneuve said. "At least five medium-range pieces and a handful of mortars."

Edward bit down an urge to swear. He'd known that it was likely, but…he pushed the wishful thinking aside and looked down at the display, silently calculating ranges and trajectories in his head. It very much looked as if they were planning to start hurling shells into the complex from an absurdly short range.

"No sign of smart weapons," he said, out loud. Even if the locals *had* had smart weapons, it didn't look as though their people would know how to use them. "They must be worried about accidentally bombarding the city themselves."

"Almost certainly," Villeneuve agreed. "But it isn't as if the complex is a small target."

Edward ground his teeth in frustration. The Marines preferred to call on mobile firepower – assault helicopters or pinpoint strikes from orbit – rather than use any form of precision artillery. It was difficult to *ensure* that the targeting was precise, particularly when the front lines were far too close together. But even primitive targeting systems could be reasonably sure of dropping shells straight down into the complex, devastating his positions. And then the enemy forces would surge forward and obliterate the remains of the defenders.

"Order the mortar teams to prepare to take them out," he ordered. It was *definitely* frustrating; the mortar crews could exterminate the gunners within range, but all the enemy would have to do was pull back and accept the risk of damaging their own city. "Once they're in position, start dropping shells on their heads."

He reached for his mug of coffee and took a sip, feeling an odd sense of *Déjà Vu*. The coffee from the garrison was still good, unsurprisingly. It had been freeze-dried and then placed in stasis, just waiting for someone to come along and start drinking. Taking some of the packets to the capital had been almost second nature. It was stronger than anything available on Avalon.

The reports kept flowing in from the various outposts. His people were tired, even though he'd ordered a third of his force to catch some sleep. He didn't dare issue sleeping pills, not when they might have to be on their feet and fighting at any moment, so they were being kept awake by incessant sniping and explosions. Sooner or later, his people would be so tired that they would fall asleep on their feet.

Or maybe I will have to issue the pills anyway and damn the risk, he thought, coldly.

"They're unlimbering now," Flora reported. "The mortar crews are taking aim."

Edward watched through the drones as the enemy gunnery crews set up. Artillerymen were among the strongest soldiers in the Imperial Army, capable of giving even the Marines a run for their money. It was a branch of the service that demanded both speed and precision as well as physical strength; looking at the enemy crews, Edward had a feeling that they hadn't been extensively drilled in preparing their weapons to fire. But then, it *did* make a certain kind of sense. The locals wouldn't have had much call for artillery when they were trying to suppress a revolt and their best crews had probably been diverted to the coast to block the CEF's advance.

"Take them out," he ordered.

The mortar crews opened fire, launching shells into the enemy city. Edward watched, as dispassionately as he could, as five of six enemy guns were destroyed in thunderous explosions, one going up so violently that it was clear that they'd stockpiled shells *beside* the guns for ease of access. The sixth enemy gun launched a shell back towards the complex – Edward braced himself instinctively – before it too was taken out. A moment later, the ground rocked violently.

"It came down in the middle courtyard," Villeneuve reported. "They smashed a lot of their statues, sir."

They'd been lucky, Edward knew. A few metres in either direction and either the Commonwealth or Wolfbane would have lost a dozen men. Or...they might have taken out part of the wall. But hopefully they'd discouraged the enemy from using guns...

A second explosion rocked the complex a moment later. "Sir, they're moving up small mortars," Villeneuve explained. "It's going to be hard to take them all out without burning through our ammunition."

Edward nodded. The Mark-VII Mortar was several hundred years old; it might have been designed for the Imperial Army, but he wasn't surprised that thousands of the weapons had leaked into the hands of local defence forces. It was one of the simplest pieces of equipment in use, even though it couldn't shoot very heavy shells. Most of the makeshift barricades would protect his men, but a lucky shot or two might be incredibly devastating.

"Warn everyone to brace for incoming fire," he said, as a third shell soared over the complex and came down on the wrong side. He found himself hoping that the enemy gunnery crew would be executed for incompetence; there had been nothing wrong with how quickly they'd primed the gun, merely with their aim. And he'd been pretty lousy when he'd first picked up and fired a gun too. "Lieutenant Coleman?"

Coleman stepped forward. "Sir?"

"Put together a team of snipers," he ordered. The enemy had tried to sweep for snipers, but they'd been driven back by a handful of mortar shells and improvised IEDs. "Not you, not this time. I want them to engage the mortar crews before they can set up and open fire."

He scowled down at the tracking display. So far, the enemy crews were firing one or two shots, then moving rapidly to another position. It suggested that they hadn't quite realised that the defenders didn't have unlimited shells to waste, not an uncommon belief among soldiers who hadn't been taught anything about logistics. But once they *did* realise the truth, they'd start setting up permanently and hammer the complex into rubble. It couldn't be tolerated.

"Yes, sir," Coleman said. He looked irked at being barred from the mission, but Edward had something else in mind for him later in the night. "I'll volunteer a pair of Marines for the operation right away."

Leo shivered as *something* struck the ground and exploded not too far away from the basement. The building quivered, dust drifting down from the ceiling, before the rumbles slowly faded away. Another explosion followed a moment later, a dull crash that seemed to reverberate through the ground. He thought he heard a whistle before a third explosion added to the chaos.

He reached out and took Fiona's hand in his, feeling her entire body trembling. She hadn't woken up until shortly after dawn; she hadn't had any time to come to grips with the reality that they were under siege. The last thing she remembered was the desperate flight back to the Residency, where she'd been sedated. And she wasn't coping with the sudden change in her circumstances very well. If it hadn't been for her, Leo wasn't sure that he would have coped very well too.

"It's awful," Fiona said. "When are they going to *stop*?"

"Once they kill us all," Leo said, his words underlined by another explosion. He couldn't help wondering just how long the Residency could stand up to the bombardment. The walls seemed solid, but they weren't made of hullmetal. "They want us all dead."

Fiona looked as if she wanted to cry. Leo reached out for her and pulled her close, despite the faint smell clinging to her body – and his too, he had to admit. There were no bathtubs available for use, even if they'd had the water. The medics had washed them down with a gel they'd sworn would kill all the bugs, but it hadn't done much for the stench. Only the grim awareness that it was likely to get worse before it got better kept him from saying anything out loud. Besides, he had the distinct feeling that the Marines wouldn't appreciate whining.

The ground shook again, violently. Leo heard a crash in the distance, followed by a female voice swearing creatively. He hugged his wife closely, wondering if the next second would be the end. Instead, an unearthly silence fell over the complex, as if the universe was holding its breath. Fiona looked up at him, hope in her eyes. He didn't have the heart to admit that the enemy were probably reloading their weapons and preparing to fire again.

There was a tap on the door, which opened a moment later to reveal the medic. Leo couldn't help noticing that blood had stained her white tunic, suggesting that there wasn't even water for the medics to clean themselves. It risked contamination, he knew, remembering some of Mindy's survivalist textbooks she'd been forced to read during Basic Training. Dirty hands spread diseases, if he recalled correctly. But there was no alternative.

"You're awake," she said, marching over to Fiona. Up close, her nametag read ZOE. "How are you feeling?"

Fiona touched the side of her head. "Thick-headed," she said, after a moment's thought. "I want to sleep and yet I can't sleep."

"That's a side-effect from the sedative," Zoe said, briskly. "Normally we would have flushed it from your system before you awoke, but we have a shortage of countervailing agents right now and it was decided that it would be better to let you sleep. Anything else?"

"No," Fiona said.

"You did pick up some bumps and bruises from your adventure," Zoe informed her. "But you should be fine. Your body may not have registered them because of the sedative; I'm afraid we had to give you a military-grade drug and…"

"Thank you," Fiona said, hastily. Another shell shook the building and she looked around, nervously. "What are we going to do now?"

"I was told that you intended to study medicine," Zoe said. "There are quite a few people in the infirmary who require some loving care. And it would take your mind off the bombardment outside."

Leo gave his wife a reassuring look. "It would be something to do," he said. "The alternative is just waiting here to see what happens."

Fiona swallowed, then stood up. Her legs were shaking, Leo realised, as he followed her to his feet. Even though she'd been in Camelot when the Crackers launched their final bid for victory, she hadn't been in the thick of the fighting. She was now…and it didn't agree with her. Leo couldn't help wondering how all the Marines were so calm when death was a mere whisker away.

"This way," Zoe said, leading them through the door and down a short flight of stairs. "There are twelve injured personnel here, including two of the maids. Three more have been wounded, but refused to step off the firing line."

Leo took in the scene before him and winced. Blankets had been laid out on the ground, each one providing *some* padding for the wounded soldiers. Several mattresses had been dragged down from the bedrooms and laid on the floor, but they seemed to be badly stained with blood and effectively useless. The soldiers looked to have been bandaged up, but it was a far cry from the clean and tidy hospital on Avalon, or even the Doctor's office on Earth. It was easy to believe that disease would spread through the complex and strike down the wounded soldiers.

One of the maids had lost a leg, he saw…and felt his stomach rebel at the sight. If he'd had something to eat, he knew he would have thrown it up at the sight of the makeshift bandage covering the bloody stump. Her back was brutally scarred, he saw as he looked away from her leg, as if someone had taken a whip to her. Given how lower-caste people were treated on the cursed world, it was easy to imagine that had been precisely what had happened. The other maid had a bandage wrapped around her upper arm, but she seemed to have no problem in moving. She'd gotten off lightly.

Fiona paled and stumbled backwards. Leo felt a flicker of sympathy; this was the reality that most of the Empire's citizens had never seen. The Core Worlds had been safe for a very long time, at least for the law-abiding citizens who didn't rock the boat or ask inconvenient questions. They never really grasped just how bad it could become... even those who watched snuff movies and other horrific entertainments intended to cater to the very worst of human impulses had rarely seen suffering on such a scale.

But Earth is gone, he thought, remembering what he'd been told. If the Wolfbane representatives had been telling the truth, Earth had been knocked flat and the entire population was dead. Leo had known that was going to happen – he'd even worked out the final steps of the Empire's fall – but it was still terrifying to realise that it had finally come to pass. The Empire had seemed so strong, so invulnerable...

"It will get worse," Zoe said, without apparent emotion. "Our small stockpile of regular medical supplies is running out fast. Right now, we have to change the makeshift bandages carefully, clean the wounds and wash the cloths with boiling water. Even with broad-spectrum antibiotics, the risk of infection is far too high."

She scowled. "There's enough bloody supplies at the garrison to provide medical care to everyone in the whole damned city," she added. "But they might as well be on the other side of the Empire."

The ground shook, once again.

"I...I'll try," Fiona said. Leo had never been prouder of her than at that moment, when she stepped up to help. "What do you want me to do first?"

"Fetch the cloths from the maids," Zoe ordered. She pointed towards a doorway leading through to the kitchens. "And remind them to make damn sure they boil the water before using it for anything else."

She paused. "And make damn sure you wash your hands first," she added. "I won't have you infecting the men either."

Fiona nodded and walked down the room, shying away from the wounded men. Leo had never given medical attention in his life; the very thought of touching wounded flesh was disgusting. Hell, he and the others in his CityBlock on Earth had never even liked to cut up meat, when they'd been able to afford it. They'd found it so much easier to buy ration bars and other pre-processed foodstuffs.

He caught sight of two of the maids as they entered, carrying a massive bucket of water between them. Colonel Stalker had apparently allowed them to stay, a decision Leo found hard to fault, even if they *were* eating up food and water. But they would almost certainly have been killed if they'd gone back to their own people. Besides, they could help the medics, allowing others to go back to the fighting.

Zoe coughed, bluntly. "You're still here?"

Leo nodded. "Is there anything *I* can do to help?"

"I'd suggest that you check in with the Colonel first," Zoe said. She looked him up and down, appraisingly. "I don't know what your shooting skills are like, but I'm sure that the soldiers would appreciate someone carrying bullets and grenades for them. Or were you planning to continue holding talks with the Wolfbane representatives while you were under siege?"

It was possible that the threat of death would encourage Lockhart to talk openly.

Leo snorted at the thought…but, on reflection, it wasn't *that* bad an idea. Whatever they learned could be transmitted to the coast, where it could be passed on to the starships when they finally returned. And besides, it would help pass the time.

"I'll ask the Colonel," he said, finally. Fiona emerged from the doorway, carrying a pile of cloths on one hand. "Thank you."

He waved goodbye to his wife, then turned and made his way towards the upper levels. The sound of shooting was growing louder, although it seemed to be irregular…and the explosions seemed to be completely unpredictable. He supposed that made sense; the enemy would be trying to rotate their firing patterns, just to keep the defenders from becoming used to them. Or perhaps he was completely wrong and something else was at work.

"Hey," a voice called. He turned to see a Marine – one of their escorts from the marketplace – standing there, staring at him. "Where do you think you're going?"

"To see the Colonel," Leo said. "Where is he?"

The Marine barked a harsh laugh. "Not up there," he said, dryly. "That would have taken you out into the open. I suggest that you follow me down to the situation room."

Leo flushed, then obeyed. Another series of explosions rocked the complex as they picked their way downstairs and into a room that had been crammed with portable equipment. Several soldiers Leo didn't recognise sat at desks, staring at display screens; others milled around the table, arguing over the map of the city. The Colonel stood in the midst of them, seemingly totally calm. Even another thunderous explosion didn't make him react.

"Take a seat, Professor," Colonel Stalker said. "I'll be with you in a minute."

He looked past Leo to the Marine. "Did you send them on their way?"

"I did," the Marine said. "And myself?"

Colonel Stalker pointed down at the map. "I have a specific task for you," he said. "Listen carefully."

Chapter
Twenty-Three

> It is common to condemn diplomats for speaking softly, rather than issuing bullish threats. However, outright threats encourage resistance as well as forcing the country issuing the threats to actually back them up or appear a paper tiger. Bad feelings can alienate future relationships between countries. Diplomats always prefer to keep their voices down.
>
> -Professor Leo Caesius, *Diplomacy: The Lessons of the Past.*

"You do realise," Watson said, as they ran through a final check of their weapons and equipment, "that they could legally shoot us if they caught us?"

Blake snorted. "I think we're well past the legalities now," he pointed out. "Besides, who have we fought in the last five years who would have honoured them anyway?"

He considered the question for a long moment, before dismissing it as a waste of time. It was perfectly true that a soldier out of uniform could be executed out of hand, on suspicion of being a spy, but he doubted that the locals would be interested in legalities. Their only real hope was to destroy the Residency and the CEF and then hope that they could play the Commonwealth and Wolfbane off against one another to prevent retaliation. Blake rather doubted that any of them would be allowed to survive if the locals won.

"No one," Watson said, confirming his thoughts. His partner checked Blake's equipment, then turned to allow Blake to do the same for him. "Are you ready?"

Blake nodded. "Let's do this."

Darkness had fallen over the city by the time they emerged from the Residency, but the moons were hidden behind the clouds, keeping the city enveloped in shadow. Blake silently bemoaned the lack of chameleon suits, but they were hardly necessary as they slipped forward, scrambled over the wall and made their way out towards the enemy lines. It was almost eerily quiet; the enemy had pulled in their guns as soon as night had started to fall, pulling back to recuperate and service their weapons. Blake doubted that would continue – sooner or later, the enemy would decide that constant bombardment would wear down the defenders –but for the moment he was glad of the peace. It gave them a chance to slip into the city unobserved.

He peered through his goggles as they advanced northwards, sticking to the shadows as much as possible. The entire region was a no-man's land, but drone overflights *had* picked up a handful of people hiding in the rubble; some too small to be adult humans. Children, Blake assumed, probably untouchables. He hoped that they'd have the sense to stay out of the fighting. But then, once the enemy forces rolled forwards, they would probably be crushed flat unless they ran very quickly

There were no signs of enemy activity until they reached a large manor-style building six kilometres from the Residency, just outside mortar range. It was hard to be sure, but a combination of drone observation and communications interception had identified it as an enemy command post, one of several. Blake found himself rolling his eyes as he took in the sheer luxury – and complete indefensibility – of the building, before deciding that the enemy might not have made *that* big a mistake. If nothing else, it wasn't as if Colonel Stalker had the manpower to come out of the Residency and assault the building openly.

He smirked to himself as he scanned the grounds with his NVGs. There were a handful of armed guards at the gatehouse, but only a handful of others patrolling the grounds. He watched long enough to take note of their patterns – and to take note of the fact that they never changed their routines – and then motioned for Watson to follow him forward, up to the wall. It might have deterred local youths, but it couldn't have slowed down a Marine for more than a few seconds. They were up and over the wall, still cloaked in shadow, without being spotted. A moment later, they were in the shrubbery and making their way towards the house. None of the guards, it seemed, had NVGs. They certainly didn't raise the alarm as the Marines slipped past them.

Watson went to work on the nearest window as they pressed themselves against the building's wall, finally undoing the latch and flipping it open with a sonic screwdriver. Blake leaned forward, stunner in hand, but no sound came out of the silent room. A moment later, he scrambled through the window and landed softly on the carpeted floor. A quick scan with his goggles revealed that the room was a bedroom, but - thankfully – deserted. It looked as though it was intended for a child.

This way, he signalled with his hands, leading the way out into the corridor. Inside, the building was astonishingly luxurious, far less tasteful than even the mansions the Old Council had built on Avalon. He found himself shaking his head as he slipped down the corridor, then froze as he saw a light in the distance. A single guard was standing there, wearing one of the most ridiculous uniforms Blake had ever seen. But there was nothing funny about the weapon in his hands.

Blake slipped forward stealthy, came up behind the guard and wrapped his hands around the guard's neck, pushing down hard enough to force the guard to black out. He caught the guard's weapon, put it to one side and gently laid the guard on the floor, then injected him with a sedative to ensure that he remained out of it. No doubt he would be caught asleep on watch, if the Marines managed to escape without being detected. In the Corps, being caught asleep while on duty was a serious offense; he had no idea how the locals would react to it, but he doubted that it would be pleasant.

Leave him, he signalled. Watson followed him up the stairs and into the master bedroom. Inside, there was a pale-skinned man in an oversized bed, alone. Blake glanced around and saw a handful of women sleeping in smaller beds, surrounding their lord and master. It struck him as something out of a bad sex VR package - not that he'd ever needed to use them, of course – but it didn't seem uncommon. Pirates took advantage of their absolute power over their victims too.

He crept forward and placed a tab against the man's neck. His breathing seemed to catch, then grew deeper. It would be hours before the drug worked its way out of his body and by then he would be in the Residency – or dead. Smiling to himself, Blake pulled away the sheets and tugged the man out of bed. The noise, as slight as it was, awakened the girls.

"Stun them," he hissed. Watson opened fire with his stunner, sending the girls collapsing back into unconsciousness. Quickly, he slung the man over his shoulder and led the way back outside, listening carefully. The noise might have been heard by another guard…

"Shit," Watson said, as someone started to shout in the native tongue. In the distance, Blake could hear the sound of running feet. "I think they're on to us."

"No shit," Blake snapped. "Follow me."

He led the way down the stairs, carrying the prisoner over his shoulder. The lights were coming on, his goggles automatically dimming to protect his eyesight. A line of guards appeared at the far end of the corridor, staring at the two Marines in absolute disbelief. Watson unhooked a grenade from his belt before they could react and tossed it into the mass of guards, blowing them into bloody chunks. It was followed by a flame grenade, starting a fire that threatened to consume the entire manor if it wasn't stopped. Blake breathed a silent prayer for the girls they'd stunned as the flames started to spread rapidly, then led the way towards the nearest exit. There was no time to waste sneaking out of a window.

More guards appeared as they used another grenade to break down the door and head outside. Watson took the lead, using his rifle to clear the way as Blake carried their captive towards the walls. Fortunately, the guards seemed to be completely confused about just what was going on; it didn't help that the MAG assault rifle was almost completely silent, depriving them of any clue as to where the sniper was hiding. Watson scrambled up onto the wall, took the captive and dropped him down onto the other side. Blake followed him, scooped up the captive and started to run. Behind him, he could hear the sound of firing growing louder. He wasn't entirely sure what they were shooting at; none of the shots were coming anywhere near the two Marines.

He glanced behind him briefly as he ran into the darkness. The manor was burning brightly now, flames licking through the windows and consuming the walls. He saw the roof start to fall in, burning all the evidence of their presence under the debris, then winced inwardly as he realised that the women might have been killed in the fire. They hadn't deserved death, he told himself. They'd been victims, just like almost everyone else on the planet.

Pushing the thought aside, he continued to run. It wouldn't be long before the enemy realised just who had been kidnapped – and why. And then they'd come after the Marines with everything they had.

Sivaganga had been sleeping an uneasy sleep when there was an urgent knocking on the door, instantly snapping him back to full wakefulness. The Prince had graciously invited him to share his lodgings, but Sivaganga knew better than to think that was a mark of favour. If nothing else, the Prince would want someone to take the blame if the operation failed completely.

"My Lord," the messenger said, opening the door, "there has been an incident."

He spilled out the whole story as Sivaganga reached for his robes and donned them, heedless of the messenger's presence. It wasn't as if he was upper-caste, after all. Someone had raided a manor and left it a burning ruin…and, according to some of the guards, they'd definitely taken one of the occupants with them. And the manor, the messenger finally got around to telling him, belonged to Ramnad Zamindari. If one of the Prince's closest allies had been captured…

"Tell the Prince I'm on my way," he said, once the tide of words had finally come to an end. "I'll be down in a few minutes."

The Prince looked terrible, he decided, as he stepped into the office. His reputation for enjoying himself in the most extreme manner was no doubt accurate; he probably hadn't bothered to sleep between ending the bombardment for the evening and hearing the news about his ally's kidnapping. His *potential* kidnapping, Sivaganga reminded himself firmly. It was quite possible that the man had died in the fire.

"This is intolerable," the Prince thundered. There was blood on his hands, which he wiped off on his nightshirt. "How *could* they penetrate our security and carry off one of my allies?"

"They are trapped there," Sivaganga pointed out, as mildly as he could. He had the uncomfortable feeling that the blood belonged to the messenger. Reporting bad news to an aristocrat was never a safe occupation. "They must be looking for other ways to weaken us."

"And they have captured one of my most capable commanders," the Prince snapped. "This hurts us badly!"

Sivaganga tended to disagree. Hotheads, in his experience, made poor commanders – or diplomats, or anything else that didn't require a heroic charge into the enemy guns. Indeed, by kidnapping the Prince's man, the off-worlders had probably done the locals a big favour...not that the Prince would see it like that. Losing one of his allies was bad enough, but it also made him look weak and foolish. Others would be tempted to challenge him and his Royal Father.

"Then we can offer to trade," he suggested. "We still have the prisoner, don't we?"

The Prince's eyes narrowed. "You propose returning our sole captive to the enemy?"

"The off-worlders would be certain to bargain for his life," Sivaganga pointed out. "And besides, we would recover him when the Residency fell."

There was a long pause as the Prince mulled it over. Sivaganga knew that he was right; they *could* use the captive as a bargaining chip, if they were prepared to admit how they'd treated him. But he knew that the off-worlders would be likely to take a dim view of torture, even if the man *was* lower than the lowest caste. They'd only see it as a sign of what awaited them if they surrendered.

But how much could *their* captive tell *them*?

"Send in a white flag once the sun rises," the Prince said, finally. "We will offer to trade captives – and then destroy the Residency, once and for all."

Sivaganga scowled. The reports from their handful of remaining agents along the coastline had made it clear that the off-worlders were starting to build up the rebels into a formidable force. It had only taken the distribution of thousands of weapons to give them a boost in confidence; indeed, there had been uprisings and brief bursts of violence all over the mainland. No matter what happened to the Residency, it would be years before the rebels could finally be put down – and that assumed that the off-worlders went away, abandoning their allies. He knew that there was no shortage to the level of dishonesty practiced by off-worlders, but would they really be so callous?

But his opinion didn't matter. The Prince had made up his mind.

Edward came down to the entrance to congratulate the two Marines personally as they returned with their prize, an unconscious man in a pair of silk pyjamas that probably cost more than Edward's annual salary. Ten minutes later, the man was transported down to the basement, cuffed to a chair and injected with a stimulant. He looked as if he didn't quite believe his eyes when he saw Edward – and realised that he was a prisoner.

"We can do this the easy way or the hard way," Edward informed him, cursing – again – the lack of truth drugs. It was unlikely that the locals had access to treatments that would nullify them – or kill anyone who was at risk of being forced to talk. "We're going to ask you questions, which you are going to answer. This device" – he snapped the monitor around the prisoner's wrist – "will tell us if you're telling the truth. If you try to lie to us, we'll hit you. Any questions?"

The man stared at him, his pale face flushing with rage. "Return me to my people!"

"Not a chance," Edward said, dryly. The captive's Imperial Standard was poor, but understandable. There had been residents of Earth's undercity with worse accents. "First question; who exactly are you?"

It took thirty minutes to work out a picture of the enemy's command structure, once the captive's defiance had been beaten out of him. The Rajah seemed to have stepped back from control, allowing his son to take the lead; Edward puzzled over it until Leo pointed out that the Rajah was preparing a fallback position. If the whole operation went spectacularly wrong, the Rajah would execute his son and swear blind that he knew nothing about the whole plan. Edward rolled his eyes when they put it together. What sort of idiot would expect him to fall for such obvious nonsense?

But the rest of the news was less encouraging. The locals were bringing up more experienced forces, intending to bring them to bear on the Residency. There were more guns coming, including ones that could be fired from well outside mortar range. It wouldn't be long, the captive said, before the Residency was reduced to rubble and all of the off-worlders were brutally slaughtered. He didn't seem to care about the prospect of starships bombarding the planet from orbit, utterly untouchable by anything on the planet's surface.

"We could go find the Prince," Coleman suggested. He sounded confident, although Edward suspected that losing one aristocrat would have taught the rest of the locals to take better precautions. "It might make it harder for them to coordinate their operations if the Prince is killed."

"Might," Edward said. He looked down at the captive. "Where would we find the Prince?"

"He moves every night," the captive said, nastily. A glance at the monitor showed that he was telling the truth. "You'll never find him."

"We'll see," Edward countered, although he suspected that the captive was right. It wasn't easy to locate a single man in a teeming city. On the other hand, it should be relatively easy to locate the Rajah…he pushed the thought aside for later consideration and stood upright. "And your people will *not* destroy us."

He ignored the snide remark from the prisoner and looked over at Coleman. "Get in touch with the intelligence staff, then keep asking him questions," he ordered. "Concentrate on tactical information, anything that might help us – or the CEF. We don't know how long we have before they bring up the big guns."

The prisoner sneered at him. "Your days are numbered, off-worlder."

Edward looked down at him. "And what," he asked mildly, "will happen to us when the walls fall?"

The prisoner hesitated, then – apparently convinced of the futility of lying – answered the question. "You'll die," he said, shortly. He sounded absolutely convinced of the truth of what he was saying. "And all traces of your influence will be wiped off the face of the planet."

"We shall see," Edward said, glancing down at his wristcom. There were five hours until the dawn, when he expected the bombardment to start again. So far, the shells hadn't inflicted any major damage, but they'd wounded his men and shaken the building's structure. "I think you won't find us an easy nut to chew. And besides, if your people overrun the complex, you will be killed in the crossfire."

With that, he nodded to Coleman and walked out of the room.

CHAPTER TWENTY-FOUR

> This can cause problems. During the lead-up to the Falklands War, the British diplomats failed to make it clear to the Argentinean Government that the British could and would fight to recover the islands. Thus believing that Britain would rant and rage, but not do anything effective, the Argentinean junta gambled on an invasion – and lost.
> -Professor Leo Caesius, *Diplomacy: The Lessons of the Past.*

"Wake up," a voice hissed. Cold water splashed across his face. "Wake up!"

Private Mathew Polk winced, trying to turn away from the water. At some point, they'd removed him from the chair and chained him to the wall, without any medical care or attention. He'd examined himself as best as he could, but all he'd been able to determine was that he wasn't going to be walking out on his own two feet. It was much more likely that he would die in the black hole chamber.

He looked up to see a dark-skinned man bending over him. "I need your name, rank and serial number," the newcomer snapped. "Now!"

Mathew fought down the urge to laugh. *Now* they asked for his name, rank and serial number, the three pieces of information that he had been told he was allowed to tell any potential captors? They'd asked for his name, but they hadn't asked for rank or serial number…had they wised up and decided to treat him in a civilised manner, or had they merely decided to refocus the interrogation?

The newcomer slapped him across the face. "Your name, rank and serial number," he repeated. "And that will be all for the day."

Mathew tasted blood in his mouth, although the pain seemed to blur into the numbness affecting the rest of his body. He was sure that the newcomer was lying, that there would be other questions once he'd shown another chink in his armour, but he needed sleep…bracing himself, he answered the question.

"Very good," the newcomer said. He barked a command in his language as he stood upright and walked back towards the hidden door. "And thank you."

A moment later, the girl arrived with a bowl of…*something* and started to spoon it into his mouth. Puzzled, Mathew accepted it gratefully, all the while trying to understand what was going on. Why had they suddenly demanded his name, rank and serial number? He shifted uncomfortably and the girl started, almost dropping the bowl on his exposed chest. Did they intend to tell the CEF that they'd captured him?

There was no way to know.

―――――

"Here we go again," Private Tomas Leloir muttered, as dawn broke over the city. "I wonder what's coming at us this time."

He gritted his teeth as warm air blew over the city, bringing with it the stench of rotting flesh and burning embers. The second day of the siege had been hellish and he had no reason to expect the third to be any better. It wouldn't be long before the enemy realised that all they had to do to win was keep bombarding the complex throughout the night, preventing the defenders from getting any sleep. Given a few days, they'd be so badly sleep-deprived that they would probably wind up shooting each other.

Rubbing his eyes, he peered into the distance, eyeing the shifting piles of debris suspiciously. NVGs had revealed some people crawling through the ruins, although none of them had come close to the walls. It would be a long time before anyone at the Residency felt safe again…assuming they survived, of course. He tried to believe that the Colonel would find a way out of the trap, but he honestly couldn't think of anything the Colonel could do. It all depended on the CEF battering its way through the enemy's lines and reaching the city before the walls fell.

He blinked as he heard the sound of a trumpet in the distance…and then stared in disbelief as an odd procession came into view. Four men, all wearing red and yellow outfits, carrying a large white flag between them. The leader, the man who was blowing the trumpet, looked nervous; the others seemed to have their eyes fixed firmly on the road. They had to know that the defenders would fire on anyone who came close to the walls, certainly after the truck bombs and the would-be ninjas. And even if that *was* a flag of truce…

"Hold your fire," the Lieutenant ordered, over the tactical network. "But prepare to take them down at my command."

There was a long moment as the strange group came closer, then the Lieutenant lifted a megaphone to his lips and started to speak. "HALT," he ordered. "WHY ARE YOU HERE?"

The group parted to allow one of the men at the rear to step forward. "I bring a message for your commander," he shouted back, although his voice sounded tinny at such a distance. "I request permission to approach the gate."

Tomas tightened his grip on his rifle as the Lieutenant briefly consulted with the Colonel. *He* had no doubt that the whole approach was a ruse, something to convince the defenders to let down their guard long enough for the enemy to launch a surprise attack. But it wasn't his job to make the hard choices, merely to carry out orders. He watched the man carefully, aiming right at his forehead. If the local plotted treachery, he'd be dead before he moved more than a millimetre.

"ONE OF YOU MAY COME TO THE GATE, IF NAKED," the Lieutenant ordered, finally. "THE OTHERS ARE TO FALL BACK."

There was a hasty consultation among the newcomers, which ended with all but one of them heading back the way they had come. The remaining newcomer slowly removed his robe, followed rapidly by a pair of underclothes that looked decent enough to pass for daily wear on Avalon, then stood upright naked. Leaving his clothes behind, he started to walk towards the gate.

"I think I've seen better strippers," one of the soldiers muttered.

Tomas couldn't help himself. He snickered. The sound broke the tension, even though a dozen rifles were still tracking the newcomer. Two of the guards at the gate left their posts and advanced forward, poking the newcomer roughly in delicate places. Tomas felt a flicker of sympathy as they even stuck a medical probe up his anus, before half-dragging him back through the gate and up towards the Residency building. He had grown to hate the locals intensely during the time he'd spent on the planet, but he had to admit that the man had nerve.

"No tip," another soldier commented.

"Keep your eyes on the surroundings," the Sergeant growled. "The show is over."

"He's completely clean," the guard reported, as they escorted the newcomer into one of the smaller rooms. Edward had chosen it because it was completely empty; the newcomer, if he was a spy, would see nothing of importance. "There wasn't even a wire."

Edward nodded, examining the newcomer for himself. He was tall, but his body had run to flab, even if he wasn't really *fat*. This was not a man for whom physical exercise was important, he decided, and probably also a man whose ancestors had been the lucky recipients of a considerable amount of genetic modification. He motioned for the guards to remain outside, then leant against the wall, trying to project an air of informality. It wouldn't do for the newcomer to realise how worried he was about surviving the next few days.

"I am Sivaganga Zamindari," the newcomer said. "With your permission, we will put aside the conventions of diplomacy."

Edward nodded, impatiently. A Zamindari was an important official, probably the equivalent of a local mayor. But then, no official on the planet could hope to command the sheer power of one of the Empire's officials, even if they weren't – nominally – aristocrats. It was probably why they affected so much pomp and circumstance…and the offer to put it aside, he suspected, was more significant than it seemed.

"I will be equally blunt," he answered. "What do you want?"

A smile twitched at the corner of the Zamindari's mouth. "We know that you are holding one of our people captive," he said. "We wish to trade for his recovery."

Edward was surprised, although he knew that he shouldn't have been. It was unpleasant to realise that the locals hadn't even *tried* to bargain for the maids, but when one of their aristocrats were taken hostage they promptly started trying to make bargains. But then, maybe they'd assumed that the maids were damaged goods or that they'd been executed out of hand. Who knew *what* went through aristocratic minds?

"Very well," he said. "What are you prepared to offer? Safe conduct back to the coast? A supply of fresh food and drink? Gold bars?"

"We have one of your people captive," the Zamindari said. Edward felt a flicker of horror, even though he kept his face under strict control. "Private Mathew Polk."

He recited the man's serial number from memory, giving Edward a chance to check it against the files on his terminal. It did match – and Polk was one of the men reported as missing, presumed dead or captured. They'd moved him up from the coastline astonishingly quickly, Edward realised, although it wasn't as if they had to worry about IEDs themselves. But then, they'd probably feared the CEF overrunning their base and liberating the captive.

"I see," Edward said, finally. "And you're prepared to trade him for your aristocrat?"

"Yes," the Zamindari said, simply.

Edward thought fast. No man left behind was one of the core principles of the Marine Corps; if they couldn't count on one another, who *could* they count on? But their captive was a priceless source of intelligence and if they sent him back, who knew when they'd have another chance to ask questions?

Coleman was putting together a plan to go after the Prince, he thought. *What would they offer for him?*

He leaned forward, tapping his terminal to record the conversation. "Do you have any other captives?"

"No," the Zamindari said. His words would be analysed by the intelligence staff, searching for signs of a lie. "And the terms of the bargain are as we have stated them."

"I want our man back and a ten-day truce," Edward said. It was worth an attempt at trying to bargain, although he doubted that he could trust them to stick to any agreement once they could wiggle out of it. "And how – exactly – do you intend to trade him for your man?"

"I am only authorised to offer your man," the Zamindari insisted. "Truces are outside my authority. If you are insistent, I will have to return to the Prince and ask him."

Edward – once again – cursed the price of high command. Every emotion in his body demanded that he accept the bargain, that he liberate one of his men from enemy captivity. But cold logic told him that it would be worthless. Even if Polk was taken into the Residency, the complex might still be overrun…and he'd be giving up his sole source of actionable intelligence. He was mildly surprised that the Prince had agreed to surrender *his* source of intelligence. No doubt their captive was more important than they'd realised.

The decision was *his*. Sure, Polk's immediate CO – Villeneuve – was also in the Residency, but Edward was the one charged with overall command. *He* couldn't allow his emotions to interfere with his judgement. Fighting back an urge to hit the man in front of him, he stood up and started to pace the room. The local eyed him nervously, but said nothing. He seemed a more experienced diplomat than Edward would have expected to find on an isolated world.

"Your offer is rejected," he said, finally. The words tore at his soul, but he forced himself to stay firm. "We would prefer not to trade at this moment."

He forced a cold smile onto his face. "After all, you *must* realise that we would be getting little out of the exchange," he added. "Don't you?"

The Zamindari showed no direct reaction. "I should warn you," he said, instead, "that our captive may fall into the hands of those who hate off-worlders at any moment…"

Edward lunged around and grabbed the man by the throat, hauling him upright and pressing him against the wall. It would have been easy, so easy, to close his fist and crush the man's neck, or simply zap him with his implanted nerve disruptor. But instead he held himself under control, somehow.

"I *know* that you all hate off-worlders," he snarled. "I *know* that you will probably have tortured him, just as you have tortured your own people whom you think have been contaminated merely by *touching* something from off-world. And I *know* that you cannot win this fight. Even if you destroy the Residency, even if you overrun the Garrison, you cannot stop the starships from reducing your world to ash. Do you really believe that Governor Brown would act to prevent the Commonwealth from punishing you for your betrayal? Or that we would act to prevent *him* from punishing you?"

A foul stench reached his nostrils as the Zamindari lost control of his bowels. Disgusted, Edward let go of his neck and let him fall to his knees.

"Take this back to your Prince," Edward hissed. "If he hurts or kills his captive, there will be nothing left of his world, but dust and rocks floating in space. We will destroy him. Tell him that, make sure he understands. There is *no* way out for him, other than abandoning this senseless war."

He stepped backwards and glared down at the cowering man. "Get up," he ordered, curtly. "And go."

The guards came in at Edward's command and hustled the Zamindari towards the door. Edward briefly considered keeping him as a prisoner, then dismissed the thought. As tempting as it was, it would be a sign of bad faith that would make it harder to hold further talks later on. Instead, he watched the man go, then turned and walked back to the situation room. He needed to speak to Villeneuve.

Sivaganga had never felt so intimidated in his life. Even when facing the Rajah or his son, he'd known that rational calculations would suggest to his ruler that wanton killing of aristocrats would undermine his throne far more than anything else. The Prince, as crude and unpleasant as he was, would understand that too. But the off-worlder...shame and rage burned through Sivaganga as he remembered the brief moment of absolute helplessness and fear. The off-worlder had been so *strong*! He could have snapped Sivaganga's neck as if it had been a twig.

He found his clothes where he'd left them, pulled them on and then stumbled away from the Residency, trying hard to keep his trembling under control. The Prince needed a report; he had to know that the off-worlders had refused the bargain…and that they'd threatened the entire planet. It was hard to comprehend, but Lakshmibai's isolation was as much a danger as it was a help. He knew, deep inside, that they had nothing to offer any of the new interstellar powers, nothing that they couldn't just *take*. And now the Empire was gone, even *land* wouldn't be particularly valuable.

Somehow, he managed to make his way to the lines without falling over. The guards met him, keeping their expressions carefully blank, and guided him into a washroom. Sivaganga washed himself clean, knowing that the true stain would never come off his soul. Even the ministrations of the Prince's women weren't enough to make him feel better.

Pushing them aside, he donned a new set of robes and made his way up to the Prince's chamber. The Prince would not respond well, either to the news about the bargain or – worse – that the off-worlders had threatened the entire planet. Carefully, Sivaganga started to work through an edited version of the truth, one that wouldn't have him facing the Prince's rage and fury. He'd have to take what he'd heard to the Rajah and pray that the old man was more understanding than his son.

The Prince listened in silence until Sivaganga had finished explaining that the off-worlders had rejected the bargain. Oddly, he didn't look surprised; it took Sivaganga a moment to realise that the Prince hadn't really expected success, even if he *did* want his ally back. But then, their captive was just a soldier, hardly a fair trade for an aristocrat.

"Then we will dispose of the captive," the Prince said, once Sivaganga had finished. "He has outlived his usefulness."

"My Prince," Sivaganga said, as carefully as he could, "he may yet have a part to play."

The Prince's eyes narrowed. "And you feel that he should be kept alive?"

"I feel that we may be unable to use him if he is dead," Sivaganga answered. There were dark rumours about just *how* the Prince worshipped the gods. Most of them were outright nonsense, he was sure, yet he'd always had a feeling that there was a solid kernel of truth in them somewhere. "A dead man is largely useless."

"Very well," the Prince sneered. If he did practice human sacrifice, he showed no particular enthusiasm for cutting their captive's throat inside a temple. But then, he wasn't stupid, merely a hothead. He understood what Sivaganga hadn't dared say out loud. "We will keep him alive, for now. But he will not be allowed to return to his people."

Sivaganga bowed his head in relief, mentally calculating how best to approach the Rajah without his son realising what he was doing. As strange as it seemed, contingency plans needed to be made. The entire planet was at stake.

And, he knew now, they'd made a dreadful mistake.

In the distance, he could hear the sound of guns booming to life.

CHAPTER TWENTY-FIVE

> However, the British victory was very limited. Argentina was not permanently defeated, nor could they realistically be forced to disarm (even merely to rid themselves of the capability to refight the war at a later date.) The tactical British success was not necessarily a long-term strategic success.
> -Professor Leo Caesius, *Diplomacy: The Lessons of the Past.*

Specialist Gareth Nix fought down the urge to cough as he crawled forwards towards the overhanging ledge. The enemy troops attacking the Residency might be of limited value, but the ones they had patrolling the countryside near the coastline were alarmingly good. Gareth knew that they knew the countryside much better than the Avalon Stormtroopers – and would have a much better idea of what was out of place. The slightest sound could betray his presence.

He smiled grimly to himself. The Stormtroopers were Avalon's first Special Forces team, a replacement – although no one said that out loud – for the diminishing number of Marines. Avalon simply lacked the capability to produce the enhancements and implants the Marines used to make themselves the best of the best, although they'd been told that humans had been producing special operations forces long before human implantation had been developed and put into active service. The Stormtroopers told themselves that their very lack of augmentation made them better than the Marines. Mostly, the Marines kept their own counsel on the issue.

Bracing himself, he reached the ledge and peered down towards the enemy encampment. It looked surprisingly familiar, reminding him of Forward Operating Bases that the Knights had established on Avalon... although he had to admit that similar problems tended to lead to similar solutions. A handful of carefully-camouflaged guns, positioned to open fire on advancing enemy forces, surrounded by a fence and roving guard patrols. The enemy seemed to dislike the idea of fighting at night, but their guards seemed as alert as ever. But then, being forced to fight a long and gruelling insurgency would have taught them a few lessons about staying on guard – or they would have been wiped out by now.

He scanned the encampment with his NVGs, then sent the first microburst transmission back to the FOB. As he expected, there was no reply for several minutes, allowing him to continue studying the enemy position and silently note its weaknesses as well as its strengths. When the reply finally came – confirming that all of the other Stormtroopers were in position – he produced the laser pointer from his belt and carefully pointed it towards the guns. The dot of light it produced was completely invisible to the naked eye, but proper sensors would have no difficulty picking it up from several miles away. Once the dot was firmly positioned on the guns, he sat back and sent a second microburst transmission. All was in readiness...

And all hell was about to break loose.

"The Stormtroopers are in position," Colonel Cindy Macintyre said. "They've designated their targets."

Jasmine let out a breath she hadn't realised that she'd been holding. Lakshmibai had been the first off-world deployment for the Stormtroopers, an exercise they'd expected to be little more than a proof-of-concept for the Avalon-raised operators. God knew that some of the Marines had made snide remarks about Stormtrooper targeting skills, remembering older units that had borne the same name. But they'd proved themselves, slipping through enemy patrols and getting into position to designate targets for the long-range guns.

"Good," she ordered. Dawn was about to break. "Send a signal to the gunners. They are authorised to open fire."

———

"Shells set to smart mode," Captain Thaddeus Rice said. "I say again, all shells set to smart mode."

"Understood," Colonel Robin Lafarge said. "Fire."

The big guns, carefully transported over the causeway and onto the mainland, fired as one, throwing a hail of shells into the air. Her crews didn't wait to see the results of their labours; they started reloading the guns at once, ready to fire a second barrage. She took her eyes off the crews and concentrated, instead, on the live feed from the guidance nodes. If something went wrong, she would only have a few minutes to act before the shells started crashing down randomly. The only real certainty was that the shells would land somewhere on the other side of the front lines.

She smiled as the command network was rapidly established, each shell's seeker head carrying a tiny portion of the burden as they searched for the pinpoint lasers that designated their targets. Once located, the command network rapidly assigned specific targets to specific shells, then started altering their trajectories until they were precisely targeted on the laser dots. The enemy shooting had been imprecise, to say the least; they had little conception of what smart warheads could do.

The first explosion flashed up in the distance as the shell slammed down into its target and detonated. Others followed, wiping out enemy guns, command posts and strongpoints. It wouldn't be complete, Robin knew from bitter experience; enemy bunkers might well be carefully positioned to limit the damage her shells could do. But it would certainly cripple their ability to reply in kind.

She looked back down at the display. Most of the exposed guns had been destroyed, but there were probably others that hadn't been located. She tapped a switch, designating several targets for a second strike, then forwarded the orders to the big guns. Moments later, a second barrage of shells were launched towards their new targets. She was rewarded by a colossal fireball in the distance as something – probably a fuel or ammunition dump – was taken out by a direct hit.

"Reload," she ordered. The Stormtroopers would no doubt have additional targets for her, once the enemy started to react. They'd know the CEF was planning to break out and strike towards the capital city, forcing them to take whatever steps were required to stop the newcomers. "And then wait for targets of opportunity."

In the distance, the flames were still rising up towards the lightening sky.

Gareth suppressed the urge to whoop and cry hurrah as the enemy gun position vanished in a sheet of flame. He ducked down instead, praying that a piece of flaming debris wouldn't come down too close to his head, while listening carefully to the command channel. It was quite possible that the enemy would start flushing out the Stormtroopers – if, of course, they realised that they were there. There was no way to know what conclusions the enemy might draw.

He peeked back over the ledge and smiled to himself as he saw the devastation. The guns were gone, while the handful of tents were burning brightly; bodies lay everywhere as the enemy soldiers attempted to cope with the sudden crisis. No doubt they'd believed that the CEF would remain in its pocket, rather than trying to take the offensive…or that it would take longer than three days to prepare the rebels to take part in the fighting. But the CEF hadn't had the luxury of time to make its preparations.

"All primary targets destroyed," he muttered into his communicator, and then started to crawl away from the burning camp. "Looking for secondary targets now."

The land seemed to come alive with the sound of firing – and explosions. He kept to the shadows, wondering just what the enemy thought they were shooting at – and smiling every time a shell rocketed in from the CEF and gave the enemy a really bad day. Not too bad, he told himself, for gunnery crews that had spent five years trapped on a tiny island, with only a handful of local girls for company. The ground shook violently as *something* detonated in the distance, sending yet another fireball billowing into the air.

He paused as he saw moving objects against the darkness, heading west. Tanks, he realised mutely; enemy tanks, hoping to intercept the CEF before it managed to break through the lines and destroy the enemy's ability to wage war. He rapidly set up his laser pointer and called in the strike, asking for a full spread of shells. Moments later, the tanks were destroyed in rolling series of explosions, leaving most of them nothing more than burning wreckage. The stench of burning flesh reached him moments later and he clipped on his mask, allowing him to slip through the chaos and make his way eastwards. Behind him, the world burned.

"The drones are reporting near-complete destruction of the enemy guns," Cindy reported. "If any others show themselves, orbit station will pick them up and we'll take them out quick."

"Good," Jasmine said. The first stage of the operation was going according to plan, something that bothered her. A plan that was going perfectly, in her experience, was generally charging headlong towards a pitfall. "And the enemy commanders?"

"Being suppressed," Cindy said. "Every time we pick up a transmission, we hurl a shell at the source. Even if they stop standing next to the transmitters, they will have some real problems coordinating their forces."

Jasmine nodded. The enemy commanders were about to learn the true meaning of fog-of-war. They wouldn't know what was happening outside their eyesight, ensuring that they couldn't coordinate a proper response to her advance. She had no doubt that individual enemy units would fight bravely to slow down her forces, but isolated from their fellows all they could do was die bravely.

"Then order the ground forces to advance," she ordered, pushing down her doubts into a locked compartment of her mind. "And provide fire support as necessary."

Corporal Sharon Jones looked at her targeting systems as the Landshark lurched into life, its colossal treads chewing up the ground as it started to move eastwards. The integrated battlespace management system obligingly provided her with a list of long-range strikes made against enemy positions, followed rapidly by a warning that many enemy strongpoints might have remained undetected. If nothing else, the absence of vehicles or radio transmitters would make it harder for them to be spotted before they opened fire.

The CO had made the deliberate decision to stay off the roads, even though it ensured that they would have a bumpier ride. Sharon approved of his decision; the Landshark was heavy enough to ensure that the enemy road network – which was primitive at the best of times – would be rendered completely useless if the tank drove down it. Some of the smaller tanks in Avalon's inventory were light enough not to have to worry, but none of them had been attached to the CEF.

She braced herself as the seconds ticked by, knowing that they could hardly hope to sneak up on the enemy soldiers. The engine might be quiet, but the sound of them crashing their way through the foliage and crushing trees and rocks under their treads could not be concealed. A shiver ran down her spine as the vehicle lurched, moving through a tiny stream as though it wasn't even there; somewhere out there, the enemy were waiting. They would be fighting back…

An alert flashed up on the display. The enemy guns – those that were left – were firing desperately, although they no longer had the sheer weight of fire that had stopped the CEF in its tracks three days ago. And they were dying almost as quickly as they revealed themselves; they might be able to hide inactive guns under camouflage, but every time they fired a shell they revealed their position to the orbiting sensors or the drones. It ensured their rapid destruction by the CEF's guns.

"Contact," she snapped, as two antitank rockets raced towards them, followed by a hail of RPGs. The hull thrummed as the weapons slammed into the tank, but inflicted no damage apart from minor scratches. "Request permission to engage."

"Permission granted," the CO said, as more rockets impacted against the hull. "Take them out."

Sharon selected the machine guns mounted on the lower armour, swung them around and fired on the enemy strongpoint. It had been solidly-built, given the time and materials the enemy engineers had had to work with, but the strongpoint disintegrated as the machine gun bullets tore through the flimsy protection. The rain of rockets and other improvised weapons stopped abruptly. Her sensors tracked a handful of men fleeing for their lives, but she ignored them. They couldn't do the tank any harm.

"More strongpoints up ahead," the driver observed, as the tank started to move up an incline. A thunderous explosion shook the vehicle, but the mine had been detonated too soon to inflict any real damage. "They're dug in well."

"Take them out," the CO ordered. "And then take us onwards."

———

Michael silently admired the devastation the tanks had left in their wake as they charged through the enemy lines, heading eastwards. Strongpoints had been broken open, guns and tanks had been smashed as if they had been made of paper and the enemy had been heavily demoralised. Hundreds of dead bodies were scattered everywhere, some clearly not even remotely prepared for a fight. He didn't know why the enemy were reluctant to fight at night, but it had worked in the CEF's favour. Their enemies had been taken completely by surprise.

He led the way up the incline, watching for traps as they checked strongpoint after strongpoint. The tanks might have smashed their way through the enemy lines, but he knew better than to think that they'd killed all of the enemy soldiers. Given time, they might regroup and start counterattacking. Or, for that matter, try to slip westwards as the front lines moved past them and hit the CEF's supply lines. A burst of gunfire from a half-smashed strongpoint forced him to duck, then motion for two of his soldiers to pin the enemy gunners down while he crawled around their position and threw a grenade into their hiding place. The explosion killed two enemy soldiers, but left a third mortally wounded. Michael hesitated, then shot the badly-burned man in the head. It was, he told himself, a mercy kill.

The sun rose in the sky as they pressed onwards, taking out dozens of enemy strongpoints. They'd done an excellent job of emplacing them, he had to admit; if they hadn't been so badly hammered by the artillery or the tanks, it would have been a very costly assault. He stopped to catch his breath, then crawled around yet another smashed strongpoint. Ahead of him, he saw an enemy soldier stumble into view, his hands in the air.

"No weapon," Sergeant Grieves observed.

Michael nodded and raised his voice, barking out a command in the local language. If he was pronouncing it correctly – whatever the locals spoke seemed to change its meaning unless the pronunciation was exact – he was telling the local to keep his hands in the air and surrender... unless he wanted to die. Michael had honestly never realised what a blessing Imperial Standard was until he'd had to learn a handful of phrases in a strange new language. At least with Imperial Standard everyone spoke the same tongue.

The local babbled something Michael couldn't follow, then waved towards yet another strongpoint. A line of battered-looking men emerged from the shelter, keeping their hands in the air. Judging by their faces, they expected to be shot out of hand, rather than taken prisoner. None of them carried obvious weapons, but Michael had been briefed on how some fanatics would cheerfully attack under flags of truce – or surrender. One bastard with a grenade and bad intentions could provoke a massacre and ensure that future surrenders wouldn't be accepted.

He keyed his radio as the flow of enemy troops came to an end. "We have thirty-one enemy troops trying to surrender," he reported. He motioned for the enemy soldiers to sit down, keeping their hands in the air. It wouldn't be very comfortable for them, but he was more concerned with the prospect of treachery. "Can you arrange a POW pick-up?"

"That's a roger," the CO said. "Secure the prisoners, then detail two of your men to act as guards. They'll be taken back to the POW camp."

Michael nodded and started to issue orders. Carefully, the prisoners were searched, then secured with plastic ties. They'd have to sit in the mud and wait for pick-up, but at least they would be alive. And, if others saw prisoners being treated decently, they would feel encouraged to surrender themselves. Or so the theory went.

Once the POWs were secured, they continued their advance through the enemy lines.

"We've had quite a few surrenders," Cindy reported. "Pick-up crews are on the way."

Jasmine looked over at her. "Any officers?"

"Not as far as we know," Cindy said. "We don't have the manpower to spare for prisoner interrogation."

Excuses, Jasmine thought, coldly. It wasn't entirely fair, but she didn't *feel* fair. Intelligence officers were always complaining about not having enough manpower…but then, Cindy *did* have a point. There were only a handful of officers, all from the garrison, who spoke the local tongue and almost all of them were needed elsewhere. If they *had* picked up an enemy officer, he would probably remain unidentified until later. Much later.

We could get the rebels to assist, she thought. *But could we trust them not to abuse their prisoners?*

She shook her head and turned back to the display. The advance was going well; the main enemy line had been breached in two places, allowing her forces to advance and smash the enemy's reserve forces. They wouldn't have a chance to counterattack, she told herself, while *she* would have a chance to prevent them from withdrawing and regrouping. Colonel Stalker would be pleased, even though there were ninety miles to go – including one city that *had* to be taken – before they reached the capital. But they would get there.

Very good, she told herself, as another enemy line was broken. *But will it be in time to save Private Polk?*

CHAPTER
TWENTY-SIX

Unfortunately, even after liberal applications of the big stick, problems don't always go away. In fact, it is quite rare for a nation to be so completely eradicated that it no longer exists even in potential. Poland was divided up between various European powers throughout history, yet it managed to return to independence several times.
 -Professor Leo Caesius, *Diplomacy: The Lessons of the Past.*

General Abhey had gone to bed a satisfied man. Siding so openly with the Prince was a risk – the Rajah was far from dead – but it seemed to have paid off handsomely. He'd stopped the off-worlder force dead in its tracks, for which he had been richly rewarded and promised far more, once the off-worlders were completely defeated. Indeed, he'd even come up with a plan to ensure their rapid and complete defeat.

Now…he found himself utterly out of touch with most of his forces, while the enemy were clearly advancing towards him. It hadn't taken long for him to realise that every radio transmission brought destruction in its wake, while the landlines he'd used to communicate between strongpoints had been cut or otherwise disrupted by the enemy. Only a handful of lines had survived, hardly enough to coordinate his forces.

He stared down at the map, trying to visualise the enemy advance before dismissing it as a useless effort. The shortage of intelligence meant that he couldn't say anything for certain, not even which units had survived the first bombardment. He'd sent off runners to nearby units, hoping to re-establish contact, but most of them had simply not returned.

It was impossible to tell if they had been killed or if they'd taken the opportunity to desert.

Placing his headquarters inside a town, he was coming to realise, might have been his sole smart move. The enemy seemed oddly reluctant to fire on his positions near civilian buildings, even ones that had been evacuated of their occupants and turned into makeshift barracks. It would certainly even the odds a little, he told himself, as he sent half of his personal guard to join the soldiers preparing a desperate defence of the town. But it was very much starting to look as though the enemy had shattered his lines.

"Take a radio transmitter to an isolated location, then broadcast a generalised signal," he ordered a runner. The young man didn't seem to realise the implications for him personally, thankfully. "The code word is Vishnu."

"Yes, My General," the young man said.

Abhey watched him go, knowing that the runner would be lucky if he managed to get out one or two repetitions of the code word before the enemy killed him. But maybe he'd be luckier than his commander. The Prince wouldn't be happy that the enemy had launched their offensive and would probably take it out on his former favourite. All the rank and money and women – he'd been promised a wife from the Rajah's household – could be taken away just as easily.

Plan Vishnu had been conceived as the ultimate fallback position. His troops – at least the ones below Pradesh - would scatter, avoiding the enemy tanks while reforming behind their lines. Once they were ready, they would harass the enemy supply lines, forcing them to divert forces to cover their rear. In the meantime, the reinforcements would turn Pradesh into a fortress that would bleed the off-worlders white.

He looked over at the last of his personal guard and scowled. "We need to make our way to Pradesh," he said, flatly. He'd have to abandon his uniform; thankfully, there were already so many refugees heading in countless directions that they'd probably pass unnoticed, as long as they didn't *look* like senior officers. "The rest of the guard can hold the town as long as possible."

Another runner came in, gasping for breath. "Hold your message," Abhey ordered. "I need you to take one to the demolition crew on the dam. They're to blow the dam as quickly as possible."

If nothing else, he told himself, a sudden torrent of water should definitely slow the off-worlders down.

The final enemy line broke as the tanks found its weak spot, then crashed right through it into relatively clear lands beyond. Michael followed, watching grimly as countless enemy soldiers fought and died – or tried to surrender. A number of would-be prisoners were actually gunned down by their own fellows, forcing the remainder to stand and fight. Michael shook his head in disbelief, then pressed onwards. Behind them, the Warriors advanced, providing fire support if necessary.

"Hold position," the CO ordered, calmly. "Take prisoners if possible; if not, take a moment to catch your breath."

"They must be trying to smash the rest of their lines," the Sergeant muttered. "And they don't want us to get too far ahead."

"Must be," Michael said, taking advantage of the pause to take a long swig of water. The sound of shooting in the distance was slowly tapering off, although he had his doubts that *all* the enemy had been captured or wiped out. There were simply too many of them. "The CO won't want cracks in our lines."

He peered into the distance, observing a thin river slowly meandering its way down to the sea. There were four bridges in view, all damaged badly enough to suggest that the engineers should put together a pontoon bridge rather than try to repair the local construction work. It struck him that there was something odd about the bridges, but he didn't quite understand what he was seeing. The bridges seemed to have been built for a far wider river.

"I wouldn't have thought that they could build a dam," Briggs observed, as the helicopter followed the river northwards. "Don't they need modern technology to build?"

"Not if you're willing to spend money and lives building one with hand-powered tools," Sergeant Andrew Wyrick observed. The dam was larger than anything on Avalon, although there was something curiously primitive about it. But then, the locals *had* tried to abandon technology altogether. "And this one clearly isn't intended to do more than help store water for the fields."

He frowned as he stared down at the dam. Dozens of tiny figures were running over it, doing...*something*. It didn't seem as though the dam *needed* maintenance...it struck him, in a moment of absolute horror, that the enemy were preparing to blow the dam. The reservoir didn't seem very full, but it wouldn't matter. Enough water was about to come downstream to severely delay the offensive.

"Alert," he snapped, switching to the priority channel. "They're planning to blow the dam; I say again, they're planning to blow the dam."

A moment later, there was a puff of smoke from the structure. For a long second, Andrew thought that the dam was strong enough to resist demolition, even with modern explosives carefully placed by experts. And then a section of the dam started to crumble, allowing water to flood through the gap and into the riverbed. The pressure on the weakening structure intensified, further wrecking the structure...as he watched, the outpouring of water brought down enough of the dam to allow it to flow freely. A torrent of water spilled downwards, heading towards the sea.

"Correction," he snapped, as he watched the flood heading westwards. "They've blown the dam; I say again, they've blown the dam."

Jasmine swallowed a curse as she saw the live feed from the helicopter – and the drones. A near-tidal wave of water was making its way downstream, spilling out over the riverbanks and flooding farmland that the locals would desperately need...and threatening some of her men with complete destruction. They'd discussed the possibility of the enemy destroying the dam, but they hadn't taken it seriously. A rational foe would know that it would hurt their own ability to recover as much as it would threaten the CEF.

These bastards don't care, she thought, numbly. She could see some advantages for a completely heartless enemy in destroying the dam. Starvation would help terminate the revolution and allow the local government to restore order relatively easily. *Why do we keep forgetting that they don't care?*

"Order our forces to take cover," she ordered, sharply. "And tell them to brace for impact."

"Get into the Warriors," Michael bellowed, as the news came in. His men jumped to their feet and ran for the vehicles, opening the hatches and diving into the infantry compartments. "Hurry!"

He understood, now, the significance of the bridges. The river had been dammed – but the dam would have to release some of the water from time to time, if only to ensure that it didn't overflow. Normally, he suspected, they would release the water gradually, making certain that a sudden flood wouldn't damage their infrastructure. Now…the entire dam was collapsing into rubble.

The Warrior came to life, motoring to find what cover it could as the ground began to rumble. Michael braced himself as the shaking grew worse, then swore out loud as the vehicle rocked violently. For a terrifying moment, it felt as if they were going to be swept away before the pressure was suddenly gone. He shook his head, then opened the hatch and jumped outside, weapon in hand. His men followed him.

He drew in a breath as he surveyed the devastation. The land was soaked; trees and crops had been utterly destroyed. Bodies had been washed into the riverbed and left there; the remains of the bridges had been swept away, leaving nothing left for the engineers to rebuild. It struck him, suddenly, that no matter how much damage the flood had done to the CEF, it would have done much more to the local forces. They hadn't had Warriors or Landshark tanks to protect them.

The prisoners, he thought, numbly. *They were exposed to the water.*

His radio buzzed. "Hold position," the CO ordered. "We are assessing the situation."

"Send bridging crews," Michael advised. "We can get across before they realise that we're coming for them."

"Jesus," Cindy breathed.

Jasmine couldn't disagree. The massive flood hadn't inflicted as much damage on her forces as she had feared, but it had devastated the countryside. In its wake, there would definitely be starvation – and anarchy. If she had been dependent on the country farms for supplies, she would have been in some trouble. As it was, it was merely a headache.

"Tell our forces to continue to push forward," she ordered, finally. "I want them across the first river before the enemy have a chance to respond."

The torrent of water hadn't been enough to damage the Landshark, but Sharon and her comrades had had a nasty moment when the onrushing water had threatened to undermine their position and send them rolling downwards to the sea. In its wake, the land was devastated – but the Landshark was utterly untouched, along with its fellows. The driver gunned the engine at the CO's command and sent it forward, towards the remains of the river. It was nowhere near deep enough to provide a barrier to the tank.

Bullets started to ping off the armour as the tank advanced through the water and onto the far side. Sharon scanned for the enemy snipers, located them hiding in the trees and fired a long burst from the machine gun back at them. The enemy had been smart and dumb at the same time; smart enough to realise that the trees on the incline would miss the flood, yet too dumb to realise that hiding in the trees merely made them easy targets. Sharon watched as their bodies vaporised under the hail of bullets, along with the trees themselves.

"Bridging crews are on their way," the CO said, as the other tanks took up position in support. "The ground-pounders will be crossing soon afterwards."

"Thought they could get Warriors through the water," the driver commented. "Or are they afraid of getting their feet wet?"

The CO gave him a reproving look. Sharon knew what he was thinking, even if he didn't say it out loud. The Imperial Army had tolerated a certain…disdain between tankers and the infantry, but the Knights had been warned in no uncertain terms that such disdain would not be tolerated. Besides, while Sharon was warm and dry inside her tank, the infantry were slogging their way through the mud and ducking bullets that could actually hurt them.

"They're not all mounted in Warriors," the CO said, finally. "And our trucks are not capable of crossing the river so effectively."

―――――

Michael detailed half of his Warriors to cross through the river and set up position on the other side, then waited for the bridging crews to arrive with barely-concealed impatience. The command network told him that reinforcements were already on the way, but they would need a bridge to get across the river. It also warned that large numbers of enemy troops appeared to be trying to advance on the far side, although very slowly… he had a feeling that the enemy had probably realised that the Landshark tanks were waiting for them.

The engineers hadn't been combat-tested either, but he was relieved to note that they were performing very well. Piece by piece, a bridge was assembled from supplies brought on trucks and pushed out over the water. Once it was in place, a Warrior drove across the structure and reached the far side, confirming that it was safe. It felt oddly rickety to Michael as he strode over the river, followed by the rest of his squad, but it would do. There would be time to get men and supplies over before it had to be replaced.

He looked up as he saw the helicopter swooping overhead, heading east. It always made him feel better when he knew that there was friendly aircraft overhead, even though the exercises they'd run had been brutally clear on the limitations of air power. In the distance, he saw shells exploding among the enemy forces, driving them back from the river. Beyond that, according to the map he'd glanced at while he was in the Warrior, there was a mid-sized town.

"Get back into the vehicles," he ordered, once reinforcements had arrived. Two new Warriors would be detailed to protect the bridge, along with three platoons of infantry and a mobile air defence system. It was unlikely that the enemy would manage an airstrike, but losing the bridge would – at best – delay the advance. At worst, the forward edge of the CEF would be cut off, unable to retreat. "We have to advance against the town."

Ekachraka rattled his cuff mournfully as he drove the truck along the drenched road. The off-worlders had taken him and his family into his service – they'd provided both food and protection – but they didn't trust him, not completely. They'd cuffed one of his hands to the wheel, with the droll comment that if he plotted treachery, his own life would be forfeit. They hadn't said that his family would die afterwards, but he'd known what they'd meant. Why else would they take his family into protective custody if they didn't want to exact revenge if he betrayed his new employers?

He couldn't believe the devastation the flood had left in its wake. Bodies were scattered everywhere; homes and entire villages had been smashed flat, their inhabitants killed or forced to flee. Surely only off-worlders could do something so evil…but he knew precisely what the Rajah had been trying to do to the rebels for years. Devastating the countryside worked better for the government than for the off-worlders.

The convoy came to a halt outside a badly-battered town. A handful of off-worlders jumped down from the lead vehicle and marched towards a warehouse that – somehow – had survived the flood. Ekachraka watched as they opened the door, revealing a mass of prisoners. They looked like drowned rats, he realised to his horror, as it became clear that the truckers were going to be transporting them back to the POW camps. He wanted to object – he knew that his lifespan would be radically shortened if loyalists realised that he was serving the off-worlders – but he knew better than to try. One by one, the prisoners were searched and then shoved into the vehicles. He couldn't help feeling that they looked altogether too wretched to threaten anyone.

He did his best to ignore the moans and brief bitter comments as he put the truck back into gear, following the other vehicles back towards the POW camps. If nothing else, he told himself, it would give him a chance to see his family…if the off-worlders were feeling merciful. He'd had only one brief meeting since entering their service.

A line of trucks passed the convoy, heading in the other direction. Ekachraka shivered as he realised that they were transporting rebel fighters, who were waving their weapons in the air as they approached the battlefield. They looked undisciplined, certainly when compared to the off-world soldiers, but he knew that they would fight. And he knew what they would do to him and his family, if the off-worlders failed to protect them. One way or another, he knew, he was committed.

He glanced in the mirror, looking at the prisoners. They definitely *seemed* beaten, between whatever the off-worlders had done to capture them and the massive flood. Maybe it wasn't too much to hope that the off-worlders would win the war. And then…everyone knew that off-worlders were inherently dishonest. The Imperial Army had promised to bring peace and yet somehow peace had never materialised. What would happen if these new off-worlders left, abandoning those who had served them to the mercies of the low-caste rebels?

But it didn't matter. One way or the other, there was no choice. He was committed.

He could only pray that the off-worlders kept their word.

CHAPTER
TWENTY-SEVEN

This was also true, to some extent, of Germany in the 20th Century. Crushing defeat in 1918 left the Germans down, but they rebuilt their power enough for a second major European war in 1939 – and, when they lost for a second time, they still returned to power decades later.

-Professor Leo Caesius, *Diplomacy: The Lessons of the Past.*

It would not have pleased the Prince, Sivaganga knew, if he'd realised that Sivaganga had taken advantage of a brief opportunity to insert his own man into the military command centre. Indeed, he would be very angry, assuming that it was the first step in a plan to subvert his authority and perhaps even rebel against the Rajah. But Sivaganga had needed information, particularly when the Prince's loud reports from the front were so clearly fabrications. If the number of off-worlders the Prince had claimed killed were added together, the defenders of the Residency would have been wiped out several times over.

But learning that the enemy force on the coast had suddenly launched an offensive was definitely worth the risk, he decided as he pulled himself out of bed and called for servants to help dress him. The Prince was probably deciding how best to massage the news to his advantage, even though it was hard to imagine *any* good spin on the information. If the spy was telling the truth, the front lines had crumbled and the enemy were advancing rapidly towards Pradesh. By the time the messenger arrived with an urgent summons, Sivaganga was ready to head towards the Prince's current centre of operations.

In the semi-darkness outside his mansion, armed guards thronged the streets, eyeing each other suspiciously. Most of them wore imperial livery, but a number clearly belonged to various aristocratic families. Seeing them here, inside the city walls, was worrying. It suggested that the families no longer trusted the Imperial Family to guard their lives – and that the Rajah didn't feel strong enough to try to remove them from his city. Sivaganga couldn't help but see it as a sign of the beginning of the end.

He scowled as he heard the sound of gunfire echoing out from the Residency. The off-worlders had devices that let them see in the dark, like cats. It was the only explanation for the fact that none of their attempts to sneak up under cover of darkness had worked, which hadn't stopped the Prince from continuing to order the suicide missions. A definite haze of desperation hung over the city and, outside the walls, the untouchables were restless. It would not be long, Sivaganga suspected, before they rioted again.

The Prince's current home was surrounded by so many armed guards that he might as well have hung a flag from the rooftop announcing his presence. Sivaganga was escorted down from the coach, searched briefly but firmly, then escorted down five flights of stairs into a basement. The Prince was standing in front of a large wooden table, pretending to study a map. Someone had drawn largely-fictitious military movements on the paper in red ink.

"The enemy have opened their offensive from the coast," the Prince said, without preamble.

Sivaganga tried hard to seem surprised without overacting. The Prince would be suspicious if he showed no reaction, but equally suspicious if he showed too *much* surprise. Instead, he looked down on the map, carefully noting the arrows that suggested that the planet's armoured forces were engaging the enemy and pushing them back, inflicting heavy casualties in the process. The Prince honestly couldn't be bothered to think of a good lie.

"However, it raises a problem," the Prince added. "We need to divert forces to Pradesh, which means taking the pressure off the Residency."

Sivaganga had to draw on every year of his considerable experience to keep his expression blank, despite the sheer scale of the insult. Just how stupid did the Prince think he was? If the enemy army was being forced back, why did they need to reinforce *Pradesh*? The city was forty miles east of the conflict zone, half-hidden within a fearsome mountain range. There was no logical reason to send additional troops there... unless, of course, the military update the Prince had given him was a complete fabrication.

He tried to think of a question that would needle the Prince a little, without pushing him too far, then dismissed it.

"I wish you to speak with the other families," the Prince said. "You will inform them that they are to dispatch their household troops to assist with the siege."

This time, Sivaganga was *sure* that he showed an unwanted reaction. If the Prince thought that the other aristocratic families would obey just like *that*, he was wrong – dreadfully wrong. They'd see it as an admission of weakness and move against the Rajah, starting the civil war Sivaganga feared. Indeed, if they realised just how bad the military situation actually was, they might just launch a coup and try to surrender to the off-worlders. The hell of it was that he was honestly wondering if that might be the best possible solution.

"They would need to be convinced that it was in their best interests," he said, slowly. "And their forces are mainly infantry, unsuited to the task of engaging armoured enemy forces."

It was worse than that, he knew. The family who had ruled Jhansi had lost most of their wealth in the wake of the refugee settlement and the Imperial Army's 'peacekeeping' operation. They were still aristocrats, but they could barely raise the money to keep their palaces in the capital intact, let alone fund household troops. He couldn't see the other families being willing to send their troops away from the capital, not when the off-worlders would chew them to pieces. It was far more likely that they would refuse to comply altogether.

On the face of it, the Rajah had a far more powerful army he could use to threaten them. But with most of his army engaged in combat with the enemy forces, the aristocrats would enjoy unprecedented freedom. Who knew *what* they might do with it?

"You are known for having a silver tongue," the Prince said. "Convince them that it is in their best interests."

"They would want specifics of our military success before committing themselves," Sivaganga said, smoothly. Unless he missed his guess, the official version would have so many contradictions that *someone* would be bound to challenge it. "May I make a counter-proposal?"

The Prince eyed him suspiciously, but gave his assent.

"Suggest to them that they share in the glory of destroying the Imperial Residency," Sivaganga proposed. "They can send their troops to join those assaulting the walls, freeing up imperial soldiers to head to the coast."

There was a long cold moment when he thought he'd finally gone too far. The Prince's face darkened so rapidly that Sivaganga was sure that his next command would be to call for the headsman, aristocratic victim or no. But the Prince controlled himself – somehow – and leaned forward. His voice, when he spoke, was very calm. Too calm.

"The Rajah was shamed when the off-worlders first established themselves in our capital," the Prince hissed. "We will not share the glory of finally removing their taint with *anyone*."

You'll have to decide soon, Sivaganga thought, coldly. *Do you want to destroy the Residency before it is too late – or not?*

He could understand the Prince's dilemma. The lands between Maharashtra and Pradesh had been restless, ever since the first rumours had spread from farmer to farmer, but so far the untouchables had refrained from open revolt. Indeed, the various families who owned most of the land had been reinforcing their security battalions in the region, just to ensure that any revolt was nipped in the bud. But if Pradesh fell to the off-worlders and their rebel allies, the untouchables would revolt and the entire countryside would go up in flames. The off-worlders *had* to be stopped at Pradesh.

But if he pulled his forces away from the Residency, he weakened the Rajah's position – and, by extension, his own.

"It *would* make them feel as though they were making a valued contribution," Sivaganga said, smoothly. "And it would free up your forces to wipe out the remaining off-worlders."

The Prince glowered at him. "Speak to them," he ordered. "Tell them that the Rajah demands their service. And tell them that if they refuse, I will not forget."

Fool, Sivaganga thought. *You're in no position to threaten them.*

But he knew he couldn't say that out loud. Instead, he bowed and backed out of the room.

The Prince, already turning back to his imaginary maps, didn't even see him go.

Private Mathew Polk was all too aware that he'd lost track of time. Chained to the wall, kept permanently in semi-darkness, it was impossible to tell just how long he'd been a prisoner. His body felt permanently sore, which suggested that he hadn't been held for more than a few days, but his universe had shrunk to the prison cell. The only diversion from his own thoughts – and madness – was his nursemaid. Her tender ministrations were all that he had to look forward to, ever since they'd stopped the interrogations.

He looked up as he heard the door creaking open – and winced as he realised that it wasn't his nursemaid. Instead, it was a tall pale-skinned man with a beard, wearing robes that made him look like a colour-blind peacock. The thought almost made Mathew smile, before he remembered where he was. Anyone wearing such clothes had to be very important indeed.

"I sent the guards away for a few minutes," the newcomer said. "I have a question to ask you."

Mathew hesitated. The guards were gone? If the newcomer was telling the truth, he could escape…but he was still chained to the wall and barely able to move, even without the cuffs and shackles. Without them, he might just be able to make to the door before the guards returned and discovered that he'd escaped. He pushed the wistful thought out of his mind and looked up at his guest. Surprisingly, he thought he saw a hint of compassion in the man's eyes.

"You have a commander," the newcomer said. "How do I get in touch with him?"

"I told you who the overall commander is," Mathew reminded him. "And you seem to have him under siege."

"That could be problematic," the man admitted. "Who is in command of the invading army?"

Mathew blinked. Invading army? The CEF?

"Yes, your friends are advancing," the man snapped. He ignored the hope that had to be plainly visible on Mathew's face. "Who should we talk to in your army?"

"Brigadier Yamane is in command of the CEF," Mathew said, finally. He was sure that he had told them that already, even though he wasn't sure why this man wanted to talk to him privately, "But you would need to make some concessions before…*he*…even agreed to talk."

"Thank you," the man said, standing up. "Don't mention this conversation to anyone and I'll see what I can do about getting you out of this cell."

Mathew watched him go, wondering if he dared hope. In the end, he told himself that it was all he had left.

Edward peered out over the city as dawn rose for the fourth day. The enemy had restricted themselves to shelling and probing attacks for the last day, but the drones had revealed more forces massing, just out of mortar range. And they'd been sweeping the city so thoroughly that Edward had refused to allow Blake Coleman to set out on another disruption mission. It wasn't worth the risk of losing him.

He rubbed his jaw where Villeneuve had struck him, feeling the dull ache pervading his body. In truth, he had expected Polk's CO to take a swing at him; he'd allowed the blow to land partly, although he was loath to admit it to himself, because he felt he deserved it. Polk might not have been precisely abandoned, but Edward knew better than to think the lost Private had any real hope of survival. Under the circumstances, he couldn't blame Villeneuve for throwing a punch. It suggested the kind of loyalty to his men that would, in a fair universe, have taken him far.

I'll have to have him promoted, Edward told himself. In the Empire, taking a swing at a CO was an automatic dishonourable discharge – if not a sentence to a penal world – but the Commonwealth couldn't afford to lose a good officer. And besides, Edward rather understood. If the roles had been reversed, he would probably have done the same thing.

You mouthed off to the Grand Senate, he thought. *And that got you sent out here.*

Lakshmibai would be a strange place to die, he knew. It was of no great importance; not to the Empire, nor to any of its successor states. Even the star's location was poor for any sort of basing rights – and besides, installing a military base elsewhere in the system would be no great difficulty. Only pirates would be interested in the system, and only then insofar as they could raid the surface for women and food supplies. Other than that, the locals could have their insular existence and no one would give a damn.

"Edward," a voice said, from behind him.

"Leo," Edward said. He turned to face the Professor, who looked very out of place on the rooftop. "You shouldn't be up here."

The Professor looked surprised. "I thought they weren't shooting at us at night."

Edward waved a hand towards the rising sun, then shrugged. "They don't seem to try to sneak snipers up until dawn breaks," he said, leading the way towards the hatch. "But we really should be under cover."

He didn't say anything else until they were back in the stairwell, heading down towards the Situation Room. "How's Fiona?"

"Coping, I think," the Professor said. "But she still gets nervous every time a shell whistles in and explodes."

"Understandable," Edward said. Most of the soldiers were used to being under fire, even if it was only in training, but the civilians didn't have that luxury. "This wasn't quite the luxury vacation she was promised."

The Professor snorted. "How do you manage to keep so calm?"

Edward smiled at him. "My first Captain used to say that *he* was in command, and if there were any panicking to be done *he'd* do it," he explained. It had been a joke, of sorts; Marines who were inclined to panic under fire were generally sorted out during Boot Camp and politely, but firmly told that the military was not a good career choice. "That kept me going until the day I woke up and discovered that I was in command."

"Oh," the Professor said. He smiled, wanly. "Colonel…can we get out of this?"

Edward shrugged. "The CEF is hammering the enemy hard," he said, as reassuringly as he could. It was still seventy miles between the CEF's current location and the enemy capital, including a city that *had* to be taken by storm. If it had been a straight drive, they'd be with them in an hour…but it wasn't going to be that simple. "They'll have to decide if they want to take us out more than they want to stop the CEF."

He glanced into a room and saw one of his soldiers snuggling with one of the maids. The rules against fraternisation seemed pointless when the odds were strongly against them getting out of the trap, although he'd made it clear that if any if the soldiers forced a maid into bed there would be hell to pay. Or, for that matter, if a soldier allowed himself to be distracted from his duties.

A soldier who won't fuck won't fight, he thought, remembering one half of the saying. It was true, but so was the other half. *A soldier who fucks when he should be fighting won't be fucking or fighting in the future.*

Shaking his head, he looked back at the Professor. "I wish I could be more confident," he admitted, "but these people are irrational. I don't know which way they will jump."

Leo felt his heart sink as the Colonel outlined the problem. He'd known just what they were facing, but he'd hoped that the Colonel might think differently. But instead, the Colonel had agreed with his private assessment of their situation.

"Thank you," he said, finally.

He left the Colonel behind and walked down to the very lowest level. They'd been lucky, he'd been told; as a married couple, they'd been given a room to share. It was tiny, compared to the luxury bedroom they didn't dare use, but compared to the sleeping quarters the soldiers were sharing it was luxury incarnate. Inside, Fiona was lying on a blanket, fast asleep. He closed the door and looked down on her.

Asleep, the tension that had lined her features had drained away, reminding him of the girl he'd fallen in love with and married. It was easy to see where his daughters' hair and eyes had come from, even if he had provided their cheekbones. Fiona looked almost young *again*.

He felt tears prickling at his eyes as he touched her forehead lightly. It was strange to realise that being in danger of a violent death had worked this miracle, stranger still to realise that he was almost grateful. As hard as her life had been since they'd left Earth, she'd escaped a far worse fate on the doomed world. Shaking his head, he lay down beside her and held her tightly. She shifted against him, cuddling up to his body. Closing his eyes, he tried to relax.

A moment later, the first shell of the day exploded outside the building.

CHAPTER TWENTY-EIGHT

> In short, historical problems do not tend to simply go away. The solutions to the first set of problems can lead neatly to the next set of problems.
> -Professor Leo Caesius, *Diplomacy: The Lessons of the Past.*

The enemy town was large enough to be a small city on Avalon, Jasmine decided, as she studied the live feed from the drones. It was barely a third of Jhansi's size – a tenth of Maharashtra's size – yet it was crammed with civilians and enemy soldiers. Ideally, she would have preferred to envelop the town and leave the town to wither on the vine, but there were too many civilians inside. They'd starve to death a long time before the enemy soldiers finally collapsed – or surrendered.

The men with guns eat first, she reminded herself. It was *possible* that the civilians would rebel against the enemy, but it couldn't be taken for granted. Nor could she assume that it would succeed. The enemy had tried hard to keep guns and other weapons out of untouchable hands and, by and large, they'd succeeded. Civilians might be desperate, but they had very little to fight with, save their bare hands.

She looked over at Cindy. "You sent them the demand for surrender?"

Cindy nodded. "I had it broadcast over the radio and through megaphones," she said. "Everyone in the city will have heard it. But there's no sign of a surrender."

Jasmine scowled. Marines fought insurgents on a regular basis and one thing they'd learned was that a small number of insurgents – or carefully-prepared troops – could keep an entire town under control until the fear they used to control the population was broken by the liberating army. The principle was the same; even if there were thousands of enemy soldiers who wanted to surrender, they'd be unable to give up without being shot in the back.

The drones had been observing the town for hours, long enough to confirm that women and children had been herded into buildings at the centre of the town, where they were effectively serving as both hostages and human shields. They'd figured out that Jasmine was reluctant to order long-range strikes against targets where civilians might get hurt, she realised; they'd actually cuffed a number of children to the rooftops, showing them clearly to the observing drones. If push came to shove, she knew, those children were going to be hurt – or worse.

Outside the centre, there were a series of defensive lines. The outer ones were manned by hastily-raised civilian 'volunteers,' who had probably been given a rifle, a few rounds of ammunition and sent out to die bravely. Further in, there were lines manned by actual *soldiers*, who would take advantage of whatever damage the volunteers had inflicted on her troops. And, beyond them, the troops that guarded the enemy commander. If he could be killed…

She shook her head. There was no easy way to take down the entire town without bloodshed.

"Send the signal," she ordered, bitterly. "The town is to be taken by storm."

Michael braced himself as the Warrior rumbled forward, guns swivelling around to target possible threats. He led his squad in its wake, silently grateful for the half-hour catnap he'd been allowed to take after they'd set up lines around the town. Without it, he wouldn't have been at his best as they approached the enemy buildings.

The slums on the edge of the town looked deserted – and permanently on the verge of falling over. Michael honestly couldn't understand why the locals tolerated such conditions; even slavers, the most despicable form of life in the universe, took better care of their slaves. But then, slavers needed healthy stock to turn a profit and the locals simply didn't care. There were so many untouchables that millions could die and millions more would step forward to take their place.

He wrinkled his nose at the smell as he glanced inside the first hovel. Inside, it was dark – and deserted. There was barely enough room for two or three people by Avalon standards, but judging by the blankets and the crudely-constructed loft, it had held upwards of ten people. He hoped, for their sake, that most of them were children, but he had a feeling that they'd been adults. How could *anyone* live in such conditions?

Leaving a green flag on the side of the door to mark the building cleared, he led the way to the next building and shone a light inside. Lights seemed to flare back at him and he almost fired a shot, before realising that he was staring straight at a pair of young girls and their older brother. All three of them were wearing rags, their faces pockmarked with scars and blemishes that could have been removed in bare minutes with modern surgery – and they were absolutely terrified. To them, he must have seemed like a creature from another universe.

"Come on out," he ordered, in the local tongue. The phrases sounded odd on his lips, but the children seemed to understand. Their faces were still fearful; they moved in a manner, he realised grimly, that suggested that all of the fight had been beaten out of them. Judging by the way the boy was limping, that beating had been only a few days ago. "You're safe now."

He pointed the children towards the embankments they'd drawn up around the town, then pushed his feelings aside and led the way onwards, moving through dozens of tiny shacks and hovels. A handful hid other refugees – or dead bodies, men and women who had simply expired in their sleep or had been murdered by their fellows. Most of them, he couldn't help noticing, looked to be old. Had their children and grandchildren murdered them when they became a liability? Off-hand, he couldn't think of anything more disgusting one could do to one's parents.

An explosion broke into his thoughts, followed rapidly by a series of shots aimed from hastily-assembled barricades. Michael cursed himself for his distraction and took cover, searching frantically for the source of the shots. Someone had ripped apart a number of slightly-better built homes and turned them into barricades, which they were using as firing positions. Others seemed to have taken up positions in various homes and begun firing through the windows, or tiny slits they'd cut into the wood. It would have been a strong position, Michael noted, if they'd had better materials to use.

He unhooked a grenade from his belt, then nodded to two of his men. They primed the grenades and threw them, then advanced forwards as explosions tore the enemy barricade to shreds. Several shots were still coming from a nearby house, so he threw a second grenade through the window and the firing stopped sharply. He glanced at the bodies – all of them were civilians, unless he missed his guess – then reached for his megaphone.

"Surrender," he bawled out, in the local dialect. "Surrender and you will not…"

The megaphone exploded in his hand. He gaped at it for a split-second, then jumped aside, swearing out loud. The enemy had at least one capable sniper, probably one of their enforcers, in position to take shots at his men. And if the sniper had aimed at his head or chest instead of the megaphone, he would be dead now.

The Warrior advanced forward, bullets pinging off the metal hull and ricocheting everywhere, and pointed its main gun towards the sniper's nest. Michael winced as the gun fired, launching a HE shell into the target. A building disintegrated with staggering force, sending the sniper falling to his death. Moments later, the Warrior's machine guns cleared the next pair of barricades out of the way.

A handful of enemy soldiers staggered forwards, hands in the air. Michael's men stripped them, bound them and then pointed them towards the edge of town. They'd have to keep their surrender, Michael told himself. If they tried to run, their own people would be likely to execute them for daring to realise that it was hopeless and surrender. He cursed again as mortar shells started plunging down in the distance, targeting the handful of Warriors. One of them was struck directly and was badly damaged, although not destroyed. The crew stumbled out, alive.

"Get back to the embankments," Michael ordered. He would have preferred to put them into service on the firing lines, but there were hundreds of Warriors stored in the Garrison, far more than they could hope to use. The crew would hopefully have a new vehicle by the end of the day. "Hurry!"

The fighting started to blur into a series of patterns as they forced their way onwards. They broke into buildings, cleared them of enemy soldiers and did what they could for the civilians they encountered in the midst of the fighting. It rapidly became impossible to predict just what the enemy would do; some surrendered after a token show of resistance, others fought to the death and had to be wiped out completely. Michael couldn't help feeling a little respect for their determination, even as it was muted by horror at what they considered acceptable treatment of civilians.

An antitank rocket raced out of a nearby house and slammed straight into the Warrior. This time, the armour was not enough to protect the vehicle and it exploded into a fireball. The crew would have died, he hoped, before they knew what had hit them. Pieces of flying metal flew everywhere, causing him to duck and then start crawling towards the enemy firing position. Despite the situation – and the tiredness pervading his body – he found himself smiling with gallows humour when he realised that the enemy soldiers had fired the antitank rocket in a confined space and the exhaust had killed all four of them.

He winced as another series of mortar shells crashed down. Thankfully, the enemy didn't seem to be very good shots; in their place, he would have taken care to have all the possible targets zeroed in before the fighting started. On the other hand, the CEF's own mortars were firing counter-battery shots and they didn't seem to have time to take aim properly before they had to move. He took cover behind a reasonably solid wall to catch his breath, then smiled in relief as he realised that reinforcements were moving up to take over the front lines.

"Get something to eat, sir," Sergeant Grieves advised him. Now that they were no longer the tip of the spear, they could unwrap a ration bar each before returning to the fight. "And make sure you have something to drink too."

Michael nodded, pulling a ration bar out of his combat dress and opening it with one hand. None of them dared let down their guard too far, not when it was all-too-likely that some enemy holdouts might have been missed. The tactical net had informed them that several enemy soldiers *had* been missed and they'd given the reinforcements some nasty moments, after they'd come out of their hidey-holes. He started as he saw movement at the corner of his eye, then relaxed slightly as he realised that it was one of his men answering the call of nature.

"At least I didn't piss myself," the soldier protested, after his comrades started ribbing him.

"You'll get your pecker shot off," another jeered, as he finished his ration bar. "I heard that replacement dicks are smaller than *real* dicks."

Michael rolled his eyes. The Commonwealth was determined to take good care of its fighting men and women – and indeed, even training accidents received the best medical care available. And yes, it *was* possible to replace a penis…but what sort of idiot would expose himself to enemy fire in the hopes they'd get a bigger one in the hospital?

"Target like mine," the first soldier pretended to muse, "how could they miss?"

"And with a target like mine," the second soldier said, "why would I want a replacement?"

"All right, you clowns," Sergeant Grieves sneered. "Party's over. Time to get back to work."

The front lines had advanced nearly five hundred metres, Michael discovered as they came out of cover and checked in with the tactical net, but he stayed on alert anyway. The enemy were shooting mortar shells off at random, while their soldiers still seemed torn between surrendering and fighting to the finish. And the buildings here were stronger, a great deal more solidly constructed than the shacks and hovels that belonged to the untouchables. They posed greater problems for the advancing forces.

He watched as a Warrior advanced down the middle of the street, guns constantly scanning for targets. The crew didn't seem to care about the threat of enemy rockets or missiles; instead, they were providing covering fire for the advancing infantry. There was a movement at the corner of his eye and he turned, weapon raised, to see a large dog cowering against one wall. Clearly, it hadn't been trained to serve in the military. And then there was a whistle and the dog lunged forward, heading right for the Warrior. Michael saw the package wrapped under its body a moment too late. The dog ran right under the vehicle and exploded.

Michael cursed out loud as he saw the warrior flip over and come crashing down, smoke and flames pouring from its exposed underside. The underside was heavily-armoured, he knew, but it hadn't been the priority that shielding its sides and top had been. He allowed himself a sigh of relief as the hatches popped open, then swore again as sniper fire picked off the crewmen before they could take cover. The enemy had devised a very deadly plan and carried it out with surprising skill.

"Target the following coordinates," he ordered, as he sought cover against one wall. The guns would respond to his call, thankfully. He'd been told that the Imperial Army had rarely allowed the people on the ground to call in artillery support, something that he was sure the Drill Instructors had made up. Who else would know that they needed support? He rattled out the coordinates, then braced himself. "Hurry!"

The ground shook as a series of shells crashed down on top of the enemy position. Michael rolled over and led the charge forward, knowing that the snipers – if they had survived – would be too distracted to fight back. Most of them appeared to be dead, along with several women in civilian clothes. Michael felt a twinge of guilt; he'd known that there was a prospect of running into human shields, but he'd told himself that it wasn't too likely. He should have known better.

It seemed that the fighting only intensified as they fought their way into the final set of defensive lines. Michael found it hard to remember why they were trying to take prisoners in the first place; if they hadn't looked so helpless, he knew that he would have gunned them down without a second thought. The massive palace that had served as the centre of the enemy's operations fell rapidly, once they realised that they had been defeated. Somehow, Michael wasn't surprised to discover the enemy leadership trying to sneak their way out of the city. They'd been dressed in drag.

Slowly, the fighting died away as the CEF took control of the town. A handful of holdouts continued to cause trouble, but they were rapidly surrounded and eliminated with pinpoint artillery fire. Most of the enemy soldiers who had survived the fighting surrendered once they realised that their commanders had deserted them, throwing down their weapons and accepting capture. Michael found his unit, tired and battered though it was, assigned to escort the prisoners out of the town until proper accommodation could be prepared for them.

Private Willis looked over at him. "Sir," he said, "is it always going to be like this?"

Michael considered the question gravely. Willis had been a newcomer to the squad, a cherry straight out of basic training. Like all such FNGs, he'd taken his share of ribbing while his squadmates made sure they could trust him at their backs. But, despite that, he'd had an air of innocence, even if it *had* been slightly tainted by his activities while on leave. Not any longer.

"It could be worse," he said, finally. "And it will be, once we hit Pradesh."

He looked over at the prisoners – and the handful of civilians who had come out of hiding to jeer at them. The level of repressed hatred was staggering, even though he knew that he should have expected it. He found himself tightening his grip on his weapon, wondering if the crowd were going to lynch the naked and helpless prisoners. How could he have blamed them if they'd wanted to show their tormentors the same mercy they'd been shown?

"Take a look at them," he added, inviting Willis to follow his gaze. "They turned this planet into a prison – and a mass grave. They're worse than pirates, worse even than the Old Council. Killing them is our duty."

He scowled at the young man's back as he returned to the rank. Michael had seen worse, as had a handful of his more experienced men, but the others had been…*innocent*. The barbarity they'd seen during the fighting was new to them. Something would have to be done about that, eventually. But, in all honesty, he didn't know what.

A shower of dirt and filth rained towards the prisoners. Michael lifted his voice, barking out a command in the local language. He mangled it twice, but eventually he managed to convince the throwers to stop. But he couldn't really blame them for wanting revenge, could he?

He linked on to the tactical net. "The prisoners won't be welcome in the city any longer," he said, after reporting the brief incident. "Is there somewhere for them to go?"

"Soon," the CO said. "Just get them back to our lines. We'll take it from there."

CHAPTER TWENTY-NINE

This is amply demonstrated by the American response to the Soviet invasion of Afghanistan. The United States armed and trained the resistance to the invaders, which eventually forced the Russians to retreat. However, the aftermath of the invasion was a devastated Afghanistan, ripe for fundamentalism which would eventually lead to a new threat to world order.
-Professor Leo Caesius, *Diplomacy: The Lessons of the Past.*

"The only thing costlier than a battle lost is a battle won," Jasmine mused, as she walked through the abandoned warehouse. Seventeen bodies had been laid out on the ground, seventeen men who had died under her command. She couldn't help feeling as if she had failed them, as if another commander would have found a way to save their lives. But she knew that *she* was the one in command.

The reporter looked over at her, but said nothing. He probably had nothing to say, she thought bitterly – nothing sensible, at any rate. What would a civilian, one who had fought with pen and ink and computer messages, know of the pain of losing someone under an officer's command? Even a resistance fighter wouldn't feel the same way. The dead might not have been Marines, but it hardly mattered. She was responsible for issuing the orders that had sent them to their deaths.

Five men killed in damaged or destroyed Warriors. Eight killed by enemy fire. Four killed by friendly fire…and wasn't *that* a joke? In the Imperial Army, even the merest *hint* of a friendly fire incident would have snarled the offensive while the commanders carried out an investigation and hired lawyers to ensure that someone else took the blame. Jasmine had already looked at the records and knew what had happened; the strikes had been called in at very close range and, inevitably, someone had become very unlucky.

And three men missing, unaccounted for.

She'd wondered if they might be prisoners, but none of the enemy commanders had known about any prisoners. The prisoners they *had* taken had died in their custody, apart from one who had been shipped up to the capital. Jasmine had almost killed them personally when she'd heard their confession. Mistreating prisoners was a precedent they could not allow to stand. But the standard response, reprisals against captured enemy POWs, was pointless when it was clear that the enemy commanders cared nothing for their men.

"When you write your book about this whole affair," she said, turning to face the reporter, "make sure you tell the universe that they died bravely and well."

"I will," the reporter promised. He didn't seem to have any difficulty looking at the bodies, even the ones who had been seriously mutilated in the fighting. "And I'm sorry for their loss."

Jasmine nodded and led the way out of the warehouse. The bodies would be shipped back to the garrison, where they would be placed in stasis or simply frozen until the starships returned. Some of the dead had probably requested burial in space, a Marine tradition that had been copied by the Knights, but the others would probably need to be returned to Avalon for proper burial. Shaking her head, she headed towards the other warehouse, noting with some twisted amusement the line of local civilians snaking into the building. The offer of basic medical care had done more to win hearts and minds than smashing their town into a pile of rubble.

Inside, all was bedlam. Mothers clutched their children tightly, while the medics briefly glanced at them and then offered what advice they could. The trucks were bringing more supplies up from the garrison, Jasmine knew, but she doubted that it would be enough to help *everyone*. In the corner, a handful of men sat with their hands bound behind their backs and cloth stuffed in their mouths. Jasmine looked over at Joe

Buckley, who had taken over security for the medical centre, and lifted her eyebrows.

"They decided that they had the right to force their way to the head of the queue," Buckley explained, shortly. He nodded to a pair of Knights who had also been assigned to guard duties. "We had a little discussion with the assholes and taught them the error of their ways."

"Glad to hear it," Jasmine said, dryly. "And the other prisoners?"

"Being cuffed and shackled at this moment," Buckley said, bluntly. "The locals may not want them in their town, but *someone* has to clear up the bodies."

He paused. "There may be a problem," he added. He looked over at the reporter doubtfully, then motioned for Jasmine to follow him into an office. "We found a number of bodies in the town."

Jasmine scowled. "The whole place is practically *littered* with bodies," she pointed out, sharply. She still remembered watching in horror as the drones revealed the bodies of a number of human shields, all killed by incoming fire. "The surprise would be *not* finding bodies."

"These bodies were killed after the fighting," Buckley said. "They were all young men, middle-caste; as far as we can tell, they didn't take part in the defence of the town. And I have a pretty good idea of who killed them."

"The rebels," Jasmine said, darkly.

"No one else has a motive," Buckley warned. "Jasmine" – he rarely called her by her first name, at least since they'd both left 1st Platoon – "the rebels might be laying the groundwork for their takeover, once the war comes to an end."

Jasmine fought down the urge to bang her hand against the wall – or summon Yin and wring his scrawny neck. Oh, she could understand the desire for revenge – and the practical aspects of eliminating the castes that would be most likely to fight against any restructuring of society – but it would only make it harder for them to take Pradesh. Hell, the local government wouldn't even *have* to lie to muster local resistance.

"Brilliant," she snarled, finally. "And we weren't even *planning* to hold the town ourselves."

She shook her head. "What do we do about it?"

Buckley didn't answer. She tossed possible options around and around in her head; they could threaten the rebels, even warn them that they might stop providing arms and support from the garrison…but Yin would know that she was bluffing. They *needed* the rebels, just to smash their way to the capital and raise the siege. Or she could ask him politely to stop, allowing him to claim that it was someone acting without his authority…which might very well be true. Insurgent groups rarely had straight chains of command.

"I'll speak to him," she said, although she knew that she wasn't in a strong position to bargain. The most she could threaten him with, realistically, was abandoning the planet altogether after recovering Colonel Stalker and his people…and that probably wouldn't bother him in the slightest. "And then we need to talk about Pradesh. I've had an idea."

"Get some sleep too," Buckley advised. "We won't be able to advance forward for another day or two, at the very least."

Jasmine nodded. Her forces had burned through a considerable amount of ammunition – and the rebels had spent it as if there would be no tomorrow. They would need time to prepare, time to bring up new weapons and vehicles from the garrison…and time to reinforce the makeshift bridges the engineers had constructed over the river. And to bring up more bridging equipment, as a second river lay between them and Pradesh. Thankfully, there was no dam to allow them to trigger a second flood.

"I'll do my best," she said. "But I won't sleep easy."

"Guard duty," Michael muttered to himself, as the Warrior sped along the road. "I'm a bloody guard."

He'd taken over the top-mounted machine gun by dint of superior authority, allowing him to feel the wind in his face. The convoy was kicking up dust and mud as it moved westwards, taking hundreds of prisoners back to the POW camps, but he was fairly safe from breathing in anything apart from the stench of decomposing bodies. It was still stunning just how much damage the flood had actually done – and just how little effort any of the locals had put into clearing up the mess.

I suppose they know that everything they do might be knocked down again, he thought, charitably. The farmers on Avalon had done much the same thing, after watching their farms burned down and their daughters kidnapped by the bandits. They hadn't had any faith in the planet's future until after the Marines had defeated the bandits and forced the Crackers to agree to terms.

They'd been promised a rest, once they returned to the FOB, although he doubted that it would be very long, Instead, it was much more likely that they'd be detailed to run a second set of escort missions within a few hours. He was still thinking about it when the first shot bounced off the vehicle's armour, far too close to his position.

"Incoming," he snapped, swinging the machine gun around to blaze at the source of the fire. The enemy had taken up position along a ridgeline, allowing them to pour fire down into the convoy. It wasn't enough to protect them from machine gun fire, he noted with some relief; the massed fire of four Warriors wiped the enemy soldiers out before they could do any real damage. He briefly considered ordering his men to dismount and scout for other surprises, then dismissed the thought. They had to get back to the FOB.

"Probably thought we were defenceless," one of his soldiers suggested. "Or maybe they just wanted to remind us that we can't guarantee our safety."

"There are *no* guarantees in this line of work," Michael reminded him, dryly. "And keep your eyes peeled for surprises. That may not be the only ambush they have in mind."

Surprisingly, the rest of the journey went without incident, although Michael refused to relax until they were actually within the outer wire surrounding the latest POW camp. The more dangerous prisoners had largely been sorted out and isolated in the early moments after capture, but he would still have been happier if the camp had been a little more complex than a few hundred square metres of ground surrounded by wire fencing. But the prisoners – naked, without tools or leadership – should be unable to escape. Besides, it was the only place where they were going to get fed.

"All right, you lot," he called, once he and his men had dismounted. "Out you come."

One by one, the enemy prisoners were unbound and then shoved through the gate into the camp. None of them looked as if they were planning to resist; indeed, they looked broken and relieved to find that they were still being guarded by off-worlders. Everyone had heard the rumours about what happened to prisoners who fell into rebel hands; Michael had allowed the prisoners to find out, hoping that it would keep them from causing too much trouble or trying to escape. It seemed to have worked.

"Good work, Lieutenant," a female voice said. He turned to see a woman whose eyes looked older than her face, wearing a faded Imperial Army uniform. She had to be from the garrison, he decided, if she was wearing that uniform. The Commonwealth had designed its own uniforms after being abandoned by the Empire. "Do you have time for a debriefing?"

Michael yawned. "My men and I require food and rest," he snapped, too tired to be diplomatic. "God alone knows when the CO will want us heading back to the front lines. I really *don't* have time to be debriefed…"

"Unless he means having his briefs removed," a soldier said, just loudly enough to be heard. "That would be…"

"Silence," Sergeant Grieves thundered. Judging by his tone, the soldier was going to regret opening his mouth. "Sir…"

"Never mind," Michael said. He looked back at the officer. Imperial Army or not, surely she deserved a little respect. "Can you hold off until we've eaten and slept?"

"There's food in the mess," the officer said. "And if you need to rest, I won't keep you."

Michael watched her go, then turned around and led the way back to the warriors. There would be a place to rest in the FOB. And then they'd be heading back to the front.

Jasmine's implanted communicator buzzed, awakening her from a sound sleep.

"I'm sorry to bother you," Buckley said, "but Yin's here, asking for you."

Jasmine sat upright, relieved that she hadn't done anything as stupid as stripping off before going to sleep. Yin still thought her a young man and she'd decided, after watching how even the rebels interacted with local women, she wasn't going to do anything to convince him otherwise. She was mildly surprised that he hadn't realised that *something* was odd about her – unlike the men, she couldn't grow any stubble on her chin – but perhaps he felt that off-worlder men removed their stubble completely.

It wouldn't be the stupidest rumour they have about us, she told herself, as she pulled her jacket over her shirt and then checked her pistol. Implanted weapons were useful, but sometimes a more visible weapon made a proper deterrent. Besides, she preferred to keep her implants as a nasty surprise for potential enemies.

"I'm on my way," she said. A quick glance at her wristcom revealed that she had slept over seven hours, right through the night. "Tell him I'll be there in a moment."

Whatever objection the locals had to working at night no longer seemed to apply, she discovered, as she stepped out of the tent. There was *still* a line of locals heading to the medical tent and another line heading towards where ration bars were being handed out. It had caused no end of friction when the locals had realised that the bars were only being handed out to people who came to the centre, rather than one person being allowed to take away a dozen bars. But she knew that the rebels would have tried to starve the less welcome parts of the community if they'd been given half a chance.

She'd set up a makeshift operational command centre in one of the few truly intact buildings at the outskirts of town. A handful of portable terminals, a generator to provide power and a processor to produce water and food…all the comforts of a Marine FOB, she'd told herself, once it was set up. And besides, she had no intention of staying in the town for one moment longer than necessary. They were already shipping up ammunition and other supplies to allow them to continue the offensive.

Yin met her in a side room, with Buckley standing by the door and trying hard to pretend to be invisible. He seemed to be succeeding, Jasmine decided; Yin was acting as if the Marine wasn't there at all, despite his immense bulk. She sat down facing the local and gave him a tired smile, then narrowed her eyes. Maybe Yin wasn't to blame for the deaths…but she wasn't going to let him off that easily.

"Brigadier," he said. "My men are in position to take over the town."

Jasmine stared at him, refusing to blink. "We found people who had been executed," she said, without bothering to be diplomatic. "Why did your people kill them?"

Yin rocked back in surprise, too much surprise. The overacting convinced Jasmine that he wasn't surprised at all. He *knew* about the murders, even if he hadn't ordered them.

"They were" – he spoke a local word Jasmine didn't know – "and deserved to be purged," he said, finally. "I cannot blame some of my people for taking the law into their own hands."

Jasmine kept her eyes on his. "And why, precisely, did they deserve to *die*?"

"They fawned on the aristocrats," Yin said. "It was them, more than anyone else, who upheld their rule. They dreamed of *becoming* aristocrats. If we kept them in the city, they would pose a security risk."

Jasmine scowled, remembering the true nature of the local religion. The middle castes were close to becoming aristocrats through reincarnation…and, for that matter, a particularly successful middle caste trader might be offered a chance to *join* the aristocracy. It was a safety valve built into their society, although it was really too small to prevent tensions eventually tearing the system apart. She could see why Yin might want to purge them…but she also knew that it could not be allowed.

"If the enemy find out what you did," she said, not bothering to pretend that she thought that he had nothing to do with it, "they will use it as a rallying cry. They will no longer surrender, but they will fight to the bitter end. And they will turn on your people too."

She showed him the images the drones had collected from the other side of Pradesh, over the mountains. Untouchables were being rounded up and sent to concentration camps, or chained up in barns for the night. It wouldn't be long before the locals started massacring untouchables outright, just to prevent them becoming a fifth column. If they heard about the slaughter of middle-caste men, they'd use it as an excuse.

"I think you should wait until after the war is over to reshape your society," she finished, hoping that he would listen to her. "Because we cannot tolerate you risking our ultimate success just because you want a little revenge."

Yin stared at her for a long moment, then bowed his head. "We will leave them alone, as long as they do not threaten us," he said. He stood up and headed to the door. "But we are your allies, not your servants. You do not command us."

Jasmine watched him go, hoping – praying – that he meant what he said. If the enemy became reluctant to surrender, the fight would be far harder – and they might not reach the capital in time.

CHAPTER THIRTY

Or, more significantly, the ending of the First World War was a diplomatic disaster. While Germany was prostrate, allowing the Allies to deal with the country as they saw fit, this state of affairs was certain not to last.
-Professor Leo Caesius, *Diplomacy: The Lessons of the Past.*

"Day Five of the siege," Edward mused, as he wrote in his command journal. The ground shook violently as another shell landed to the north of the complex, but he ignored it. "Supplies of weapons and ammunition critical. Medical supplies and food not too far behind."

He scowled at the book with some irritation, silently cursing the long-dead Marine Commandant who'd insisted – and had it written into the regulations – that every CO had to keep a personnel command journal as well as the unit's log. Thankfully, a later Commandant had ensured that the journals were kept sealed until the writer was dead, but it was still a nuisance. Edward had never cared for writing his thoughts down on paper, certainly not in the middle of a war zone. And yet it wouldn't have felt right to unilaterally countermand the regulation. He was *still* a Marine.

"Wolfbane forces have fought well beside ours, with most integration problems ironed out by the desperate need to cooperate," he added, scratching out the letters one by one. He hadn't even known how to *write* until he'd joined the Marines. The Undercity didn't really offer any education to its inhabitants, save the school of hard knocks. "It leaves me certain that their ultimate commander is at least as competent as Admiral Singh. I sincerely hope that we can agree on borders we can both accept."

Another explosion, closer this time, set the light bulb swinging over his head. He glanced upwards, then closed the book and returned it to the box he'd brought with him from Avalon. It had been given to him on the day he'd been promoted to Captain and assumed command of Stalker's Stalkers, one of three gifts that came directly from the Commandant. The box was sealed, utterly impossible to open without either Edward's DNA or knowledge of the override code. It should be stored safely in the Slaughterhouse, where the box would be sent after Edward's death.

Or it should be sent there, he thought. The Wolfbane representatives hadn't known what had happened to the Slaughterhouse – or, indeed, about many other worlds apart from Earth itself. It was impossible to know what might have happened in the Core, with Earth gone. Many of the Core Worlds were just as overpopulated as Earth. They might well be overwhelmed by civil chaos of their own.

There was a tap on the door. "Come," he ordered. The door opened to reveal Blake Coleman, with a maid following him. "Success?"

"Yes, sir," Blake rumbled. "Mad here has agreed to assist with my proposal."

Edward studied the maid thoughtfully. It was hard to place her age, but she was clearly a young woman – with the slender figure that seemed to be the local ideal. Her skin was paler than the other maids, almost pale enough to make her pass for one of the highest caste. It was easy to see why she was popular – the brown eyes were enough to make him melt – but less easy to see why she might have volunteered for the mission.

"Mad," he said. The girl nodded. Despite her composure, it was clear that she was thoroughly terrified. "Do you understand what we're asking you to do?"

"Yes," Mad said. Her voice was very soft, so quiet that Edward had trouble hearing her. "I understand."

Edward met her eyes. "Why do you want to do this?"

Mad's eyes flashed with sudden anger. "Look at me," she hissed, somehow keeping her voice low. "I'm *mixed*. Father...*took* mother and gave her me. I don't fit in *anywhere*."

"I see," Edward said. Her skin colour would have marked her out as the bastard child of a higher caste man, but not ensured that she was *treated* as befitted someone of such status. It was easy to see why she'd been pushed into maid service; no doubt the thought of ordering someone so pale around was a pleasure to members of the lower castes. "And you understand what might happen to you if you get caught?"

The girl gave him an oddly-scornful look. "Would that be any different from what they would do to me if the walls fall?"

"No," Edward said, after a moment. The girl was brave enough, he had to admit. "Please wait outside."

He waited for the girl to leave the room, then looked up at Coleman. "Do you think she's up to it?"

"She's the only one who claimed to know someone we could talk to," Coleman admitted. "We're short on options, sir."

"I know," Edward said. He hated sending *anyone* into danger, particularly an untrained civilian who would be more of a liability than an asset. But Coleman was right. They *were* running critically short of options. He glanced at his wristcom, noting that there were still five hours until dusk. "Get some sleep and make sure that she does too. Then…good luck."

He watched Coleman go, then looked down at the latest report from the CEF. Brigadier Yamane was preparing to thrust over the river towards Pradesh, at which point she would have to gamble on her hastily thought out plan to take the city. And if it failed, Edward knew, the CEF would have to fight its way through, block by block…with all the attendant civilian and military casualties. It would be a bloody meatgrinder that would rival Han for sheer awfulness.

Damn it, he thought, as he stood up to inspect the defences. *But we don't have much time left.*

Blake dropped down from the wall and glanced around, pistol in hand. There was no sign of anyone moving, not even a handful of people hiding in the ruins surrounding the Imperial Residency. Perhaps the smell had driven them away, he told himself, silently grateful for the benefits of modern medicine. They'd all had their senses of smell surgically reduced by the medics, ensuring the stench couldn't get to them.

He looked up and nodded. Mad dropped down a moment later, right into his arms. He glanced down at her face – deliberately blackened until she was almost as dark as Blake himself – and then put her on her two feet. There was no time for clowning around, not when they had several miles to walk without being detected.

"Stay behind me and keep to the shadows," he muttered. "And don't say a *word*."

She followed him, surprisingly quietly by his standards, as he led the way through the ruins and up towards the enemy lines. The enemy seemed to have drawn back a little, purely to allow them to police most of the city…a curious reaction, Blake had thought, when the guards weren't anywhere near their two greatest security threats. But it allowed him to ensure that they slipped through without being detected. He relaxed slightly as they reached the poorer part of town, where there were still a handful of civilians on the streets. If they saw him in the semi-darkness, they'd mistake him for another civilian.

Better not let them see my skin, he thought, sourly. *It would be curtains for sure.*

Earth had no racism, at least not based on skin colour. Centuries of inbreeding and genetic modification had produced a population that tended to blur the ethnic traits together into one collective whole. But it still existed on many of the outer worlds, including the ones that based themselves on a standard largely-mythical ethnic background. He'd been on Edo during one short period of leave and seen how the locals looked at anyone who lacked the features their ancestors had spliced into their DNA.

But most such worlds had no underclass. Here, the darker the skin, the lower the caste…something that bothered Blake on a very fundamental level. His homeworld had no such nonsense; the Marine Corps was a raving meritocracy, but if he'd been born here he would have been condemned to hew wood and draw water for his entire life. There would have been no education, no chance of bettering himself…hell, if they sensed the urge for a fight that had propelled him into the Corps, they would probably have killed or gelded him out of hand. Mad had told him what happened to untouchables who grew too rowdy. It sickened him.

He kept to the shadows as the quality of houses slipped rapidly. From the maps, he knew that the poorest members of the lower castes – but not the untouchables – lived right up against the edge of the city walls. He'd been at a loss to know how the walls were intended to deter anything until he'd realised that rioting untouchables probably wouldn't have access to high explosives or even primitive gunpowder. Given time, he could *teach* them how to make gunpowder, although he hoped that the fighting would be over before that became necessary.

Mad motioned for him to stop, pointing to a house right on the edge of the walls. Blake lurked behind, one hand on his pistol, as Mad slipped up to the building and gently knocked on the door. A hatch opened, revealing a woman wearing a scarf that concealed most of her features. There was a brief exchange between them and then Mad waved for Blake to come forward, into the building. The door closed with a dull thud.

"This way," Mad said, giving the woman a handful of local coins. "There's a tunnel under the walls."

Blake scowled as he was led down into the basement and through a tunnel that looked to have been carved out by hand. It didn't seem very secure at all; indeed, he was surprised that the constant shockwaves caused by the explosions hadn't caused it to collapse. He'd crawled through tighter spaces while boarding starships, he told himself as he slipped forward, but it didn't really help. It was a relief to finally emerge on the other side, where another woman waited for them. Her face was a dark brown, illuminated by a candle she held in her hand.

Mad spoke briefly to her, then led Blake up a flight of stairs and out into the streets. The difference struck him at once; inside, the buildings were relatively solid, outside they seemed permanently on the verge of falling down. There was rubbish and human waste everywhere, although he couldn't help noticing that no one seemed to throw out food. The NVGs revealed a handful of people sleeping in the open. They were lucky, he told himself, that the weather was temperate all the year round. They'd freeze to death in colder climates.

"This is my home," Mad said, as they reached a tiny shack. There was a note of…*bitterness* in her voice. "I was born here."

The minute he looked inside, Blake knew why she was bitter. It was a tiny house, barely more than one room…with a cage hanging from the ceiling. A pair of teenage girls seemed to be sleeping *in* the cage. It took him a moment to realise that it was the only way to protect their reputation, although somehow he doubted that it would matter. How *could* anyone live in such an environment?

Mad motioned for him to sit on the floor – he didn't dare lean against the wall for fear of bringing it down – and chattered to the four teenage boys in the room. One of them left moments later, the others stayed where they were, watching Blake through fascinated eyes. It was easy to tell that they had their doubts, but they didn't seem inclined to make a fuss. Besides, he had the distant feeling that they viewed Mad as hopelessly compromised anyway.

The door opened, revealing an elderly man. "You're from the Residency," he said, as soon as the door was closed. His Imperial Standard was poor, but understandable. "And *she*" – he nodded to Mad – "saw fit to bring you here. What do you want?"

Blake studied him for a long moment. The man was old, but his eyes were sharp and there was clearly nothing wrong with his brain. He knew that Blake wouldn't have been sent to the untouchable slums unless he wanted something…but any form of contact with the off-worlders could have the most dire repercussions. Blake wouldn't blame him in the slightest for being unwilling to commit himself before he saw something to make him believe that he wouldn't simply be abandoned.

"Part of our force is held under siege in the Residency," he said, bluntly. There was no way to know how much the man knew of what was going on outside the city. The upper castes might have tried to keep a lid on the news, but rumours spread faster than Blake could shed his shipsuit when confronted by a pretty girl. "The remainder is advancing on the city."

"On the other side of Pradesh," the man said. "It is yet to break through the gap."

Not ignorant, then, Blake noted.

"It will," he said, confidently. He had every faith in Jasmine Yamane who had, after all, commanded the operation that had brought down

Admiral Singh. "Mad informs me that you are one of the underground leaders here. We would like to work with you to bring down the government."

"And save your own people," the elderly man mused. He threw Mad a long considering look, then peered back at Blake. "And how are we to know that you won't use us and then throw us aside."

Blake kept his voice level. "Right now, the caste government is tottering," he said, remembering the reports from the CEF. "If you take advantage of its weakness to rise against it, you would not only bring it down faster, but earn yourself a place at the table to sort out the post-war world."

"And if we rose too soon, we would be crushed," the old man pointed out, mildly. "What can you offer us now?"

"They think that they have disarmed you," Blake said, evenly. "We have looked at the tools and equipment they allow you to use and we know better. You have weapons, you just don't know how to put them to use. We can teach you how to use them – and how to obtain better weapons of your own."

He leaned forward. "Once they get through Pradesh, there's a straight run to the capital," he continued. "We can and we will ship weapons forward, to arm you and your people for an uprising. You would be able to face your tormentors on even terms for the first time in your life."

"We will not act until your forces are in position to support us," the old man said, finally. His eyes narrowed. "If we take this to…*them*, we would be assured of some reward."

"A bullet in the back of the head, perhaps," Blake suggested. "Maybe that would make a change from torture followed by sudden death."

He met the old man's eyes. "The starships will be back," he said. "There is no way that your government can overrun the garrison, or convince the starships that the whole affair was a dreadful misunderstanding. When they arrive, this world will be destroyed – unless the Residency is saved and a new government is in place to take over the reins of power. You *could* betray us, of course you could. But you'd only be betraying yourselves along with us."

"A convincing argument," the man noted. He reached out and caught Mad's eye, pulling her to her feet. "I need to talk to my daughter, if you don't mind."

Blake watched him leading Mad away, feeling oddly disbelieving. Mad was his *daughter*? But if that was true, who was her mother? Or was she merely his adopted child? He pushed the thought aside a second later, looking around at the teenage boys. They stared back at him with a mixture of curiosity and defiance. To them, he had to seem like a character out of a story – a man who was like them, yet superior in every way.

And you should know better than to think of yourself like that, he scolded himself. *Even the best Marine can be killed by a ten-credit bullet fired by an idiot.*

It was nearly twenty minutes before they came back into the room. "She believes that you can teach us," the man said. "When do you intend to begin?"

"As soon as you wish," Blake said. The plan hadn't called for an immediate return to the Residency. If he'd been rejected, he would have explored the city and then holed up somewhere until night fell again. "Mad can supply you with our shopping list."

"You can't stay here," the man warned. "Mad can't stay here either. They know that she stayed inside the Residency. If she were to be found outside, it would raise far too many questions. We shall find a place for her to stay elsewhere."

He turned, barking orders all the time. "And your clothes look *too* good. Come with me. And walk as if you have a hunchback. You look disgustingly healthy for one of us."

Smiling to himself, Blake followed. The resistance seemed to have a good awareness of security, thankfully. He would have bet good money that the delay in the man's arrival had been caused by a careful check of the surroundings, just to make sure no snatch team lay in wait. It was good to be working with people who understood the risks.

His smile grew wider. If nothing else, he was going to finally *do* something that might do more than delay the inevitable. And it would also satisfy his desire for a fight.

CHAPTER THIRTY-ONE

The Allies could have treated Germany gently, admitting that they all shared the blame for the war, or they could have broken Imperial Germany back into its pre-1871 state. Either one would have made a German war of revenge unlikely (or at least harder).
-Professor Leo Caesius, *Diplomacy: The Lessons of the Past.*

"This place should be suitable," the engineering crew said. "We'll start work at once."

Michael nodded. The Ganges River was a far more formidable obstacle than the first river they'd crossed, being deep and wide enough to prevent a Warrior from simply motoring across the riverbed and appearing, dripping wet, on the far side. As the river was the only natural barrier between the CEF and Pradesh, the enemy had dug in along the far bank, establishing guns and bunkers everywhere they could. It seemed to have stopped the CEF cold.

He smirked. The main body of the CEF had stopped on the near side and were shaking their fists at the enemy defenders, but his unit had advanced southwards until they found a place where the river could be bridged easily. No doubt the enemy had scouts out watching for any attempt to outflank the defenders, yet they would have some trouble reacting to the CEF's move. Their tanks and other vehicles couldn't move without being seen by the drones and hammered by long-range guns.

The bridge grew rapidly until it touched the far side. As before, it seemed dangerously fragile, but he knew that it was remarkably solid. He led his platoon across the bridge to secure the far side, then waved to the Warrior drivers, inviting them to bring their vehicles over the river. Once they were over, two of them would remain to provide security while the others would follow him back down to take the defenders in the rear.

Hopefully we've outflanked their IEDs too, he thought, remembering how another Warrior and four trucks had been lost to IEDs over the past few days. Small bands of enemy soldiers were still roaming the countryside, emplacing IEDs along the roadsides or terrorising small villages that might otherwise have sided openly with the rebels. They would all be wiped out in time, Michael was sure, particularly as the rebels brought more and more armed men into their forces, but until then they would continue to be a nuisance.

"I'd love to go climbing there," one of his soldiers muttered, as they advanced northwards, following the river down towards the sea. "Do you think there are Mountain Men there?"

Michael snorted. Avalon's Mountain Men were cranky old hermits – or so he had been told; he'd never met one. They were generally unfriendly to visitors, rarely leaving the mountains even for medical attention; it was an open question how they courted and married their wives. But they also stayed out of politics...here, he suspected, the hills were alive with rebels and bandits, taking advantage of the terrain to hide from the local government.

Or maybe not, he thought, looking towards the forbidding peaks that dominating the eastern skyline. *Those mountains don't look hospitable at all.*

"You can ask the locals, once we've won the war," Sergeant Grieves said. "Until then, shut up and soldier."

"The flanking movement seems to have succeeded," Buckley said. "They're heading right towards the enemy lines."

Jasmine nodded. It had been a gamble, but the enemy seemed obsessed with preventing them from heading right for Pradesh, destroying bridges and digging in along the direct route. She'd hoped that meant that they wouldn't be so fixated on any *other* possible angles of approach...and her gamble seemed to have paid off. The enemy didn't seem to have noticed that over seven hundred infantrymen and their vehicles had already crossed the Ganges and were bearing down on them.

"Order the artillery to open fire," she ordered. "And then the tanks are to advance directly towards the enemy."

"Understood," Buckley said.

Thirty seconds later, she heard the big guns begin to fire.

Michael sucked in his breath as he saw the explosions in the distance as the big guns pounded the enemy with high-explosive shells. There seemed to be fewer secondary explosions this time, as far as he could tell; the enemy might have realised – finally – that parking fuel or ammunition close to their guns wasn't a bright idea. He heard, moments later, the sound of enemy guns trying to return fire, although their shooting seemed ragged. The drones spotted the gunners and targeted their positions for the next barrage from the other side of the river.

He keyed his radio. "We're moving in," he reported. "Keep a *very* close eye on our position."

They'd practiced advancing under cover of a moving barrage on Avalon – a hair-raising operation at the best of times – but a retreating barrage was something new. The prospect of an accident that led to friendly fire taking out one or more of his soldiers had haunted his thoughts ever since he'd been briefed on the battle plan, yet he knew that it was a risk that had to be taken. It was clear that the enemy had at least three to four thousand men in the area, badly outnumbering his force. If they rallied before the tanks made it across the river, the whole operation might go spectacularly wrong.

"Fire," he ordered.

The Warriors lurched forward, aiming to take the enemy position in the rear. Michael watched with cold approval as enemy troops were picked off before they realised that they were under attack, or scattered in horror as they discovered that they were surrounded. He felt his face twist into a smile as he saw several of the black-clad enforcers; no one had realised it, but their first targets were where they were intimidating the ordinary soldiers into maintaining their positions. The enforcers scattered or died, their command authority dying with them.

He fired a shot at a soldier who was trying to take aim at one of the Warriors and activated his communicator. "Call for surrender," he ordered. If the enforcers were gone, perhaps they could wrap it up before the tanks arrived. "Tell them that they won't be hurt."

The Warriors started to broadcast the surrender offer, telling the enemy soldiers to throw away their weapons, lie down on the ground and put their hands on their heads. Michael saw a number obey, but others kept running or tried to fight. It was hopeless, he knew, yet they fought anyway. The sound of shelling died away as the tanks came out of the water, machine guns constantly scanning for new targets. Moments later, the enemy position was effectively in their hands.

"Move the prisoners outside the position," Michael ordered, as the firing came to an end. "And keep a sharp eye on them."

He shook his head ruefully as he counted the bedraggled prisoners as they were led out of their former position and told to sit down in a nearby field. There were nearly two thousand of them, far more than anyone had expected to capture. He left them in the hands of Sergeant Grieves, then went to join the parties exploring the remains of the enemy positions. Not all of the makeshift bunkers had stood up well to the barrage, he discovered. Several of them were crammed full of dead soldiers, who had been killed through shock or overpressure. He shuddered, fighting down the urge to be violently sick as he staggered away from the scene.

Good thing we did manage to outflank them, he decided, as he glanced at some of the stronger bunkers. They'd held, protecting their inhabitants…and keeping them in an excellent position to fire on anyone trying to cross the river. *If we'd had to charge right into the teeth of their fire, we would have been massacred.*

He looked back at the mountains and shuddered. Pradesh was waiting for them – and Pradesh could not be outflanked. It was a fight that would give most of the advantages to the defenders, while all of the CEF's technological advantages would be negated by the urban location. Ideally,

Pradesh would be left to starve…but that wasn't an option. Whatever else happened, he knew, the coming fight was going to be a nightmare.

The bridging crews moved up as soon as the enemy fire died away and started work on a new series of pontoon bridges. Jasmine watched – tired even though she hadn't fought herself – as the bridges were put into position in record time, allowing reinforcements and supplies to flow across the Ganges. Her forward elements had already advanced, ensuring that the enemy couldn't mount a counterattack without being detected and repulsed. In their place, Jasmine would have tried to launch a counterattack at once to destroy the new bridges, but that wasn't really an option. The enemy had no sizable forces on the near side of Pradesh.

They do have insurgents, she thought, grimly. Only thirty minutes ago, there had been a report of another ambush, aimed at a truck convoy heading east. No one had been hurt, let alone killed, but it had spooked the drivers. And they weren't always *that* lucky. *We're being worn down, piece by piece.*

It would have been better if she had been prepared to rely totally on the rebels, but she wasn't sure she dared. There had been no more targeted killing, at least as far as they knew, yet there had been quite a bit of intimidation – and hundreds of higher-caste survivors had headed to the coast and begged to be taken to one of the holding islands. Jasmine suspected that the rebels had told them that if they didn't leave, they would be killed…which was, as Buckley had pointed out, really fucking stupid. The rebels were composed of former slaves, servants and refugees. They didn't know the first thing about running a farm, maintaining complex equipment or even building a government. Hell, most of the rebels who had tried to learn how to drive just hadn't had the patience or aptitude for it.

The hatred has sunk in too deep, she told herself, with a shudder. *Would Avalon have ended up like this, if we hadn't been there?*

She scowled. The Cracker War had come to such a favourable conclusion because the Marines had beaten the Crackers on the battlefield…

and because the new government had offered the Crackers reasonably decent terms, separating the radicals from those who merely fought for justice. Despite the long history of the rebellion, it had been possible to form a new order that had accepted all of the planet's factions. But here… somehow, she doubted the hatred between the castes would melt away so quickly. They'd hated each other for nearly a thousand years.

But, in the end, it wasn't her problem, even though she felt responsible for it. Her problem was getting to the capital, liberating Colonel Stalker and the Imperial Residency…and then pulling back to the garrison to wait. The planet would have to take care of itself. God knew that the Commonwealth couldn't impose a permanent solution on people so determined to wipe each other out.

Shaking her head, Jasmine keyed her wristcom. "I want to see everyone who's assigned to Operation Pony," she said, shortly. They'd taken over a farmhouse to serve as a temporary HQ. "Report to HQ as soon as possible."

General Abhey was mildly surprised that he still had a head on his shoulders. The Prince was not known for accepting excuses for defeat and his father, according to the General's family in the city, was looking for someone to serve as a scapegoat for the Prince's failure. As far as he knew, the only thing that had saved his life was the simple fact that the Prince dared not draw any more attention to problems in the west than could be avoided. There were already questions being asked by the highest aristocrats in the land.

He scowled down at the latest report from his observers in the field, mentally comparing it to the official bulletins being issued by the Prince – and found it somewhat lacking. The official story was that the enemy had been halted on the Ganges; unofficially, the enemy were already *across* the Ganges and heading east. He'd scattered small teams of soldiers throughout the countryside to impede the advancing spearheads as best as they could, but he doubted they would slow the offworlders for long.

The next report concerned the reaction of farmers to his desperate search for food and other supplies. Even the big estates, the ones run by the lower aristocracy, had been reluctant to allow the soldiers to take their chickens, pigs and goats, not to mention their seed corn. It was their livelihood that was being taken away, including their ability to replant their fields next year. But there was no choice, General Abhey knew; the off-worlders could not be allowed to take supplies from the countryside. Anything that slowed them down worked in his favour.

He scowled, darkly. The smaller farmers – even the ones who had been former soldiers – were practically in open rebellion. Several of his agents had been murdered, others reported that food and seed corn had been hidden…and they didn't even have the power to punish offenders. Some farmers had been killed, naturally; others would escape punishment until the off-worlders were defeated…if, of course, the off-worlders *were* defeated. The way they were going, he was more worried than he cared to admit about Pradesh. What if they had one of their fabled city-busting bombs with them?

The thought failed to cheer him up, so he looked at the latest message from the Prince instead. It was full of bombast, alternately insisting that the off-worlders would be destroyed with ease and threatening him and his family if he failed to hold the line. General Abhey gritted his teeth, fighting down the urge to throw the message into the fire. Who knew who happened to be serving the Prince as well as their General? Spies could be everywhere, watching and waiting for the first sign of disloyalty.

He crossed to the window and peered out over the city. Pradesh was constrained by the mountains, which meant that it had had to expand upwards instead. The city's designers had produced a series of towering apartment buildings, all of which were crammed with refugees from the farms, but there wasn't enough room for all of them. Even the streets were clogged with people; Pradesh, once the cleanest city on the planet, was threatening to turn into a disease-sodden wasteland.

It was heavily defended, he told himself. He had four thousand soldiers dug into the buildings to the west, while they'd armed and given basic training to thousands of refugees…who could, at the very least, soak up bullets aimed at his trained men. Their families, of course, had been secured and were held in a basement to the east, just to ensure they remembered which side they were on. But, in truth, if he'd had any hope of them making a difference, he would have lost it after the results of the first battles.

Everything he could muster had been massed to hold the line. There were guns, mortars and even a pair of helicopters, carefully preserved for this battle. He'd even had IED teams emplacing weapons, although there had been four accidents already before the enemy even began their offence. And he'd even placed human shields in strategic locations. It seemed impossible that the off-worlders could just push through the defences, but so far they'd smashed every force that stood up to them. He knew he had few reasons to be hopeful.

In the distance, he saw smoke rising up in the west…

They're not far away, he thought, bitterly. *They're not far away at all.*

Cursing the Prince under his breath, he strode out of his office and down towards the temples, where a giant statue of the city's patron god glared out over the fortifications. It had been a long time since he'd entered a temple willingly, no matter where he'd been, but today he had the feeling that an offering of food and drink to the god would be appropriate. If nothing else, it would show his confidence…and, perhaps, if the gods really did exist, remind them which side they were supposed to be on.

The priests were already praying for victory, leading the city's upper-caste women in a complicated prayer. He'd ordered the city's official priests to follow the official position and, so far, they were obeying… which was more than could be said for some of the others. Several of them had started ranting and raving to packed crowds, proclaiming the off-worlders to be the punishment of the gods on a disobedient planet. The General had felt a pang of guilt at their words – he had paid no attention to the gods himself, whenever it could be avoided – but he'd still had to have the priests dragged away and locked up. They couldn't be allowed to encourage the fatalism spreading through the city. Even the ones who lashed themselves publically, offering their blood in recompense for sins against the gods, were dangerous.

He paused, staring at the women. Their devotion shamed him; they knew what fate awaited them if the city fell, yet they were still praying to the gods instead of sinking into despair. Who knew? If they prayed hard enough, perhaps the gods *would* help. If they were real, of course. The giant golden statue, only a few metres shorter than the one in the capital, was only a representation of the god. They might be elsewhere, but watching, always watching.

And if they don't help, he thought, cursing his own disbelief as well as his absent master, *the off-worlders will destroy their order and replace it with chaos.*

CHAPTER THIRTY-TWO

Instead, they saw fit to belittle Germany – doing the Germans a considerable injury – without ensuring that Germany would never be in a position to take revenge.
-Professor Leo Caesius, *Diplomacy: The Lessons of the Past.*

Jasmine was barely aware of Emmanuel Alves entering the room. All of her attention was fixed on the Stormtroopers, the helicopter pilots and a handful of resistance fighters who could pass for enemy warriors. Absurd as it seemed, she had to admit that the enemy caste system – and its perverse obsession with skin colour – actually worked in their favour. A dark-skinned person with a weapon would look so badly out of place that guards would *know* to open fire.

She had had her doubts about the Stormtroopers, even though she knew that the number of full-fledged Marines available to the Commonwealth was shrinking, either through assignment to specific positions or combat losses. They couldn't have undergone the intensive hell of the Slaughterhouse, let alone the implantation process; the technology to produce Marine-class implants simply didn't exist on Avalon. But they had proved themselves, she knew, and they'd have a chance to prove themselves again. It wasn't as if she had a company of Marines to throw into the breach.

"This is Pradesh," she said. The enemy city was both large and confined, the worst possible situation for urban combat. There would be hardly any room to manoeuvre, for one thing, and the enemy would know the territory far better than her people. "As you can see, the city blocks our path to the capital. It is effectively a bottleneck. We cannot go around it. We have to go *through* it."

They knew all that, of course, she reminded herself. But she needed to say it out loud.

"They have sealed their gates and stopped taking people in from the west side," she continued. "However, they are still taking in people from the east. This gives us an opportunity to get a handful of infiltrators into the city. Your mission will be to gain entry, then hit the defenders from the rear. Find the enemy CO and assassinate him, sow chaos as opportunity arises…you know the drill. Anything to cripple their defences and make it easier for us to gain control of the city."

She looked over at the resistance fighters. "You'll have to do the talking," she said, hoping that they could understand her. Yin had sworn he'd find her men who spoke Imperial Standard, but not all of his promises had been worth something. "Can you pose as soldiers long enough to remain undetected?"

"Yes, My Lord," the leader said, in passable Imperial Standard. He *still* thought she was a guy…if it helped them take her seriously, so much the better. "We deserted from the army long ago, but we still know how to act like soldiers."

Jasmine kept her face expressionless. She hated this, hated relying on allies who might be a broken reed…but the only alternative was a frontal assault on the city's defenders. The results would be a bloodbath far in excess of any recent battle, apart from Han. But then, if Pradesh was so heavily defended, she hated to think what hitting their capital city would be like.

One problem at a time, she told herself, sternly.

"Good," she said. "The helicopters will drop you off on the other side of the mountains, before daybreak. How do you plan to convince them that you're legit?"

The leader snickered. "There are always stragglers from every forced march," he said, darkly. "No one will be surprised if we claim to have been left behind."

Jasmine snorted. How could such an undisciplined army hope to survive? She knew exactly what the Drill Instructors would have said if she'd fallen too far behind, probably after giving her a kick up the backside to force her to move faster. After all, just because soldiers were slowing down didn't mean that the *enemy* forces in pursuit were going to slow down.

But it did explain some of the odder skirmishes her forces had reported as they closed in on Pradesh. They'd overrun enemy squads who had fired off a few shots for the honour of the flag, then surrendered. If they weren't used to moving quickly – Jasmine knew from experience how hard it could be to retreat if one wasn't used to falling back – they might not have been able to break the habits of a lifetime before it was too late. And if it worked in their favour, *she* wasn't going to complain.

"Volunteers only," she said, addressing the Stormtroopers. "No one will hold it against you if you back out."

Somehow, she wasn't surprised when the entire squad volunteered for the operation.

"You think they can see us coming?"

Sergeant Andrew Wyrick considered the question as the attack helicopter lifted up into the darkening sky. The locals didn't seem to have *any* form of radar, not even the standard air-search radars that were normally attached to all military deployments. Indeed, the only form of sensor anyone had seen them deploy was heat-seeking missile heads that had been fired at various helicopters. In theory, cloaked in darkness as they were, the helicopters should be invisible.

"Depends if they have any passive sensors," he said, finally. Flying in unfamiliar territory would require them to use the radar to navigate – and a passive sensor rig could pick up on it and track them without betraying its location. "Toggle the sensor network; I don't want any of the transports using their own radar. Let them think that we're just on a roving patrol."

He peered down at the darkened landscape, noting the near-complete absence of lights west of Pradesh. The city itself was a glow against the horizon, as if they were trying to mock the advancing off-worlders by not turning off the lights. He couldn't help eyeing it nervously, even though he knew that they would be giving the city a wide berth. There were horror stories of helicopters that had been illuminated by lights on the ground – and then shot down by enemy guns.

The helicopters – three attack helicopters, two heavy transports – climbed higher as they headed southwards, moving further inland. According to orbital observation, there was hardly a remaining settlement for seventy miles, not after the enemy had started scorching their own planet to prevent croplands and farm animals from falling into rebel hands. He shuddered – the savagery of the war far outmatched anything on Avalon – and then steered the helicopter east, heading over the mountains. There was no sign of lights amidst the rocky peaks either, just pockets of air turbulence that made the helicopter shake angrily. He was used to it, but he couldn't help wondering how the resistance fighters were coping. It seemed that none of them had flown before.

"Look," Briggs said, quietly. "Take a look at that, boss."

Andrew sucked in his breath as they cleared the mountains and peered down on the eastwards side of Pradesh. The enemy countryside was nowhere near as developed as Avalon – they didn't have the technological base that even the average stage one colony would have – but there were definitely hundreds of lights scattered across the landscape. He took a look at the map, mentally tagging the lights with names and linking them to settlements that had been identified from orbit. It was probably an illusion, he knew, but it all seemed so safe and tranquil.

An illusion, of course, he sneered at himself. *Even if we weren't here, it would be far from tranquil.*

"I've identified the LZ," Briggs said, staring down at his display. "Ready to sweep the area?"

"Take us in," Andrew ordered.

The attack helicopters drew ahead of the main force, heading down towards the LZ. Orbital observation had stated that it was a suitable location, but Andrew – and the mission planners – knew better than to take that for granted. There might be hidden surprises that would make it unsuitable, just waiting to surprise them. He brought up the radar, swept the location carefully, then switched it off. No return fire blazed towards them.

"Seems clean," he said, finally.

He swung the attack helicopter into a holding pattern, then signalled the transports. "All clear," he said. "Good luck."

Specialist Gareth Nix silently cursed the designer of the helicopter's air filtering system as the aircraft rattled down towards their targets. The Stormtroopers each had hundreds of hours in helicopters, but most of the resistance fighters had been sick as soon as they hit their first patch of turbulence. Judging from their faces, they'd been convinced that the helicopter was about to heel over and slam straight into the ground. It was probably just as well that they couldn't see outside, given how close they'd been flying to the mountains. Some of them would probably have fainted at the sight.

He slipped on his NVGs as the helicopter landed with a bump. "Keep your heads down," he muttered, as he stood up, clutching his rifle in one hand. The enemy-designed rifle felt oddly unfamiliar, but carrying a MAG-47 would be a good way to betray their true identity. "Follow me out, one by one."

The noise of the rotor blades sent chills down his spine as he ran out of the helicopter, scanning for potential threats. Apart from a handful of wild animals – all Earth-origin, according to the briefing – there was nothing. He turned back and watched as his Stormtroopers joined him, followed by the resistance fighters. They looked shaky; a handful even stumbled and fell as they tried to run. As soon as the last fighter was out, the helicopter revved up its engines and headed back into the night sky. They were alone.

He motioned for his Stormtroopers to spread out, keeping one eye on the resistance fighters as they fought to control themselves. The stench of vomit still surrounded them, despite the fresh night air blowing from the east. He waited, despite his growing impatience, until Singh – their leader – finally pulled them into some semblance of order. If they'd been trying to slip into a Civil Guard base, Gareth would have despaired. Surely even the Civil Guardsmen would have noticed vomit-stained idiots trying to make their way into a secure area.

"They won't care," Singh assured him, when he voiced his concerns. There was a hint of bitterness in his tone, although it didn't seem to be directed at the off-worlders. "They will think that we found a farmhouse to house us for the night. It isn't uncommon."

Gareth didn't doubt it for a second. The ill-disciplined enemy troops seemed to spend half of their time preying on their own civilians, rather than chasing rebels and bandits across the countryside. One group had been caught in the midst of raping a pair of refugee girls, as if they'd thought that getting out of sight of the advancing off-worlders would be enough to ensure their safety. He suspected that any group that did force a farmer and his family to host them for the night would make themselves very unwelcome very quickly.

"I hope you're right," he muttered. He glanced at his GPS, then pointed to the west. "Let's move."

The thought tormented him as they marched forward, heading towards the road leading down to Pradesh. On Avalon, a soldier who turned up late – either from leave or during an exercise – could expect to face some pretty searching questions. Gareth knew from experience that only life-threatening excuses would be accepted; being with a woman, too much alcohol or even forgetting the time were not considered acceptable. But here…didn't they *care* about their military? Indiscipline in peacetime only led to indiscipline in war.

Of course they don't, he thought. *The last thing they want is an effective military, particularly not one that might be capable of overthrowing the government…*

He pushed the thought aside as they reached the road and started to walk down it, just as the first glimmers of dawn appeared over the horizon. By the time they reached the first refugee camp – it was more like a prison – on the east side of the city, sweat was trickling down his back. The local military clearly hadn't realised that it was possible to produce uniforms that protected their men from the heat – or, if they had, they hadn't bothered to try to obtain the equipment to produce them. If the temperature had been any hotter, he suspected, the refugees would be in real danger.

But they were in danger anyway, he knew, as they glanced into the camp. Some of the refugees looked as though they were trying to be defiant, but others looked…*beaten*, as if the worst had already happened and all they could do was endure. A handful of men and women had been stripped naked, their dark skins showed the signs of multiple whippings. The children seemed to be physically unharmed, but he dreaded to think what would become of them, if they survived the war. Quite a few of the kids looked to be on the verge of starvation. The fear in their eyes when they saw the uniforms the Stormtroopers were wearing was sobering to behold.

"They might have made recruits," Singh muttered, as they approached the city – and the guards on the gate. "So they uprooted them from their homes and dragged them here, planning to work them to death. If we don't get there first."

Gareth pushed that thought aside as they reached the gate and confronted the guards. They wore red and green uniforms that made them perfect targets; indeed, most of them simply didn't *look* very alert. Singh stepped forward and talked to the leader, gesturing wildly – and rudely- as he explained their delayed arrival. After he made an obscene motion with his pelvis – and passed the leader a handful of coins – the gates were opened, allowing them to enter the city.

He couldn't help feeling a little claustrophobic at the sheer masses of people on the streets, both civilians and soldiers. There were strips of bedding everywhere where people were trying to sleep under the stars, buckets of slops being hastily removed by dark-skinned untouchables and hundreds – perhaps thousands – of children running through the streets, kicking tin cans around as if they didn't have a care in the world. They were paler than the children in the refugee camp outside, Gareth realised. Chances were that they were getting treated better too.

Their parents looked more concerned, he noted. There was a thick scent of fear in the air; no matter the lies told by town criers and radio broadcasters. They *knew* that the off-worlders were massing on the other side of the wall, ready to break through and storm the city. And they knew that many of them were likely to be killed in the crossfire. He shook his head, tiredly. If the population had rebelled against their rulers long ago, it would never have come to this.

"You spoke to the guards for a while," Gareth observed, as soon as they were out of earshot of the guards. "What did you tell them?"

Singh's face darkened. "I was telling them about the charms of a young farm girl," he said, the bitterness returning to his voice. It struck Gareth suddenly that Singh was speaking from experience. He'd *been* an enemy soldier, after all. "How pretty her eyes were, how small and dainty her breasts were, how tight her holes were…and how much fun we had with her, all night."

Gareth wasn't sure he wanted to know, but he asked anyway. "Is that why you deserted?"

"My family were *Kshatriyas* – warriors," Singh admitted. "My father was a soldier; my mother was specially bred and trained to give birth to soldiers. My father offered to sponsor me into his old unit, one of the display formations that show off the planet's military prowess through parades and other shows of force. I'd heard too many stories of actual fighting and protecting the population, so I managed to get myself sent to an enforcement unit instead. My father was furious and cut me off from my family.

"The first week on patrol, we found a farmhouse and forced ourselves on the inhabitants," he added, softly. "They weren't untouchables; they were reasonably prosperous *Shudras*. And they had a daughter. She was pretty, but young; barely mature. I don't know how young. My commander grabbed the girl, stripped her bare and thrust her into my arms. He said…he said that it would be a fine welcome to the unit."

Gareth shuddered. Throughout the Empire, the standard age of consent was sixteen – but there were plenty of worlds that drew the line elsewhere. On a world where lower-caste people were considered less than animals, he had a sick feeling that the line might not exist at all, providing the perpetrator was high and the victim was low. He didn't want to hear the rest of the story, but Singh went on relentlessly.

"I tried to refuse," Singh explained. "He turned ugly, demanded to know if I thought that I was better than him. If I didn't touch the girl, I would be hurt, maybe killed…I broke; I took her by force, telling myself that it was better that I did it, rather than one of them. But after I was finished, they all took turns; by the time they were finished, she was dead. It wasn't what I'd been promised. I deserted shortly afterwards."

He straightened up. "I slipped them a bribe not to report our arrival to our CO," he said, changing the subject. "Which is good, because our CO hasn't heard of us. As long as we don't go too near the west wall, we should be relatively safe."

"Good," Gareth said. The story had put him in the mood to kill someone. Preferably the entire planetary leadership, for starters. He'd heard similar stories from people who had been press-ganged into pirate crews, people who had been forced to commit crimes just to ensure that they could never go back to civilisation. "Let's go find out where the enemy commander is holed up."

CHAPTER THIRTY-THREE

> While helpless, Germany was made to assume the blame for the war – and pay colossal (and unrealistic) reparations. Hitler was able to turn German rage to his advantage and, once elected into power, start building up to refight the war.
> -Professor Leo Caesius, *Diplomacy: The Lessons of the Past.*

"They're in position," Buckley said, quietly.

Jasmine let out a breath she hadn't realised she'd been holding. She'd established her lines near the wall, close enough to intercept anyone trying to sneak out of the city, distant enough to avoid the worst of the sniper fire from the walls. But she knew that the coming battle was going to be bloody, whatever else happened. The enemy commander – she found herself wishing, absurdly, that she knew the man's *name* – had allowed some of the refugees to sleep on the far side of the wall. They, not his people, would be the first victims of her onslaught.

She turned and looked at him. "No response to our surrender demand, I take it?"

"Just sniper fire," Buckley reported. He didn't tell her that he'd already made that report, but his body language said it very clearly. "The Warrior retreated, without damage."

"So they're still there, like a cork shoved up someone's ass," Jasmine said, taking refuge in the vulgar language. Her own reluctance to attack wasn't helping, she knew. The last report from the Imperial Residency suggested that the Colonel was running out of time. She braced herself, silently damning the cruel necessity, then keyed her wristcom. "Begin Operation Pony; I say again, begin Operation Pony."

Gareth had surveyed the enemy CO's headquarters several times before the orders came in; despite himself, he had to admit that the enemy commander had shown more tactical acumen than his predecessors. The building he'd chosen as a base was tough – and nowhere near as much of a target as the palaces and temples at the heart of Pradesh. And it was surrounded by soldiers in full battledress, rather than the ridiculous uniforms worn by some of the household troops. But it was still their target.

"As soon as the shooting starts," he ordered, keying his communicator, "we move."

Michael braced himself as the order came in, then issued his first command. The Warriors revved up their engines and prepared to move, just as the Landsharks swivelled their main guns around and unleashed a devastating barrage towards the enemy wall. It shattered under the impact in a dozen places, cascading inwards as the high explosive shells ripped it to pieces. He said a silent prayer for the helpless civilians, caught up in the midst of the fighting, then issued his second command.

"Advance."

As one, the Warriors started to advance towards the city. The infantry followed behind the AFVs as their machine guns started to chatter, throwing enemy snipers off the walls and ripping them to shreds. There was a long pause, then the Landsharks fired again, smashing what remained of the west wall. He saw hundreds of people running, some badly wounded, and muttered another prayer for them. The sound of shooting grew louder as some of the enemy troops finally began to respond, firing from secure positions. Michael issued additional orders, calling for rockets to shatter their bunkers, then followed his men into the city.

And then he turned his thoughts to staying alive.

"They're coming, Most Honoured General."

"I have no doubt of it," General Abhey sneered. The noise from the west would have been quite enough to inform him, even if shells and guided rockets hadn't been falling into the city, shattering some of his hidden guns. They'd definitely been spying on his forces, although he wasn't quite sure how. There was so much about their technology that he didn't even begin to understand. "Inform the front lines that they are to fight to the death."

"They will, Most Honoured General," his aide said.

General Abhey gritted his teeth. The man had been assigned to him by the Prince, supposedly as a sign of respect. How many others of the warrior caste were entitled to issue orders to a *Brahmin*? But he knew better. The aide's *real* job was to spy on him and report back to the Prince. And he was a shameless ass-licker who couldn't have fired a gun to save his life.

"Good," General Abhey growled. A thought struck him and he smiled. "Order the refugee brigade to be sent in. And I want you to go in person to see that it is done."

The aide blanched, then tried to hide it. "General, I..."

"I need someone I can trust to handle it," General Abhey said, watching as the younger man tried to find an excuse to stay away from the fighting. "You're a respected aristocrat. They'll listen to you. Go."

The young man hesitated, then left. General Abhey allowed himself a secret smile, then turned back to the table and gazed down at the chart of the defences. The young fool – and his patron – hadn't realised that he'd concluded that there was no point in actually trying to *command* the battle, not when the enemy was advancing with such power. He'd merely issued orders that all of his people were to resist until they could resist no more.

And now all he could do was wait. Wait and see how well his planning matched up against the sheer power of the off-worlders.

The guards on the gate were jumpy, but they didn't take much notice of Gareth and his men until it was far too late. Clearly, although they didn't bother to fight by any civilised standards – insofar as warfare was civilised – they'd never considered the possibilities of someone else wearing their uniforms. Skin colour was all they had to separate friend from foe and, as Singh proved, it really wasn't good enough. The guards on the gate were rapidly dispatched without loss to his forces.

"Get in there," he snapped, pulling the grenade launcher out of his bag. It was enemy-issue, several generations behind the weapons on Avalon, but it seemed simple enough. He fired a grenade right into the guardhouse and watched it explode into a fireball. "Clear the building!"

Leaving a third of his team to hold the ground floor, he led the way down into the basement, rolling grenades ahead of him. There was no time to take prisoners, according to the briefing – and besides, after seeing what they'd been doing to their own civilians, he didn't *want* to take prisoners. Explosions shook the building, clearing the way. He crashed through a door into a large staff room, glanced at the map on the table… and then ducked as an officer wearing an absurd uniform opened fire on him. The officer was shot down a moment later by one of Singh's men.

Singh poked him, suspiciously. "You think he was their commander?"

"I hope so," Gareth muttered. He checked the man's uniform for rank stripes, but the locals didn't even seem to have evolved a common system for denoting rank. The Marines, Imperial Army and Civil Guard all shared the same basic system; he honestly couldn't understand why the locals didn't have one of their own. "He's certainly wearing enough gold braid."

He tore the map off the table, folded it up and stuck it in a pouch, then led the way into the next room. Several other officers were standing there, staring at the raiders as if they'd seen monstrous ghosts. Gareth bit down on what he wanted to say and simply shot them in the head, one by one. One of them tried to surrender, but Singh ignored it, blowing the man's head off with a single shot. Gareth found it hard to blame him.

"They're confused out here, sir," the observer reported. "But I think someone is trying to organise them."

Gareth smiled, coldly. Let them try to organise a counterattack when their CO was dead and there was a major attack pushing in from the west. He knew from talking to Singh that the local troops were not expected to show any initiative; hell, it was quite possible that most of them hadn't even been issued any ammunition for their weapons. It seemed absurd, but he had to admit that the enemy commanders might have a point. Some of their press-ganged soldiers would happily shoot them in the back, rather than turn their guns on the enemy.

Still, there was no point in sticking around. He pulled a thermal grenade off his belt and set the timer, then emplaced it in a cabinet of paperwork, then waved to Singh and the rest of the troops. They'd definitely outstayed their welcome.

"Targets of opportunity," he muttered, once they were outside the building. The observers had called in a handful of shells from the big guns, scattering the forces massing in position to see and interdict their escape. Behind them, the building was already starting to burn, destroying the files the enemy CO had collected. "Let's see what we can find."

Michael heard the chanting as he advanced into the city, even over the thunderous sound of the gunfire from the Landsharks. He glanced at Sergeant Grieves, who seemed equally perplexed; neither of them could pinpoint the source of the sound. It seemed to be coming from all around them. And then he saw the first wave of men hurling themselves towards the advancing soldiers.

My God, he thought, stunned. *They're mad!*

They charged, firing as they came. Michael stared for a long moment, then barked a command. The Warriors opened fire with their machine guns, scything down the men like blades of grass, but others kept coming, running right into the teeth of their fire as if they honestly didn't care about their lives. Michael fought the urge to be sick as they were ripped apart, blood and guts showering everywhere…and still more came. They seemed unstoppable.

"Mortar strike," he snapped into his communicator. "Danger close; I say again, danger close."

There was a pause, then shells started to fall ahead of them. The lines of enemy suicide attackers seemed to vanish, the last of them shot down by the Warriors seconds after they entered range. Michael stared in disbelief at the sight in front of him; the streets were literally awash with blood, a handful of survivors moaning among the blood and guts. He honestly couldn't understand how *anyone* had survived. Dear god, not even the cruellest pirate had ordered his men into such a bloodbath. Behind him, he heard several of his men puking their guts out.

It *burned* at him not to be able to advance, but he knew that his squad had been badly shaken by the experience. He tapped his communicator, requesting reinforcements, then ordered them to fall back to a defensible location. They needed time to recuperate.

Somehow, he had the feeling that they weren't going to get it.

"They used *human wave* attacks?"

"Yes, Brigadier," Major Adamson reported, through the communications network. "There were thousands of them, mainly untrained civilians. Three of our squads were actually overrun and…"

Jasmine could fill in the blanks. "Destroyed, I presume," she said. She remembered Han and shuddered. "Are they hopped up on something?"

"Unknown," the Major admitted. "It's quite possible, but we won't know until we get the results from blood testing."

"Get samples back to the medics," Jasmine ordered. Han had been bad…but she'd been a newly-minted Rifleman then, not the CO. She'd never really been able to comprehend the full horror of the nightmarish battle until afterwards, when all of the after-action reports and assessments had been distributed. No wonder the old sweats had been so glad to be redeployed back to Earth. "And then move reinforcements up to hold the line."

"The rebels want to add their own forces to the mix," Buckley offered. He gave her a long look. "They might be able to take some of the pressure off us."

Jasmine considered it, briefly. At best, the rebel forces were light infantry, ill-suited to the concrete hell Pradesh was becoming. But she knew that she didn't have many reinforcements on hand, certainly not without drawing down the patrols sweeping the roads for bombs and other unpleasant surprises. And it would allow the rebels to feel as if they were making a contribution.

"Tell Yin that he can funnel his people in, but make sure that there's a fire controller with each group," she ordered. "If they get into real trouble, we can fire covering shells to get them out."

"Understood," Buckley said.

The ammunition dump was poorly defended, much to Gareth's surprise. But then, most of the enemy soldiers were running around trying to hunt down the insurgents or fighting to prevent the CEF from breaking in. He attacked at once, leading his team to shoot down the guards and take possession of the dump, then glanced inside. It was a minor miracle, he realised a moment later, that the enemy hadn't had a major disaster already. They'd stacked explosives and detonators together.

"Give me a moment," he muttered, as he rigged up a timer. It didn't take long to produce a basic IED. "Let's go."

He led the way out and into the side streets, brushing past countless refugees who were trying to hide from the fighting. Moments later, there was a colossal explosion as the ammunition dump went up, shaking the ground hard enough to smash windows and send fragile buildings crumbling to the ground. He keyed his communicator, sending in a report, then led the team into a building to take a breather before launching the next offensive.

"Move towards the front," the CO ordered, finally. "The rebels are taking the lead."

Offhand, Andrew couldn't recall seeing a more wretched city. He'd been in Camelot during the battle and he'd thought that was bad, but this was far worse. A third of the city seemed to be on fire as the CEF and its rebel allies pushed their way inwards, while the remainder seemed to be in absolute confusion. The colossal fireball that billowed up from the city a moment later sent the helicopter wobbling unsteadily through the sky for a moment, before Andrew regained control and peered down, looking for likely targets.

There were none – or, at least, it was impossible to pick them out. A tidal wave of refugees seemed to be fleeing the city, heading east towards the capital. He found himself hoping that they found some safety, although he knew that it was unlikely. They'd be a plague of locusts swarming out all over the land, eating all that they could find…it wouldn't be long before starvation threatened the population.

"Picking up laser pointers," Briggs reported. "Our teams on the ground are reporting in. They want strikes ASAP."

Andrew scowled. Firing into a burning city, with visibility a joke under a haze of smog…it wasn't something he was comfortable with. But they had their orders. They just had to hope that the Forward Air Controllers knew what they were targeting.

"Fire," he ordered.

"They're fighting like demons, but they're no good at clearing houses," Major Adamson reported. "No sense of tactics at all."

Jasmine nodded, watching the live feed from the drones. The rebel fighters were brave, no doubt about it, and the prospect of victory forced them forward…but they didn't have the slightest idea how to conserve their strength. It was as if they'd forgotten how to *think* in the midst of fighting, of finally getting a chance to wrap their hands around enemy necks.

At this rate, there won't be much left of the city by the time we're through with it, she thought. The FACs kept calling down strikes on buildings that were defying the rebels, blasting them into rubble…and often killing civilians in the process. Jasmine would have offered a truce long enough to evacuate the civilians, if she'd thought that the locals would accept it. But she knew that they would have only taken it as a sign of weakness.

There were a handful of prisoners…but, compared to previous battles, only a handful. The intelligence staff were interrogating them now, trying to determine what had made them surrender and the others hold out. It would be nice to think that they would come up with something that they could use to encourage a surrender, but Jasmine knew better than to hope too much. The odds were against it.

"Cycle up our reinforcements," she ordered, grimly. According to the drones, there were riots brewing in the untouchable holding pens on the other side of the mountains. They would be massacred if the CEF didn't break through to the pens in time. "And continue bombarding them with the offer to accept surrender."

"All right, you lugs," Michael bellowed, despite the tiredness pervading his body. The orders were clear, allowing no room for misinterpretation. "Get up; we're going back in!"

His soldiers clambered to their feet with varying degrees of enthusiasm. They'd had a rest, some food and a drink, but they still looked tired. And yet there would only be rest once the fighting was over. In the distance, the thunderous sounds of guns, rockets and explosions only showed that the enemy had nowhere to run. They were trapped in the bottleneck, unable to retreat in good order.

"The rebels have done a good job of clearing some of them out of our way," he added, as an update came in over the network. And they'd paid a heavy price to do it, he *didn't* add. "We now have to take part in the final push."

Bracing himself, he checked his weapons and body armour – he'd found a bullet caught in his armour after leaving the FEBA, one he hadn't even noticed hit him – and then led his men back to the war.

CHAPTER THIRTY-FOUR

> In the meantime, the Allied coalition against Germany was allowed to lapse. America went into isolation, Italy (unsatisfied with its booty from the war) switched sides, France and Britain drifted apart and – war-weary – refused to stand up to Hitler when he could have been stopped relatively easily. The net result was a refought war and a devastated continent.
>
> -Professor Leo Caesius, *Diplomacy: The Lessons of the Past.*

The news from the front fell into two categories. There were the official updates from the Prince's commanders, which proclaimed great victories, and the more useful messages from his spies, which warned that Pradesh was slowly falling to the off-worlders. Somehow, Sivaganga Zamindari was unsurprised when the Prince's invitation to hear the reports of the battle as they came in was rescinded. The Prince wouldn't want his allies to hear the news of his defeat.

But it did allow him a chance to pay a call on the Rajah. No one dropped in on the Rajah without an appointment, but requesting an interview might have tipped off the Prince that Sivaganga was planning to go behind his back. Eventually, he announced his intention to request the Rajah's blessing for the betrothal of his son to the daughter of another aristocrat and departed for the palace. If the Prince suspected something, he did nothing to prevent the Rajah from agreeing to the interview.

The Rajah's palace was heavily guarded, he was relieved to see. Armed guards stood everywhere, watching new arrivals suspiciously; Sivaganga was searched twice before he was even allowed to enter the building, then escorted up the stairs and into the smaller appointment chamber by two burly eunuch guards who watched him closely at all times. They took his sword, shoes and even his headgear before allowing him to step inside… and he was grimly aware of their presence, even after he faced the 'Rajah' for their private appointment. It was far too likely that one of them might have been pushed into spying for the Prince.

He wished, as he went through the series of elaborate bows, that he could speak to the Rajah alone – and indeed, by the standards of the aristocracy, he *was*. But the guards and servants had eyes and ears; ignored by their masters, they could go anywhere and hear anything. He wanted to ask the Rajah to send them away, but he dared not even raise the topic with his monarch. It would have ensured his immediate execution.

"My Lord and Master," he said, as he completed the bows with a prostration that left his head just under the Rajah's foot. "I must talk with you on an urgent matter."

The Rajah eyed him calculatingly. No one stayed Rajah without cunning, courage and a certain amount of ruthlessness, not when there were so many who wanted to be Rajah themselves. The elderly man had to watch his son carefully, knowing that one day his heir might become impatient and seek to take the throne by force…and then there were other aristocrats who thought that their blood made them better candidates for the throne. It was a cutthroat system, Sivaganga knew, one that encouraged distrust and suspicion. There were times, he had to admit, when he wondered if there might be a better way.

"Talk," the Rajah ordered, waving him upright.

Sivaganga settled back on his knees with a sigh of relief. His body had felt older, somehow, as the news of the first defeats had started to flow in from the west. Prostrating himself in front of his master was painful, all the more so as he knew the Rajah's power was starting to crumble. But was the Rajah himself aware of it? What had his son told him?

He took a long breath and began. "My Lord and Master, the news from the front is not good," he said. "Pradesh is on the verge of falling to the off-worlders. Once the city is gone, there are no defence lines in place between Pradesh and the capital – and your Royal Person."

The Rajah's face showed no expression. Sivaganga wondered, bitterly, just what was going through the Rajah's mind. He wasn't ignorant, unlike the untouchables; he would have noticed that the locations of the staggering off-worlder defeats were constantly moving eastwards, towards his capital. The mountains might have blocked most of the rumours from the west, but enough had made it through to make the population restive. And there were eager young aristocrats already sharpening their knives.

"They have also been arming and training rebels," he added. Their intelligence *did* have a good idea of what had been stockpiled in the off-worlder garrison. If the rebels gained access to the armoury, they would become unstoppable. "Right now, we must start considering that the war may not develop to our advantage."

The Rajah leaned forwards. "Are you saying that we have lost?"

Sivaganga heard someone gasp behind him. He didn't look round.

"The off-worlders will find new recruits when they break through the mountains," Sivaganga said. "*We* will have to arm men who are…unlikely to serve us with great enthusiasm, or recruit more household troopers from the aristocracy. They are unlikely to slow the off-worlders down until they reach the capital – and a fight in the capital would utterly tear the city apart."

He didn't add – because he knew that the Rajah would know – that the loyalty of the aristocracy would almost certainly collapse. Instead of sending their troops to join the defence of the planet, they would see to their own safety – or, perhaps, seek to topple the Rajah and try to come to terms with the off-worlders. What did they have to lose?

"Let Us assume that you are correct," the Rajah said, after a long chilling moment. "What do you propose that We do?"

"Seek a truce, now," Sivaganga said. It was, effectively, throwing the Prince to the wolves…but it wasn't as if the Rajah was short on sons. They just weren't old enough to be named as heirs to the throne. "Tell the off-worlders that we will pay reparations, provided that they leave your dynasty in control. Offer them whatever they want – your daughters, your wealth – in exchange for survival."

The Rajah stared at him long enough for Sivaganga to wonder if he'd gone too far. Offering the Rajah's daughters to the off-worlders was bad enough, but surrendering his wealth – the source of his power – was worse. Without it, the Rajah's position would be crippled. He would have problems recruiting more soldiers, which would make him vulnerable to an internal coup.

"If your assessment of the situation is correct," the Rajah said, finally, "it is already too late."

"We still have something to bargain with," Sivaganga said. "They would have to batter their way into our city in time to prevent us from destroying the Imperial Residency. We could use that as leverage against them – and once the forces have stopped advancing, we can keep talking sweetly to them until they leave the planet. And then we can settle accounts with the rebels."

He knew that wasn't going to be easy. Even if the off-worlders left the planet completely, there would still be years of fighting ahead – and no guaranteed victory. Perhaps it would be best to come to a truce with the rebels…but he knew that the Rajah would never even consider the possibility. They were nothing more than untouchables, after all. There was no point in treating with them as equals.

The Rajah considered the proposal. Sivaganga felt a moment of pity; his son controlled most of the military now, placing him in a particularly strong position. Even if he accepted the peace proposals, the Prince would still feel betrayed. It was quite likely that he would seek to take power for himself immediately.

And he can't be killed, because that would leave the Rajah without a strong male heir, Sivaganga thought, grimly. *His death would leave the Rajah vulnerable until his other sons reach their majorities.*

"We will inform Our son that We will send representatives to the Residency," the Rajah stated. "But We must obtain a settlement in line with Our dignity."

Sivaganga braced himself. "Most Humble Lord," he said, taking his life in his hands, "you may not have any dignity when the off-worlders reach your city."

The Rajah, astonishingly, smiled. "But without retaining my dignity" – he spoke of himself in the first person, surprising Sivaganga – "my position is weak and it will fall. The prestige of the Rajah must not be allowed to slip."

It has already slipped, Sivaganga wanted to shout. Did the Rajah really believe that the rest of the aristocracy were unaware of the looming disaster? Sivaganga wasn't the only aristocrat making covert preparations to send his family out of the city. Once Pradesh fell, the rest of the aristocrats would either start running to their estates or launch a coup against the Rajah and his son. Time was running out.

"I understand, My Lord," he said, bowing again. "If I may make one final suggestion?"

The Rajah quirked an eyebrow, invitingly.

"There is an off-worlder prisoner held in the Prince's dungeons," Sivaganga said. He'd had to talk the Prince out of killing the off-worlder several times. The next time, he might fail – and be forced to watch as the off-worlder was crucified by the Prince's guards. "I wish to suggest that you take him into your personal custody."

The Rajah stroked his beard, considering the possible consequences. "I will see to it," he said, finally. "You are dismissed."

Sivaganga nodded, then bowed and knocked his head against the carpeted floor. He prayed, as he started to crawl backwards, that the Rajah could rein in the Prince before it was too late – and that it was not already too late. Surely, the off-worlders didn't *want* the planet. No one had been interested in their world, save as a dumping ground for unwanted refugees. Maybe they could go back to being ignored.

He shuddered as he was led out of the Palace. In the distance, he could still hear the sound of guns from the Residency. It wouldn't be long before they were coming out of the countryside too.

Mathew opened his eyes, somehow. He knew that he was dying, knew that his body was gradually breaking down through hunger, thirst and ill-treatment. The food and water they supplied was insufficient, while they hadn't even *bothered* to provide medical care. Part of him was mildly surprised that he was still alive – he half-expected that he would never wake up, every time he closed his eyes – but the rest of him found it hard to care. His thoughts kept wandering all over the universe, reminding him of his childhood on Avalon.

It had crossed his mind that he was going mad, that he might *already* be mad, but so what? If it helped him cope with his new world, the tiny and smelly cell that he knew he would never leave, it might even come in handy. He'd wanted to laugh, like a madman from one of the immensely bad entertainment programs shipped to Avalon before the Fall of Earth, but his throat was too dry to do more than cough. Perhaps, he told himself, this was the day upon which he would die.

He heard, in the distance, the sound of angry shouting. Someone had once told him that being immersed in another culture would allow him to learn their language, but he hadn't picked up even a single word. Not that it mattered, he knew; if he escaped, he would stick out like a sore thumb. Even the pale-skinned higher castes looked different from a baseline Avalon native. Their features were sharper, for one thing. He tried to tell himself that just because they *looked* cruel didn't mean that they were. But the evidence suggested otherwise.

The shouting grew closer, then came to an abrupt halt. Silence fell; Mathew found himself straining his ears to hear something – anything – from outside the cell. There were a faint series of thuds and a sound that reminded him of a body hitting the floor, then nothing. It struck him that he might be being rescued, that the CEF might be storming the building, but he knew that it was unlikely. If the city was under attack, his captors would not have hesitated to kill him to prevent the CEF from liberating him. Even so, the flare of hope in his chest refused to fade away as someone started working on the door.

It wasn't soldiers from the CEF, he realised numbly as the door fell open. The newcomers wore bright gold uniforms, making them shine even in the darkened cell. Mathew knew that they would have made excellent targets if he'd had his pistol, but as it was all he could do was sit helplessly and wait to see what happened. The first newcomer strode over to his side, examined the chains securing him to the wall and then barked orders towards the door. A moment later, the mute girl who'd taken care of him appeared, blood running down the side of her face from where she'd been struck. She carried a key in one hand, which she passed to the newcomer before falling to her knees and prostrating herself in front of him. For a terrible moment, Mathew thought that he was going to crush her head under his boot before he turned and unlocked the chains. They fell clear…but the moment Mathew tried to move, his body screamed in protest.

The newcomer scowled, then barked more orders. Two of his men came forward and picked Mathew up between them, carrying him through the door and up the stairs. Outside, there were several guards lying on the floor, beaten and bloody. Mathew couldn't prevent himself from smiling, no matter the pain, as he saw one of his interrogators nursing a broken jaw. It seemed that the newcomers had knocked the guards down and out.

Outside, the sun was so bright that Mathew flinched away from the light. How long had he been in the cell? It had felt like months…the only clue he had that it might not have been so long was the simple fact that his chin hadn't grown much stubble during his confinement. But did beatings and starvation slow it down? He honestly couldn't remember. Instead, he took a breath of fresh air – despite the faint stench of smoke and decomposing human bodies – and relaxed. If they were taking him to his death, at least he'd seen the sun again before he went.

They stopped outside a strange wooden box, about the same size as an aircar, and opened a door. Inside, there were two benches, one covered with cushions. His captors carried him into the box, placed him down on the cushions and placed straps over his body. A moment later, the girl was shoved in beside him. Someone had tied her hands together in front of her and wrapped a long cord around her ankles. Mathew stared in disgust; she was no threat to them, yet they insisted on treating her like a dangerous criminal.

The doors slammed shut a moment later, leaving them alone. Mathew wished he could say something, but his mouth refused to work. Seconds later, the box lurched and rose into the air, then started to shake regularly. It took him a moment to realise that the newcomers were actually *carrying* the box, with him and his nursemaid inside it. They'd never heard of cars, he realised, even though he was sure that there would be oil deposits somewhere underground. But then, human labour was cheap here.

He found himself feeling sick as the vehicle kept moving, but thankfully there was nothing in his stomach to vomit up. The girl reached out and touched his forehead gently, then looked away, her dark eyes shadowed and pale. She knew that he was dying…he scowled inwardly, trying to understand just why they had her in the prison. Did they believe that he would be less likely to hurt her if he tried to break loose? Or was she the daughter of a prisoner who had been put to work? He pushed the thought aside as the vehicle finally came to a stop and was lowered to the ground. There was no way to know what was about to happen, but he had the feeling that he was about to find out.

The door opened, revealing more gold-clad guards. They pulled the bench out and carried it – and Mathew – through a large set of doors into another room. The girl followed, her hands and feet still bound. Mathew tried to throw her a sympathetic look, then was distracted by an older man peering down at him. Moments later, most of his cuffs were removed and the man was poking and prodding at his wrists.

"Young man," the man said, in passable Imperial Standard. "Can you understand me?"

Mathew had to swallow twice before he could answer. "Yes."

"Good," the man said. "I'm a doctor, here to examine you. I suggest that you refrain from causing trouble. The guards will not hesitate to replace your chains if you pose a threat."

"I can barely move," Mathew said. "Why am I here?"

"To be healed," the doctor informed him. "Lie still and let me work."

Mathew wasn't reassured. What sort of medical treatments did they use on this godforsaken planet? Leeches, bleedings and amputations? On the low-tech worlds, he knew, a broken arm could cripple someone for life. Here, if there were any modern medical treatments, they were reserved for the aristocracy. He'd seen quite a few untouchables begging because there was nowhere else for them, their lives destroyed by injuries that could be cured in a few days on Avalon.

"Heal her too," he said, quickly. "Her tongue, too."

"She was silenced," the doctor said. There was no pity in his voice. "I cannot help her to talk again."

Can't, Mathew thought, *or won't?*

Chapter Thirty-Five

> Such issues illustrate the complexities of international diplomacy, for several different nations were involved, each one with different interests. It proved impossible to hold together a coalition indefinitely without a very clear threat – and there were plenty of times when that threat was far from clear.
> -Professor Leo Caesius, *Diplomacy: The Lessons of the Past.*

"The north wall is starting to weaken," Flora commented.

Edward nodded, rubbing his eyes. If anything, the enemy bombardment had intensified over the past two days – and their reluctance to continue the fight at night had vanished. The constant shelling had been keeping his people awake and tired, despite the use of stimulant capsules and sleeping pills. Supplies of them were running low too, just like everything else.

If only we could get supplies into the city, he thought. But every time he looked at the problem, it became clear that it wasn't possible. The helicopters would be engaged by enemy fire as soon as they came into range. *As it is, we can't hold out much longer.*

"We might need to start pulling people out of your compound," he said, sourly. Thankfully, the central compound hadn't been threatened yet, but it was only a matter of time. "You can double up with us."

Flora sighed. Whatever differences had existed between the two forces had melted away as the siege took its toll. Commonwealth and Wolfbane personnel lived and fought together, covering each other as the enemy tested the defences time and time again. And they would die together,

Edward and Flora both knew, when the defences finally collapsed. It was only a matter of time.

"We can't move too many supplies now," she warned. "They're hitting us hard."

Edward nodded. Anyone out in the open was vulnerable, either to a mortar shell or a sniper shot. The enemy snipers had been creeping forward again, despite Marine sharpshooters attempting to take them out. One of them had picked off a Commonwealth soldier only yesterday, firing from over a kilometre away.

He looked down at the datapad, which listed the remaining supplies. Food and water was on half-rations already, but it could be stretched to two more weeks at most. It was ammunition that was the real problem, he knew; at current rates of consumption, they would run out altogether in less than two days. And if the enemy charged the walls again, the ammunition would run out at terrifying speed. At least they didn't seem to realise that the defenders had only a handful of mortar shells left.

"But we can't afford to lose the north wall either," he said. Yesterday, a shell had come alarmingly close to blowing a hole in the wall completely. Another hit and the wall would crumble into dust, allowing the enemy to charge right into the compound. "We have to balance our responsibilities."

He rubbed his eyes, wishing for sleep. Offhand, he doubted he had kept such hours since the Slaughterhouse – and he'd been a younger man then, at the peak of human physical condition. It was worse for the Professor and the other civilians, he knew. Some of them were staggering around like zombies, unable to awaken fully and yet unable to sleep. If this went on, they'd end up shooting at shadows – or each other. He'd already had one soldier start shooting madly at enemies only he could see.

And his Sergeant knocked him out, Edward thought, dryly. *At least he's getting some rest.*

"Take command of the defences," he ordered, pushing the thought aside. "I'm going to tour the building."

The sight that greeted him as he made his way through the complex was pitiful. Most of the maids were so tired that they were trying to sleep, despite the endless explosions shaking the building; most of his soldiers weren't much better off. Thankfully, they were used to the stench of unwashed human bodies or it would have been a great deal worse. He looked into the infirmary and saw the medic – and her volunteer assistants – doing what they could for the wounded. Most of them required the garrison's medical centre, not what they had.

"Sir," a soldier said, tiredly. "Are…are they still out there?"

"I'm afraid so," Edward said, kneeling down beside the speaker. He was so *young*, utterly fresh-faced, barely old enough to shave. It was easier to understand, now, what the old sweats had said when they'd talked about old man's guilt. He'd sent this young man off to war, where he'd been wounded – and was still at grave risk of dying. "What's your name, son?"

"Eliot," the young man said. He cleared his throat. "Private Eliot Rosenberg, 3rd Avalon Infantry Battalion."

"You guys did well up there," Edward said, seriously. "Without you, we would have been overrun."

Rosenberg smiled. "As good as the Marines?"

"Definitely," Edward said. Rosenberg and so many others would have made prime candidates for the Slaughterhouse, if they could have sent them there. Most of the best candidates came from the Outer Worlds, even though Edward himself came from Earth. "You held the line for us."

"Thank you, sir," Rosenberg said. He hesitated, then leaned forward so he could speak quietly. "What are the rules on marrying someone from this world?"

Edward hesitated. When had Rosenberg had the opportunity to meet someone…oh, of course. "One of the maids, I presume?"

"Yes," Rosenberg said. "She's wonderful, takes good care of me…"

"I don't think that the immigration office would object, if she chose to marry you," Edward said, making a mental note to have an older sergeant have a few words with the young man before he committed himself. War brides, in his experience, weren't always as interested in their husbands as they were in escaping their homeworlds. "But are you sure she wants to go with you?"

"I think so, sir," Rosenberg said. "But I haven't asked her yet."

"Good luck," Edward said, standing upright. "And heal quickly."

He nodded as he saw the rifle lying beside the blankets. If the enemy broke in, the wounded would sell their lives dearly…although he knew that they would die. Wounded, unable to move, a single grenade would kill them all. If the ammunition shortage grew worse, he might have to recall those weapons…but for the moment they'd have a chance to claw the enemy before they went down.

Silently wishing the young man good luck, he headed over to the next wounded soldier. If they'd been injured under his command, the least he could do was visit them where they lay…

…And pray that he wasn't lying when he told them that the CEF was on the way.

Blake Coleman had his doubts about the security of the warehouse the rebels were using as a base, but he had to admit that it served a useful purpose. The untouchables ran the city's sewer system, among other things, and they used them to move throughout the city unseen by their masters. It didn't take long before Mad's father explained to him that the warehouse was actually *linked* to the sewers.

"Pay attention," he said, once his class was assembled. Seventeen young men, all bright…and doomed to a life of servitude by the colour of their skin. "If you get any of this wrong, the odds are that you will die painfully."

Mad translated as he looked meaningfully towards a large table, crammed with all sorts of household junk. He hadn't lied to Mad's father when he'd told him that the untouchables had all sorts of weapons in their hands, they just didn't know how to use them. But then, there were tricks *he* would never have thought of if he hadn't been introduced to them on the Slaughterhouse. He had no idea who the long-dead MacGyver had been – a Marine Pathfinder, he assumed – but he'd had all sorts of ideas for making deadly weapons from common materials. His book was banned all over the Empire, if only because it would give resistance fighters ideas.

"Most soldiers – and certainly all generals – will tell you that you need proper weapons to fight," he added. "That is a myth, spread by men who want their potential victims to feel helpless and cower before their might.

There are no dangerous weapons, just dangerous men. With the proper mindset, a weapon can be constructed from almost anything and put to deadly use. Without it…not a chance."

He surveyed their faces for a long moment. They were eager to learn, he saw, but would they have the nerve to use it? Their caste had been downtrodden so long that they might be unable to fight when the time came. Or they might flinch at the wrong moment, only to be gunned down before they could recover. All he could do was teach them…and pray.

"This is a bottle of cleaner," he said. Unsurprisingly, some of them sneered at his explanation. They all *knew* that it was used to clean aristocratic toilets. "Useless for anything else, right?"

He grinned as he picked up a second bottle. "This is a bottle of a different cleaner," he added. "Separately, they're harmless. Together…well, you can build a pretty effective bomb out of them, with a few more pieces of junk."

Piece by piece, he put together a very simple IED. It would have horrified the local government if they'd understood just how much power they'd inadvertently placed in the hands of the untouchables, even without additional weapons brought in from the CEF. Once it was ready, Blake allowed them to look at it for a few minutes and then took it apart, carefully separating the dangerous components.

"You're supposed to be good with your hands," he said, to a trio of men who were unpaid mechanics. "You should have no difficulty in sourcing the material and then putting together more of these beauties for yourselves. Once ready, you can set them up in certain places and then detonate them when the time comes. Just remember, once an IED is emplaced, removing it can be damn difficult."

Once Mad had translated his speech, he went on to explain pressure plates and even radio detonators. Unsurprisingly, they picked up the concept at once and started discussing it amongst themselves in their own language. Blake waited for them to quiet down while he put together his next trick, then held it out for them to see. The tiny fan was fashionable among the upper castes, a neat way to keep oneself cool in public, but the can of liquid he'd attached to the device didn't look friendly at all.

"The liquid here is yet another cleaning fluid," he explained. After the bomb, no one was inclined to doubt him. "However, if you happen to superheat the liquid, it turns into gas – gas vile enough to make people seriously ill if they breathe in enough of it. Useful?"

He grinned at their expressions, then pushed on. "You probably already know that basic cooking oil can catch fire," he added. The locals used oil almost constantly, along with rice and noodles. It almost seemed to be their staple dish. "What you don't know is if you mix it with *this*" – he held up yet another bottle – "you get a liquid that burns hot enough to cause real damage."

One by one, he went through his series of tricks and traps for their benefit, feeling almost like a stage magician as he unveiled them one by one. Flour could make an effective bomb, treated properly; basic gunpowder was relatively simple to make, given time. He even took a moment to outline the most effective techniques for sabotaging the defences, pointing out that dirt or sugar in the fuel tank could rot vehicle engines. It was hard to believe that untouchables were actually allowed to serve in vehicle sheds and other military complexes, even if they weren't allowed weapons. The opportunity for sabotage was remarkable.

"Make sure that you are careful where you practice," he concluded. "If you are caught, you'll wish that you had blown yourself up."

He watched them go, mentally unsure if he was doing the right thing. Knowledge was power – and the right sort of knowledge could undo a government or bring down a regime. Marines *didn't* teach locals such tricks, not regularly. They would only have ended up being used against the Empire.

And us, he thought, sourly. *What would the Crackers have done with such knowledge?*

"Thank you," Mad said, very quietly. "You gave them hope."

Blake nodded, sourly. Once the balloon went up, many of those young men – and the young men they were going to teach, spreading the knowledge as widely as possible – would die. If the latest news from Pradesh was accurate, the CEF would be at the city walls within the week. By then, he needed to have the rebels ready to act…despite knowing that it would cost them heavily.

I should have stayed a Rifleman, he thought, numbly. *I was happy there.*

Darkness fell quickly, revealing flames drifting up in the distance from the Residency. Blake looked towards it and shivered, then allowed her to pull him out onto the streets. The sheer level of despondency and hopelessness still stunned him, even though the rebels had shown him proof that not *everyone* had been beaten down. It was worse than Camelot's Red Light District had been, back when they'd first arrived on Avalon. At least there the population had had booze to drown their sorrows. Here, the locals were not allowed alcohol. It was on the prohibited list.

Which didn't stop the aristocrats indulging themselves, he reminded himself. They'd discovered a crate – a full crate - of an alcoholic brand of Firewater Mead in the Residency, dating back to ten years before the Empire had abandoned Avalon. Blake had hoped that the Colonel would share it out among the men, but instead it had been put aside to serve as a makeshift disinfectant. It was, in his opinion, a waste of a crate worth more than the combined salaries of the entire company.

"You handled them well," Mad said, softly. She pulled her cloak around her face, concealing her pale skin. "They were very impressed."

"Good," Blake said. "I just hope they listen to me."

Something…*changed*. Finely-honed combat instincts came to the fore, warning him that there was trouble ahead. He glanced around surreptitiously, looking for a possible threat; someone was moving up ahead, moving right towards them. Several people, he realised as they came closer, wearing ragged clothes and dark expressions. Their eyes were fixed on Mad. One of them looked at Blake and made a gesture with his hands, ordering him to flee at once. Blake stared at him in disbelief. Did they really expect that he would *run*?

Of course they do, he told himself. Mad had said enough about her upbringing to convince him that it hadn't been a safe environment for *anyone*. The rebels co-existed, uneasily, with wolves who prayed on the untouchable sheep. He felt a hot flash of anger as the man threatened him with a knife no larger than his finger; it wasn't enough to be treated like dirt by the upper castes, the untouchables had to be treated badly by their own kind. It had been the same in Earth's undercity – and a thousand other places across the Empire.

One of them reached out for Mad's breast. They were going to rape her right out on the street, he realised, as he reached forward and casually snapped the knife-bearer's wrist. He let out a yelp, more in shock than in pain, and started to cradle it; Blake moved forward, pulled the would-be rapist forward and slammed the palm of his hand into the man's throat. He felt the man's neck break; he dropped the twitching body and moved on to the next target, who was desperately trying to retreat. Blake slammed a kick into his chest and heard several ribs break. The man fell to his knees, vomiting up blood.

The remainder of the gang broke and ran, fleeing into the shadows. Blake watched them go, mentally debating whether he should give chase. They were vermin, sick monsters who preyed on their own kind, yet he knew that if he killed them all there would be replacements on the streets within the day. Shaking his head, he looked over at Mad and discovered, to his surprise, that she seemed calm. But then, she *had* worked for the aristocracy, where she met rapists who just happened to have titles all the time.

"We'd better move," he said, bitterly. "Come on."

"Thank you," Mad said, as they made their way through the darkened streets. *Now* she sounded shaken. "You...you killed them."

"Some of them," Blake said. The one who had come at him with a puny knife might have survived...but not for long. The streets were unforgiving to the weak and it was unlikely that he would be able to get proper medical care. "The others got away."

He paused. "What about the bodies?"

Mad looked at him as if he'd said something stupid. "What *about* the bodies?"

Blake winced, inwardly. There were so many bodies lying around that no one would notice a couple more. Even if someone did, who were they going to report it to? The untouchables wouldn't want the household troops invading their slums, would they? He smiled at the thought, then followed her back to the shack they'd been given. It was better than a Civil Guards barracks, although *that* wasn't saying much. And it was nicely anonymous.

"We're going to get supplies soon, I hope," he said, once they were inside. He'd checked the house for bugs the day they'd moved in, finding nothing. "And then we can have some real fun."

He scowled. If only they were in time…

CHAPTER
THIRTY-SIX

The Invasion of Iraq presents an illustration of how different national imperatives can interact. America believed the invasion to be necessary for national (and global) security. France, Russia and China, however, believed that the invasion was a direct blow against their interests, thus their refusal to support the invasion.

-Professor Leo Caesius, *Diplomacy: The Lessons of the Past.*

There had been no response from the Prince as darkness fell over the city, convincing Sivaganga that the Rajah had succeeded in calming his wayward son. The shelling might not have stopped, but the off-world prisoner was safe and there were no immediate prospects of trying to rush the Residency. With that thought in mind, he went to bed next to his mistress and tried to sleep.

He was jerked out of a sound sleep by the sound of someone breaking down the front door, followed, several seconds later, by the sound of shooting. Jumping out of bed, he scrambled for the pistol he'd hidden in the dresser, even as his mistress moaned and tried to hide under the bed. The door exploded inwards seconds later, just as Sivaganga was trying to load the pistol; three dark-clad men led the way in, clubs in hand. He dropped the pistol to the floor, but that didn't stop them grabbing him, wrestling him to the bed and then twisting his hands behind his back so they could cuff him. A moment later, they rolled him over until he was staring into the face of one of the Prince's personal guards.

"By Order of His Most Imperial Majesty, you are under arrest for treason against the Rajah," the man said, in tones of heavy satisfaction. He searched Sivaganga roughly, tearing away the gold braid on his nightshirt. "And your entire family is being taken into custody."

He pulled Sivaganga to his feet and force-marched him down the corridor and down to the lobby. His wife was already there, along with several of the servants, all handcuffed and looking miserable. He saw a handful of bodies lying in one corner and realised that some of his servants had tried to resist, although it had clearly been futile. His mistress was pushed down beside him, followed rapidly by all seven of his children. The younger ones were crying inconsolably.

Sivaganga found his voice, somehow. "I am an aristocrat of the…"

The Prince's guardsman slapped him across the face, hard. "You will be silent," he snapped, angrily. "The Prince will hear your pleas later."

He motioned for a pair of guards to keep an eye on the family, then left to coordinate the search. Sivaganga watched helplessly as a small army of guards – he couldn't understand how the Prince had amassed such a large force so quickly – ransacked the house. A number stole various pieces of art and stuck them in their pockets, daring the house's owners to protest. The guards who stayed with the prisoners were almost worse. They both leered at the women, even the younger daughters. They'd never have another chance to see upper-caste women in a semi-naked state.

This must be how the untouchables feel, Sivaganga thought, in a sudden sharp moment of bitter empathy. How long had it been since he and his peers had gone into the untouchable shacks, pulling out the prettier girls and using them as they pleased? The untouchables had been put on the world to suffer, they'd told themselves, but in truth they'd only cared about their own pleasure. He knew now how untouchable fathers must have felt, seeing their daughters dragged away to be raped and abused. They'd been helpless…and ashamed of their own helplessness.

It was a relief when the guardsman came back and barked orders to his men. The servants would be taken to the city's jail, the women and children would be taken to a safe house…and Sivaganga himself would be taken to the palace. He was dragged to his feet and forced out into the darkness, then shoved into a coach and chained to the wood. Surely, he told himself, as the vehicle started to move, the rest of the aristocracy would do something. They wouldn't stand for their wives and children being abused.

But it was hard to cling to that thought when he was all alone.

The vehicle came to a halt and he was dragged out. He caught a glimpse of the Rajah's Palace before he was pushed forward, into the building and down a series of corridors that led to the large throne room. Somehow, it wasn't a surprise to see the Prince lounging on his father's throne, twirling his father's sceptre in his hands. He seemed very pleased with himself.

"You're a fool," the Prince said, as Sivaganga was thrown at his feet. "Did you really believe that I didn't have spies in my father's chambers?"

His smile grew wider. "And shouldn't you prostrate yourself before me? I *am* your Rajah."

Sivaganga felt his blood run cold. The Prince had *killed* his father?

"It's a little hard to prostrate when one's hands are cuffed," he managed to say, desperately. The Prince seemed to have gone completely off the rails. "What have you done?"

"My father had a great deal of faith in his precautions for selecting guards and servants," the Prince said, with some amusement. "And the faith was well-placed, I must admit. Not a one of them were prepared to share even snippets of information with me. But there are other ways to listen to secrets, if you know how to do it. And if you happen to be in charge of most of the security department."

"You bugged your own father," Sivaganga said. Of course…the Prince might have hated off-worlders, but he'd also had a childish fascination with their technology. And his father had even *encouraged* him. "So you know…what?"

"I know that you urged him to make peace with the off-worlders," the Prince said. "I know that you none-too-subtly urged him to forsake *me*. I know that you crossed the line from giving advice to outright treason. Your life is forfeit."

Sivaganga suddenly felt very tired. "You're a fool," he said. "The war against the off-worlders is going badly. You should know just how close they are to our city. Our power totters on a knife-edge…"

"*My* power," the Prince snapped. "I am the divinely-anointed Rajah, descended from the man who led our people to a world where they could replant the faith and grow towards perfection. I am the apex of the ladder that climbs towards heaven. You, for all your breeding, are as far below me as the lowly earthworm, striving towards the sun."

He's cracked, Sivaganga realised. A chill ran down his spine. *Defeat and the threat of being handed over to the off-worlders has unhinged him.*

"You have to listen to me," Sivaganga insisted. "This war is unwinnable. Surrender now and they might just let you live…"

"We surrendered when they told us that we had to take in refugees," the Prince thundered, sitting up straighter on the throne. "We surrendered when they insisted on landing a *peacekeeping* force to keep the rebels under control. We surrendered when they demanded an island they could use as a permanent base, then installed a space station so they could keep a permanent eye on us. And we even surrendered when they told us that the island would never be returned."

His eyes blazed fire. "We will not surrender again!"

Sivaganga desperately turned his head, trying to meet the Prince's eyes. "Even if it means the destruction of everything? The entire planet?"

"The gods will not let us die," the Prince insisted. "We have allies, powerful allies. We will never perish."

Allies? Sivaganga stared at him in disbelief. The Commonwealth? Wolfbane? Another off-world faction? Or was the Prince simply making it up? It was certainly possible that he was demented enough to convince himself that he had allies who would even the gap between his forces and the enemy starships. Without them, the Prince's regime would last until the starships returned to orbit, whereupon it would be destroyed from high overhead.

He stood up and used his foot to roll Sivaganga over, until he was lying uncomfortably on his back. "Your treachery will not go unpunished," he hissed. "You and your family will anoint the altars of our gods with blood."

Sivaganga felt his blood run cold. "You're going to sacrifice them?"

"You have always claimed to be of high blood," the Prince informed him, leering. "What finer food could we offer the gods? And your daughters, according to my doctors, are virgins. They will make appropriate sacrifices for when the time comes."

"No," Sivaganga said. His daughters were virgins...he'd preserved them, restricting their lives to ensure that they went unsullied to their husbands. He'd never dreamed that it would ensure that they went to the altar tables instead. "Please, no..."

The Prince reached down and grabbed his nightshirt, yanking him upwards. "I have heard enough of your objections," he snapped. "Your death will show the rest of the aristocrats that I am not to be toyed with, merely obeyed. And if they don't...their household troops will be badly outmatched by my own forces. Resistance will be crushed."

He looked up at the guard. "Take him to the cell," he ordered. "And leave him there to wait for daybreak."

"They've stopped firing," Edward observed. There had been breaks in the enemy fire before, but never something so all-encompassing. And dawn was slowly breaking over the city. It was strange to see them *halting* at daybreak. "Are the drones showing anything interesting?"

"Negative," Villeneuve said. "They just seem to have stopped."

Edward looked over at Flora, who looked back. She looked as puzzled as he felt.

"Get the ready squads primed," Edward ordered. If the enemy were preparing a rush, he'd be ready to meet them. "And then start prepping the mortars too."

Mathew was half-asleep, the girl curled against his chest, when the door burst open, revealing four black-clad men. They picked him up, chained his hands and feet, and then half-carried him through the door and down the long corridor. One of them caught the girl and pulled her along behind him, holding onto her arm tightly. She didn't try to struggle, despite the obvious pain. Mathew felt a pang of bitterness, then puzzlement; they'd treated him – finally – and then they'd chained him up again?

Bright sunlight greeted them as they stepped out of the building, reflecting off a colossal golden statue. Mathew stared at it, trying mentally to guess its height; he would have said that it was at least fifty metres high. The goddess – he assumed that the statue represented a woman, as there were faint bulges on her chest – shone brightly in the morning light. It was surrounded by crowds, all staring at him. A man in a red robe pointed to Mathew and said something in the local dialect. The crowds started shouting abuse at him a moment later.

Telling them who I am, Mathew thought. And yet there was an undertone of fear in their voices, a suggestion that all was not well. He looked over the city and saw smoke rising up in the distance…and more smoke, far past the city's walls. *They're on the way.*

His escorts led him towards the base of the statue, where he found himself staring at a number of young – and completely naked – women, their hands tied behind their backs with golden cords. They looked completely out of it, as if they weren't even aware of their surroundings; they weren't even trying to hide from his gaze. The red-clad man peered down at Mathew, then started to speak to the crowd again. They jeered and catcalled at the women, as if their punishment was deserved. But what were they doing…?

The first woman – a young girl, barely entering her teens – was led forward and made to lie down on a silver table in front of the statue. Mathew felt a shiver of horror running down his spine as he realised that it was an *altar*, a moment before a golden knife slashed down and cut the girl's throat. The crowd let out a yell as the girl died, the red-clad man somehow chanting loud enough to be heard over the racket. A moment later, her body was removed and dumped at the base of the statue.

Mathew tore his gaze away, looking at the other statues. None of them seemed benevolent; they all seemed to be eyeing the prisoners – the sacrifices – with hungry eyes. What sort of creatures did these people worship, he asked himself; why had they not found a kinder god? But, as the next girl was dragged up onto the platform, he realised that he wasn't going to be able to answer the question. He was about to die.

He elbowed his nursemaid, who had been trying to press herself into his chest. "Go," he hissed, pushing her away. *She* wasn't tied or chained; she could make her escape, even though the rest of them were doomed. "Get out of here."

The girl gazed up at him, her eyes fatalistic. Mathew realised, suddenly, that she'd known what was about to happen – and that she'd accepted it. Death was better than her existence as a mute slave in the prisons, she seemed to have decided; perhaps she was right. He managed to squeeze her shoulder, then stared up at the red-clad man. A third girl, who had looked old enough to be Mathew's age, was being led forward to die. She seemed more aware than the others, trying to both fight and cover her breasts with her hair, but it wasn't enough. The priest pushed her down onto the altar, then cut her throat with a practiced motion. Mathew watched the blood drain out of her corpse and shuddered. There were only five more girls to go before it was his turn.

"Damn you," he shouted, finding his voice. "Kill me instead."

There was a pause...and then the crowd started to jeer again, shouting and screaming as if they wanted to lunge at Mathew and tear him apart personally. The priest, if he had understood, took no heed. Instead, he had the next girl brought up and placed on the altar, ready to be sacrificed. Mathew looked away, unwilling to watch as the girl died.

"I'm sorry," he muttered, thinking of his parents. They'd been so proud of him...would they be so proud if they knew that he was about to be sacrificed? And his girlfriend on Avalon? Would she mourn for him, he wondered, or would she simply move on to the next guy in her life? He hoped that she would be happy, whatever she chose. "I'm so sorry."

Sivaganga had run out of tears after watching his youngest daughter die. The Prince had held his head personally, holding his eyes open and forcing him to watch, smiling darkly at his discomfort. The deaths were almost...*exciting* for the Prince, he realised; he'd been a devotee for years, without ever being allowed to revel in it openly. One by one, his daughters died…

"Don't kill the off-worlder," he said, bleakly. It was hard to care any longer. Let the entire world die! His wife and daughters were dead…and the gods alone knew what had happened to his sons. "You mustn't…"

The Prince smiled at him, unpleasantly. "And if I told you that your daughters would live – sorry, your *remaining* daughters would live – if you condemned the off-worlder, would you do it?"

Sivaganga shook his head, wishing that his hands were free and that he had a weapon. Any weapon. At least he could have killed the Prince before he died.

The Prince frowned, cocking his head as if he were listening to someone. "You may have your wish," he said, finally. He clapped his hands together, drawing the guards back to him. "Have the off-worlder and his little pet returned to the cells."

Sivaganga stared at him. "Why…?"

"That's for me to know and you not to know," the Prince said, nastily. He motioned to a second set of guards, who grabbed Sivaganga by the arms and pulled him forward. One of them elbowed him in the chest when he tried to spit out a last curse, finally telling the Prince what he thought of him. "Enjoy your future life as an untouchable."

It was impossible to fight as Sivaganga was dragged down towards the statue. His last two daughters were standing there, both weeping silently as the drugs wore off. He felt a flush of shame on their behalf, stripped naked and exposed in front of a jeering crowd of lower-caste civilians. The Prince, calculating as well as cruel, intended to humiliate them so completely that other aristocrats would think twice about open revolt. But then, given the number of private guards the Prince had brought into the city, open revolt would be quickly crushed in any case.

He watched helplessly as his oldest daughter – she had already been engaged to another aristocrat – was dragged up and placed on the altar. This time, he managed to look away as the knife came down and ended his daughter's life. The crowd still bayed for blood…it wasn't every day they saw aristocrats die. And some of them probably believed that the sacrifice would help defeat the off-worlders.

At least the Prince spared the off-worlder, he thought, puzzled. *But why?*

The Prince's laughter echoed over the field as Sivaganga was dragged forward by the guards. He caught sight of his daughter's body, then looked away as he was pushed down onto the bloodstained altar. The priest leaned forward, whispered a very ancient curse in his ear, then raised the knife high above his head. It glittered in the sunlight as he held the pose, playing to the crowd. A moment later, he slashed down…

…and Sivaganga knew no more.

CHAPTER
THIRTY-SEVEN

> Americans regarded the general European unwillingness to assist (although more European countries supported the invasion than opposed it) as a betrayal of American support for Europe during the Cold War. From an emotive point of view, they were right; from a cold-blooded real politic view, they were wrong. Geopolitics dictated Europe's response to the operation.
> -Professor Leo Caesius, *Diplomacy: The Lessons of the Past.*

The devastation stretched as far as the eye could see.

Jasmine refused to allow any emotion to appear on her face as she walked through the remains of Pradesh, followed by the reporter, Yin and Joe Buckley. There was barely a building left standing in the westward side of the city, while even the eastward side had dozens of shattered buildings and countless bodies scattered around. The enemy had fought hard before finally breaking, killing thousands of civilians in the crossfire. Pradesh was no longer habitable.

Teams of POWs, their legs shackled, were working to clear the roads running through the heart of the city. The family that had owned the city had started out poor, but clever; controlling the sole sizable path through the mountain range had allowed them to levy a tax on every shipment that crossed their territory. By the time Pradesh had been reduced to rubble, they'd been one of the richest aristocratic families on the planet. Now, Jasmine wondered idly, it was hard to say what would become of them. The remains of Pradesh would be handed over to the rebels, once the CEF had resumed its advance.

"Over forty *thousand* bodies so far," Buckley reported, consulting his terminal. "Mostly enemy males, but quite a few women and children too. And a number of suicides too."

Jasmine shuddered. The locals didn't seem to believe that women should fight, but there *had* been incidents where women had charged the advancing soldiers during the fight for Pradesh. Perhaps it wasn't too surprising, she reminded herself; the local government had told the women that the off-worlders would rape and kill them if the city fell. Maybe it explained the suicides too; local women were rarely taught how to fight back if confronted by a would-be rapist.

The soldiers of the CEF hadn't raped anyone, as far as she knew, and would have been executed if they had, but the same couldn't be said for the rebels. Quite a few rapes had been reported, leaving her with the dire suspicion that there were plenty of others that had gone unremarked. The untouchables had been treated as human animals for so long, with their masters claiming free access to their wives and daughters, that it was perhaps unsurprising that they'd taken the opportunity for some revenge. Even so, it was still sickening, all the more so because their victims were innocent. She'd complained to Yin, but he hadn't been too concerned.

"Keep moving the bodies out to the mass graves," she ordered, tiredly. At this rate, they were going to leave mass graves studded all over the planet – and the Commonwealth would be about as welcome as Admiral Singh had been on Avalon. "And our own losses?"

"Seven hundred deaths or serious combat injuries," Buckley told her. "Plus a large number of minor combat injuries that have been treated, but with the victim returning to duty at once."

Jasmine nodded, brusquely. The Marines had invested a great deal in devising medical treatments for their people, treatments that they'd tried to duplicate for the Commonwealth's ground forces. If someone made it to a medic, he was likely to survive, even if they had to shove him into a stasis tube until they could get him to a proper hospital. But the garrison's limited medical facilities were being overwhelmed and they simply didn't have the medics to keep up with the wounded.

"Reconfigure our units so they can be redeployed," she ordered, knowing that it would provoke resentment. Soldiers who fought as part of a specific unit became very attached to the unit, something that promoted brotherhood among the men. But several of her units had taken serious losses, enough to render them combat ineffective. Their remaining troops would have to be assigned to other units before they could return to the fight. "What about the untouchable camps."

"There was a slaughter," Yin snapped. His voice was bitter; the rebels had hoped that they could liberate their fellow untouchables before it was too late. "They just…"

Jasmine nodded. She'd seen horror, but watching enemy soldiers carrying out a mass rape and slaughter – while being utterly unable to do anything about it – had been hellish. They'd seen children crushed under tanks, men killed by nerve gas and women literally raped to death. And then the enemy soldiers had melted away into the eastwards countryside, long before her forces could catch up and exterminate them. Instead, they'd had to remove the few survivors from the camps and burn the rest.

The real mystery was why the enemy hadn't unleashed nerve gas against the advancing CEF. Her troops did have the standard Imperial-issue immunisations that would handle *some* nerve gases, but the rebels would have been wiped out if the gas had been deployed carefully – or at least forced to retreat while the CEF cleared the way. And the enemy might have got lucky and picked a gas that *did* affect her troopers. The only answer she could think of that seemed even remotely plausible was that the enemy had been worried about gassing their own troops at the same time.

But that would be out of character, she thought. *They've never shown the slightest hint of concern for their own people before.*

"I want the higher-caste prisoners to be executed," Yin said, breaking into her thoughts. "They have *got* to learn that we won't let this pass without retaliation."

Jasmine gritted her teeth. Most of the city's aristocrats had left before the fighting began, but a number had been captured. For the moment, they were isolated from the rest of the POWs; Jasmine had intended to let the intelligence officers talk to them and see if the prisoners knew anything useful. She doubted it – half of them were women and children – but it had to be tried. But she hadn't even considered that Yin might want to use them to send a message.

It *was* generally agreed in military theory that retaliation was the only way to deter atrocities such as civilian slaughter or prisoner mistreatment. Certainly, the strict ROE normally issued to the Marines made an exception for such actions. But it relied upon facing an enemy who gave a damn what happened to his own population and she would have bet half her salary that the local government wouldn't care *what* happened to the rest of their population. They certainly hadn't bothered to moderate their approach when the rebels started taking vast stretches of land.

"I understand your reluctance to act," Yin said, into the silence. "But there are *millions* of untouchables left under their control. We have to make it clear that if they want a war of extermination, the gods will make sure that they have one!"

"Perhaps you could threaten your prisoners," Buckley suggested. He smiled at Yin, although Jasmine – who had known him for over five years – saw a hard edge to the expression. "The problem with killing hostages is that they're useless after you kill them."

Yin snorted, rudely. "Our mere existence threatens them," he pointed out. "They never stopped trashing our women or killing our men."

Jasmine wasn't so sure. The rebels had been largely concentrated on the westward side of Pradesh; there had been few uprisings on the eastward side, where most of the ruling caste lived and ruled. To some extent, the rebellion had been out of sight and out of mind, particularly as it was far too close to the Imperial Garrison. But now, the rebels were breaking through the mountains and heading down onto the plains, rumours of their arrival spreading from plantation to plantation. Their advance might concentrate a few minds.

Particularly if they do see aristocrats dying, she admitted, silently. The problem with terrorism – and killing the POWs would be an act of terrorism, no matter how justified it seemed – was that it was easy to miscalculate. Jasmine had seen terrorists intimidate their victims into abject submission, even when the victims grossly outnumbered the terrorists, but she'd also seen the victims of terrorism lash out, intent on exterminating the terrorists once and for all. And if a few thousand innocent people were also exterminated…in the heat of their rage and fury, they wouldn't care until it was too late.

She held up a hand. "You can kill the adult men," she said, finally. "And you can make it clear to the enemy that you have done so. But the women and children are to remain alive."

"They are not *innocent*," Yin snapped. "My wife was scalded because her mistress poured boiling water on her, just to remind her of her place. Maids have been beaten for failing to take care of the aristocratic brats…"

"That is not negotiable," Jasmine said, coldly.

Yin locked eyes with her for a long moment. "I could pull back my men," he said, in a tone that matched hers. "See how far you get without us?"

Jasmine quirked her eyebrows. "On the very edge of victory?"

It *was* an effective threat, she knew – and she knew that he knew it. If the rebels melted away into the countryside, the CEF's supply lines would be cut by the enemy insurgents. At the very least, she would have to detail her infantry to provide extra escorts for the convoys, which would limit her ability to advance. Her forces were already short on ammunition after taking Pradesh.

But she couldn't become partner to a massacre.

"Very well," Yin said, folding. "But understand this; once the war is won, the aristocrats will be exiled. They can live on their own on the other side of the sea."

Jasmine nodded. There were three continents on the planet and only two of them were inhabited. The third could easily become a home for refugee aristocrats, a place where they could try and build a civilisation of their own. Jasmine knew that it would be hard – few of them knew how to farm, or even hunt without proper weapons – but it was better than being lined up and executed after they lost the war.

"We can provide transport," she said. "And you will be rid of them."

She watched Yin go, then sighed. Taking Pradesh had also given them access to one of the enemy's radio broadcasting towers, allowing them to bombard the enemy lines with propaganda. Yin would have to announce the death of the male aristocrats on the radio, just to ensure that the enemy knew that it had happened…and to offer them a chance to end the war without devastating the countryside any further. But somehow she doubted that the enemy just intended to surrender.

"Check in with the scouts," she ordered. "Have they reported anything new?"

Buckley worked his headset, then shook his head. "Nothing," he said. "The enemy force just seemed to have melted away."

"Let's hope so," Jasmine said. "Are the helicopters ready to leave at last light?"

"Yes," Buckley informed her. "They can make it to the capital and back before the sun rises."

The warehouse was used to store rice, much to the delight of the rebel fighters. Michael had been astonished when they'd started to clear it out, even though the rice seemed to be infested with small ant-like creatures that suggested that it was contaminated. Singh had assured him, while directing parties to take the rice to be cooked, that it was still perfectly safe to eat. And it had *looked* clean when his men had been offered it, but he'd still declined. He would sooner stick with ration bars and MREs.

Once the warehouse had been cleared – the resistance fighters had wanted to feed the surviving civilians as well as themselves – it had been turned into a makeshift prison for twenty-seven men, women and children. Michael was surprised that they had been assigned to guard duties, even though he had lost a third of his men in the desperate fight for Pradesh, but Sergeant Grieves had pointed out that the pale-skinned men and women were probably aristocrats. Their safety could not be guaranteed if rebel forces took them into custody.

None of them *looked* very aristocratic, Michael decided, studying them. Their clothes were a cut above those worn by the average citizen of the city, made from finer materials in brighter colours, but their expressions ranged from shock to numb horror. He couldn't help wondering if Avalon's council had felt the same way when their plans had come crashing down and they'd been arrested by the Marines. It would be worse for the locals, he decided, as he looked away from a girl who was silently weeping. They knew precisely what the rebels would like to do to them.

He looked over as a rebel messenger entered and whispered frantically to Singh. Whatever he said must have been important, because Singh called several of his men over and started to issue orders in the local language. Michael felt a chill running down his spine as he watched, unable to avoid a sense that something was about to go badly wrong. They'd already had to chase away local civilians who'd wanted to hurt or kill the aristocrats; what, he wondered, was about to happen?

Singh turned to face him. "By order of our leadership, and yours, the male prisoners are to be taken out and shot," he said. "We are to take them now."

Michael barely heard some of the prisoners starting to object. "No," he said, flatly. "You cannot take them out and kill them."

"We have agreement from your commander," Singh insisted. The rustling from the prisoners grew louder as women clutched hold of their husbands. "We can and will take them."

Michael keyed his handcom. "Command, this is Volpe," he said, briskly. "We have a situation."

He ran through the complete story, keeping a sharp eye on Singh. His men were ready to fight, but in close quarters any exchange of fire would rapidly turn into a bloodbath – and undermine relationships between the rebels and the CEF. It was two minutes before he received a response, directly from Brigadier Yamane.

"You are to hand over the adult male prisoners to the rebels," she ordered. There was absolutely no emotion in her voice. "And you are to remain in charge of the other prisoners."

Michael hesitated. "Brigadier…"

"That's an order, Lieutenant," Yamane said. "Carry it out."

Michael glared at Singh as he closed the channel. "*You* can take them out of here," he snapped. "We'll just stay here and watch."

Singh nodded and directed his men to seize their targets. The male prisoners fought, assisted by their wives and children, but it was useless. Michael looked away as one of the women was knocked down, blood pouring from her mouth, and fell on the ground. The prisoners were dragged out, leaving their families behind. They looked utterly broken.

"Damn you," Michael muttered, although he wasn't sure who he meant. The rebels, the CO…or even himself, for doing nothing and allowing it to happen? But what could he have done? "I want to leave this godforsaken place."

Sergeant Grieves clapped a hand on his shoulder. "So do we all, sir," he said. "So do we all."

The square, according to the translators, was called Chop-Chop Square, where the enemies of the local government were beheaded. Jasmine watched coldly as the rebels, now in possession of the space where so many of their number had died, prepared to put it to use one final time. A platform was set up, complete with a small headrest and a large axe. The only difference, according to Yin, was that the executioner wore no mask.

Jasmine refused to look away as the first aristocrat was dragged up onto the platform and forced to kneel, placing his head on the headrest. He looked to be in shock, she decided, which was probably a good thing. The executioner lifted his blade, holding it high in the air to catch the sunlight, then brought it down with staggering force. There was a dull thumping sound as it cleaved through the aristocrat's neck and hit the headrest. The victim's head fell off and landed on the platform, bouncing around until it fell off the side and into the crowd.

Sickening, Jasmine thought. But wasn't that a little hypocritical? Public executions were held on Avalon too. And yet, the criminals on Avalon were interrogated under lie detectors and truth drugs, then tried by a jury of their peers. The local government had executed people for trumped-up reasons…and the rebels were executing aristocrats purely for being aristocrats.

She looked over at the reporter and saw her disgust mirrored on his face. He didn't seem to be taking it any better than her; Jasmine had a private suspicion that his report of the CEF's deployment would be strongly negative, at least when he was covering this part of the mission. It would annoy the military, she knew, but she couldn't blame him. Her own report would strongly suggest abandoning the planet, leaving the rebels and aristocrats to kill each other on their own.

One by one, the remaining aristocrats died. One walked to the headrest with a sneer fixed on his face, which didn't even waver as the axe came down. Another cried and pleaded for mercy, offering everything from money to women if the rebels would only spare his life. A third seemed to have fainted and had to be positioned on the headrest by the guards. Finally, when the bloody business was concluded, Jasmine walked away without looking back.

"The sooner we finish this," she muttered to Alves once they were out of earshot, "the sooner we can leave this planet."

"Amen," Alves said.

CHAPTER
THIRTY-EIGHT

> During the Cold War, there was a common foe, which provided a strong incentive to paper over differences between Western Europe and America. Unfortunately, those differences did not go away. When the Cold War ended, European reliance on America ended (at least for the moment) with it. This ensured that Europe had considerable freedom of action during the run up to the invasion.
> -Professor Leo Caesius, *Diplomacy: The Lessons of the Past.*

General Bhagwandas knew that he was lucky to serve his Prince. He might have been born to the warrior caste, but he was still very low…barely above a worker, his classmates had jeered at him during basic training. Native talent only took one so far if there were more aristocratic officers competing for promotion and if the Prince hadn't taken an interest in his career, Bhagwandas knew that he would have been lucky to be promoted at all. But the Prince *had* taken an interest in him and he'd become, in turn, the Prince's loyal servant.

So why, he asked himself, did entering the throne room feel as though he was entering the den of a dangerous animal?

The Prince was seated on the throne, chewing a piece of unidentifiable meat from a tray that had been set up beside him. Bhagwandas bowed, then prostrated himself, wondering just what the meat actually *was*. It hadn't been until the sacrifices had begun that he'd realised that the Prince was a Thug, a devotee of Shiva…and that he'd formed most of his private army out of Thugs. Such worship, officially frowned upon if not banned, accounted for their devotion to the Prince. He was one of them in a way his honoured father could never be.

And rumour had it that the Thugs devoured human flesh and drank human blood...

"My Prince," he said, without rising. "I bring news."

"Speak, General," the Prince said. There was a faintly unstable tone in his voice, a hint that he might have slipped into madness. "What are the off-worlders doing?"

"They have secured Pradesh and are probing eastwards," Bhagwandas said, wondering if he was about to be dragged out and placed on the sacrificial altar himself. Two days after the sacrifices and the city was still quivering in fear. The Prince had wanted to intimidate the aristocrats and he'd succeeded, magnificently. "We believe that they are bringing up supplies now, reinforcing their forces, before they resume their advance. Once they begin..."

"They will be on us," the Prince whispered.

"Yes, My Prince," Bhagwandas said, staring at the floor. "They will reach the walls of the city within two days at the most, perhaps less."

He scowled. He'd dispatched soldiers to lay traps and set ambushes, but there were no convenient rivers on the near side of the mountains. And the road network was much better; the off-worlders would find it much easier to advance, spreading out their forces to prevent ambushes from giving them bloody noses.

And the untouchables are revolting, he thought, silently. The security forces had lost control of dozens of plantations, allowing the untouchable serfs to slip away into the countryside or start aggressively attacking their higher-caste masters. And they were no doubt watching his men as they tried to hide IEDs along the roads. The off-worlders and their rebel allies would have plenty of help when they finally advanced on the city.

"I have seen it," the Prince said. "You may rise."

Bhagwandas straightened up, rocking back on his haunches. There was an unholy gleam in the Prince's eye, a suggestion that he hadn't – yet – lost the game. Bhagwandas knew that the forces he'd raised and trained for the Prince would fight hard, but they didn't have the firepower to do more than slow the off-worlders down. They would be rapidly wiped out if they fought the invaders in the countryside.

"Pull all of our forces back into the city," the Prince ordered. "We will fight them here, in the sight of the gods. Here, we will not lose."

"My Prince," Bhagwandas said, carefully, "the city will be devastated."

"There must be a *sacrifice*," the Prince insisted. "We will stand ready to offer our city, the jewel of our world, to the gods. They will heed us at the last. I have seen it."

Bhagwandas watched in horror as the Prince produced a smoking pipe and held it to his lips, taking a long breath. The smell was chillingly familiar; in small doses, it caused euphoria, but in large doses it tended to cause hallucinations. A smart man would know better than to allow himself to become addicted to such a drug. But the Prince...

He's mad, Bhagwandas realised. But there was nothing he could do about it. The Thugs patrolling the city wouldn't hesitate to kill him if the Prince ordered it. He was *their* Prince, after all. And Bhagwandas's family were the Prince's hostages, ensuring his good behaviour; he couldn't even flee the city and find somewhere to hide. All he could do was obey.

"And assemble our forces for a final attack on the Residency," the Prince ordered. "This time, it will *fall*!"

Andrew peered down from high overhead as the four helicopters made their way east, heading towards the glow on the horizon. The landscape seemed dark, but every so often there was a fire burning brightly where someone had set fire to a plantation house before fleeing into the darkness. From time to time, the threat receiver picked up hints of enemy radio signals, but they never stayed active for very long. It seemed that most of them were heading back towards the city.

"I'm picking up the Marine beacon," Briggs said. "They're two miles from the city."

"Take us lower," Andrew ordered. It was a gamble; the capital city was lit up brightly and it was possible that they would be seen as light reflected from their hull. "And keep one eye out for trouble."

The LZ was a clearing in the midst of a small forest of trees. Andrew disliked it on sight, but he had to admit that he understood why the

Marines had considered it a suitable landing space. It would be difficult for the enemy to bring more than light infantry to intercept the helicopters, if indeed they *had* been betrayed. And the helicopters carried more than enough firepower to make intercepting them a very dangerous exercise.

He smiled as the sensor revealed the hidden beacon, followed by a signal that was utterly invisible to anyone without the right equipment. Bracing himself, he moved the helicopter to one side, then sent the signal to the two transports. They started to settle down into the clearing while the attack helicopters patrolled, watching for trouble. The signal was right, but it was easy to imagine how the operation might have been betrayed…

Blake watched from his hiding place as the two transport helicopters settled down into the clearing, their rotor blades whipping through the air. The noise was overpoweringly loud; it seemed impossible that they hadn't been heard in the city, even though it *was* over two kilometres away. But the enemy had far too much else to worry about to allow them to interfere.

"Stay here," he muttered, and stepped forward. One of the attack helicopters moved overhead, its weapons trained on him as he advanced. They'd be ready in case the enemy had somehow forced him to work for them. He raised his voice to be heard over the rotor blades. "Advance."

"Retreat," a droll voice shouted back. "How are you, you old bastard?"

"Joe," Blake said, in delight. "What are you doing here? I thought that you were holding Jasmine's hand."

"She let me take a break," Buckley said. He nodded to the helicopter crew, who started unloading the heavy crates onto the ground. "Do you have people standing by?"

Blake nodded, reached into his pocket and produced a small flashlight, flicking it on and off once. Moments later, a handful of untouchable resistance fighters appeared, ready to pick up the priceless cargo. Buckley motioned to the boxes, allowing them to take them into the forest, where they would be emptied and the contents smuggled into the slums. There was enough light weapons and ammunition to fight a small war, Blake noted with some relief. Despite what he'd told his students, military weapons *were* more effective than civilian makeshift bombs.

"We brought a handful of trained fighters from the west," Buckley informed him, as four dark-skinned men jumped out of the helicopter. A fifth looked pale enough to pass for warrior caste. "They know how to use the antitank rockets and heavy machine guns."

"Good," Blake said. Teaching the insurgents how to use the Imperial Army's standard-issue rifles and pistols would be easy; teaching them how to use more advanced weapons would take some time. Having people who knew what they were doing and could speak the local language would speed matters up a little. "And the advance?"

"We're pushing down gently into the eastern side of Pradesh now," Buckley said, as the last of the crates was dumped onto the ground. "Once dawn breaks, we'll pick up speed; ideally, we'll be at the walls of Maharashtra within a day. But there is no way to be sure."

Blake nodded. At full speed, the Landsharks and Warriors could be at Maharashtra within hours at most, but the enemy could easily have deployed mines and IEDs to slow them down, even if there *weren't* any natural barriers the enemy could turn into a death trap. But all of the reports from his spies suggested that the enemy forces were withdrawing into Maharashtra itself, preparing for another urban fight. He knew that his insurgents would make that a deadly gamble for the enemy CO, but it was still going to be a bloody slaughter.

"We should be ready to assist you by then," Blake said, instead. It was astonishing just how thoroughly the untouchables pervaded the city. Didn't the enemy *realise* what a security breach they were allowing? But then, untouchables did all the shit work. If they were barred from the city, the aristocracy would have to get their lily-white hands dirty. "But the matters on the ground are not good. We don't know *what* happened to the Rajah, yet his son is very firmly in charge."

"Not for long," Buckley said. He stepped backwards, into the helicopter. "Have a good one!"

"You too," Blake said. "And give my love to the CO."

He turned and walked away from the helicopter, hearing the noise of their rotors grow louder as they started to lift off the ground. Part of him wanted to contemplate the prospect of leaving the world behind, but he knew there was no time. Their supplies had to be moved back to the city before daybreak. The humans who would carry the load were already in place, ready to move.

"There's a *lot* here," Mad said, in awe. She was staring down at an opened crate, inspecting a series of pistols. Judging by their shiny appearance, they had either belonged to headquarters staff or had simply never been issued to a user. Blake was inclined to suspect the latter. "But is it enough?"

"It should be," Blake assured her. He closed the crate, then hefted it into the air. "Let's move."

"That's the supplies dropped off," Buckley said, over the intercom. "Blake's forces should be a great deal more formidable in a few hours."

"Let's hope so," Jasmine said, watching grimly as a Landshark was manoeuvred through the narrow streets of Pradesh. They'd had to knock down several dozen surviving buildings just to provide room for the massive tanks to make their way through the pass. No doubt the locals would have yet another reason to complain about the CEF after the war. "We're going to be there soon."

The drones over the city had revealed that Blake was right; two-thirds of the enemy force seemed to be digging into Maharashtra. But the rest of their force seemed to be mustering for yet another assault on the Residency, an assault that the defenders were ill-prepared to resist. Time was definitely running out, as if the enemy had decided that if they couldn't win the war, they might at least spite the CEF by destroying the Residency. Jasmine knew that they had to move – and move fast.

"They should be able to hold out long enough for us to get there," Buckley reassured her. He understood her feelings, even if she didn't dare say them out loud. "And the rebels have been very helpful."

Jasmine smirked. The slaughter *had* convinced the great mass of untouchables that they had to kill or be killed. Not only had they risen up against their oppressors, but they'd been removing IEDs or warning the CEF of where they were hidden. She knew that they would still have to be careful, but the uprisings would make it much harder for the enemy to interfere with their advance...at least until they reached the city walls. Maharashtra had a population of over seven million, according to the Garrison's database...and it had only been increased by refugees fleeing into its walls. There might have been more room to manoeuvre, but hitting the city would turn into another bloodbath like Pradesh, only bigger.

She shook her head, tiredly. Whatever happened, whatever choices they made, people were going to die.

"I presume," she said, "that there has been no response to our surrender demands?"

"None," Buckley confirmed. He sounded faintly irked. "I would have told you at once if there had been."

"I know," Jasmine said, accepting the unspoken reproof. She glanced at her wristcom – four hours to daybreak – and then cleared her throat. "Get back here as quickly as possible, then get some sleep. We advance at dawn."

She closed the channel, then looked over at the reporter. "Are you all right?"

"Just tired," Alves admitted. "And still a little shocked."

Jasmine didn't blame him, particularly as it seemed that the slaughter hadn't done anything to moderate the enemy government's treatment of the untouchables. There were reports of other slaughters that had provoked the uprisings, slaughters that would have spread out of control if the enemy hadn't been forced to face the CEF. It would grow worse, Jasmine knew, before it grew better. If, of course, it ever did.

"We should release a gene-modification virus," Alves said. "Give all future children the same skin colour. Destroy their system once and for all."

It *was* an attractive thought, Jasmine had to admit. No matter how irrational discrimination by skin colour was, it probably wouldn't go away overnight, no matter who won the war. Why should it, when it was such an easy way to identify one's enemies? Maybe dark skin would rule in the future, rather than light skin, but the basic system would still be the same. But changing it…

"It sometimes has side effects," she said, remembering horror stories from some of the early days of settlement. There had been planets founded by ethnic settlers who had wanted to ensure that their descendents kept what they considered their authentic features. Sometimes it had worked. At other times, there had been long-term genetic damage that had blighted the lives of their descendents. One group of settlers had wanted albino-pale skin, on a planet cursed with bright sunlight for most of the year. "And it isn't our decision anyway."

"But can these people *make* such a decision?" Alves asked. "They are too hung up on the idea of skin colour determining one's place in life to think about the advantages of changing it."

Jasmine considered it for a long moment. The hell of it was that she didn't really disagree with him, although the cynic in her pointed out that skin colour wasn't the *only* reason humans found to discriminate or kill their fellows. Maybe the planet's population would find a new reason and then use it as an excuse whenever anyone asked. No, knowing humans as well as she did, there was no *maybe* about it.

"It isn't our job to make these decisions for them," she said, with a sigh. "That's what allowed the Grand Senate to turn Earth into a nightmare. They started making decisions for everyone and then enforcing them on those who didn't want to participate. Maybe they had good intentions, at the start. But eventually the power they claimed became an end in itself."

She shook her head. "No," she added. "We cannot make such decisions for them, even though we think we know best. No matter how much they need it. We dare not open that can of worms."

With that, she headed over to the makeshift HQ. She needed sleep before time ran out.

Michael watched from the open hatch as the Warrior started to make its way down the road heading eastwards from the city. The landscape was different here, he noted; long stretches of farmland and plantations, broken only by lines of trees that marked barriers between different fields. There were few people working there, he saw; instead, many of the farmhouses seemed to have been burned to the ground, their owners forced to flee or brutally murdered by their former serfs.

"What a fucking mess," he muttered, as he swung the machine gun from side to side, watching for threats. The trees hadn't been planted too close to the road, but there were too many places to hide IEDs. It was reassuring to know that the Landsharks were following close behind, yet the Warriors weren't anything like as armoured. An IED might be powerful enough to destroy one of them or flip it over, stunning or killing the soldiers inside. "They could be anywhere."

He glanced down at his terminal, then returned his gaze to scanning the roadside as they advanced onwards, heading towards the capital.

Towards Maharashtra.

CHAPTER THIRTY-NINE

> Put simply, nations that saw an advantage in remaining close to America (Britain, Poland, Spain) joined the coalition force. The nations that preferred to keep their distance (France, Germany) refused to send troops to Iraq.
> -Professor Leo Caesius, *Diplomacy: The Lessons of the Past.*

"They're coming," Edward said, as he watched the display. The shelling had only intensified as dawn rose above the city, while the drones revealed new enemy forces moving into position, readying themselves for a charge. Behind them, small armoured cars were being prepared. They'd back up their infantry...and shoot them in the back if they retreated. "Tell them... tell the soldiers that we will hold out as long as we can."

He glanced at the live feed from the CEF as Villeneuve and Flora started to issue orders to their men. Brigadier Yamane was pushing it, but Edward knew that it would be at least an hour before her forces could reach the city – and then she would have to fight her way through the defenders to reach the Residency. At best, it would be tight; at worst, she would arrive too late to save even a single one of the defenders.

A strange place to die, he thought, as he checked and rechecked his service pistol. They just didn't have the rifle ammunition to spare for him to carry a rifle with him, not any longer. *I thought it would be on Avalon.*

He'd long since come to terms with his own mortality, after seeing some of his fellow recruits die on the training range. Others had died too on a dozen worlds; it struck him that his training platoon, the twelve of them who had graduated the Slaughterhouse so many years ago, had lost half of its members between graduation and Edward's exile to Avalon. They'd died upholding the Empire and the honour of the Terran Marine Corps, but they'd died. Only one of them – dogface, they'd called him; it bothered Edward that he couldn't recall the Marine's *name* – had retired and gone out to the Rim. God alone knew where he was now.

You always knew that the time would come to pay the piper, he told himself. It was an oddly liberating thought. There was no need to command an operation spread out over an entire planet, or to wait behind in safety as his Marines put themselves in harm's way; he could and he would fight to the last, knowing that there was no longer any point in holding back. *If the time has finally come...*

Edward had never been particularly religious. It was hard to be religious in the undercity – and harder still when he'd seen countless atrocities committed in the name of one religion or another. But now, knowing that he was on the verge of death, he understood what people saw in religion. There was a comfort in believing that there was life after death, that there was an omnipotent and omniscient entity weighing each soul in final judgement...and that good deeds would be rewarded and bad deeds punished. He thumbed the Rifleman's Tab on his collar, wondering if he should bury it for recovery and shipment to the Slaughterhouse, before dismissing the thought. It had come at too high a price to be simply abandoned at the last.

"Take command," he ordered Flora, picking up the other pistol from the desk. "Let me know when they begin their offensive."

The shelling only grew louder as he walked down the stairs and into the infirmary. A handful of walking wounded were being organised to help fend off the final attack, but the others were largely helpless. He caught sight of the Professor's wife and felt a sudden wave of pity for the woman. She hadn't expected to be caught in a trap when she'd joined the mission, had she? And yet her work with the medic had been good. Maybe it would even be the making of her.

He stepped into a side room and saw the Professor, looking down at his terminal. Edward knew that he'd downloaded thousands of terabytes worth of files from the Imperial Library before leaving Avalon, but he was surprised that the Professor had found time to read. But then, he wasn't really able to do much else to help. And the weapon he'd been given had been passed to one of the walking wounded.

"Time is about to run out," Edward said, flatly. The Professor looked up sharply, then gently placed the terminal on the desk. "Take this."

The Professor took the pistol and stared at it, in puzzlement. "Why...?"

"If they break through, use it on your wife and then on yourself," Edward told him, bluntly. The drones had picked up the most horrifying scenes as the local ruler sacrificed to his gods, including countless untouchables and even a few of the aristocrats. He had no doubt that anyone dragged kicking and screaming from the Residency would be sacrificed as well. "I suggest that you do not hesitate."

"I can't shoot my wife," the Professor objected. "I..."

"If she falls into their hands, she will be raped," Edward said, in no mood to dance around the subject. "And then they will cut her throat and allow her blood to feed their gods. You will be saving her from a fate worse than death."

"And giving her an earlier death," the Professor muttered.

"I know," Edward said. He reached out and clapped the Professor on the shoulder. "I'm sorry. If I'd known..."

He shook his head. There was no time for musing on what might have been. All they could do now was sell their lives as dearly as possible.

General Bhagwandas studied the plans of the Imperial Residency carefully, then contemplated the troops the Prince had assigned to the mission. The remaining aristocratic household troops would be going in first, followed rapidly by the Prince's own soldiers, who would use the household troops to soak up bullets. In the meantime, armoured cars would sweep the walls with machine guns, providing cover for the advancing soldiers, while the shelling would grow even stronger. It should work, he told himself. The off-worlders *had* to be running out of ammunition by now.

And we're coming at them from all points of the compass, he added. *Even they cannot hope to defend the entire wall.*

He picked up the telephone – no radios now, not with the enemy force heading towards the city – and gave a simple order.

"Go."

"They're coming."

Private Tomas Leloir braced himself as the first enemy soldiers came into view. They were wearing even more colourful uniforms – if that were possible – and advancing openly, not even *trying* to seek cover. A single machine gun would have scythed them all down in a second, but they were terrifyingly short on ammunition. He lifted his rifle and took aim, gritting his teeth. They'd been told to make every shot count.

Behind the soldiers, a row of small armoured vehicles advanced forward. Tomas bit down a curse, hearing the ripples of dismay running through the line, as the other soldiers caught sight of them. The vehicles were primitive, little more than civilian cars with armour nailed over their exterior to provide some protection, but their rifles wouldn't even *scratch* them. And the machine guns that poked through slits in the armour would be more than enough to sweep the defenders off the walls.

"Take aim," the CO ordered. He sounded calm, somehow. They'd all seen the images the drones had taken of the sacrifices; they all knew what would happen to them if they fell into enemy hands. "Fire on my command."

There was a long pause, then the enemy opened fire. The soldiers lifted their rifles and blazed away, showing a wanton disregard for ammunition that Tomas could only envy, while the armoured cars opened fire on the walls. Bullets pitted into the solid walls, then came screaming over the top as the gunners adjusted their aim. Tomas fought the urge to cringe back as tracers blazed through the air, barely a metre over his head. The enemy were steadily finding their range.

"Fire," the CO ordered.

Two rockets lanced towards the armoured cars, followed by a salvo of mortar fire…and then nothing. Tomas realised, even as he picked off his first target and moved on to the second, that was the end of the mortars.

They'd destroyed a dozen armoured cars, but more were pushing forward behind the burning wrecks, threatening to run over their own people in their eagerness to get to grips with the enemy. Behind them, a second force of soldiers appeared, all clad in black. This group seemed to be more professional, using the debris and burning vehicles as cover as they advanced forward.

One of the vehicles seemed to jerk to one side and then come to a halt; the others kept coming, lowering their muzzles until they were pointed almost directly at Tomas and his comrades. He wanted to crawl backwards as fire blazed only millimetres above his head, but somehow he kept himself still. Moments later, there was a colossal explosion in front of them. Risking a peek, he saw that the gatehouse had been destroyed and one of the armoured cars was inching its way into the compound. Black-clad men thronged around it, looking for targets.

"Prepare grenades," the CO ordered, as the first armoured car was joined by another. Two more explosions shook the ground, both on the other side of the complex. A third, seconds later, blew another chunk of the wall to dust. The enemy were definitely inside the compound. "And *throw!*"

Tomas threw his grenade, trying to roll it under one of the armoured cars. Several other soldiers had the same idea, leaving five more armoured cars nothing more than burning debris. Dozens of enemy soldiers were caught in the blasts, but the enemy seemed to have an unlimited supply of manpower. A quick glance from side to side told him that four of his comrades had been hit, three of whom were definitely dead. The fourth would almost certainly die if they didn't get him into a stasis tube.

"All units, pull back to the centre," the CO ordered. His voice still seemed calm, somehow. "I say again, all units pull back to the centre."

Throwing a second grenade to cover their retreat, the soldiers picked up their wounded comrade and headed towards the passageway into the central compound. Behind them, the enemy forces rallied and continued their advance.

The Commonwealth side of the Imperial Residency had fallen.

"They've just punched out the north gate's defenders," Flora said. There was a grim note to her voice as she struggled to coordinate her people. "My forces are falling back."

Edward nodded. Given the sheer weight of firepower the enemy had flung at both sides of the compound, it was no surprise that they'd broken through. Both the Commonwealth and Wolfbane forces had spent the last few days rigging traps for the enemy forces, but the callous disregard for their own people the enemy commanders had shown suggested that the traps wouldn't do more than slow them down a little.

"Get them into the central compound," he ordered, "and fire off our last mortar shells. Let them think that we have plenty more in reserve."

Somehow, he doubted that it would be enough.

The temptation to second-guess himself was overwhelming. What if he'd convinced the diplomats to agree to a meeting in deep space? Or if they'd kept the starships in orbit? Or if they'd held the meeting in the garrison? Or if Wolfbane had brought along its own military force, instead of just the Residency guards? Or what if...

He pushed the thought aside. It was futile and pointless. All he could do now was fight.

Leo sat on the blanket, his head between his legs as the sound of explosions grew louder and louder, until they merged together into a single never-ending sound that seemed to reach inside his head and *twist*. Pain throbbed in his temples as he stared at the gun, the gun the Colonel had given him. He couldn't shoot his wife; he couldn't kill his wife...and yet cold logic told him that the Colonel was right, that Fiona might have cause to be grateful if he killed her. But he couldn't force himself to kill her...

Shaking, he covered his head and prayed that it would all be over soon.

Tomas heard the sound of firing grow louder as the enemy came up behind them, but all of his attention was fixed on the gateway into the central compound. A handful of guards were providing covering fire, forcing the enemy to fall back in disarray, but he knew that it wouldn't be long before they ran out of ammunition too. He led the way through the gate and watched as it was slammed closed, then they kept running towards the central building.

They made it inside and he stopped, gasping for breath. The medic was already looking at his comrade, but from the expression on her face he knew that they were too late. If the bullets hadn't been enough to kill him, the race into the central compound had definitely finished the job. Another one of his comrades was dead.

"Get to the next location," a voice ordered.

Tomas looked up and saw Colonel Stalker – their CO, despite his rank. He hesitated, then asked the question he knew that he would never have dared ask if they were not about to die.

"Sir," he said, "why are you still a Colonel?"

Colonel Stalker smiled, surprisingly. "It never seemed right to promote myself," he explained. "And the Empire is unlikely to promote me in the future."

His smile grew wider. "Go to the next location," he repeated. "We may as well hold out as long as we can."

Tomas nodded and led his three remaining comrades towards the window they'd been assigned as a firing slot. It was far from perfect, but whoever had designed the Imperial Residency had obviously never thought about creating fortresses. If he had, Tomas was sure, the entire complex would have been built out of hullmetal and would have been completely impregnable to anything short of a nuke. And the locals had no nukes.

He caught sight of two of the maids carrying ammunition and hastily grabbed a pair of magazines for his rifle. Both of the maids looked terrified…and yet there was a certain resolve about them, a willingness to see the fighting through to the bitter end. Tomas hoped, as he noticed the knives they carried on their belts, that they were prepared to cut their own throats if the compound fell. He knew precisely what the local troops would do to them before they were sacrificed to the gods.

"Thank you," he said, quietly.

The maids bowed and retreated. Tomas watched them go. In their dresses, everything was covered…but as they moved, he could see their hips and bottoms moving in a natural seductive rhythm. He felt a sudden flush of lust which he ruthlessly pushed aside. He'd been told that it happened, when death was close…but then, death had never been *close* before.

"Nice ass," one of his comrades noted. He leered cheerfully towards the retreating girls. "Do you think we have time…?"

"No," Tomas said. He paused. "Well, maybe *you* do."

They shared a laugh, then turned back to the window, preparing themselves as best as they could.

The end could not be long delayed.

General Bhagwandas swallowed a curse as the next set of reports came in from his commanders. Having broken into the two off-world compounds, his soldiers were starting to loot and burn rather than reforming for an assault on the final part of the complex. The Prince's picked men had been promised vast rewards for so long that the soldiers had clearly decided to take what they could get, despite the best efforts of their commanders. But the fight was almost over.

He glanced down at the map showing the estimated position of the enemy relief force and smiled. They would not reach the Imperial Residency in time to make a difference.

"Bring up the reserves," he ordered. The Prince would be happy when the Residency fell, he hoped. Maybe there would even be time to save his family before the rest of the off-worlders arrived. "They are to advance and crush the enemy beneath their feet."

He paused. "And order the gunners to stop shooting," he added. Normally, no one would care about friendly fire, but the important thing now was to bring down the Residency and destroy its inhabitants. "The infantry can finish the task now."

Silence fell, so suddenly that it was almost a physical blow.

"They've stopped," a voice said. Edward recognised the speaker as one of the walking wounded, there to serve as part of the last-ditch defence. "Do you think they've decided to back off?"

"I doubt it," Edward answered, shortly. The drones were picking up a whole new force of black-clad infantry advancing on the double. He'd hoped that the looting would keep the enemy busy for some time, but it seemed that they had more troops in reserve. God alone knew how many they'd lost – he was sure that it was over a thousand – yet they just kept coming. "I think the final push is about to begin."

"They'll be on us in minutes," Flora agreed. She laughed, softly. "I told the Governor that we should have held the meeting in deep space."

"Too late now," Edward commented. Maybe he should have asked her more about Wolfbane, now that their backs were pressed firmly against the wall. But it was definitely too late.

He looked around the tiny compartment. "Gentlemen, it's been a honour," he said. There was no point in holding onto hope any longer. "Fix bayonets."

CHAPTER FORTY

This caused problems – which were not smoothed over by the diplomats. Bad feelings threatened to tear apart the complex network of alliances that bound the West together. In the end, it could have been disastrous.
  -Professor Leo Caesius, *Diplomacy: The Lessons of the Past.*

Blake could *hear* the sound of fighting in the distance as he climbed out of the tunnel and back into the city. The latest update from Colonel Stalker had not been good; the Residency was under heavy attack, with ammunition running out. If it ran out completely, the complex would fall within minutes.

He glanced back at the rest of the untouchable freedom fighters, hoping – praying – that their brief training sessions would be enough. They would be no match for Marines, or even soldiers from the Imperial Army, but all the reports suggested that the local security troops were brutal rather than competent. Blake wasn't so sure that the untouchables could fight – they'd had all resistance beaten out of them over generations – but there wasn't anything else for them to use. The CEF was still some distance from the city gates.

"Send the signal," he ordered. "The attacks are to commence in ten minutes, if I don't send the order before then."

He led the way outside, marvelling at the nightmare that seemed to have gripped the city's streets as the fighting raged on. Mobs of people swarmed the streets, while the handful of security troopers in the lower-caste areas were completely overwhelmed. Homes were being looted and burned to the ground, people from different castes were being beaten, raped and killed...absolute chaos seemed to be breaking out. No one challenged them as they made their way through the streets, despite the combination of local military uniforms and dark skins. No doubt, he told himself, the local civilians were having too much fun shedding the last veneer of civilisation to bother with their own security.

A fireball rose up into the air from the direction of the Residency, followed rapidly by two more. The ground shook a moment later, violently. Blake briefly wished he had a direct link to the Residency, to find out what had happened, before pushing the thought aside ruthlessly. All he could do was get his people in place and then attack, hoping that there was time to save the Residency. Looking at the chaos, he tended to doubt it.

He braced himself as a trio of enemy soldiers swaggered by, drinking and singing a song in their own language that Blake would have bet half of his salary was thoroughly obscene. Deserters, he guessed; men who'd decided that they would sooner flee than fight. Maybe they'd seen one too many human wave attacks, maybe they realised that their commanders had gone insane...or maybe they were just cowards. He muttered orders for the team to give them a wide berth, even though none of them seemed to be carrying weapons. They were too drunk to realise that they were heading right into the most dangerous part of the city, wearing hated uniforms.

More explosions shook the ground as they headed towards the palace that served as the enemy command post. Blake had seen the drone images, but they hadn't prepared him for the sheer staggering immensity of the building – or the awareness that it *was* nothing more than a palace. Government House on Avalon was much smaller, even though it served as the centre of government as well as the home of the Governor. The Imperial Palace on Earth was bigger – if it was still intact, which Blake doubted – but it was the nerve centre of an empire that stretched across hundreds of thousands of light years. He couldn't believe just how much money the local aristocracy had wasted on their homes, when their population was poor and starving.

They saw the lower castes as less than human, he thought, in a rare moment of insight. *They weren't there to be cared for, merely to be used.*

He inspected the defences quickly. There were several dozen soldiers at the gate, looking alarmingly competent; there was no way of knowing what might be inside the wall, waiting for them. Ideally, Blake would have preferred to sneak over the wall, but there was no time. Instead, he keyed his communicator, issued orders...and waited.

Maharashtra was burning.

Andrew sucked in his breath as the three attack helicopters swooped over the city. A third of it seemed to be on fire, while the rest of it seemed to be under mob rule. He could see thousands upon thousands of people running through the streets, while the security forces concentrated their attacks upon the Residency and guarding the upper-caste areas. Even if the fighting ended within seconds, even if the Commonwealth or Wolfbane didn't seek revenge for the dead diplomats, the city would never be the same again.

"We have our orders," Briggs said. "We're to clear the way for the insurgents."

"Understood," Andrew said. He would have preferred to engage the forces attacking the Residency, but the attackers and the defenders were so closely mixed together that it would have been impossible to separate the two sides. "Taking us in...now!"

He braced himself for ground fire as the helicopters started their attack run, but nothing rose up to greet them apart from a handful of rifle shots, which clanged harmlessly off the armour when they hit the helicopter at all. The targeting selector came online, isolating the enemy guardposts, the walls...and, behind them, a handful of armoured vehicles. Someone had clearly been giving some thought to the defence, he decided, as he unleashed the first spread of rockets and cannon fire. But it hadn't been enough.

"Targets destroyed," Briggs informed him. A series of explosions billowed up from under the helicopter as the rockets found their targets. "But the palace is untouched."

"Good," Andrew said, as the helicopters climbed back up into the air. He keyed his radio. "The path is clear; I say again, the path is clear."

Blake allowed himself a smile at the reaction of Mad and the other untouchables to the helicopter strike. It was raw power on a scale they couldn't even begin to comprehend, any more than the local commanders could grasp the sheer firepower of even the smallest Imperial Navy starship. There was nothing left of the defenders, apart from a handful of burning vehicles and dead bodies. Most of them had been simply vaporised.

"Send the signal," he ordered. There were untouchables scattered throughout the city, primed to attack its infrastructure and leadership... and probably lose their lives doing it. If there had been more time to prepare, Blake knew that they could have taken out the enemy leaders and perhaps even taken the city itself, but instead they were being forced to rush. "The attacks are to commence at once."

He hefted his rifle, grinned at their shocked faces, and led the way towards the palace. As ordered, the helicopter pilots had left the building alone, even though they'd strafed the gardens as well as the defenders. He winced as he saw the burning armoured cars – they would have been a nasty surprise if they'd attacked without air support – and then felt an odd twinge of sadness as he saw the lake. One of the rockets must have landed in the water and exploded, he realised; there were dead fish floating on the surface. Once, the garden had been elegant and lovely. Now, it was just a wreck.

"Hurry," he ordered, as they ran through the garden and up to the main doors. "We have to get to the enemy CO before it's too late."

General Bhagwandas picked himself off the floor with the inescapable conviction that the world had just turned upside down. One moment, he'd been supervising the final attack on the Residency; the next, the entire building had been shaken so violently that he'd lost his footing and fallen to the floor. One of his aides had banged his head on the table, he realised as he caught hold of the stonework and used it to pull himself to his feet; the aide had cracked his skull badly enough to kill him. Blood was flowing freely from a gash on his forehead.

He reached for his telephone, only to discover that it didn't work. It should have provided a direct link to the Prince, but there wasn't even a dial tone. There was a groan as another of his aides stood upright and started to drunkenly weave towards the door. General Bhagwandas barked commands, only to see the young man stagger and fall to his knees. A third aide, showing more independence of mind, was trying to work the radio. As he made contact with some of the other bases around the city, his face paled.

"General," he said, "there are attacks everywhere."

"Give me that," General Bhagwandas ordered. He took the radio and started to issue demands for information. "See what you can pull out of the other systems."

The news flowing in wasn't good. Some bases refused to respond completely, others reported insurgents – all untouchables – attacking their soldiers and wreaking havoc. The news made him shudder as he realised the full extent of their enemy's perfidy; the untouchables might not have been allowed to handle weapons, but they did the cooking and cleaning in all of the military bases. They were everywhere; cleaning barracks, scrubbing toilets, even washing vehicles. And hardly anyone would take note of their presence. After all, they were just untouchables. The outcasts of the gods.

Other news came in from his spotters all over the city. Palaces were being attacked; aristocratic families were being killed by once-faithful servants. The untouchables seemed to have planned carefully, committing themselves to bringing down the upper-castes when help finally arrived. And the off-worlder army was advancing towards the city at terrifying speed, utterly untouchable by anything he could put in its path. Their entire position was disintegrating.

And he could no longer hope to direct anything.

"Pick up your weapons," he ordered, bitterly. His family were still hostages, held in the Rajah's palace. Somehow, he would have to liberate them and make his way to the estates he owned, well away from the rest of the population. He could rest there, perhaps offer his services to whatever government took over the planet. "It's time to go."

Blake wanted to advance carefully into the palace, turning over every nook and cranny for unwanted surprises, but the untouchables seemed to lose all discipline as they realised that they could finally lash out at their hated masters. They poured into the palace in a terrifying stream, shooting madly at the few remaining guards and servants, smashing artworks and tearing down paintings in a chilling orgy of destruction. Blake could understand the temptation to destroy so much belonging to the oppressors, but not at the expense of the mission.

The interior of the palace was stunningly luxurious. Gold and silver artworks were everywhere, even hanging from the ceiling. It seemed as though the owners of the palace had spent generations building up a collection of artefacts; wooden toys, pieces of art and – everywhere – statues of their gods. One room was decorated with staggeringly explicit paintings showing every possible sexual act, including several Blake had never even *considered* before, let alone tried. Several of them looked more likely to cause serious bodily harm rather than sexual satisfaction.

"The men are allowed to enjoy themselves with the lower-caste women," Mad explained, as she followed him through the chamber. "But the women are expected to remain unsullied until marriage. The decorations are intended to teach them what they need to know."

Blake snorted. The Commonwealth was an open society, accepting just about anything as long as it took place between consenting adults in private. But this world seemed utterly and absurdly hypocritical. They didn't have reliable contraception, let alone medical treatments that would cure sexual diseases and ensure conception. What was the point of insisting that their women remain virgins when their men might easily pick up something nasty from the lower-castes and infect their wives?

They don't have DNA tests either, he reminded himself. *They have to ensure that the girls are virgins or parentage might be in doubt.*

The next room was a set of small chambers, barely larger than the tiny rooms assigned to officers at the barracks. Blake glanced inside briefly, then started as he saw something moving…he had his rifle tracking the target before he realised that it was nothing more dangerous than a pet monkey. The beast eyed him with disturbingly human eyes, then started making loud and unpleasant noises. Blake shook his head, then headed onwards, searching for the enemy command post. The palace was just too big to be searched quickly.

He checked his radio. There were only a handful of reports coming in, but most of them agreed that the enemy position was falling apart. Attacks that started *inside* bases and garrisons were always the hardest to deal with, Blake knew from bitter experience; even if the enemy managed to rally their forces, it would be hard for them to know who to trust. Besides, some of his other strikes had been targeted on the primitive telecommunications network. The primitiveness of the system might have saved it from targeted air strikes, but it had also ensured that it couldn't respond well to losing a few nodes.

"Come on," he ordered. "We have to find the bastards."

General Bhagwandas picked up a handful of grenades and hooked them onto his belt, then motioned for his three surviving aides to follow him down the stairs. The sounds from inside the building suggested that it was being raided by the enemy and that there was no longer anyone in place willing and able to defend it. All they could do now, he told himself, was run and hope that they could recover his family before it was too late.

The sounds of people looting grew louder as they headed down the stairs, towards the entrance to the underground network that allowed the aristocrats to meet and talk in secret. Part of him burned with rage at the thought of untouchables ransacking the palace, molesting the concubines and slaughtering faithful servants, part of him prayed that it would keep them busy long enough for him and his aides to escape. The palace was surely large enough to distract any number of untouchables, particularly ones more interested in looting than revenge.

And then, as they headed down the stairs, he saw the figures at the bottom.

Blake saw the enemy soldiers at the same time and lifted his rifle, opening fire on the two aides. It was hard to be sure – the enemy troops seemed to wear more gold braid than even an Imperial Army General – but he suspected that the first two were bodyguards and the third was a CO. The aides weren't remotely prepared for a fight, he realised; he shot them both down before they could get a single shot off in any direction. Their CO stumbled backwards, his face pale and wan, then lifted his hands into the air.

"Don't move," Blake barked at him. Mad echoed the message a moment later. "Hold still."

He stepped up to the man, resisting the temptation to roll his eyes. *This* was a General? The man was grossly unfit, with a uniform that – no matter how carefully tailored – couldn't even begin to hide his paunch. He didn't even try to resist as Blake removed the grenades and added them to his own collection, then searched him thoroughly. With the grenades and the pistol, Blake realised, the enemy officer could have forced the insurgents to kill him...if he had tried.

"I have information to offer you," the man babbled. "But I need something from you..."

"You're in no position to make bargains," Blake snapped. "Call off the attack on the Residency."

"I can't," the man confessed. The way he cringed as he said it, as if he expected to be shot a moment later, convinced Blake that he was telling the truth. "The communications network is gone."

He took a breath, desperately. "I know where the Prince is," he said, his voice shaking with fear. "I can lead you to him. But you have to help me find my family."

Blake stared down at him in disgust. This...utterly worthless officer had launched the assault that threatened to destroy the Residency and kill Blake's CO...and he was trying to bargain? The planet could have been saved if someone in a position of power had overthrown the government before it was too late, but instead they'd just gone along with their Prince and obeyed orders. And now, without the enemy communications network, it would be impossible to impose a ceasefire.

"Take us to the Prince," he ordered, finally. "And may your gods help you if you're not telling the truth!"

The door burst inward, revealing a howling mob. Private Tomas Leloir threw the first grenade into the mass of people and had the satisfaction of seeing several of them blown apart by the blast, just before the people behind them pushed through and came at the defenders. They fought desperately, but the tidal wave of rioters – driven on by enemy soldiers – was too strong. The defence crumbled and Tomas fell to the floor. Strong hands tore at his armour, ripping it away. Someone barked orders in the enemy language, including several words he vaguely recognised. They didn't intend to treat him as a lawful combatant.

Desperately, he reached for the final grenade and pulled out the pin, just as they rolled him over. Feet came down, stamping on his legs and arms, but it was already too late.

"Fuck you," he whispered.

The grenade exploded a moment later.

CHAPTER FORTY-ONE

What, then, are the lessons from the past? First, bear in mind that countries have different geopolitical imperatives. Second, bear in mind the limits of the possible. Third, bear in mind the dangers of backing someone into a corner. Fourth, bear in mind the importance of keeping one's own priorities at the forefront of one's mind.
-Professor Leo Caesius, *Diplomacy: The Lessons of the Past.*

"They've overrun the lower floors," Flora remarked.

Edward nodded. They'd sealed as many of the interior doors as they could, forcing the enemy to follow a specific path into the building. He knew that the remaining defenders would give a good account of themselves, but time was definitely running out. If nothing else, he told himself, Blake Coleman and Jasmine Yamane would ensure that the planetary government paid a high price for their treachery.

Jasmine gritted her teeth as she looked down at the live feed from the Residency. The final part of the complex was under attack, the enemy – heedless of their shattered command network – pressing the assault as hard as they could. Their final death throes might bring the Residency down with them, she realised bitterly. It was time for a desperate gamble.

"Signal the tanks," she ordered. "They are to go to full speed and enter the city."

It *was* a gamble, she knew. There would be no time to sweep the roads for IEDs or other unpleasant surprises – and something a Landshark could just shrug off could disable or destroy a Warrior. But they hadn't come so far, through so many difficult battles, to fail at the final hurdle. They would liberate the Residency or die trying,

"Order the helicopters to clear the path as much as possible," she added. "I want the enemy utterly incapable of mounting any resistance."

———

Corporal Sharon Jones sucked in her breath as the Landshark went to full power, charging forward across the countryside and down towards the city. On paper, the Landshark could travel at over 100km per hour, but she'd never ridden on a tank that moved so fast outside exercises. The vehicle bucked and yawed as it raced forwards, tearing up the road as it moved. She muttered a silent prayer for the Warriors, which would be following in their wake, and then concentrated on her guns. The city walls were looming up ahead of them.

Against unarmed untouchables or even much of the resistance force, the walls would have been an effective defence. They might not have been made of hullmetal, but they were solid, capable of absorbing bullets and even RPGs without being badly dented. But a single shell from the Landshark blew a hole in the wall large enough to drive the vehicle through. Behind it, hundreds of refugees and enemy soldiers scrambled for cover as the tanks advanced. An enemy AFV appeared briefly, its guns swinging round to open fire, before the Landshark sideswiped it. The enemy vehicle was flipped over and sent crashing into the nearest building.

The CO tapped a switch and a recorded message started blaring out of the tank's loudspeakers, warning the civilians to get the hell out of the way. In the crush, Sharon realised in horror, many of them would never be able to leave before they were crushed or killed in the crossfire. Civilian vehicles – mostly human-powered – were smashed as the tanks rode forward, crushing everything in their wake.

"Barricade dead ahead," the CO said. "Sharon; one HE round, if you please."

Sharon nodded as the barricade came into view, fighting down the urge to snigger. It might have been effective against infantry, but against a tank it was worse than useless. The enemy gunners manning the barricade were brave enough, she had to admit, but they might as well have been firing spit balls. She fired once and watched, grimly, as the barricade vanished in a tearing explosion. Behind it, more enemy civilians ran for their lives as the tanks charged onwards. She found herself looking away from the displays as hundreds of people, unable to escape, were killed in the crush.

"They're trying to regroup behind us," the CO said. "But we have to keep going. "The Warriors will deal with them."

Sharon nodded. The tank shook violently as it crashed into a series of stalls – thankfully, abandoned by their owners – and then clipped a house, sending the brick building crumpling over into a pile of dust. Other buildings followed, shattering into ruins as the tanks advanced onwards. The Residency wasn't *that* far away.

Michael would have been impressed by the sheer scale of the devastation the tanks left in their wake if the enemy hadn't been reforming behind them. Countless enemy soldiers, unable to even scratch a Landshark, were trying their hardest to take out the thinner-skinned Warriors and the soldiers tucked up under their armour. He found himself swinging the guns around and firing madly, even as innumerable shots came flashing back at him. Sheer luck protected him from being hit.

Explosions billowed up in the distance as fire controllers called in long-range strikes from the CEF's mortars. It didn't seem to slow the enemy down; there were thousands of them, all seemingly intent on destroying as much as they could. He saw a Warrior explode so violently that he knew that there was no point in searching for survivors, the wreckage left behind for later recovery. The gun barrels felt hot to the touch as he kept shooting madly.

The arrival at the Residency shocked him. He passed the gun to another soldier, then jumped off the Warrior and looked around as the rest of the squad formed up behind him. The complex was in ruins; there were so many holes in the walls that an entire squadron of tanks could have been driven through and into the complex without meeting any opposition. Luckily, the tankers had already smashed their enemy counterparts...

"This way," he snapped, and led his men towards the central building. "Hurry."

Edward sensed the exact moment they'd won. The enemy force, the one trying to batter its way into the situation room, suddenly seemed to waver and collapse. He took advantage of their confusion to hurl his last grenade into their midst, then relaxed slightly as the CEF's troops stormed the building. One by one, the remaining enemy soldiers and rioters were rooted out and captured – or killed. He fought down the urge to sag in relief as the complex was declared secure. There was too much else that had to be done.

He climbed into the nearest tank and glanced down at the Force Tracker. The CEF held the roads leading into the city, but very little else. Blake Coleman's resistance force was running around unsupervised, while the outside resistance fighters, their forces augmented by rebels from the eastern side of Pradesh, were streaming into the city. There were roving bands of enemy soldiers everywhere, some trying to fight, some trying to escape and some just trying to loot. Law and order, such as it was, seemed to have collapsed completely.

"I picked up a message from Blake," Watson said. The Marine had insisted on shadowing Edward as he left the complex, even though the area had been declared clear. "He's intending to capture the Prince."

"Good," Edward said, savagely. There were few things he wanted more than five minutes alone with the mad aristocrat who, according to prisoner interrogations, had started the war. "Ask him what support he requires, then provide it."

Blake allowed himself a sigh of relief as the news came in from the Residency. The CEF had reached there in time, saving seventy men and women from a dreadful fate. Now, he told himself firmly, as he led his group towards the Rajah's palace, it was time to catch the person responsible for the nightmare that had claimed so many lives.

The streets were surprisingly clear, he discovered, as they walked onwards. Most of the local population seemed to have fled, while the rioters seemed to have decided to take on the remaining enemy soldiers rather than loot. Or maybe there was something else going on…he pushed the thought aside as they reached the Rajah's palace and examined it thoughtfully. There was no guard, even at the guardpost. The entire complex looked deserted.

Maybe he's fled, Blake thought, coldly. It would hardly be unprecedented for an enemy commander to flee, leaving his men to their fate. God knew that there were plenty of officers exactly like that in the Imperial Army, men and women who cared more for their positions than for the lives of their troops. But the Prince had nowhere to go. If their babbling captive was correct, his life was forfeit no matter who captured him. His fellow aristocrats would be the least forgiving of all.

No guards appeared to block their path, no shots were fired, as they advanced up the road and entered the palace. Inside, it was almost more luxurious than the last palace, although it *was* a little more tasteful. A low growl startled them, revealing the presence of a giant tiger who eyed them disdainfully and then strolled off down the corridor. Blake stared in disbelief, then shot the animal in the head. It had been a magnificent creature, he knew, but they couldn't have it wandering the streets and developing a taste for human flesh.

They took every precaution as they slipped up the stairs, but it seemed unnecessary. The building was as dark and silent as the grave. Blake felt his senses tingling in alarm as he peered into a side room, then he almost swore out loud as he saw the bodies. There were over seventy girls – the oldest couldn't have been more than twenty – lying on the ground, quite dead. They'd arrange their gorgeous outfits around themselves as they'd fallen, presenting an image of true beauty even in death. Blake had seen horror, but this…this was true horror.

Blake rounded on the captive. "Who are they?"

"The concubines," the captive stuttered. "Each one comes from a noble family, each one competes to see who can bear the child of the Rajah. Those who become pregnant are taken from here and given the very best of treatment until they give birth. Should they give birth to a boy, their status is assured."

Blake stared at him. "And if they give birth to a girl? Or never give birth at all?"

"The girls can be married off to the Rajah's favourites," the captive insisted. "But those who don't give birth have earned the displeasure of the gods."

"I can guess what that means," Blake snarled. He stared down at the captive until the man wilted. His fear seemed excessive until Blake realised that he must look like the captive's worst nightmare, an untouchable with a gift for violence and a complete lack of mercy. "Why are they dead?"

"They must remain pure, untouched, so that the Rajah can sow his seed in them," the captive admitted. "Faced with the risk of capture, they took poison rather than remain alive to face disgrace."

"You sicken me," Blake hissed.

He took one last look at the girls, then led the way down towards the Throne Room. A second set of dead bodies greeted them as they entered the antechamber; a hundred young men, wearing nothing apart from tight loincloths. There was something about them that was badly wrong, Blake realised, but it wasn't until he took a close look at one of them that he realised that they'd been castrated. The disgusting sight made him want to close his legs protectively. No doubt losing their manhoods had been the price for serving in the Rajah's palace. The faint stench that hung in the air, no longer obscured by perfume, suggested at least one of the other prices they paid for being his servants.

The Rajah wanted to be really sure that he was the father of his mewling brats, Blake realised, shaking his head in disgust. The guards had died by poison, just like the concubines. *Those guards couldn't fuck anyone.*

The doorway to the Throne Room was wide open, a faint mist – Blake's implants stated that it was harmless – drifting out into the antechamber. Blake lifted his rifle as he stepped inside, then paused as he saw the Prince seated on the throne. Not entirely to Blake's surprise, the Prince was definitely alive. Someone like him would have insisted that others commit suicide, but chosen to avoid ending his own life.

"Stand up and step away from the Throne," Blake ordered. There was a dark glint in the Prince's eye he didn't like at all. He activated his communicator, ensuring that the Colonel would be able to see what was happening. "You are in our custody."

"They told us that we could best you," the Prince whispered. His Impcrial Standard was precise, almost perfect. "They promised us support."

Blake leaned forward. "Who promised you support?"

"They did, of course," the Prince said. He smirked, reminding Blake of a naughty little boy. In some ways, the Prince had never really grown up. "But perhaps we just did not go far enough to earn their favour."

Blake thought fast. *Who* had promised the Prince support? An offworld faction? Wolfbane, pirates…or someone else? Or was he mad enough to believe that his *gods* had promised him support? If that was the case, Blake knew, there would be no point in trying to draw anything out of the Prince. He was quite mad.

"Stand up and step away from the throne," he snapped, activating the laser sight on his rifle. A beam of red light appeared, targeted on the Prince's forehead. "I won't ask again."

"I sacrificed thousands," the Prince mused. He didn't even seem *aware* of the threat. Blake couldn't help wondering if he was drugged – or worse. "I sent countless untouchables to the gods. I sent nearly a hundred aristocrats to the gods. But the gods saw fit to reject my sacrifice. I understand now."

He looked up, his dark eyes meeting Blake's. "I sent unwilling victims to the gods," he said, loudly. "The gods did not accept them. A willing victim must go to the gods."

There was a click. Blake realised, too late, that the Prince had been waiting for them before committing suicide himself.

"Through my sacrifice," the Prince insisted, "the world will be cleansed in fire and made whole."

Blake grabbed Mad and started to run, but it was already too late.

Seconds later, the world exploded into fire.

Edward swore out loud as the Rajah's palace disintegrated into a colossal fireball, rising up high above the city. The last few moments of Blake Coleman's meeting with the Prince made it far too clear what had happened. He'd mined the entire building, then waited for someone to come drag him off the throne…and then blown the entire building sky-high.

"Blake," Brigadier Yamane said. "Sir…"

"He's gone," Edward said, gently. He'd seen too many good men and women die in his time, but there was something worse about losing Coleman. The battle had been won; he'd died through treachery, when he should have been able to retreat and join the rest of his comrades. "Pass the word; the CEF is to pick up everyone in the Residency, then pull out. We'll establish a FOB a kilometre from the city itself."

He wanted to do something about the chaos enveloping the city, but he didn't even begin to have the manpower necessary to stop the rioting, looting, raping and killing. The oppressed and downtrodden wanted revenge, while their former masters were desperate to escape; Edward doubted that the rebels would honour the agreement to send their former masters overseas, even if it would end up helping them in the long run. Instead, he had a feeling that the revolution would eat itself rather than find a compromise everyone could live with.

"Understood, sir," Yamane said. She'd evidently had the same thought. "We have troops along Route One; I'll have them reinforced, then we can pull them out along with the rest of the Residency staff."

Edward nodded. There would be time to mourn Blake Coleman in the future, once they were out of danger. Now, all that mattered was pulling their people out of the city and away from the chaos. Shaking his head, he picked up a terminal and inspected the live feed from the drones. It was unlikely, he realised, that many buildings would be left untouched by the time the rioting ran its course.

He smiled as the hatch opened, allowing the Professor and his wife to climb into the colossal tank. Leo looked pale, but his wife seemed more assured of herself…being a medic, being *useful*, had done wonders for her. Edward promised himself, silently, that she would have her chance at training to become a *proper* medic, then he looked back at the terminal. There were more enemy forces moving towards Route One, with uncertain intentions. Without the Prince, there was no one who could say *stop*.

And we still don't know what happened to Polk, he reminded himself, bitterly. Losing someone in combat was bad enough, but at least they knew what had happened to him. Having a POW go missing was worse. Polk could be dead, killed in the chaos, or he might still be a prisoner. There was no way to know. His family would never receive closure, never be able to mourn their son properly. The thought nagged at his mind as he forced himself to relax.

The tank lurched into life, taking them away from the Residency. Edward found himself wondering, grimly, what might happen to the talks now. God knew that nothing had really been decided by the time the shit hit the fan. But then, they *had* worked together against a common foe…

Time will tell, he decided. *It always does.*

CHAPTER
FORTY-TWO

A very wise general once remarked that one should know the enemy as well as one's self. This is true of all fields, but very true of diplomacy. Understanding the enemy's strengths and weaknesses – and how the enemy looks at the world - is of vital importance.

However, a note of warning. One should never accept an enemy's narrative unquestionably. Nor should one fail to bear in mind that, in the end, diplomats represent one country – the one that issued their credentials. To lose sight of that is to lose sight of what it means to be a diplomat.

Unfortunately, many diplomats have done just that.

-Professor Leo Caesius, *Diplomacy: The Lessons of the Past.*

"Fucking hideous mess."

Michael nodded, unable to find it in him to reprimand the soldier who had spoken so rudely. The sight before them was horrifying; even the grim awareness that it could have been much worse didn't soften the blow. He couldn't help thinking that they were doing the wrong thing, no matter what the CO said about there being no alternative. And yet there was a part of him that said that they should just go, abandoning the cursed world to its fate.

The refugees were all upper or middle caste; men, women and children, uprooted from their homes and ordered to march to the camps with the clothes on their backs and very little else, not even food and drink. Their bodies were injured – some of them had been beaten quite badly – and their clothes were torn or in some cases ripped away completely, but it was the look in their eyes that haunted Michael. They'd never believed that they could lose power so quickly and completely, nor that the torments they'd inflicted on their lesser would one day be inflicted on them. And now it had happened…

There was a man leading a family of five; his wife and four children. The younger children seemed unaware of the seriousness of the situation, but the others were terrified, glancing at the off-worlders as if they expected to be brutally raped and murdered at any moment. Behind them, there were five or six boys who had lost all contact with their family; there was no way to know if they were alive or dead. There was a girl who had been beaten so badly that her face was unlikely to recover, another girl whose ears had been torn away from her skull…and countless rape victims, very few of whom would receive any treatment. The medics, Michael knew, were badly overworked.

"Sickening," he muttered, in agreement.

Once the first wave of looting and worse had come to an end, the rebel leadership had taken command and started sweeping the upper-caste out of the capital city. The camps had barely been set up in time to take them; no matter what the off-worlders said, the rebels weren't going to deny themselves the pleasure of uprooting their enemies for any longer than they absolutely had to. Michael and his squad had been rushed to provide some security for the camps, fearing that rogue – and not so rogue – groups of rebels would take advantage of them to exterminate their enemies in large numbers. The settlements on the islands, he'd been warned, would take months before they were ready to accept newcomers.

Michael had his doubts about how long it would be before the upper-caste population was reconciled to the new state of affairs. Few of them had any experience with farming and even fewer were willing to learn how to actually feed themselves. They'd been pampered from birth till death; even the warriors, the ones who were supposed to *fight*, had had a large retinue of servants to hew wood and draw water. Maybe they could hunt on the unsettled continent, or learn how to fish, but Michael suspected that most of them would starve. The rebels might even have that in mind as the final objective…unless, of course, the former upper-caste population chose to return and work under those they had once despised.

His wristcom buzzed. "The algae-farms are up and running," the CO said. "We should be able to start feeding them soon."

Michael nodded. The former lords and masters of the universe – or at least of this planet – wouldn't starve. But eating algae-based products... they might consider starvation preferable, particularly when compared to the delicacies they were used to.

Too bad, he thought, sourly. *The alternative is worse.*

"So we have a basic agreement," Leo said. "Our governments will have to ratify it, but the agreement is in line with what they wanted."

He smiled. Holding the remainder of the talks on the garrison's island was inconvenient, but it was a great deal safer than the Imperial Residency. The talks hadn't progressed too far – they hadn't received some of the concessions the Commonwealth had wanted – but at least they had a rough agreement on a border. Trade, he'd decided, could wait until there was more trust between the two parties.

"So it is," Flora agreed. The Wolfbane Representative smiled back at him. "I believe that my government will also convey its thanks to your people, particularly the ones who saved our lives."

Leo nodded, as if he could take credit personally for the CEF's last-minute rescue. "I think it should show that we are capable of working together," he assured her. "And that we do have interests in common."

The interests, he knew, didn't include Lakshmibai. Lakshmibai might have served as the seat of the talks, but neither the Commonwealth nor Wolfbane was genuinely interested in providing further support to the planet. In future, if there were a need for talks, they would be held on the garrison or an uninhabited island. The rebels and their former masters could sort themselves out without further off-world interference.

"Indeed we do," Flora agreed. She took her copy of the treaty and stood up. "And I hope that you and your wife recover from your experience. Being under siege is never pleasant."

Leo felt his smile widen. He'd never seen Fiona more animated in years. Even though they were safe now, she was still helping the medics with the thousands of refugees, trying to provide some medical care before they were transported to their new home. She'd even talked about becoming a full-fledged doctor when they returned home. And she'd accepted Avalon as *home*.

"I think we'll be fine," he said. He rose to his feet and held out a hand. "And thank you."

"There is no way we can get you back to Earth," Edward said, addressing General Joseph Raphael and his handful of officers. "You know as much as we do about conditions between Wolfbane and Earth."

He scowled. The Commonwealth Navy had talked, time and time again, about sending a mission from Avalon to Earth – or at least to the Slaughterhouse – in hopes of finding out what was going on in the Core Worlds. But it would take six months for a heavy cruiser to make it to Earth and nothing smaller could hope to do it, at least not without refuelling. And there was no certainty that they would locate operating cloudscoops along the way.

But it would have to be done, sooner or later.

"The Commonwealth is prepared to take you into its service," he continued, "or allow you to retire to one of our worlds. I believe that Wolfbane will be happy to take you too. The choice is yours."

Raphael frowned. "Can we take the women with us?"

"If they want to come, they can come," Edward said. He wasn't entirely comfortable with the idea of taking them back to Avalon, but they'd definitely earned a chance to try out for Commonwealth citizenship. And, without them, the garrison would probably have collapsed and fallen into local hands long ago. "But we need your answer by the end of the day."

He watched them go, then looked down at the final report from the capital. A team of SIE experts had combed what was left of the city, but they hadn't been able to answer the two most important questions that nagged at Edward's mind. Had the Prince received off-world support for his mad uprising? And what had happened to Private Polk?

They *had* found hints that the Prince had had access to more advanced off-world tech than the rest of the planet, but Edward knew that proved nothing. There was no reason why the Prince couldn't have simply purchased it from a trader – Edward had yet to meet the trader who had moral or ethical qualms over selling advanced technology to repressive regimes – rather than receiving help from an off-world faction. And yet…the Prince had seemed convinced that *someone* was helping him. Madness…or a sign that something had begun on Lakshmibai that they had yet to comprehend? There was no way to know.

And Private Polk?

It *was* clear that he had been threatened with becoming a sacrifice… and then had been reprieved. *That* was out of character for the Prince, so much so that some of the prisoners had commented on it. But again, it proved nothing. The destruction of the Rajah's palace had wiped out every last trace of those they'd known to be in the building, as well as those they hadn't. In the end, like the other unanswered questions, there was no way to know.

"Damn it," Edward muttered, as he closed the terminal. "Damn it to hell."

———

The tropical beach had been a favourite resort for the garrison's staff, even during the worst of their isolation. Jasmine had been amused to discover that the small island was surrounded by sharp rocks, each one capable of tearing a local boat open and throwing the crew out into the sea to drown. It provided a security that reassured the stranded garrison's staff, as the only way to reach the island was through helicopters – and they could intercept any helicopter the locals sought to send to the island.

Colonel Stalker had ordered her to rest and relax after they'd buried Blake Coleman – as per his last wishes, they'd carved a memorial for him on another uninhabited island – but Jasmine found it hard, almost impossible. There had been a time when the chance to relax, to wear a bikini and enjoy the bright sunlight, would have been very welcome, but now she found it almost impossible to decompress. As a Marine, she had moved from trouble spot to trouble spot, following orders…and then moving away. Now, she'd been responsible for thousands of young men, some of whom would never see Avalon again. If the Colonel hadn't threatened to dump her on the island and abandon her there for a week, she wouldn't have gone on leave.

"I made drinks," Alves said, passing her a tall glass. It felt cool to the touch; she sniffed it suspiciously, before deciding that it was unlikely to be able to harm her. "The base liquid was in the garrison; I just brought it out and added fruit."

Jasmine snorted. They'd found plenty of stuff in the garrison's immense stockpiles that seemed to serve no useful purpose. Compared to that, alcohol – even alcohol so expensive that the Imperial Navy could have bought a corvette for the price of a crate – was almost normal. The only surprise was that it hadn't been drunk by the officers and men who'd been left behind when the Imperial Army pulled out.

"Thank you," she said, taking a sip. It tasted faintly of coconut… and something she couldn't identify. Being unable to get drunk, like all Marines, had deterred her from developing expensive tastes in alcohol. "This is good."

Alves smiled as he sat down next to her. "My small skill at making people feel at ease is confirmed," he said, warmly. "I had to download the recipe from the garrison's database, though. I confess!"

Jasmine surprised herself by giggling. "Why was *that* in the database?"

"God knows," Alves said. He looked over at her, gently. "Do you want to talk about it?"

"Talk about what?" Jasmine asked, although she had a pretty good idea. "And why?"

"It can be good to talk," Alves pointed out. "And, for what it's worth, I won't breathe a word of whatever you say. You'd kill me."

Jasmine eyed him suspiciously. There were horror stories from the Imperial Army about experienced soldiers who had spoken to the wrong person and wound up banned from combat operations…or, worse, treated as having mental problems. The Marines didn't have that problem, but they still found it hard to open up to someone outside their brotherhood. How could they understand?

"When you go into a new platoon," she said, finally, "the old sweats will give you a very hard time until you prove yourself. They don't know if they can trust you. If you weren't already hardened by the Slaughterhouse… but you'd be alone, just you against your new teammates. Blake…rode my ass hard. It wasn't until after my first real test that he lightened up and we became friends as well as comrades.

"He liked to fight," she added, after a moment. "When he wasn't fighting the enemies of the Empire, he was picking fights with other soldiers and guardsmen. He was never interested in promotion, never tried out for becoming an NCO…all he wanted to do was fight. And fuck. I lost track of the number of times he got yelled at for spending too much time with women when he should have been with us. And when he got promoted… his heart wasn't really in it."

She shook her head. "We all die, sooner or later, but Blake's death was…senseless," she concluded. "One more of us gone. How long will it be before there are no Marines left?"

"There will be others, surely," Alves said. "You can rebuild the corps…"

"Maybe," Jasmine said. "But it would take us years to rebuild the Slaughterhouse."

"Your boss told you to relax," Alves said, finally. "So lie back and relax."

Jasmine snorted again. "You started it," she pointed out. "But you're right."

She looked at him thoughtfully. He'd never been unhealthy and now, after two months on a very hostile world, he was fit and wiry. Carefully, she reached for him and pulled his body towards her, careful not to pull too hard. At least he didn't seem to be flinching away…she kissed him and, after a moment, he returned the kiss.

"Lie down," she ordered, sitting up. A moment later, she was straddling him. "This definitely counts as relaxation."

Carefully, she undid her bikini and leaned forward until she could kiss him again.

Mathew opened his eyes.

He was lying on a soft bed, staring up at the ceiling. The glowing lights overhead suggested, very strongly, that he was on a starship. But the restraints around his wrists suggested that he was still a prisoner.

"Ah," a voice said. "You are awake."

Mathew turned his head, trying to find the speaker. She was a middle-aged woman, wearing an Imperial Navy uniform. The red cross over her right breast, he knew, marked her as a medic. But who *was* she?

"I'm afraid that you're still a prisoner," the woman informed him, "but we did take the liberty of repairing the damage the barbarians inflicted on your body. You were in quite a mess when we took possession of you."

Mathew hesitated, listening carefully. The dull background throbbing suggested that the starship was in Phase Space, heading…he had no idea where. But if he was a prisoner, it was clear that they weren't heading to the Commonwealth. Wolfbane? Or somewhere else?

He found his voice. "Who…who are you?"

"My name doesn't matter," the woman said. Her voice hardened. "But I am sure you will have heard of my commanding officer. Her name is Singh.

"Admiral Singh."

The End

AFTERWORD

The Boxer Rebellion (or Uprising, depending on which terminology you use) is not considered politically-correct history. I certainly never learned about it in school. It is a fascinating story with many lessons for the present-day world, yet in the West it is regarded with a mixture of shame and embarrassment. After all, didn't we oppress the Chinese to the point where they rose up against us?

To summarise a complicated story, the Boxers were a secret society in China dedicated to throwing out the 'Foreign Devils' – the Westerners (and Japanese) who had attacked China, forced concessions out of the weak government and seemed bent on eventually carving up and partitioning up China between them. They believed that they had magic powers which could be used against the outsiders; more importantly, several members of the Chinese Government *also* believed them (and feared that the Boxers might become an anti-Manchu movement too.) In 1900, with China suffering under the combination of a drought and outside interference, they struck. A series of attacks on foreigners culminated in the siege of the foreign embassies in China's capital, Peking (Beijing). To some extent, those attacks were aided and abetted by the government.

In response, the major Western powers (and Japan) put together a multi-national force, which marched into China and eventually saved the embassies before they could fall to the Chinese (which didn't stop newspapers at the time reporting that the embassies had fallen and printing obituaries for the various ambassadors). The force then rampaged through Peking, looted heavily and forced the Chinese to pay reparations for the uprising. In the long run, the Boxer Rebellion helped weaken the Chinese Government still further, to the point where it collapsed a few years later.

It is something of a mystery just how serious the Chinese Government *was* about the affair. On one hand, it would be hard to find a Chinese official who actually *liked* the Westerners; on the other, the balance of military power should have ensured the destruction of the embassies a long time before the relief force arrived in Peking. Is it possible that the Chinese Government, having realised that the Boxer claims to supernatural protection were bunk, decided to ensure that the Westerners were *not* wiped out? The destruction of the embassies would certainly have galvanised Westerners who wanted to divide China up between them, destroying the local government completely. In truth, we will probably never know.

Modern eyes tend to side with the Chinese in the affair. It is true that the West did force its way into China, which wished to remain isolated from the world. It is also true that the diplomats behaved very undiplomatically, that missionaries demanded special concessions for their Chinese converts and various Western powers took pieces of China to use as their own territory (such as Hong Kong.) To us, the whole affair seems very embarrassing, a case of shameless imperialism at its worst.

And yet it is also true that the Chinese behaved badly too. Chinese pretensions to being the sole source of global civilisation rang hollow in the ears of ambassadors who knew that the Chinese were no match, militarily speaking, for the West. Indeed, the Chinese Government was almost sickeningly ignorant of the outside world, addressing – at one point – Queen Victoria as a Barbarian Chieftain. Even when China's back was to the wall, the Chinese Government continued to tell itself that the outsiders were merely coming to pay homage to the Son of Heaven, or that their armies could be beaten easily. China bears a large measure of responsibility for the poor relationship between her and the West.

But leaving that debate aside – because it can be argued both ways, suggesting that there is merit in both sides of the case – what are the lessons of the Boxer Rebellion?

First, trouble can seem to come out of nowhere. It is true that only a handful of foreigners (and perhaps Chinese officials) predicted the uprising, despite numerous signs of impending trouble. Hindsight is, of course, clearer than foresight; it's easy to blame someone for missing signs that, in retrospect, seem clear. In modern times, who predicted either 9/11 or the Arab Spring?

Second, local governments might covertly support the rebels, fearing that otherwise they might turn against their own governments. In modern terms, we have Pakistan's curious relationship with the Taliban and Pakistani extremists – and sizable sums of money flowing from the Gulf Oil States to various extremist factions. If there were a major anti-foreigner uprising in Saudi Arabia or Pakistan, which way would the local government jump?

Third, a display of weakness or irresolution can invite attack. Prior to the Boxer Rebellion, Italy made demands on China – which, in an unusual show of determination, the Chinese Government rejected. Firm and resolute actions might well have prevented the whole uprising from growing out of hand. In modern times, America's hesitation in dealing with rogue governments merely encourages them to press further.

Fourth, resolute action can prevent a tragedy. The advance of Western forces (I believe) helped convince the local government not to allow the embassies to collapse. In modern times, the American failure to rescue the hostages in Iran – and, later, the delay in coming to the aid of Libyan rebels – only encouraged the enemies of civilisation.

It is said that those who do not learn from experience are condemned to repeat it. How right they are.

[Those interested in reading more about the Boxer Rebellion might wish to consult *The Fists of Righteous Harmony: A History of the Boxer Uprising in China in the Year 1900* (Henry Keown-Boyd) and *The Boxer Rebellion: The Dramatic Story of China's War on Foreigners that Shook the World in the Summer of 1900* (Diana Preston).]

There is a popular trope in military fiction (both general and SF) that tends to brand Ambassadors and Diplomats as cowards, traitors or simply idiots. The 'Ass in Ambassador,' as TV Tropes names it; the diplomats are the ones who talk, talk, talk and compromise, compromise, compromise... seemingly unaware that they are giving away far too much for far too little. A typical example would be Reginald Houseman of David Weber's *The Honour of the Queen*, whose effective ignorance of his own ignorance leads him to offend his hosts and threaten to damage relations between them and Houseman's state. As one of the other characters points out, Houseman's suggestion basically boils down to giving their hosts sworn enemies more economic muscle to beat them to death with.

From Houseman's point of view, there was great merit in his suggestion. It did not, however, take into account the antagonism between the two worlds, or that both sides were not always capable of acting rationally – or, for that matter, that the enemy world was governed by fanatics who brutally oppressed anyone who didn't agree with them. Houseman was a caricature of the Ivy League Diplomat, merged with a hefty dose of 'the know-it-all who doesn't.'

This is not, sadly, averted in the real world. History is replete with examples of weak diplomacy leading to wars. Chamberlain of Britain was desperate to avoid war, so much so that he missed the bus when it came to fighting and winning a war (in 1936 or 1938) when it could have been won with minimal bloodshed. His problem, put simply, was that he failed to comprehend the true nature of Hitler's regime. There would be war as long as Hitler was in power.

However, the diplomats have other problems. Their job is to maintain the lines of communication between their state and their host state. Offending their hosts gratuitously is a good way to damage relations (and, if they go too far) to end their careers. This is nicely illustrated by the FBI's operations in Yemen, prior to 9/11, where the FBI team clashed constantly with the US Ambassador to the country. They saw themselves as investigators, digging out the truth; the ambassador saw them as clowns who knew little of local realities and would merely offend their hosts. In a sense, both the investigators and the ambassador were correct. Their objectives clashed quite badly.

A secondary problem lies in competition between diplomats and military men (in American terms, the State Department and the Pentagon.) Passing the buck to the Pentagon, for whatever reason, might make the State Department look like a failure. This led to problems when diplomats on the ground realised that certain problems were intractable, but their superiors were unwilling to press for military action. As weird as it seems, the State Department regarded the Pentagon as its natural enemy (and vice versa) rather than accepting that they had to work together. This makes perfect sense if you realise that they also compete for funding from the American Government.

A third problem lies in the fact that foreign governments often do not have the ability to do what the foreigners want, no matter how simple it seems. Saudi Arabia did not move against terrorists (and their funding networks) in Saudi after 9/11 because it would have risked considerable upheaval and civil unrest, perhaps even the fall of the House of Saud. The government was reluctant to commit suicide on America's behalf. It was not until terrorists started striking within Saudi itself that the government found the nerve to take the offensive against them.

They also have interests of their own. Pakistan's links to the Taliban are considered borderline treacherous by Americans, not without reason. The United States has, after all, supplied (and still supplies) Pakistan with billions of dollars worth of aid. However, the United States can simply withdraw from the region; the Pakistanis have to deal with the Taliban indefinitely. If extermination isn't an option, the Pakistani Government has to come to an accommodation with them. What choice do they have?

As I write these words, American Embassies in a number of countries are being closed in light of an undisclosed terrorist threat. As physical manifestations of American soil (legally, embassies are part of the country they represent), they are tempting targets for attack by anti-American factions. Nor can the United States always count on the host governments to provide protection, even though – legally – the protection of foreign embassies is the responsibility of the host government. (The governments that do take this seriously are not ones the United States has a problem with, although it is worth noting that the American Embassy in Moscow was never attacked.)

This is a wise precaution. Ever since President Carter failed to respond vigorously to the Iranian Hostage Crisis (which stated with an attack on the American Embassy in Tehran), American and other Western embassies have been seen as fair game. Problems in one country can often lead to attacks on American Embassies in another; the Mecca Uprising of 1979 led to attacks, including the burning of the American Embassies in Pakistan and Libya. The fact that America had nothing to do with the uprising (which was carried out by Sunni fundamentalists of the same strain that would eventually lead to Al Qaeda) was of no concern to the demonstrators. And the local governments did *nothing* to stop the attacks.

Iranians have problems understanding why their country is so distrusted by the West, particularly America. After all, they argue, the average Iranian has no hatred for the United States. The answer is simple; Iran, in choosing to assault the embassy and start a major hostage crisis, stepped outside the bonds of civilised discourse. No one would have blamed the Iranians for evicting every last American official (it would be their right, under diplomatic protocol) but taking hostages and threatening their lives was unacceptable. Iran acted in a manner that showed a total disregard for international norms, a manner that was not even emulated by Hitler, Stalin or Imperial Japan, none of them paragons of good behaviour.

President Carter's paralysis in the face of looming disaster did much to cement the poor reputation of the United States. When the going got tough, it was whispered, the US got going, not a message to encourage America's friends and allies across the world. It is true that a more vigorous response might have risked the lives of the hostages, but it is also true that it might have convinced the more rational elements of the Iranian Government that backing the extremists would merely lead to pain. Even if the hostages died, exacting payment for their lives would have strengthened the United States' reputation and made future such crises unlikely.

It is this that allowed host governments to think that they could get away with allowing mobs to threaten, ransack and destroy Western Embassies. And, unfortunately, in many cases they have been correct. The attack on Benghazi in 2012, which included the death of the American Ambassador, might not have happened if it had been made clear that such attacks would draw a vigorous response.

There are no shortage of excuses for such attacks. I don't see any such excuses as valid; the concept of diplomats remaining untouched is a core principle of international relations, allowing nations to actually *talk* to one another face-to-face. Choosing to accept such attacks (and the host country's disregard for the safety of foreign diplomats) is a dangerous misstep.

It must not be allowed to continue.

Christopher G. Nuttall
Kuala Lumpur, 2013

If you liked *To The Shores*, you might like

THE COWARD'S WAY OF WAR

"In today's wars, there are no morals. We believe the worst thieves in the world today and the worst terrorists are the Americans. We do not have to differentiate between military or civilian. As far as we are concerned, they are all targets."

-Osama bin Laden

Sometime in the near future, a dying woman is discovered in New York City – infected with Smallpox. As the disease starts to spread, it is discovered that terrorists have unleashed a biological weapon on the American population – and brought the world to the brink of Armageddon.

Against this backdrop, an extraordinary cast of men and women fight desperately for survival in a world gone mad. Doctor Nicolas Awad struggles desperately to contain and control the outbreak; President Paula Handley struggles to rally the shattered country for war and preserve something of the American way of life. On the streets of New York, Sergeant Al Hattlestad and the NYPD try to keep order and save as many as possible, while survivalist Jim Revells takes his family and tries to hide from the chaos.

But the nightmare has only just begun…

CHAPTER ONE

... Among the many difficulties faced in countering such weapons is that the deployment system – i.e. an infected person, willingly or otherwise – is extremely difficult to detect. No reasonable level of security – up to and including strip and cavity searches – can detect an infected enemy agent. The issue becomes only more complicated when one realises that the infected person may be unaware that he or she is infected and, therefore, will show no sign of guilt or fear when investigated.

-Nicolas Awad

New York, USA
Day 1

"Did you enjoy the flight, sir?"

Ali Mohammad Asiri pasted a smile on his face as he looked up at the flight attendant. He had visited America several times before, yet he would never get used to American women and how they chose to dress. Just looking at the attendant – her nametag read CALLY – made him grimace inside, for it was clear that she had no sense of modesty. If one of Ali's sisters had dared to wear such an outfit in front of a strange man, he would have beaten her into a pulp. The Americans were truly a shameless people.

"Yes, I did, thank you," he said, in fluent English. As much as he wanted to reprove the harlot for her dress sense and her forwardness, he didn't quite dare. The orders had been quite specific and completely beyond question. He was to pretend to be a playboy, one tasting the seductive western world for the first time, and do nothing to attract attention. It was odd that leering at a flight attendant was less likely to attract attention than politely turning his eyes away from her, but orders were orders. Besides, he was skilled at concealing his true thoughts. Growing up with a father who adored the Americans – and the money they brought into the Kingdom – had left him very aware of the possibility of betrayal. "It was an excellent flight."

Cally grinned down at him, apparently unaware of his inner thoughts. "I'll be sure to pass your compliments on to the pilot," she said. It had been a boring flight really, with no excitement beyond a short landing in France before flying on to New York. "Is this your first time in New York, honey?"

Ali winced inwardly at her words. "No," he admitted. He would have preferred to claim ignorance, but there was no way of knowing just who Cally truly worked for or even if she would get curious and check his records. "I visited three times before and enjoyed myself, even though I was a child the first time around."

Cally shrugged and headed off to bother another passenger, leaving Ali to slump into his chair in relief. The passengers were disembarked row by row and herded off the plane and into the flight terminal, many of them heading back to the United States after a holiday or business trip abroad. Even in a time of economic recession, the Americans looked fat and disgustingly healthy compared to some of the fighters he had seen at the training camp, but then the devil was fond of rewarding his servants in this life. It was the afterlife that they had to beware, or so Ali had been taught, back when he had rediscovered his faith. Allah saw all and stood in judgement over it all.

He stood up when the flight attendants waved at him, picking up his small carry-on bag as he moved. There wasn't much in it – increasingly burdensome flight regulations had made it impossible to carry anything useful onto the plane – but he had been warned not to let it out of his sight. The Great Sheikh had made it clear that Ali must not lose his documents, even though he hadn't offered any specific instructions as to the disposal of those documents. Indeed, Ali had no idea why he'd been ordered to take a short holiday to New York City and spend a few days just relaxing and enjoying himself. When he thought about the privations being suffered by the fighters in Afghanistan, Iraq and Pakistan, he felt nothing, but guilt. How could he enjoy himself – insofar as it was possible for a believer to enjoy himself in a sinful city – when his brothers were suffering at the hands of the infidel?

But orders were orders.

Ali remembered – as he followed another female flight attendant – how he'd first met the Great Sheikh. He'd been a young man then, barely aware of the greater world outside his home city, yet bitterly aware of his father's lack of faith. His father worked with infidels, did business with infidels, profited from infidels…and ignored his duties to Islam. The young Ali, more influenced by a strict believing uncle than his father, had wondered if his father had had plans to use the infidel lust for money against them, but as he'd grown older he had come to realise that his father just loved their money. He had grown to manhood aware of his family's shame – and of how his world was slipping away from him – and desperate to change it, somehow. His uncle had introduced him to a more fundamentalist mosque and it had all grown from there. Ali had thought to go to Pakistan – Iraq wasn't a safe place for believers these days, not with an increasingly effective Iraqi Army wiping out *Jihadi* cells almost as soon as they were formed – but the Great Sheikh had had other ideas. Ali was a young man with an unblemished record, one that would sound no alarms in the American security forces. He could be far more useful elsewhere.

The Great Sheikh himself was a great man. He had fought alongside the great Osama bin Laden before the unleashing of righteous wrath on New York City, over seventeen years ago. Since then, he had fought in Iraq, Pakistan and even Europe before he'd finally been ordered to return to his homeland of Saudi Arabia and start forming new cells for overseas operations. Ali, like many other young men, had been captivated by his words, for they had nothing in their lives to live for. Ali had graduated from education with a degree in Islamic Studies that had proven to be worthless in the real world, while there was no hope of marriage or children. His father had refused to help his believing son any further, after reminding Ali that he had urged him to take a more useful – and sinful – course. Instead, one of his daughters was – against all Islamic Precepts – slowly assuming control of the family business. Her husband, a weak man easily dominated by his wife, might have control in name, but in reality it was all hers. It made Ali's blood boil. How could any man be so weak?

"You will do nothing to attract attention," the Great Sheikh had said, the first time Ali had flown to America under his orders. Ali had expected to be contacted while in the United States for a martyrdom operation, but nothing had ever materialised and he'd returned home, half-suspecting that the Great Sheikh would be angry with him. Instead, he'd been thanked and urged to return to his studies, before being sent on a second trip a year later. "You will be a typical sinful lad" – at this point, the Great Sheikh had winked at him – "and pretend to enjoy yourself. You will have no connection with us that anyone can see."

Ali could only assume – as he passed through the security checks – that the Great Sheikh had given him the mission because he knew that Ali wouldn't be tempted by the many temptations of the West. It was sad, but true that many of the fighters had been tempted – and fallen – by alcohol, or drugs, or women. Some of the tales whispered by veterans from many campaigns against the infidel had been horrific, suggesting that they'd embraced sin in all of its many forms. Ali had said that that might explain why they'd lost; how could they expect Allah to bless their mission if they broke His rules? The Great Sheikh had taken a more pragmatic view. If someone was willing to fight the infidel, all such failings could be ignored, at least until the *Dar-ul-Harb* became the *Dar-ul-Islam*, when purity would be the order of the day. Ali longed for such a day, for it would give his life meaning. He didn't fit in with the modern world the Americans and their European lackeys had created.

The security checks took longer than they had the last time, causing him to worry about what the Americans might have found, even though he knew that he was carrying nothing that might implicate him in the cause. He had no banned material, no pamphlets castigating the West and the fallen Muslims who accepted the West's domination of their souls… he didn't even have a copy of the *Qur'an*! He had protested when the Great Sheikh had ordered him to carry only western material, but the Great Sheikh had been insistent. He was to do nothing to attract attention. He was merely a tourist visiting New York City and it had to remain that way.

Eventually, the Americans finished their checks and allowed him to pass through the security barrier and into John F. Kennedy International Airport. It was the busiest international air passenger gateway to the United States, according to the Americans themselves, making it ideal for the network's more undercover purposes. There was no point in trying to sneak in – and perhaps being caught by the Coast Guard – when they could just fly into America perfectly legitimately. It was something, Ali had been told, that made people like him extremely valuable. As a 'clean' man, with nothing to alert the Americans to his true masters, there was no reason for them to delay his entry into their country. Even the growing paranoia about Arabs and Muslims in America couldn't delay his operation. It did help that he had no intention of doing anything in New York City.

Waving goodbye to the TSA agent who had searched his bag, Ali headed down to the taxi rack and climbed into a taxi being driven by a Pakistani immigrant. He was tempted to speak to the man in Arabic, but again, it risked attracting unwanted attention. Instead, he gave the man instructions to head directly to the Marigold Hotel and settled back to enjoy the ride. It always amazed him how orderly American streets were compared to the roads back home, where everyone drove as if their lives depended on it. New York had a remarkable skyline, even though it was nothing more than a sign of American decadence. It was temping to order the driver to take him to where the Twin Towers had once been – before they had been knocked down by the 9/11 Martyrs – yet he didn't quite dare. The Great Sheikh's instructions had been specific. He was not to do anything that might attract attention and that included visiting the site of 9/11, or any other Islamic site in New York.

The movement had spent a considerable amount of money booking him a suite at the Marigold Hotel, allowing Ali to relax in the lap of luxury. He had to repress another surge of guilt as he paid and tipped the taxi driver, before strolling into the Marigold as if he owned the place – and, with the amount he was paying, the staff were happy to treat him as if he *did* own the hotel. Ali allowed himself to act like a Prince he had seen once, tipping the staff as they showed him to his suite and helped him to unpack. The wink from the maid suggested that she would be willing to go above and beyond the call of duty – in exchange for an additional gratuity, of course – but Ali just wanted to sleep. He dismissed the staff, lay down on the comfortable bed and went to sleep.

When he awoke, several hours later, he felt famished and ordered a plate of food from room service. The suite came with a computer and he logged on to a popular and free email account, sending a single email back home to inform his brothers that he had arrived. The email would pass unnoticed, even by the never-to-be-sufficiently-damned American NSA and its dreaded interception skills, for there was nothing in it that might attract attention. Who would notice – or care about – an email from a newly-arrived tourist to his friends back home? He resisted the temptation to log onto some of the cause's websites – that would definitely have attracted attention – and shut down the computer. There was a knock at the door and a maid appeared with a tray of food, much to Ali's relief. He shook her hand, pressed a tip into her fingers and shoed her out of the room, before settling down to eat. It was still early afternoon in the United States, but it felt much later. The jet lag was kicking in.

After he had eaten his food, he left the hotel and played tourist. New York had plenty of interesting sights to see, even if he had been specifically barred from going anywhere near an Islamic site. He kept his feelings off his face as he walked through endless museums and art galleries, wondering at all the energy surrounding him. The Americans had no sense of shame or decorum. He spied a pair of Americans wearing army uniforms and shuddered inside, remembering tales from brothers who had narrowly escaped death at the hands of men wearing similar uniforms. The Americans flaunted their power for all to see.

But then, he told himself, what could one expect from unbelievers? When all one had was the glory of one's own self – instead of the glory of God – why would they not flaunt what they had? The temptations of the mundane world were great, yet the price was agonisingly high. He saw a homosexual couple walking hand in hand and shuddered again, remembering the day when a pair of such sinners had been put to death back home. The Americans seemed to embrace sinners. Tired, he started to make his way back to the hotel, wishing – once again – that the Great Sheikh had given him something more worthy to do. Perhaps, the next time he came, he would have orders to spend his life dearly in reminding the Americans that judgement existed, or perhaps he would be part of a team that would bring the United States to its knees.

He stepped onto the underground and rode for several stations before reaching the one closest to the Marigold. Despite himself, he couldn't avoid feeling a childlike sense of fascination with the transport system, even though the other commuters looked bored or angry. He found himself rubbing shoulders with the American melting pot – Latinos from Mexico and South America, Chinese and Vietnamese immigrants from the Far East, men with skins so dark that they looked as if they had come from Africa – and fought hard to keep the distaste off his face. He reminded himself, again, that it wasn't his duty to question the Great Sheikh and his orders. He would carry them out, even if they made no sense.

Back at the hotel, he had a long bath and then settled into bed for the night. The Great Sheikh had ordered him to play tourist for his entire visit, which meant visiting the American cinemas and watching some of their filthy films and other entertainments, perhaps even visiting some of their dance clubs and dancing…could there be any greater sin? The Great Sheikh had told him that sins committed in the name of Allah, with no actual intention to sin for the sake of sinning, were no sin, yet Ali would have preferred to avoid them. If the Great Sheikh had told him why he was following such absurd orders, it would have been easier, but what he didn't know he couldn't tell. Ali was confident that he could survive an American interrogation, no matter how rigorous, yet others had believed the same.

He rubbed at his forearm as he turned over and switched off the lights. The tiny bump had materialised only a day before he'd boarded the flight in Saudi Arabia, a sign that he'd been bitten by an insect in the night. It didn't really hurt, but it twitched from time to time, reminding him that it was there. Ali pushed the pain aside and ignored it. After what some of the movement had suffered over the years at the hands of the Great Satan and its allies, complaining about an insect bite seemed absurd. Shaking his head at the thought, he closed his eyes and went to sleep. He had a long day ahead of him tomorrow, doing nothing.

There had been over five hundred men and women on the aircraft that had brought Ali to the United States. As darkness fell over the eastern seaboard, many of them returned to their homes in New York or headed onwards to other destinations within the United States. The people he had met on his first day in New York – the flight attendants, the security officers, the taxi driver, and the hotel staff – likewise dispersed themselves over the city, relaxing after a hard day at work. Some went to their homes to sleep; others went to party or to relax with their friends. In the end, it hardly mattered.

None of them – not even Ali, who had carried it to America's shores – knew that the most destructive attack in America's long history had begun. None of them knew that they were carrying the seeds of destruction within them. And, because none of them knew this, none of them took any precautions. The attack spread rapidly across the city and outside, across the United States. An attack on a scale to dwarf Pearl Harbor had begun and no one had even noticed.

But they would.

And soon.

Download a Free Sample from the Chrishanger…

www.chrishanger.net

And then download the full novel as an eBook!

Printed in Great Britain
by Amazon